READERS LOVE EUGENIA RILEY'S
A TRYST IN TIME!

"*A Tryst In Time* quite simply took my breath away! The characters were so defined and full of life that I could feel their joys and sorrows. I must admit, I cried."
—Miss L.R., New Orleans, LA

"This book is simply the greatest thing since pizza. I loved it!"
—Ms. J.D., Chicago, IL

"Thank you for such a *wonderful* story! If it hadn't been midnight when I finished your book, I would have written you then, when my emotions were raw and my tears still fresh!"
—Miss B.R.S., Reading, PA

"There are only two things wrong with this book: I lost sleep, and the book ended. Magnificent!"
—Mrs. C.A., Greenfield, CA

"Most paperbacks are *not* memorable. *A Tryst In Time* is both memorable and captivating!"
—Miss V.N., Pittsburgh, PA

IN HER PLACE

"So," Missy taunted, "are you going to sweep me off up those stairs and ravish me, now that you've abducted me?"

"Don't tempt me!" Fabian snapped.

She expelled an exasperated sigh and crossed her arms over her chest. "All right. Why don't we just have it out, now that I've stepped all over your silly macho pride?"

He took a menacing step toward her, and, even in the scant light, the hard glitter in his eyes was unnerving to her. "You really like to provoke me, don't you, Missy?"

"So what if I do?" she shrugged with bravado. "Now, aren't you gong to follow suit like every other bumpkin tonight and tell me I've forgotten my place?"

"Oh, I've a place in mind for you," he said in a soft voice that sent a chill coursing through her.

"And where is that, *pray tell?*" she mocked.

He stared her straight in the eye. "In my bed."

Other *Leisure Books* by Eugenia Riley:

A TRYST IN TIME

TEMPEST IN TIME

EUGENIA RILEY

LEISURE BOOKS   NEW YORK CITY

*This book is dedicated, with love,
from my daughter, Noelle, to the
memory of Brian—*

Heaven will never be the same.

A LEISURE BOOK®

January 1993

Published by

Dorchester Publishing Co., Inc.
276 Fifth Avenue
New York, NY 10001

The author extends special thanks to Virginia Brown and Linda Kichline of Memphis, Tennessee.

Chapter One

Missy Monroe was talking on the phone with her fiancé, and her mind was on ball bearings.

"Yes, Jeff, everything is set for the wedding tomorrow," she said tensely as she puffed away on a cigarette and scowled at the production schedule on her desk. "Mom and Dad seem to have all their ducks in a row, and I'm completely packed."

"I can't wait to see you in your bikini on that beach in St. Croix," Jeff said. "I'm sure I won't be able to keep my hands off you."

"You've managed to do so up until now," she responded dryly.

"Now, Missy. You know I want to wait until after we're married and make everything perfect," Jeff assured her gently.

Missy stifled a groan. "Ah, yes. Old-fashioned

11

gallantry, right here on the brink of the twenty-first century. How did I manage to deserve such a wonderful man as you?"

Jeff chuckled. "Sweetheart, are you teasing me?"

Missy sighed, setting down her cigarette and taking a quick gulp of scalding-hot coffee. She grimaced as her stomach rebelled at her fifth cup of the bitterly strong brew so far that day. "Actually, I think I'm just being honest."

"Then I might also wonder how I've come to deserve such a fine woman as you."

Now Missy did groan. "If you wonder about that, Jeff Dalton, you're a masochist."

He chuckled. "And you, darling, are being far too hard on yourself, as usual. Are we still on for dinner tonight?"

Tossing back her hair, Missy rubbed the tense muscles at the back of her neck. "Sure. If I can just get that shipment out the door to Detroit by then."

A note of concern entered his voice. "Missy, you work too hard. You know you don't have to continue at this pace once we're married. Between us, we have plenty of money."

"But I'll always want to work, Jeff."

"What about the children we want?"

She shrugged. "What do you think nannies are for? I'm not giving up my career."

There was an awkward pause, then Jeff said resignedly, "Of course, darling."

Missy rolled her eyes as she watched the plant manager step up to her doorway. "Look, George Schmidt is here, so I'd better run."

"Certainly. Give my best to George. Pick you up at seven?"

"Great."

Hanging up the phone, Missy stubbed out her cigarette and glanced anxiously at George. "Well? Will we make the deadline?"

George—a large, balding man in his late forties who appeared to be perpetually exhausted—flashed his boss a sheepish smile. "Sorry, Missy, but two more of the grinders just went down."

"Damn it!" Missy lurched to her feet, confronting George angrily. "How can you let something like this happen? If we don't get that shipment crated and ready for the hotshot by five, we're going to lose the order! I told you to monitor the preventive maintenance on those machines! One more fumble like this, mister, and it'll be your—"

"My what, Missy?" George interjected with tired patience.

All at once, Missy made a strangled sound, gritting her teeth in an effort to control her surging temper. She stalked off to the window, folding her arms tightly across her roiling stomach and staring moodily at the Mississippi River in the distance. She couldn't believe what she'd almost said to George—the very last person on earth whom she needed to alienate today!

Across from her, George Schmidt observed his young boss with a world-weary eye. Missy Monroe was a stunning blue-eyed blonde with a perfect cameo face. She wore a crisp suit of lightweight blue wool, and her shiny long hair was impeccably coifed about her face and shoulders. A person would never know just by looking at her that this twenty-five-year-old woman was a headstrong, spoiled little brat. Around the plant, Missy was called, unofficially, "The Bitch."

13

George had known Missy all her life. When Howard and Charlotte Monroe had first started Monroe Ball Bearings twenty-five years ago and had brought their infant daughter with them to the plant, he had even changed Missy's diapers a few times. Yet George had always felt concerned that the kindly Monroes had spoiled Missy outrageously, giving in to their willful child's every whim. Now, the 100 employees of the plant were reaping the consequences of Howard and Charlotte's total indulgence of their only child.

Ever since Missy had taken the helm of Monroe Ball Bearings two years ago, she had run the establishment with an iron fist, subjecting the staff to endless threats, unreasonable demands, and frequent temper tantrums. She never went so far as to fire anyone, but several qualified middle managers had already thrown up their hands and quit after bearing the brunt of one of her tirades. The loss of trained staff had hurt the enterprise, and probably as a result, Missy had recently made at least a token attempt to curb her notorious, hair-trigger temper. Rumor even held that she had attended a few therapy sessions.

Now, she turned to George with a contrite smile. "Look, George, I'm sorry. You've been like a second father to me, and I can't believe what I almost said to you. I don't know what I'd do if I lost you. I don't know why you put up with me sometimes. I'm such a bitch."

George didn't comment on what both of them knew to be true. Instead, he said, "Missy, you can't expect machines that are being run twenty-four hours a day, seven days a week, not to break down."

She waved him off. "I know."

"But we'll make that deadline, even if I have to grind the last few bearings with my teeth. Look, you've got wedding plans to complete, so why don't you just go on home?"

A crooked smile pulled at her mouth. "I'm being a pain in the neck, right?"

"Try a little lower," he suggested dryly.

She pointed toward him in a mock gesture of a firing gun. "Gotcha." She bit her lip. "By the way, are you certain you can handle everything while I'm away in the Caribbean?"

"We've been over this a thousand times." He winked at her. "Believe it or not, you're not indispensable around here. Almost, but not quite. Now, you just go on and marry that fine young man of yours and be happy." With a touch of sadness, he finished, "I really wish you *could* be happy, Missy."

She thrust her fingers through her hair. "I know. That would make life a lot easier for all of us, wouldn't it?" Watching him turn to leave, she added with unaccustomed tentativeness, "See you at the wedding tomorrow?"

He grinned. "Sure, boss. I wouldn't miss it for the world."

Moments later, Missy's mood was dour as she zipped along the freeway, heading toward her family's home in east Memphis. Last month, when the lease on her condo had expired, she'd moved home to prepare for her wedding; after she and Jeff were married, they planned to live at his apartment while they built a house in town.

Before leaving the office, she had dictated a memo to her assistant, giving George Schmidt another hefty bonus, his third so far this year.

She smiled ruefully. Each time she exploded at her capable plant manager, she tried to bribe his forgiveness through another fat check, or a generous chunk of company stock. Her temper was becoming expensive, and George was becoming rich. No doubt, he deserved it for putting up with her.

Why did she have to be such a bitch? Recently, her therapist had been trying to get her more in touch with her own feelings, to help her figure out why she suffered from so much repressed anger and passive hostility.

As nearly as Missy could figure, it was because she really *was* a pain in the neck—and, most critically, because no one here really needed her. She felt strangely out of sync in the world in which she lived, like an odd puzzle piece left over after a perfect picture had already been formed. Her gentle, long-suffering parents didn't need her; she'd been a thorn in their sides all her life, and she knew they would have preferred a much more docile sort of daughter. Monroe Ball Bearings didn't need her, either—George Schmidt was quite capable of running things without her, and she was little more than a squeaking cog there.

Most depressing of all, her fiancé, Jeff, didn't need her. Jeff was a kind, sensitive, honorable man; but Missy knew he was marrying her mostly due to the longtime urging of both their parents. Theirs would be the joining of two old Memphis families, as well as the merging of two viable industries here in this important commercial center of the South. Monroe Ball Bearings and Dalton Steel Tubing. It all seemed as natural and inevitable as baseball and apple pie.

Yet Missy had to face the fact that Jeff simply

did not excite her. Their relationship was devoid of conflict, since he almost always agreed with her on everything. Of course, Missy would never have dreamed of marrying any other type of man, since she was a hard-charging, liberated woman who wouldn't take any nonsense from anyone. She had been drawn to Jeff initially because he was so gallant, completely different from the jerks, male chauvinist pigs, and outright bastards she had dated in the past.

Still, Jeff was almost too much of a gentleman. Sometimes she perversely hungered to have a shoe-throwing fight with him, a really low-class scene, if only to clear the air. And the lack of sex in their relationship bothered her. Perhaps she could do something about that tonight. . . .

Heaving a guilty sigh, she lit another cigarette. Jeff was a living doll, and she was certainly a self-centered shrew to be thinking such unkind thoughts about him. Besides, surely all she was experiencing were pre-marital jitters. All her doubts would vanish once she and Jeff were married and off on their Caribbean honeymoon.

Missy did look forward to marrying Jeff tomorrow morning in her family's historic home. Missy and her parents lived in a huge Greek Revival mansion that originally had been built in the 1840s and was once part of a cotton plantation owned by some distant relatives named Montgomery. In fact, Missy's mother had once given her a box containing a few old letters belonging to a distant cousin from the 1850s, Melissa Montgomery, after whom Missy had been named. Missy had loved reading Cousin Melissa's descriptions of the carefree life-style of that era, and she had often daydreamed about living in those dashing antebellum times. Indeed, Missy was wearing a replica of Cousin Melissa's wedding dress tomorrow. The box had also contained a faded daguerreotype of Cousin Melissa in her wedding gown, and Missy had been amazed by her resemblance to her distant relative. It had been almost as if she were staring at herself, magically transported to another time.

She laughed at the thought. Wouldn't everyone here love it if she did disappear?

Cousin Melissa's wedding day had been February 29, 1852, according to an inscription on the back of her picture. Leap year. When Missy had discovered that 1992 was also a leap year, she had found the symbolism irresistible and had set her own wedding date accordingly. Wouldn't her grandchildren laugh one day when they discovered that she and Cousin Melissa had married in the same house, in the same wedding gown, on the same day—February 29—only 140 years apart?

The sense of being in another time was certainly with Missy as she turned into the circular driveway of her parents' palatial home. The two-story mansion loomed before her with its fresh white paint, stately fluted columns, and gleaming dark green shutters. Honeysuckle curled about the trellises, and, around the grounds, magnolias, dogwood, and azaleas were already sprouting lush blooms. At the front of the house, two workmen were washing windows in preparation for tomorrow's wedding. Missy's heart took a sudden, unanticipated dip at the thought.

She parked her green Jaguar in front of the house, got out, and hurried up the front steps, taking deep breaths of the crisp, nectar-scented breeze. Inside the foyer, she noted that several maids were busy cleaning fixtures and polishing the fabulous rosewood antiques in the double parlors and dining room. The mingled smells of furniture polish, glass cleaner, and roses laced the air.

She spotted her father standing beyond her at the newel post, at the base of the fabulous spiral staircase. Tall, slender, and gray-haired, Howard Monroe was intently polishing the newel button with his handkerchief.

Missy smiled. She had always been fascinated by the newel stone, which was green malachite shot through with odd, concentric circles. She remembered when she was a small child and her father had first told her of the legend of the newel button, of how in the "olden days" the button had been placed on the newel post in honor of the mortgage on the house having been paid. Her father had also mentioned that this particular button was supposed to be a polished fragment from a genuine Egyptian amulet.

Howard glanced up at his daughter and smiled. "Well, hello, dear. Glad to see you home early, for a change. All set for the wedding tomorrow?"

Missy hurried over to hug her father, stretching on tiptoe to plant a kiss on his cheek. "George hustled me out of the plant. I was being a nuisance, as usual."

Her father chuckled. "I take it he'll be receiving another generous bonus?"

"You take it right." She glanced about. "Where's Mom?"

"Settling some last-minute details with the florist and the caterer." He coughed awkwardly. "I do hope that George is still planning to attend the wedding tomorrow?"

"I didn't manage to scare him off, if that's what you're so tactfully asking." Missy sighed. "Oh, Dad, you and Mom have been so good to me, and I've always been such a pain."

Her father eyed her quizzically. "You haven't been that bad, dear, not really."

She rolled her eyes. "Not even when I got expelled from boarding school for smoking in the library? Or the time I hid in one of the delivery trucks—and ended up in New Orleans? Or the day I got my driver's license and totaled your Cadillac?"

Her father chuckled. "Why this latent attack of conscience, my dear? It's not like you to be so self-deprecating." His gaze narrowed. "I do hope this sudden remorse is not a result of your therapy. Aren't those sessions supposed to make you feel *better* about yourself?"

"Oh, I don't know, Dad . . . I suppose I *am* trying to take a hard look at myself." She frowned morosely. "Maybe I'm just feeling sorry for Jeff, and thinking of what a rotten wife I'll make him."

Her father slanted her a reproachful look. "I see no one forcing that young man to the altar."

Missy twisted her fingers together. "But he's only marrying me because both our families have always wanted this match. Jeff's so honorable— in a way, it's almost as if he's a man of another age."

"And aren't you marrying him for those very sterling qualities?"

"Yes. But, the question is, why is he marrying *me*?"

Howard gave her hand a quick squeeze. "Now, my dear, give your young man more credit than that. It doesn't stretch my credulity one bit that he would fall in love with such a lovely creature as yourself. You may have your faults, Missy, as we all do, but at heart, you're a very worthwhile young woman. And you must know that your mother and I have always loved you, too."

"I know you do, Dad." She glanced up at him uncertainly. "Even though I'm nothing like either of you?"

"Missy, you've always had such unrealistic expectations. You're being too hard on yourself."

"That's what Jeff said." *Much worse, I've always been too hard on you, and on Mom*, she added to herself guiltily.

Howard gave the newel button one last swipe with his handkerchief. "There. Now everything will shine tomorrow—even this lovely old stone." He stared at his daughter lovingly. "I can't tell you how proud I'll be to escort you down this staircase."

Missy smiled bravely at her father, and the two looked into the newel stone together. . . .

Chapter Two

Memphis, Tennessee—February 28, 1852

In the same house, 140 years away, Melissa Montgomery stood with her father by the same staircase, and both of them were staring at the same newel stone.

Melissa was a stunning, blue-eyed blonde with a perfect cameo face. Her long hair was upswept in a proper bun, and she wore a high-necked frock of dark blue brocade, with full, sweeping skirts that covered even the tops of her black kid walking shoes. Her father was a robust graying man with sparkling blue eyes and a trim goatee; he wore a black frock coat and matching trousers, a green moiré vest, and a black silk cravat.

Using his snowy white handkerchief, John was polishing the newel stone, which a workman had attached to the post earlier that day. The oval of green malachite had been placed on the post in honor of the mortgage on the house being paid in full.

"There," John said proudly, admiring the green bull's eye that now gleamed in its sterling silver holder. "We have double cause to celebrate, my dear. Today, I'm losing a mortgage, and tomorrow, I'm gaining a son-in-law."

"Yes, Papa," Melissa said demurely, even as she inwardly cringed at the thought of wedding Fabian Fontenot tomorrow, in accordance with the marriage contract that had been made between their families at her birth.

"Ten years, and at last this place is truly ours," John went on, glancing about at the double parlors to their left and the dining room to their right. All three rooms sported lavish French Revival furniture, imported rugs, and gleaming crystal chandeliers. Several maids bustled about, cleaning and polishing in preparation for tomorrow's festivities.

Melissa followed her father's scrutiny with a wan smile. She glanced again at the newel post, fingering the button of green malachite, which was shot through with odd, concentric circles. For a moment she could have sworn she saw the button wink up at her, almost like a mysterious conspirator. "Where did you get this stone, Papa? It's so lovely."

"Do you remember Finias Haggedorn, my friend who traveled so extensively throughout Egypt? He brought me this bit of malachite following his last expedition."

"How fascinating."

Leaning toward his daughter, John confided with a twinkle in his eye, "Finias swears the stone is a fragment from a genuine Egyptian amulet.

It's even supposed to possess magical properties."

"Truly?" Melissa replied. "You know, a moment ago, I could have sworn I saw the stone—"

The rest of Melissa's comment was curtailed as the front door swung open and Lavinia Montgomery swept inside, the ostrich feathers on her hat bobbing as she crossed over to her husband and daughter. Following the slim, still youthful matron was a beleaguered-looking manservant who was trying to juggle at least half a dozen boxes.

"Hello, darlings!" Lavinia trilled gaily, removing her gloves as she pecked the cheeks of her husband and daughter. With a nod at the servant, she continued crisply, "Joseph, you may take all of those boxes up to Miss Melissa's room." Winking at her daughter, she added in a confidential whisper, "My dear, wait until you see the luscious lingerie I bought you to complete your trousseau!"

"Thank you, Mother," Melissa said dully.

Lavinia glanced chidingly from Melissa to John. "And what are the two of you doing standing here by the newel post like a couple of hat trees? You both have duties to attend to, I might point out."

John chuckled. "Now, Vinnie, don't get on your high horse. Your daughter and I were having ourselves a bit of a ceremony."

"And what sort of ritual is this, pray tell?" Lavinia demanded imperiously. "May I remind you that the only ceremony that matters is the one to be carried out here tomorrow after church?"

John smiled. "True, my dear. But I think it's also important that your daughter and I take a moment to note the placement of the newel button on the post—in honor of the mortgage being paid."

"Stuff and nonsense," Lavinia insisted stoutly. "Melissa is getting married tomorrow, and all you can think about is mortgages and these absurd, trivial rituals."

"Trivial?" John boomed. "Are you now calling the home where we raised this lovely child trivial? May I remind you that you're the one who insisted that we build this Greek Revival monstrosity?"

"Now *you're* calling our home a monstrosity?" Lavinia queried.

"You called it absurd," John pointed out heatedly.

"I certainly did not! I merely called the *ritual* absurd—"

"Mama, Papa, please!" Melissa interjected fretfully. "Must you bicker so, on the very eve of my wedding?"

"My point exactly," Lavinia blustered on, with a firm nod at her husband. "Here you are, spending your time blessing newel buttons and other such folderol, when we've a wedding to prepare for!" She glanced sternly at her daughter. "Why, the situation is most grave, John. Just look at the girl—at twenty, she's practically a spinster, and we can't afford to leave anything to chance."

"My dear, what a callous thing to say to the child," John chided.

"The *child* needs a husband, just as you and I need grandchildren," Lavinia snapped back.

"Well, you needn't reduce things to such a crude level," John argued. "Think of your daughter's sensibilities, for heaven's sake."

"The girl is marrying Fabian Fontenot," Lavinia

25

continued, undaunted. "I'm sure her sensibilities have been thoroughly scandalized by now." She pinched Melissa's cheek. "What a sly devil he is. You lucky girl."

As Melissa stifled a cry of horror at her mother's words, John's features darkened. He shook a finger at his exasperating wife. "Lavinia, I'll tolerate no more of this loose talk. Why, a body would almost assume you're in love with that young man—"

"Why even assume?" Lavinia asked outrageously.

"Lavinia Montgomery! If I weren't a gentleman, by thunder, I'd have you across my knee for such treason. . . ."

As her parents continued bickering, Melissa stood miserably at the sidelines. As always, she felt totally left out of their lively banter, an outsider in her own home. Though her parents had always treated her well, Melissa had felt all her life that they were disappointed in her as a daughter, and that they would have preferred a spunkier offspring. As for her marriage tomorrow, she had long ago concluded that her parents were much happier that they were gaining Fabian Fontenot as a son-in-law than they were that she was gaining a husband.

"He is coming for supper tonight, isn't he, dear?" Lavinia interjected, breaking into Melissa's thoughts.

"I beg your pardon?" she asked.

"Fabian? Isn't he coming for supper tonight?" Lavinia repeated impatiently.

"Fabian told me he would stop by after the evening meal—to discuss our wedding trip," Melissa related awkwardly.

"Ah, wonderful," Lavinia cried, clapping her hands. "Dessert."

"Now, Lavinia," John scolded.

Melissa left her parents to bicker and slipped away up the spiral staircase. On the second floor, she swept quickly to her room, entered, and shut the door. She glanced around at the familiar haven where she had spent so many happy hours reading, sewing, praying, or just day-dreaming. She watched the sunlight dance across the Persian rug and gleam on the polished rosewood furniture, the bright cheeriness of its rays seeming to taunt her. She glanced at the lingerie boxes stacked on her dresser—and abruptly burst into tears.

Crossing the room, Melissa threw herself across the bed and sobbed disconsolately. As much as she had tried to put on a good show around her parents, she was terrified at the prospect of marrying Fabian tomorrow. He had made her life utter hell all through their courtship. No matter how hard she had tried to please him, she simply could not. He scoffed at her sensibilities and bellowed at her constantly. Her attempts to placate him only enraged him all the more. Though she hated to admit it, she had to acknowledge now in her heart that Fabian was a beast and that the two of them had nothing in common. Their marriage was surely doomed—

And yet Fabian would be coming to see her tonight, to discuss plans for their wedding trip! The very idea made her quake and sob all the more.

Melissa fervently wished she could somehow escape her fate. Yet she was deeply religious and devoted to her family, and she would not dream of disappointing her parents, or of dishonoring the marriage contract made at her birth.

Now, if only she could survive her marriage to Fabian!

"Melissa, child, what ails you?"

At the dinner table that night, Melissa glanced apologetically at her mother, after having just spilled her third goblet of water during the meal. "I'm sorry, Mother," she murmured, then turned apologetically to the graying manservant who was mopping up the mess with a linen towel. "Here, Joseph, let me . . ."

"Restrain yourself, daughter!" Lavinia scolded so vehemently that both Melissa and Joseph shrank back. "Why do we have servants, if not to tend to such mishaps?"

"Yes, Mother," Melissa said, planting both hands firmly in her lap and slanting Joseph a lame smile.

Meanwhile, Melissa's father was dabbing at his mouth with a napkin and flashing a sympathetic grin at his daughter. "Now, Vinnie, don't be so hard on the girl. She's simply experiencing pre-marital jitters. Very natural."

"Pre-marital jitters, my hat!" Lavinia snorted. "The way the girl is fumbling her way through dinner, she'll surely dump a tureen of soup over poor Fabian's head on their wedding night."

Even Melissa gasped at that horrifying image.

John was poised to comment when Eli, the butler, stepped into the room and announced, "Mr. Fabian Fontenot has arrived."

No sooner had Eli pronounced his words than a tall, dark, masterfully handsome man strode in. "Good evening, John, Lavinia." His intense gaze flicked over to Melissa, and he added with a touch of cynicism, "My darling Melissa."

While Melissa stared back at Fabian, wide-eyed, John and Lavinia sprang up to greet their guest.

"Fabian, boy!" John boomed out, pumping Fabian's hand and pounding his back.

"My dear, you're just in time for dessert," Lavinia added to her future son-in-law with an adoring smile.

"Thank you for your hospitality," Fabian returned in his deep, resonant voice, "but actually, I've come by to have a word with my future bride." He shot another meaningful glance at Melissa, who stared back at him like a frightened doe.

"Ah, yes, boy, you two have a wedding trip to plan, don't you?" John put in. "Are you spiriting our daughter off to some truly romantic haunt?"

"I hear Paris is so lovely in the spring," Lavinia added wistfully.

Fabian fought a grin. "Well, suffice it to say, your daughter's wedding trip should prove a fine surprise," he muttered dryly. He started toward Melissa. "My dear, shall we have our little chat out on the gallery?"

She managed a tremulous nod.

"Isn't it a bit cool to sit on the porch tonight?" John asked.

Lavinia waved him off. "John, don't put a damper on them. Can't you tell that these two love birds are dying to be alone?"

"Actually, sir," Fabian remarked to John, "the night is rather mild."

He nodded. "Very well, then."

Fabian took Melissa's shawl from the back of

her chair and draped it about her shoulders. She stared up at him and struggled not to cower in his daunting presence.

"Shall we?" he murmured mockingly, extending his arm.

Melissa gulped, but obediently shot to her feet. "Of course, F-Fabian," she stammered. She placed her clammy fingers on his arm.

"John, Lavinia, if you'll excuse us?" With these polite words to his parents-in-law-to-be, Fabian towed his fiancée from the room.

"Ah, a match made in heaven," Lavinia breathed raptly.

John appeared more skeptical, stroking his goatee as he eyed his wife. "You know, I do wonder, my dear."

"Wonder what?" Lavinia asked.

"If we're not imposing our own expectations on the child."

Lavinia was aghast. "Why, John! What an absurd thing to say!"

"Is it?" His frown deepened. "Vinnie, no one ever asked the child if she wants Fabian Fontenot for a husband—"

"How could she not want him? The man is a god!"

John slanted a reproachful glance at his wife. "Perhaps I'm questioning whether we chose a husband for Melissa for our own good instead of for hers."

Lavinia rolled her eyes. "John! What folderol! The two are obviously meant for each other. Why, the girl was fairly trembling with joyous anticipation as they left the room together."

John appeared unconvinced. "Was it anticipation? I wonder."

* * *

Out on the dusky, cool front porch, Melissa sat tensely on the swing, clutching her shawl tightly about her as she watched Fabian pace. Lost on her was the beauty of the sunset, the sweet scent of the jasmine and the calling of a night bird. Her entire being was focused on her tyrant of a fiancé and what preposterous thing he might say or do next.

Striding about with hands clasped behind his back and scowling formidably, Fabian appeared as volatile and unpredictable as a storm about to unleash its fury. Oh, Melissa well knew he could be charming and agreeable, as he'd been with her parents in the dining room. Yet he also had a hair-trigger temper and a brooding, mercurial nature—all of which Melissa was painfully aware, after their two-year-long courtship.

Often, guilt gnawed at her that she did not find him more appealing. Fabian certainly turned every other female head in Memphis, and he had never missed an opportunity to flirt with the fairer sex, even in her presence. It often dismayed Melissa that, far from becoming jealous at her fiancé's overtures toward other young ladies, she often wished he'd simply choose some other Memphis belle to wed.

He was certainly a prime candidate—big, broad-shouldered, and muscular, with thick, curly dark brown hair, deep-set brown eyes, and features that appeared as if chiseled from some ancient bust of male perfection. Melissa knew that most women would swoon in joy at the prospect of sharing the marriage bed with him—

Instead, Melissa quaked in fear, the very intensity that set other female hearts to palpitating making her shrink in horror. The few times Fabian had kissed her had been unqualified disasters. He had been bold, demanding, totally impatient with her maidenly qualms; she had been overwhelmed, on the verge of hysterics. If such were her reaction to a mere kiss, their wedding night would surely be an utter trial for her and a terrible disappointment for him.

He turned to her with a strained smile. "You are all packed for tomorrow, I presume?"

She twisted the fringe on her shawl. "Yes, Fabian."

His challenging gaze impaled her. "You're certain you want to follow through with this?"

Melissa was taken aback, feeling sweat break out on her upper lip. "What other choice do we have? After all, the contract was signed at my birth."

"Indeed, it was," he drawled. "We mustn't neglect our duty, must we, you and I?"

Melissa bit her lip. "Fabian, is there something you wish to say? I mean, you seem rather tightly wound tonight."

"Do I?" He crossed his arms over his chest in a gesture of belligerence. "Tell me, are you not curious regarding our wedding trip, my pet?"

She stared at her lap and muttered, "I'm sure that anywhere you wish to take me will be fine with me."

Anger darkened his face. "My, my. Do try to restrain your joy at the thought of wedding me."

She glanced away awkwardly. "I'm sorry, Fabian. I did not wish to make you feel . . . unwelcome."

To her chagrin, her apology only snapped his meager patience and exacerbated his fury. He charged on her aggressively. "You did not want to make me feel *unwelcome*? How could I possibly feel that way? You merely quake in terror and revulsion every time I come near you! You only shrink in horror ever time I kiss you! Why should I feel the least bit *unwelcome*, my sweet darling, when you're about as eager to marry me as a felon being carted off to the gallows!"

Melissa was fighting tears at his harsh, cruel words. "Fabian, I—I apologize if I've seemed—distant. But, please, must you bellow at me tonight, on the very eve of our wedding?"

"Must I bellow?" Fabian was shouting now. "Damn it, woman, where is your righteous indignation? Have you no spine at all? Is that calf's jelly holding you together? I swear, I've never known a woman who was more mealymouthed and lacking in spirit! If I brought a cast-iron tea kettle crashing down upon your head, you would only apologize for being in my way!"

Melissa stared at him distraughtly, wringing her hands. "What is it you want, then? Why is it I can never please you?"

Fabian clenched his fists and somehow restrained an insane impulse to blurt out the truth. Instead, he said resignedly, "The die is cast. It seems we cannot escape our fate."

Melissa nodded miserably. "That is true."

"We'll wed in the morning, then," Fabian continued morosely, "and tomorrow afternoon, we'll depart on our—blissful honeymoon."

Melissa gulped, her curiosity at last outweighing her fear. "Where is it you are taking me, Fabian?"

A smile of vengeful pleasure lit his face. "Why, I'm taking you on a safari to Africa, my sweet darling."

"A—a safari! To Africa!" Melissa was aghast.

"Indeed. We're sailing for the Gold Coast, where we shall hunt elephants with friendly Nigerian natives."

"Fabian! Surely you jest."

"Not at all. So you don't think you'll enjoy traipsing through the wilds of the brush country with me, my sweet?"

"It is not that at all!" Melissa cried. "I find your choice of a wedding trip—bizarre, to say the least—but I would be willing to abide by your wishes—only—"

"Only what, pray tell, my sweet darling?" he sneered.

Huge scalding tears filled Melissa's eyes. "How can you even think of shooting those big gentle elephants!"

He muttered a blistering expletive. "Oh, for the love of heaven! So I've offended your tender sensibilities, have I? I knew before that you were a prig, but now I'm certain I'm marrying a coward—and a hothouse flower."

These comments brought Melissa surging to her feet. She trembled in hurt and mortification. "How can you say such a thing!"

"I say it because it's true!" he barked. "Now, the question is, will you obey me and go to Africa like a dutiful wife, or shall we simply call off this travesty of a marriage?"

Melissa's lower lip was quivering violently. "Fabian, they're only elephants! How can you shoot them?"

"Quite easily, my pet," he snapped. "With an elephant gun."

"B-but they no more deserve to be shot than—than I do!"

He raised an eyebrow at that. "Don't tempt me."

Melissa was choking on sobs. "Very well, then, Fabian Fontenot! I'll go with you to Africa! But do not expect me to join in your cruelty!"

She fled into the house.

"Ah, hell!" Fabian groaned.

He remained behind, slamming his fist into a pillar and cursing himself as a sadistic beast for making Melissa cry.

Actually, Fabian had no intention of taking Melissa to Africa. But some perverse part of him had been trying for ages to provoke her into breaking their engagement. Why did she always give in to him on everything? Why did she never truly fight him, or tell him to go to hell, as he sometimes so richly deserved? He hated himself because this gentle creature always brought out the worst in him. Fear gnawed at him that their marriage would be a disaster. But no matter what unforgivable thing he did, Melissa had never even considered calling off the wedding. And even he couldn't be such a cad as to break the contract made so long ago between their families.

Sorrow lanced Fabian's heart as he remembered his mother and father. He'd lost his parents two years ago, in a yellow fever epidemic. He now shared the family plantation home with his aging grandparents, who were frail and infirm, as well as deeply entrenched in Old-World traditions. Fabian knew that if he backed out of the arranged marriage now, he would break his grandparents' hearts—not to mention disgracing the memory of the dear mother and father who had made the contract in the first place.

He was bound, then—bound by guilt and honor.

While he might try to goad Melissa into rejecting him, he could never subject her to the humiliation and disgrace of a broken engagement at his hands.

He lit a cheroot, his gloom growing as deep as the shadows of the night. Every time he touched Melissa she cringed from him. She was a shy, retiring maiden who needed to be wooed and seduced; he was a man of strong urges accustomed to taking precisely what he wanted—a man with no patience whatsoever for a jittery virgin.

Their marriage was clearly doomed, yet there was no help for it.

Late that night, when all the house was dark, Melissa crept down the steps in her traveling cloak, with her valise in hand. Hers was a flight of utter panic and despair, and she had no idea where she was going. But, for the moment, her terror at the thought of wedding Fabian outweighed all other concerns.

Next to the newel post, she paused, as she again seemed to glimpse that odd light winking at her from the stone. She remembered how thrilled her father had been during their small ceremony today, how proud both her parents were regarding her planned marriage to Fabian tomorrow. Her heart welled up with painful, conflicted emotion—

Suddenly, Melissa realized that she couldn't disappoint her parents—she couldn't run away from her troubles. Fabian had been right—there was no escaping their fate. With tears streaming down her face, she stared into the newel button and whispered hoarsely, "I wish I could be anywhere but here!"

Melissa rushed back up the stairs to her room, where she spent the rest of her night in a purgatory of desperate weeping and futile prayer.

Chapter Three

One hundred and forty years away, Jeff Dalton and Missy Monroe stood by the same newel post, kissing. The two had just returned from an evening of dinner and dancing. Missy wore a black cocktail dress and pumps, Jeff a navy suit, a white shirt, and a tie.

Missy was trying her best to pour herself into the kiss, clinging to Jeff and pressing her mouth firmly onto his. Jeff's response was far more restrained, his lips remaining tightly pressed together, his hands perched tensely on her shoulders.

At last she pulled back in exasperation. "Jeff, what's wrong with you tonight? I might as well be kissing a block of ice, for all that you respond to me!"

Jeff chuckled, flashing charming dimples. "Just trying to restrain myself, darling, so tomorrow night will be very special."

Missy breathed a frustrated sigh and took his hand. "Let's have a nightcap in the living room."

"Sure. Whatever you say."

Inside the lovely old double parlors, Missy poured them both snifters of brandy, and they settled down with their drinks on the rosewood settee flanking the blazing fire. Jeff took off his jacket and loosened his tie. For a few moments, the two sipped their drinks in silence and absorbed the ambience of the elegant rooms.

Missy glanced at Jeff, reflecting on how handsome he was, with his thick blond hair, his blue eyes, and his finely chiseled features. He was tall, with a lean, muscular build that looked great in swim trunks. She had often mused that they would have beautiful children together someday. While Missy was devoted to her career, she had always secretly mourned her upbringing as an only child, and had longed to have several children of her own. Of course, she would never be willing to give up her career, but she firmly believed that her work would be no impediment to her having a family—

If Jeff would ever father her children! She swirled her brandy and frowned at the thought, realizing that it really bothered her that she and Jeff were marrying tomorrow and they still hadn't slept together. Perhaps she was using him in this marriage, but he would clearly benefit from the arrangement, too—

What if her stud were a dud?

Jeff set his snifter down on the coffee table and flashed her a tired smile. "Guess I'd best be going, Missy. We've a big day ahead of us tomorrow."

She touched his hand. "Jeff, do you really want this marriage?"

He appeared taken aback. "Why, of course I do."

"I just don't know sometimes," she said sullenly.

"Missy—you must know I'm devoted to you," came his gallant response.

She still appeared unconvinced, pressing her fingers on his shirtfront. "Then how 'bout just one more kiss before you leave?"

He smiled placatingly. "Sure, darling."

Jeff took Missy's snifter and set it down on the coffee table. Then he drew her into his arms and slanted his mouth tenderly over hers. But Missy had lost all patience with his chaste kisses. Her bold fingers pulled at his shirt buttons; her tongue pressed eagerly into his mouth, darting in and out in shameless invitation.

Missy heard Jeff groan, felt his arms tighten about her. For a brief, exhilarating moment, she was sure she had won. Taking encouragement from his raspy breathing and the eager press of his body, she undid several buttons on his shirt and ran her fingertips over his bare, muscular chest. She could have laughed her triumph when his tongue plunged with sudden hunger into her mouth. Her hand moved wantonly lower, beneath his waist, then her fingers curled about something deliciously hard—

She gasped with joy and delirious anticipation. This man was clearly no dud!

Then, even as she was reaching for his belt buckle, Jeff abruptly pulled away, stood, and crossed the room to the window. Standing with his back to her, he buttoned his shirt and straightened his tie. "Missy, we mustn't," he said hoarsely. "Your parents—"

"Are sound asleep upstairs," she finished impatiently. "As for you, Jeff Dalton, either you've started carrying a nightstick or you're hiding one wedding present I'm determined to open tonight."

He turned on her in sudden anger. "I don't find your crude attempts at humor the least bit amusing, Missy."

She lunged to her feet. "Then why are you marrying me?"

For a moment, Jeff was tempted to blurt out the truth. Then he thrust his hands into his pockets and said resignedly, "I'm marrying you because it pleases you—and because it pleases our families."

"And what about you?" she pursued aggressively. "Does this marriage please you?"

He sighed. "Why else would I have proposed, Missy?"

"I'm really not sure." She eyed him quizzically. "Are you a virgin, Jeff?"

His face darkened. "Certainly not!"

"Well, I'm not either," she asserted without shame.

He laughed dryly. "I'm certainly well aware of that fact."

"Then what's the big deal about our making love?" she demanded.

"Are you afraid that you'll get less than you bargained for?" he asked darkly.

"Well maybe I am!" she retorted. "I'm not really sure at this point whether you'll ever honor your obligations as my husband."

"Damn it, Missy!"

Prior to this moment, Missy had been certain that she knew Jeff Dalton. But it was a white-faced stranger who now quickly crossed the room,

41

pulled her into his arms, and kissed her with surprising passion.

A moment later, he pulled back, blinking at her as a muscle worked in his jaw. "Don't worry, Missy," he assured her bitterly. "I'll rise to my duty."

Numbly, she watched him stride out of the room. Never had she known Jeff Dalton to be possessed of such turbulent emotion.

"My God, where did *that* come from?" Missy whispered.

Jeff didn't feel proud of himself as he drove away from the Monroe home. By nature, he was a patient, gentle man, but tonight, his fiancée had managed to goad him into an anger and passion that he now deeply regretted.

He recalled her ruthless questions: Why was he marrying her? Was he a virgin? He smiled ruefully. He supposed he was a virgin—almost. Wouldn't Missy laugh if she knew the truth? If she knew he had made love to only one woman during his entire lifetime? If she knew that he was marrying her now to please other people, not himself?

For, as much as Jeff had tried to play the role of the amorous, attentive fiancé, he knew that this marriage, far from being a love match, was a merger, a cold-blooded business deal. All his life, his parents, patriarchs of Dalton Steel Tubing, had yearned to join forces with Monroe Ball Bearings. For some time, Jeff had resisted them, and then, about two years ago, when his father's health was rapidly failing, he'd given up and acquiesced. Tomorrow, his widowed mother would see their dream realized, and Jeff would consign himself to a loveless marriage. He was nothing if not a dutiful son.

Was he being fair to Missy? A bitter laugh rose up in him. Oh, yes, he was being eminently fair. Missy wanted a merger, too. Her only qualm seemed to be whether or not he would father the children she longed for to perpetuate her dynasty.

There, too, he would fulfill his duty, even if his heart would never be in this marriage.

Where was his heart? At that critical question Jeff felt tight emotion welling up in his chest.

Jeff was twenty-six years old. He had an MBA from Harvard Business School. He worked tirelessly and successfully as general manager of his family's firm. To the world, he presented a cheerful and charming façade.

Yet he was a man dead inside. He had died on the fourth of July, six years ago, on the night he had lost the woman he loved.

Abbie had been only eighteen, full of life and vitality, humor and trust. He had loved her since high school, had dated no one else after he went off to college. He had written her poetry and read it to her in the gazebo behind his family's summer house.

He'd been home that summer before his junior year, and their love had deepened into a maelstrom of passion. He had tried so desperately to resist her, wanting for both of them to be virgins on their wedding night.

On July 2, she'd seduced him, in two hours of glorious passion in the back seat of his car. Jeff had never known that such ecstasy could exist. He had begged her to marry him at once. She had refused, telling him that he had to put his education first. It had been their first and only fight. She had demanded that they both take a week or so to cool off.

Nevertheless, two days later, on July 4, he had called her, begging her to meet him so that they could talk things over. She had made plans for the day, having signed up to paint houses in a poor neighborhood with members of her church. But she had promised to meet him late that night, at their favorite spot in Audubon Park—

She had never made their meeting. As Abbie drove to the park, a drunk driver had hit her car head-on, and she'd been killed instantly.

Jeff's world had been utterly shattered. It was still shattered. If anyone ever read the dark, hopeless poems he wrote now, he'd be carted off to an asylum.

Abbie had been the only woman he ever loved, the only woman he'd ever made love to.

Now, he would commit himself to a marriage where his feelings would always be safe, shut away, sacrosanct.

Where was his heart? It lay at Memorial Park Cemetery, with an angel who would never see nineteen.

Chapter Four

The next morning a feeling of unease dogged Missy as she sat at her dressing table. Her hair was styled in lush ringlets atop her head, and she had already donned her lingerie and petticoats and had applied light makeup, in keeping with the old-fashioned dress she would soon put on. Yet as she stared at her reflection in the mirror, she saw a tight-lipped young woman with worry lines surrounding her mouth and eyes—not a blushing bride.

Today was her wedding day, yet Missy's mood was far from blissful. She remained perplexed by Jeff's behavior the previous night, and she still wasn't really sure why he was marrying her. She had suspected for some time that he didn't love her, and she knew in her heart that she didn't love him.

Why, then, was she going through with this?

Because Jeff is handsome and charming. Because

he treats you like a lady. Because you can always get your way with him.

A dozen sound reasons for marrying him flooded her mind. The marriage was expedient, a sound and logical business merger. Love didn't matter as much as accomplishing her goals—

Why, then, couldn't she shake this feeling of vague dissatisfaction?

Missy told herself she couldn't have it all. No one could. Oh, she'd been around a few men who'd sparked feelings of passion in her. Yet those same men had been chauvinistic jerks who had really wanted only to boss her around.

Jeff represented safety, security, respect. Those were the things that really mattered in life, weren't they?

"Good morning, dear," a pleasant feminine voice trilled out, breaking into Missy's turbulent thoughts.

Missy glanced over her shoulder, watching a plump, middle-aged woman enter the room with a breakfast tray. "Good morning, Mom."

"How are you doing today, sweetheart?" Charlotte Monroe continued, crossing the room. She was already dressed for the wedding in a stylish ensemble of lavender silk.

Missy groaned as she watched her mother set before her a tray with enough pancakes, bacon, and orange juice for three men. "I'm doing fine, Mom—as long as I don't gain five pounds before I try to squeeze into my wedding gown."

Charlotte laughed. "Darling, you're much too thin. So, are you all set for the most exciting day of your life? No last-minute jitters?" She smoothed down a curl on Missy's brow. "You do look rather preoccupied."

Missy restrained an urge to snap at the woman who had hovered over her all her life. Instead, she muttered, "You know I'm not the jittery type." She took a gulp of coffee and grimaced.

"Are you all packed for the Caribbean?"

"Yes, Mother."

"And have you had all your shots?"

Missy rolled her eyes. "What shots?"

"You mean you didn't even ask the doctor? What if you were to contract malaria or something?"

Missy's eyes implored the heavens. "Mother, we're going on a cruise to the Virgin Islands, not on a safari to Borneo."

Charlotte appeared unconvinced, laying an index finger alongside her cheek. "Well, I'm not sure, dear. There must be an inoculation or two that you need. . . ."

Missy set down her lipstick and frowned up at her mother. "Mom, will you please quit worrying and help me into my wedding gown? Isn't the man due any minute now to take my photograph?"

"Well, yes, but . . ." Charlotte chewed her bottom lip. "I just hope we haven't forgotten anything."

Missy stood. "Believe me, Mother, we haven't. After all, you must be the only matron in Memphis with a smoke alarm, a snakebite kit, and a fire extinguisher in every room of your house."

This comment coaxed a smile out of Charlotte Monroe. She swept over to the closet, taking out Missy's wedding dress and then following her daughter to the full-length mirror. Pulling the lovely, old-timey masterpiece of satin, lace, and seed pearls over Missy's head, she uttered an ecstatic sigh.

"Oh, darling, how wonderful you look!" Charlotte cried, dabbing at tears with her handkerchief. "The seamstress did a splendid job of copying Cousin Melissa's wedding gown, didn't she?"

"She certainly did," Missy replied, glancing at the daguerreotype of Cousin Melissa, which sat framed on her dresser. A shiver coursed through her as she stared at the visage of a woman who could have been her exact twin, except for a rather sad, vulnerable quality in her distant cousin's eyes. Gazing back into the mirror, Missy admired the styling of her copied gown—the high neck, fitted bodice, tight waist, and full, sweeping skirts. The entire effect was delicate, feminine, and so old-fashioned that Missy felt almost as if she had stepped back into another time. Indeed, she now so resembled Cousin Melissa's daguerreotype that a more superstitious person might have sworn that she had just materialized from the faded photograph. The thought brought a proud yet fleeting smile to her lips.

Why did she feel so blue?

As a knock sounded, both women called out, "Come in," and Howard Monroe entered the room, wearing an elegant black suit.

Grinning with pride, Howard crossed the room to his daughter and wife, pecking both their cheeks. "My dear, I've never seen a lovelier bride."

"Thanks, Dad," Missy said. "You look quite handsome yourself."

"Well." Howard clapped his hands. "The photographer is here, and a few of the guests have already arrived."

"How wonderful!" Charlotte trilled. Abruptly, she wrung her hands. "Oh, do you suppose we've forgotten anything, Howie?"

"Now, Charlotte, quit fretting, everything is fine," Howard assured her. He turned to his daughter. "Mr. Christopher is setting up his equipment on the upstairs back balcony."

"Great," Missy replied with a frozen smile.

Moments later, Missy stood posing for the photographer on the crisply cool veranda, with the bright sunshine of the late February morning pouring down upon her. The scent of delicate perfumes drifted up from the garden below her, and a choir of birds sang sweetly in the trees.

But as the photographer snapped his shutter, Missy's smile remained stiff, frozen . . .

Melissa Montgomery sat at the dressing table in her underclothes and wrapper. With her hair styled in lush ringlets atop her head, she stared red-eyed into the mirror. She felt—as Fabian had so aptly put it last night—about as eager to marry him as a felon being carted off to the gallows. She glanced across the room at her wedding dress, hanging from the door of her armoire, and sorely wished she could get up the courage to don it.

Melissa had spent the night sleeping fitfully and sobbing into her pillow, as her puffy features now attested. She remained incredulous and horrified that Fabian planned to take her off on a honeymoon to Africa to shoot elephants. Never in her life had Melissa touched a gun, and she wasn't about to do so now. But surely she would burn in hell for being a part of Fabian's scheme. Indeed, nightmares of squalling, stampeding elephants— the poor beasts storming across the African plains as Fabian chased them with a blazing gun—had haunted her dreams all night. She felt more sympathy for the elephants than she felt for herself. At least Fabian wouldn't shoot her—

Or would he? she asked herself in a sudden panic as she recalled some of his surly comments last night.

"Good morning, dear!" a cheerful feminine voice called out.

Melissa jumped and jerked about on her stool, watching her mother sail into the room. Lavinia was already dressed for the wedding in an elegant frock of mauve silk.

"Good morning, Mother," Melissa managed.

With a frown, Lavinia took in her daughter's swollen features. "What's this, daughter? You look as if you're about to attend your own funeral, not your wedding."

As she faced her mother, Melissa's lower lip trembled violently and she burst into tears.

"My heavens!" Lavinia exclaimed, handing her daughter an embroidered handkerchief. "I can understand pre-marital jitters, but you're turning a case of nerves into a full-fledged crying jag."

"I'm sorry, Mother," Melissa choked out.

Lavinia patted the girl's heaving shoulders. "Is it tonight that you're fretting over?"

"Yes . . . No . . . Oh, I don't know!" Melissa wailed.

"I recommend a double dose of brandy before retiring," Lavinia put in confidentially. As Melissa stared at her mother in shocked surprise, she added stoutly, "I realize that you've never touched spirits, but I think some medicinal fortitude may be in order under the circumstances—"

"Oh, dear!"

"Don't worry, Fabian will know precisely what to do."

"That's just what I'm afraid of," Melissa sobbed.

Lavinia might not have even heard her, for all she took note. "Oh, you lucky girl!" she trilled gaily, crossing over to the washstand and wetting a cloth in the basin. She wrung out the rag and returned to her daughter's side, blotting Melissa's face. "Now chin up, daughter! Chin up! The man will arrive shortly to take your daguerreotype. And I'm sure the guests will be descending upon us forthwith, as soon as church is released."

"I do so wish we'd gone to the service this morning," Melissa fretted.

Lavinia raised an eyebrow. "On your wedding day? And risk seeing the groom? I know you don't approve of having the wedding on Sunday, but it's really the only time when everyone is in town, and, besides, Reverend Sloan must leave for the camp meeting tomorrow—"

"Yes, Mother."

"Now, I'll call Dulcie to put on your gown."

Half an hour later, Melissa stood on the back veranda, posing for the photographer in her fabulous gown and veil as the bright sunshine of the late February morning poured down upon her. A potpourri of delicate nectars drifted up from the formal gardens, and a choir of birds sang sweetly in the trees.

Yet, as her image was etched for posterity, Melissa's smile was stiff and frozen.

All too soon, Melissa stood at the top of the dramatic spiral staircase with her father. Her veil was in place, her bouquet in hand. Below her in the huge double parlors, Fabian, the minister, her mother, and several dozen guests waited for her to descend. She stared down at Fabian, noting his grim, impatient expression, and felt the contents of her stomach making a quick, sickening ascent up the back of her throat—

Even as panic and nausea threatened to overwhelm her, the strains of the Wedding March drifted up from the piano.

"Ready, dear?" her father asked with a proud grin.

Wild-eyed and fighting back queasiness, Melissa stared at her father and found herself thinking again, *I wish I could be anywhere but here. . . .*

"Well, Melissa?" he prodded with concern. "Are you all right?"

She flashed him a frozen smile. "Of course, Father. I'm ready."

Melissa's slippered foot ventured forward. Yet instead of contacting the step, her shoe caught on her hem. She did a wild little dance, flailing out with her arms then screaming as she lost her balance—

As her father tried unsuccessfully to grab her and the horrified guests watched, Melissa tumbled head over heels down the stairs, her body abused and bruised by each sharp step. Watching wallpaper and banister spindles whirl past her, she clawed out for a handhold, but grasped only empty air. She continued to roll and pitch headlong until she hit her head on the newel post, lost consciousness, and landed in a heap at the foot of the stairs.

There was a collective gasp, a split-second of appalled silence, and then Melissa's parents, Fabian, and fifty alarmed guests rushed toward the fallen woman. In the panicked atmosphere, no one saw the newel button wink as if it alone were in possession of a mischievous secret. . . .

*   *   *

Missy Monroe stood at the top of the spiral staircase with her father. Her veil was in place, her bouquet in hand. Below her in the huge parlor, Jeff, the minister, her mother, and several dozen guests waited breathlessly for her to descend. Missy watched Jeff smile up at her. He looked very handsome in his old-fashioned morning coat and matching trousers, and yet she could see sadness and a certain resignation in his eyes.

The strains of the Wedding March drifted up from the piano.

"Ready, dear?" her father asked with a proud grin.

Missy glanced again at Jeff's less-than-ardent countenance, then stared at her father. Ironically, she found herself thinking, *I wish I could be anywhere but here . . .*

"Well, Missy?" her father prodded.

Missy flashed him a frozen smile. "Sure, Dad."

Missy's slippered foot moved forward. Yet instead of contacting the step, her shoe caught on her hem. She did a wild little dance, flailing out with her arms and then screaming hysterically as she lost her balance. . . .

Chapter Five

The calendar on the bedside table read "February 29, 1992."

A throbbing pain tugged Melissa Montgomery toward consciousness. She blinked and gasped as her eyes struggled to take in the blurry room. Her head hurt like the very devil, and her body felt as if she'd been pounded with a rolling pin.

Images swam before her, of bizarre people dressed in outlandish clothing. At first, she thought she was in the midst of a bad dream. Then her vision cleared, awareness dawned, and she gasped in fear and horror—

She was lying in a strange bed in a strange room—it was her room, yet it *wasn't* her room at all. The windows were in the same places, yet the drapes were different, straight lined and crisply pleated. The walls were papered in a floral print she'd never seen before; the rug was a plush mauve that crept from wall to wall. The furniture had peculiar, squared-off lines and was vastly different from the carved rosewood pieces she was accustomed to—

And the people! Four utter strangers surrounded her bed, the ladies with short hair and wearing scandalously short dresses, the gentlemen in their equally curious suits and odd, polished shoes. Even as she tried frantically to take all this in, one of the gentlemen stepped forward and flashed a small beam of light into her eyes. As she cowered back in fear and clutched the covers, the man turned to the other gentleman and frowned.

"Well, doctor?" the second man asked.

"Her reflexes seem normal," the doctor said, "but we'll take X rays just to be sure."

Melissa realized she was on the verge of hysterics. Who were these people and what madness were they babbling about? Why was she here? Why was there a small black box on the bedside table, with queer red numbers blinking at her like demons? Why was a shaft of warm air blowing down upon her face, even though there was no window nearby? What were all these bizarre lamps with huge chimneys glowing with soft white light?

"Where am I?" she managed to say at last.

"Oh, you poor dear!" One of the strangers, a plump, graying woman with a kindly face, rushed forward and took Melissa's hand. "Don't worry, Missy, darling, Mother is here!"

"M-Missy? M-Mother?" Melissa gasped, staring mystified at the woman, whom she had never seen before in her life.

"Oh, dear!" the woman gasped. She turned to a tall, gray-haired man. "Howard, she doesn't know me!"

Frowning, the man named Howard stepped forward. "Missy, dear, it's Dad. Surely you must remember—"

"D-dad?" she cut in, more confused than ever.

He turned to the man with the small light. "She doesn't know us, Edmund. Her injury is obviously quite serious."

"I tend to concur," Edmund said as he scratched his jaw.

Even as Melissa continued to take in the scene, wild-eyed, another middle-aged woman stepped forward, this one tall and thin, with pinched, unpleasant features. She peered down at Melissa critically, then turned to the plumper woman. "Well, it looks like she'll live, Charlotte. I've always argued that a good bop on the head might straighten out this little shi—*my niece*— but we can't have the girl stumbling around with amnesia." She peered at Melissa again. "Why, she doesn't even look like herself."

Now all four of the people stepped closer to stare at Melissa intently. Melissa shrank away from them, her eyes huge with apprehension and bewilderment.

"You, know, Sister, you have a point," said the man called Dad. "She does appear somewhat different."

"Why, she looks five years younger," the aunt declared.

"Surely it's just the rushing of blood to her face," the one named Mother added.

The doctor was scratching his jaw again. "We'll know more after the X rays."

"X rays?" Melissa cried. "What X rays?"

"Don't you even remember falling down the stairs, my dear?" Dad asked gently.

"Yes, that I do remember," Melissa replied politely. "Although I must assume that I suffered a rather singular landing, to say the least."

There was a moment of stunned silence, then the others whispered and consulted among themselves. "Why is she talking this way?" the aunt demanded of the mother. "She sounds as if she's rehearsing for *Jane Eyre*, for heaven's sake."

"Oh, dear, this is not good at all," the mother fretted back, wringing her hands.

"I tell you, we must take those X rays at once," the physician added.

Even as Melissa was struggling to take all this in and hang on to her sanity, the bedroom door abruptly swung open and a tall, handsome blond gentleman strode in. At once, Melissa's gaze became riveted upon the newcomer. He wore a gray morning coat and matching trousers—attire much more familiar to her. At once, his presence comforted her and even assuaged her fear. She watched, mesmerized, as the beautiful gentleman crossed the room.

"I called the emergency room just as you asked, Dr. Carnes," he was remarking to the physician, "and they said to bring her on in. Of course, I insisted that they dispatch an ambulance."

"Good thinking, Jeff—and thanks," the physician replied.

The blond man paused before the bed and stared down at Melissa with a warm, surprised smile. "Why, Missy, darling, thank God you're awake!"

Melissa stared up at the man named Jeff and felt her heart skip a beat as she took in his warm smile and charming dimples. When he took her hand and kissed it, her heart soared at the tenderness of his touch, the magic of his lips. Suddenly she no longer cared where she was, or even *who* she was.

For Melissa had lost herself in the most kindly, perfect male face she had ever seen in her life—she was drowning in fathomless blue eyes where she longed to dwell forever.

"Poor, darling Missy," her handsome prince murmured. "That was such a terrible fall you took. Are you sure you're all right now?"

By now, Melissa was certain she had died and gone to heaven. But she did not care, for she had just met the man of her dreams.

Melissa smiled up at Jeff Dalton and replied, "I am doing just splendidly, thank you."

The newspaper lying on the bedside table was dated "February 29, 1852."

A throbbing pain tugged Missy Monroe toward consciousness. She blinked and gasped as her eyes struggled to take in the blurry room. Her head hurt like hell, and her body felt as if she'd been battered with a two-by-four.

Images swam before her, of bizarre people dressed in outlandish clothing. At first she thought she had stumbled into a bad dream—or onto the set of the Memphis Players. Then her vision cleared, awareness dawned, and she gasped in fear and horror—

She was lying in a strange bed in a strange room—it was her room, yet it wasn't her room at all. The windows were in the same places, yet the drapes were different, styled of red velvet with heavy, outdated swags. The walls were papered in an odd, old-fashioned print she'd never seen before; the rug was different, a time-worn Persian. The furniture was intricately carved and looked as if it had come from a museum—

And the people! Four utter strangers surrounded her bed, two women with long hair arranged in buns and wearing gowns that looked as if they'd come straight off the sets of *Gone With the Wind*, and two men in equally outdated suits. Even as Missy struggled desperately to take all this in, one of the men—a Stygian-looking character with a goatee—stepped forward with two small metal contraptions that looked like pill boxes.

"I tell you, the young woman has taken a bilious fever," the man declared to the others, "and that is surely the reason she lost her balance and took that spill. I shall just bleed her with these leeches, and clear her system of the poisons. . . ."

As Missy watched in wide-eyed dread, the man opened one of the contraptions, revealing razor-sharp teeth—and then aimed those vicious teeth squarely at her arm!

"Back off, you quack!" she screamed at the lunatic looming over her, waving a fist at him.

The man instinctively jerked back, and both of the women gasped. "Lavinia," the older of the two said anxiously, "what madness has taken my grandchild?"

"Now, Mother, don't fret," the one named Lavinia said stoutly. "My daughter has taken a bad fall, and she's merely lost her head for the moment."

"Well, let's do hope that she finds it—and posthaste," the older woman pronounced stiffly.

Missy, meanwhile, was gaping at the two strange women. "Grandchild? Daughter?" she repeated incredulously. "Are you two a couple of nut cases or something? What on earth are you babbling about, and where in the hell am I?"

Now everyone gasped.

"Lavinia," the older woman said with a frown, "my grandchild is ranting like a madwoman and cursing like a creature of the streets. I fear the fall has affected her memory."

"It's certainly affected her tongue—for the better, I'd say," Lavinia replied with an astonished smile.

"Now, Vinnie," the other man scolded. "Don't torment the child—she has been through enough already."

The grandmother peered at Missy intently and shook her head. "There is something very queer about all this. She looks different—older, somehow. The fall must have aged her."

The woman named Lavinia waved her off. "Oh, who wouldn't gain a wrinkle or two from a hair-raising plunge like that? Don't worry, Mother, Melissa will be herself in a day or two. Don't you agree, John?"

The man named John stepped forward. "Melissa, dear, it's Father. You've had quite a bad accident, my dear."

Missy had followed this outlandish conversation with an expression of utter mystification. "No lie," she snapped sarcastically.

"But—er—the question is—don't you remember us, my dear?" he continued.

"No, I don't remember you!" she declared. "But I do know a looney tunes when I see one, and the name is Missy, you dope!"

All four of the strangers appeared utterly baffled, and murmured to one another. At last, the man named John cleared his throat and asked, "Don't you even remember falling down the stairs?"

"*That* I do remember," she retorted nastily. "But as for this little detour into the Twilight Zone—why don't you all just give me a break?"

The others were exchanging perplexed glances, when, suddenly and violently, the bedroom door flew open and the most handsome man Missy had ever seen in her life came charging across the room and bellowing—at her! At first Missy was so mesmerized by the man's physical beauty—his tall, muscular body, his Adonis perfect features and deep-set brown eyes—that she didn't really hear his words. Then the force of his diatribe penetrated her whirling mind, and she listened in seething silence.

"Enough, Melissa!" he roared, waving a fist. "I have had all I can abide of your silly frailties and your vapors. It is bad enough that you have disgraced your family with that clumsy, histrionic tumble down the stairs. What is totally unconscionable is that you have tried to rid yourself of this marriage in such a cowardly manner. Well, you agreed to this travesty and so, by damn, you are going to go through with it. Your selfishness has kept the guests waiting quite long enough, thank you. So get your lazy *derriere* out of that bed, come downstairs, and marry me!"

By now, Missy assumed she had died and gone to hell. She had certainly just met Satan incarnate. "Marry you?" she scoffed to the Neanderthal looming over her. "Are you nuts? It'll be a cold day in hell before I marry a horse's patooty like you! You, mister, are a jerk!"

As comments of shock and utter confusion rippled through the room, Missy watched the woman who called herself her grandmother faint dead away to the floor.

Chapter Six

"Where are you taking me?" Melissa gasped. "And what are those?"

Back in the present, Melissa was staring horrified at her presumed mother, who was trying to hand her some odd garments. The strange "aunt" and the men had just left the room, and Melissa was still totally confused regarding where she was and what was going on. She remained incredulous that these people claimed to be her family, and the fact that she was half-dizzy from the pain splintering her head, not to mention sore all over, did not help her state of mind in the least.

"My dear, it's only a pair of panties, a bra, and a slip," the mother assured her gently. "You must put these on so we can go to the hospital and get you checked out."

"Checked out? What is that?" Melissa gasped.

"You know, dear, take X rays," the woman explained patiently.

Melissa shook her head violently, grimacing at the pain her sudden movement brought on. "I want no part of these rays."

"Oh, dear," the woman replied. "You have a concussion, for sure. Just look at that goose egg on your head."

"A concussion?" Melissa's voice quivered with fright as she fingered the sore bump on her forehead. "Whatever it is, I don't want it."

"But you don't have a choice, dear. You have to have it—I mean, you already have it. Oh, my, this is so very difficult," the woman fretted. She gently took Melissa's arm, tugged her to a sitting position, and spoke urgently. "You must dress, Missy. The ambulance will be here any minute."

"Ambulance?"

"To take you to the hospital."

"But I don't want to go to a hospital! I'm not even sure who you are or where I am," Melissa wailed.

"Now, dear, I realize you are confused. Who wouldn't be, after a tumble like that? Just remember that you are at home, with your mother, your father, your aunt, and your dear fiancé, Jeff."

"My dear fiancé, Jeff?" Melissa repeated in an incredulous whisper.

"Yes, darling. Surely you must remember taking that fall down the stairs, right before you were to marry him?"

"Merciful heavens! I was to marry . . ." In an awed voice, Melissa finished, "*Him?*"

Charlotte patted her hand. "There, there, dear, I'm sure it will all come back to you in time. But for now we must get you downstairs. We mustn't make the amubulance wait—"

"Can you not offer a repast to the driver and

give the horses some oats?" Melissa cried desperately.

The woman named Charlotte stared at Melissa in utter shock. "Oh, heavens, this is so much worse than we feared." She tugged the girl to her feet. "Now you must dress, darling."

Staggering on her wobbly feet, Melissa noted for the first time the skimpy attire she was wearing—a sheer pale blue gown that left her arms naked and barely covered her knees. "What manner of garment is this?" she demanded.

"It's your nightgown, dear." The woman rolled her eyes. "Actually, you have no idea of the frustrating time Aunt Agnes and I had getting you out of those strange undergarments—"

"What strange undergarments?"

"Why, that corset, the camisole, and those weird pantaloons, or whatever they were. Agnes and I agreed that it was the oddest selection of lingerie we've ever seen in our lives. Indeed, we were stunned that you took this old-fashioned wedding dress business all the way down to your—er—unmentionables. Oh, well." The woman extended the risqué garments again. "Now, if you'll just put these on—"

Melissa's eyes grew huge as she studied two skimpy bits of sheer lace that obviously purported to be a corset and drawers. "But I cannot wear those!" she gasped. "They are scandalous!"

"Oh, dear."

Despite a long, bewildered litany of protests, Melissa was at last persuaded to don the under things and the "slip," along with a pair of miraculous sheer stockings that covered her from toe to waist, a highly improper dress with a short skirt, and the strangest pair of shoes she had ever seen.

Her head was throbbing with pain and confusion as her new "mother" led her from her room and down the upstairs hallway. She glanced in disbelief at the odd, thick carpet and alien wallpaper, at the strange flat lamps that were attached to the ceiling and glowed so softly.

How could this place be her house, yet *not* be her house? Dear God, where on earth was she, and who were all these strangers into whose clutches she had fallen—literally? Had she died in the fall she'd taken? If so, where had she gone? To purgatory? The unnerving thought made her wince aloud.

"Now, now, dear, it's not that much farther," the woman named Charlotte soothed.

The older woman held Melissa's arm tightly as they maneuvered their way down the stairs. Glancing downward at the foyer, Melissa spotted the doctor, her new "father," and her presumed aunt. Next to them stood the gentleman named Jeff, her supposed fiancé, and despite Melissa's fears, she took heart at the sight of him. She smiled at him shyly and he smiled back.

Just as the two women were reaching the downstairs corridor, two men in white coats entered the house with a stretcher. The doctor firmly took Melissa's arm and led her toward the men, saying, "Now, young lady, if you'll just lie down here—"

But Melissa dug in her heels, her eyes frantic as she glimpsed the horror awaiting her outside. Next to the steps was hunched a huge white metal beast with an evil, blinking red eye!

"Help!" Melissa screamed. "It's a monster!"

Throwing off the doctor's hand, Melissa fled for her life up the steps, while the others watched her with expressions of utter stupefaction. Within seconds, she had disappeared upstairs.

The doctor scratched his chin. "Perhaps we should try a different approach here," he muttered.

Missy charged up dizzily from her bed. The others had left her seconds before so she could rest. She laughed bitterly at the very thought. How could she rest when she had clearly landed in the jaws of hell?

For the first time she noticed that she was wearing a voluminous cotton gown that dragged the floor and looked as if it had belonged to her grandmother. Her head throbbed as she struggled to take in her surroundings. Everything in the room appeared as if it had come from another century—the antique furnishings and old kerosene lamps, the Persian rug, the mother-of-pearl accessories on the dressing table, the porcelain basin and pitcher on the washstand.

What on earth was going on here? Had someone played a huge joke on her, dropping her off at some historical re-enactment village? But how could that be if she was still in the same house? And who were these deranged people who claimed to be her family and fiancé?

Missy rushed over to the French doors that led to her upstairs balcony. She flung them open and stepped outside.

"Oh, my God!" she gasped.

In front of her, where the Johnsons' house should have been, was a huge field. She spotted at least a dozen blacks in work clothing and straw hats; the men were bent over, preparing the earth for planting. To the north, beyond a formal garden and trees, were strange outbuildings and numerous log cabins; half a dozen black children raced about, playing with a dog. In the distance, a horse and buggy were clipping down a narrow plank road where Poplar Street should have been.

"Holy cow!" Missy cried. "I've died and gone to Tara."

Melissa awakened with a splitting head. She had a vague memory of having hysterics, and of a couple of people holding her down while the doctor stuck her with a huge needle. That was the last thing she remembered before oblivion overtook her, and she felt half-tipsy even now.

She staggered to her feet. Again, she glanced, mystified, at her queer surroundings, at the weird furniture with its odd, square shapes and the strange black box staring at her from across the room, its face resembling a shiny blank picture.

Where on earth was she? And who were these strangers who kept insisting they were her family and her fiancé? Not that she minded the fiancé so much, but she had to figure out what was going on here!

She wobbled over to the French doors leading to the veranda and opened them.

"Oh, my God!" she cried.

The Montgomery family cotton plantation was gone. In its place stood several huge, fantastical-looking houses. Metal monsters, resembling the terrifying ambulance, were parked on strange, smooth gray driveways. Small children, dressed in weird outfits, ran about the green yards, laughing and throwing balls to one another. Overhead, ominous-looking black wires were strung across the skies on poles.

Melissa turned from the horrifying scene with a gasp. She paced the room, her mind whirling. She had clearly died in her fall. She had awakened in an entirely different world. But how could that be if she was still in the same house?

At last she paused by the bedside table. She picked up a weird object, slim, black, and smooth, like a polished piece of wood, whose front was dotted with numerous buttons, neat checkerboard-type squares painted different colors, and frightening messages.

"Power, cancel, stop, TV, VCR, record, eject," she read, dropping the bizarre object, as if it had just burned her. She picked up another odd contraption, a wedge of wood to which was attached numerous white sheets on a silver ring.

The first paper read "February 29, 1992."

"1992!" Melissa cried.

She ripped off the slip of paper and stared at it, stupefied. Beneath it, another sheet read "March 1, 1992."

Melissa crumpled to the floor in a swoon.

Missy was about to start hyperventilating. She paced the room madly. Where in the hell was she? *When* in the hell was she? Nothing was where it was supposed to be! Nobody was *who* they were supposed to be—including herself! Missy had never before in her life been afraid of anything, and yet now she actually trembled at the thought of leaving the confines of this house and finding out what other horrors awaited her here—wherever, whenever, here was!

She was losing her mind! She had entered the *Outer Limits*!

Oh, God, she thought, stopping in her tracks. What if she truly had died in that fall?

Then she spotted the newspaper on the bedside table. She raced over to it, picked it up, and stared at it frantically.

"*Memphis Daily Appeal*," she read aloud. "February 29, 1852."

"1852!" she cried.

Missy began to hyperventilate.

Certain she would quickly pass out, she began flinging open drawers and tearing through the old-fashioned lingerie and lace-trimmed handkerchiefs.

"Doesn't anyone have a paper bag in this asylum?" she panted.

Missy made a dive for the bed, yanked the pillow out of its pillowcase, threw the pillowcase over her head, and began choking violently on flecks of stray goosedown.

Melissa burst into the parlor, waving the remote control at Howard and Charlotte. "There is a man upstairs in a black box and he was watching me dress," she informed Howard hysterically. "You must go upstairs and shoot the villian, Father." She stuffed the remote control into his hand. "And take this with you—it is what made him appear in the first place. I presume he must now be stopped, canceled, or ejected—only I had no idea which button to push!"

With these words, Melissa collapsed onto the couch, thrust herself into Charlotte Monroe's arms, and began weeping disconsolately.

"Oh, dear," Charlotte Monroe said, patting the girl's back and glancing at Howard. "I think we'd best call the doctor again."

*   *   *

"A *chamber pot*?" Missy ranted at the hastily summoned black maid who now cowered before her. "Are you nuts? Do you actually mean to tell me there's no indoor plumbing in this looney bin? What kind of way is this to run a nightmare?"

Chapter Seven

"I suppose the wedding will have to be postponed now," Howard said.

"Of course—how can we ask the girl to marry a man she doesn't even know?" Charlotte asked.

"Oh, I don't think it's so terrible that she doesn't know me," Jeff remarked.

"Most peculiar," Agnes pronounced.

Late that afternoon, Howard, Charlotte, Dr. Carnes, Aunt Agnes, and Jeff were all gathered in the living room, drinking coffee and trying to figure out what had happened to their "Missy." The doctor had just returned and re-examined her, following Charlotte's frantic call. Jeff had stopped by again after driving his mother home.

"For that matter, she doesn't know any of us," Charlotte continued. "She even asked me—most politely—to call her Melissa."

Agnes harrumphed. "Missy has never been polite in her life."

"That's true." Charlotte's hand flew to her mouth. "I—uh—I mean, she certainly seems to be well-mannered now."

"This asking to be called 'Melissa' is also strange," Agnes went on. "Missy has always hated her name."

"Well, I like it," Jeff defended. " 'Melissa' has a lovely, old-fashioned ring to it, don't you think?"

Everyone nodded.

"She runs off screaming every time we mention taking her outside the house," Howard put in. "We're never going to get her to the emergency room at this rate."

"Indeed," Dr. Carnes concurred. "I'm most concerned regarding her amnesia. That's a very nasty blow to the head that she took. We could be dealing with a number of serious conditions here—a severe concussion, a blood clot on the brain. This young woman obviously needs to have her head examined."

"Are you suggesting a psychological condition now?" Charlotte asked.

The physician would only shrug. "I need those X rays, and the sooner the better."

Jeff, who had been listening with a frown, now lunged to his feet. "Well, I disagree."

"Jeff!" Charlotte gasped.

He faced the others resolutely. "I'll not have Missy—Melissa—terrorized this way."

"Terrorized?" Agnes repeated.

"She's obviously very vulnerable right now, very confused," he explained. "I'll not let anyone force her to leave this house until she's ready."

"That's taking a very great risk, young man," the doctor reproved.

"Do you have any proof that this concussion

or blood clot even exists?" Jeff pursued aggressively.

"No ironclad proof," the doctor conceded. "Her period of unconsciousness was brief, and there are no signs of pupil enlargement or discharge from the ears. However, only medical tests can rule out any serious complications. And there's her psychological state to consider—"

"Indeed, there is," Jeff cut in. "And what is the risk to her psychological well-being if we force her to leave this house? The poor girl is bewildered by everything. She doesn't know what a car is, what a television or radio is, or who any of us are. Why, one of the maids told me she started shrieking when the vacuum cleaner was run. It's almost as if she's never had any contact with the twentieth century."

"I agree," Charlotte piped up. "Why, when I was trying to convince her to go into the ambulance, she was murmuring some lunacy about offering the horses a repast. Very politely, of course."

"And there's the man in her television that she insisted I should shoot—or cancel—I'm not sure just what it was she wanted there," Howard observed with a puzzled frown.

"She does seem off her rocker," Agnes agreed. "When I went by her room to check on her a few minutes ago, I found her pounding on the wall near the intercom. She insisted that some poor musician was trapped behind the wall."

"Oh, dear!" Charlotte gasped.

The doctor had been listening with a deep frown. "You've all brought up some very valid points. Somehow, we must impel this young woman to go to the hospital—"

"That will only scare her to death," Jeff pointed out.

"I think the boy is right, Edmund," Howard put in. "If we force Melissa to undergo tests, it might drive her over the edge."

"Very well," the doctor conceded wearily. "If you folks are willing to chance it. Just remember that it's against my better judgment."

After the doctor left, the four others stared at each other in perplexity. "So what do we do now?" Charlotte asked.

"I say we leave the girl alone," Agnes suggested. "What's a little insanity, when the fall has obviously knocked the brattiness right out of her?"

"I say we let Melissa recover in her own way, in her own time," Jeff said.

"So she's 'Melissa' to you now," Agnes remarked wisely to Jeff. "You know, the girl does seem like a totally different person."

No one present had the courage to comment on what a blessing *that* was.

As Jeff drove away from the Monroe home, his mind was swirling with thoughts and questions regarding the woman he now knew as "Melissa." He felt as if he'd suddenly, miraculously, been presented with a new fiancée. "Missy" had tumbled down the stairs earlier today, and a vastly different woman—a kindly, soft-spoken woman who asked to be called "Melissa"—had awakened in her bed upstairs.

Had he misjudged Missy before? Had all her worthwhile qualities been buried somewhere in her subconscious, waiting for the fall to shake them to the surface? Whatever the reason, the result had left Jeff feeling both amazed and captivated.

The old Missy had never needed him, but this new Melissa did. Even though he'd only been with her for a few minutes today, he'd had ample time to assess the depth of the change in her. She was now so helpless, so confused and frightened, qualities he'd never before seen in his independent "Missy"—qualities he loved in this new Melissa.

Loved? Was it possible that his heart was not encased in ice, after all? He realized that he couldn't wait to see her again, to let her lean on him, to help her through this trying period.

For the first time in six long, lonely years, Jeff could feel his heart melting that first, tiny bit.

"I suppose the wedding will have to be postponed now," Lavinia said.

"Of course," John added. "How can we ask the girl to marry a man she doesn't even know?"

"Perhaps it's not such a tragedy that she doesn't know me," Fabian remarked.

"Most peculiar," Grandmother pronounced.

Fabian, John and Lavinia, the physician, and Grandmother Montgomery sat together in the parlor, discussing Melissa's current, bizarre mental state.

"She talks out of her head constantly," John went on. "She doesn't seem to know any of us— or even where or who she is."

"And this queer vocabulary she uses," the physician put in. "What is all this madness about 'nut cast' and 'looney tunes'?"

"It's almost as if she's a different person," Grandmother Montgomery remarked. "Didn't I tell you, Lavinia, that she even looks different now?"

"That you did, Mother," Lavinia agreed.

Leaning toward Lavinia, Grandmother continued in a mortified whisper, "And those scandalous underthings she had on when we undressed her. . . . Why, I've never seen the likes! So skimpy and shocking, I threw them all in the rag bag!"

While Lavinia frowned and patted Grandmother's hand, John said, "When I went upstairs to check on her a few minutes ago, she insisted I call her 'Missy.' What an odd name. And then she demanded that I bring her some strange object—I believe she called it a telephone."

"Are you certain she did not mean telegraph?" the doctor suggested helpfully.

"A telegraph in a bedroom?" John countered, raising an eyebrow. "Be serious, Fletcher."

"I hear she threw a chamber pot at the maid," Grandmother Montgomery added. "I tell you, the child is demented."

Abruptly, Lavinia laughed. "Oh, come on, all of you, be serious. Of course the girl is still our Melissa. Only she has spirit now, following her fall. I'd say that's a vast improvement." She turned to Fabian. "Don't you agree, darling?"

He grinned at her. "I'm not saying I like being called a jerk, or a horse's patooty. I'm not altogether sure just what those terms mean—although I do have my suspicions. Nevertheless, I must admit that the fall seems to have brought out Melissa's better side. However, I am baffled by her confusion and memory loss." He turned to the physician. "What do you think, Dr. Fletcher?"

The physician leaned forward intently. "I still maintain that her collapse was caused by a bilious fever. The fever caused the dizziness, which subsequently brought on her fall. I must warn you all that the poisons are likely eating up her brain even as we speak. If only you would allow me to bleed her—"

"Oh, stuff and nonsense!" Lavinia put in, waving the man off. "I've never held with those torture devices you call leeches—"

"Then it's on your head, Lavinia, if the girl succumbs," the doctor put in gravely. "Whatever malady has consumed her, in time she will either recover, die, or be rendered fit only for the asylum." He stood with his black bag and clapped on his stovepipe hat. "Since I've a baby to deliver, I bid you all good day."

A grim silence fell in the wake of the physician's departure. Lavinia leaned toward John and confided, "I shall certainly pray that Dr. Fletcher is not planning to apply those leeches to the poor infant—or its mother. He seems determined to bleed someone today."

"What are we to do about Melissa?" Grandmother asked.

"She's 'Missy' now," John reminded them.

"Why do anything?" Fabian put in. He stroked his jaw, then grinned lazily. "As a matter of fact, I rather like her just the way she is."

"She *is* different," Lavinia murmured.

No one present had the nerve to comment on what a blessing that was.

Later, as Fabian rode toward his family's neighboring cotton plantation, his thoughts were on the woman who had two hours ago called him a jerk. He felt amazed, amused—as well as intrigued and captivated.

It hardly seemed possible, but the fall had obviously brought about a dramatic change in his fiancée. Gone was his mealymouthed, meek little

"Melissa"; in her place was spunky, hot-blooded "Missy"—

A woman he was dying to get to know better.

Had he misjudged her before? He now knew that the woman he'd thought of previously as dull as dishwater and cold as ice possessed a passionate nature, an inner fire hot enough to burn them both. Had her accident indeed brought her better qualities to the surface at last?

He grinned. Tomorrow he would begin their courtship anew. He would woo her and win her, and he would pray that this confusion— this sudden, wondrous transformation in her— would never end.

A ripple of excitement coursed through his loins. Only hours before he had dreaded the idea of taking a cringing virgin to bed. He had planned to keep a mistress following his marriage, and to do his husbandly duty by Melissa only often enough to get an heir on her.

But now that she had changed . . . Damn! What a little spitfire she had become! Her manner and attitude, her impudent, outspoken little mouth, just begged him to give her exactly what she deserved—a vigorous and thorough bedding!

The twinge in his manhood hardened into a tormenting ache. *Missy*. He liked the sound of that—

"Well, Miss *Missy*," he murmured aloud, tipping his hat. "Your seduction will be my pleasure."

Chapter Eight

"Oh, what a beast!" Missy cried.

She sat on her bed upstairs with an open black journal clutched in her trembling fingers. She had just finished reading the diary of her distant cousin, Melissa Montgomery, the very woman whose daguerreotype had sat on her dresser at home—wherever, *whenever*, home had been! She had read an appalling account of the poor woman's torture and terror at the hands of the savage beast, Fabian Fontenot, in the year 1852—

Only the story was happening *now*. The story was happening to her!

Setting aside the diary, Missy got to her feet and began to pace. It was all too much! She could barely even comprehend it all!

Unless some sadist had engineered the most clever and devious practical joke in all of history, she had somehow been transferred to the year 1852, and into the life of her Cousin Melissa, the distant relative who had so greatly resembled her. From reading the diary, Missy had confirmed that both weddings had been scheduled for this very day, February 29. And from what the others living in the house had already told her, this "Melissa," too, had taken a fall down the stairs on her wedding day and had hit her head. That meant that they had both taken their falls at precisely the same moment, only a hundred and forty years apart—

Afterward, this "Melissa" had disappeared. She, on the other hand, had somehow been "flashed back" here. Now, everyone was assuming that she was this "Melissa." How in the hell . . . ? Had she died and been reincarnated into the past?

Leap year! she thought suddenly, her eyes wild with crazed realization. Both 1992 and 1852 had been leap years! There was even a bizarre logic and humor in the entire unbelievable mess!

And if she truly had "leaped" here, into the past, where on earth was Cousin Melissa?

The answer seemed so obvious that Missy began to tremble.

"Oh, my God!" Melissa cried.

She sat in her bedroom on the strange bed. Next to her on the mattress lay a framed, faded daguerreotype she'd found on the dresser. It was the very picture she'd had taken earlier today— only "today" appeared to have been at least a hundred years ago!

Even more appalling, clutched in her fingers was a small, peculiar portrait she'd found in the drawer of the night table. The piece of stiff, heavy paper looked like a photograph—except that it had all the bright colors of a painting! How could this be? Everyone knew it was impossible to produce a photograph in colors!

Most astounding of all, the small portrait was of a woman who could have been Melissa's twin—she had long, curly blond hair and bright blue eyes. Had it not been for the paint on the woman's lips, the rouge on her cheeks, and the outlandish clothing she wore, Melissa would have sworn she was staring at herself. The woman was smiling, and her arms were entwined around the neck of Jeff Dalton! The inscription on the back read "Missy Monroe and Jeff Dalton at gallery opening on Beale Street, January 13, 1992."

1992! It couldn't be true! It simply couldn't be!

Yet the evidence was rapidly mounting that something was terribly amiss here. In Melissa's lap lay the appointment book of this woman named "Missy Monroe," who obviously had lived in this very house—a house that was Melissa's house, yet wasn't. According to the appointments jotted down, "Missy" had lived in the year 1992 and was planning to marry Jeff Dalton on this very day, February 29—

Only something had gone wrong! From what the others had told her, this "Missy" had taken a tumble down the stairs on her wedding day, just as she had. Somehow "Missy" had disappeared afterward. She, on the other hand, had been transferred here, into Missy's home and life, and now everyone was assuming that she was Missy!

Merciful heavens! It was all too mind-boggling! She was living another woman's life one hundred and forty years in the future!

"Holy cow, this *is* Tara!" Missy gasped.

She stood on the grounds behind the plantation

house, her figure partially obscured by a hedge of blooming azaleas, as she watched a wagonload of black men come in from the fields on a buckboard pulled by two work horses. The wagon lumbered off toward a row of log cabins in the distance.

"Unbelievable!" she muttered.

Missy had decided to go exploring, to confirm or disprove her theory that she had traveled back through time. So far, since she had awakened in this strange purgatory, she had not seen an automobile, a utility pole, a light switch, a telephone, or even a toilet. Any suspicion that she was merely lost or misplaced in her own time was rapidly evaporating. Even on the old "reenactment" plantations she had visited with her parents, there were modern conveniences—cash registers in the gift shop, telephones, rest rooms, air conditioning, and all the rest. She might be in the same geographical place, even in the same house—but she wasn't in the same time!

She took a moment to calm her raging nerves and glanced downward at the ridiculous attire she wore. Upstairs, she had rifled through the armoire, examining in amazement the many old-fashioned silk and satin dresses hanging there. It had taken her forever to find a plain dress without the usual mile-long skirts. Another eternity had passed before she'd managed to don a set of strange, scratchy underwear—a lacy camisole, bloomers that covered her from toe to waist, and a heavy, voluminous petticoat. Afterward, she had struggled into the straight, lined gingham dress with its too-tight waist and a pair of high-topped walking shoes that even her grandmother would have scorned. Presentable at last—

or so she hoped—she had sneaked downstairs, tripping on her long skirts several times as she headed out the back door to investigate.

What she had seen so far had hardly comforted her. Though the house itself had been vaguely familiar, the grounds behind it were incredible! Beyond the gardens, half a dozen outbuildings had loomed before her. She had already explored a smokehouse, a spring house, and—briefly and nauseatingly—a privy. Now, glancing to her left, she watched a couple of black women with armloads of produce head into a stone building that was obviously a kitchen. She remembered her now-deceased grandmother once telling her that in "olden times" kitchens had been segregated from the main house in order to prevent fires.

Mercy! This clearly wasn't 1992!

Trying to ward off the panic that constantly hovered at the edge of her mind, Missy lifted her skirts, maneuvered her way past the kitchen, and approached a huge shedlike building. She opened one of the large, creaky doors and stepped inside.

"Good grief!" she gasped.

Inhaling the scents of leather, axle grease, and dirt, Missy stared in amazement at the many old-fashioned conveyances lining the building— a two-wheeled buggy, a large, custom carriage, a gig with a folding top, and assorted work wagons. On the walls were hung harnesses, bridles, wagon wheels, and whips. Never before in her life had she longed to see a jug of antifreeze or a discarded hubcap—but oh, she did now!

Muttering an expletive, she left the building and shut the door. Moving around the side of the carriage house, she spotted a slave in the distance; he was shooing a horse outside a stable. Not far from him, another black man was leaving a corn crib with a sack of grain.

That was it, then. She had definitely been whisked into the past, and was living with the very distant relatives who had built the house she had known as "home" back in 1992. Since she was obviously the physical twin of her counterpart "Melissa," the only person who was mystified by all this was herself!

"What on earth am I going to do?" she wailed.

She wondered if her parents and Jeff even knew she was missing back in the present. But if what she suspected were true . . .

Despondently, she trudged back toward the house. So she'd been transported to another time. She supposed worse things must have happened—although she couldn't think of one at the moment. Exploring the nineteenth century could even prove interesting in some respects. At least she wasn't dead—or so she hoped.

But her problem remained getting out of this mess. How had she traveled here in the first place, and how would she make her way back to the place and time where she belonged?

She had to face it: She had not a clue regarding how she would get back to her own family. She might be stuck here forever—with that chauvinist from hell, Fabian Fontenot! Maybe she had died and *he* was her punishment!

Should she tell someone about her dilemma? She laughed. These country bumpkins would never believe her—they'd only cart her off to an asylum—or bleed her with those vile leeches until she had the pleasing demeanor and complexion of a zombie.

No, she'd best keep her mouth shut and investigate her surroundings, play out the bizarre role fate had assigned to her. She would get to know these people better, and look for answers.

And if that horse's patooty, Fabian Fontenot came around again . . . She smiled grimly. As long as she was stuck here, she might as well give that louse just what he deserved for being so mean to poor Cousin Melissa.

"Will you kindly quit ringing and shouting at me?" Melissa cried to the telephone receiver she held at arm's length. "And whoever you are, I'd advise you to get out of this device before you suffocate!"

Dropping the frightful object, Melissa retreated to the door of her room, where she'd been examining a gadget called an "Off-On" when the contrivance called a "phone" had started blinking and ringing at her again. Never in her life had she seen such bizarre contraptions!

Now, she flipped the "Off-On" to and fro, staring mesmerized at the ceiling fixture that kept glowing with mysterious light, then extinguishing itself, with each flip of the switch!

Heavens! What was the source of this miraculous light that had no need of matches or wicks and simply beamed down upon command?

During the last few hours, while she was supposedly resting, Melissa had been busy exploring her room. She had studied half a dozen astounding gadgets and whatnots. While avoiding the frightening box the maid had told her was called a "TV," she had experimented with another, smaller box that produced strange music at the flip of a switch; she had played with an amazing machine that punched out letters on a sheet of paper when a body hit the corresponding key; and she had toyed with another tiny machine that performed arithmetic feats on command.

Equally astounding had been the moments she'd spent exploring the room the maid had called the "bathroom," with its revolutionary indoor plumbing. Recently (whenever "recently" had been), Melissa's family had received a letter from a distant relative in St. Louis; Cousin Minerva had written of the fantastical new sewer system there. But Melissa had never experienced such wonders firsthand—until today. Indeed, the toilet had proved so fascinating that she had flushed it five times; the huge tub had contained both hot and cold running water, plus two mysterious units called a "whirlpool" and a "Shower Massage"—and the possibilities there had both boggled her mind and frightened her. She had decided she would explore these new wonders later on, when she got up her nerve. After her unnerving experiences with the "TV," and the "phone," she didn't doubt that a man might materialize from the bathroom wall if she somehow activated the "massage" unit.

Melissa cracked open her door and peered out into the hallway. Once she saw that the coast was clear, she slipped into the corridor. Though she was too frightened to venture far, she had promised herself she would explore the grounds outside the house, in an effort to learn a little more about the amazing world where she had awakened.

Tiptoeing down the hallway, she felt half-naked in the scandalous clothing she wore—the same outfit "Mother" had earlier insisted that she don.

She prayed that no one would spot her.

Arriving at the first floor, she could hear voices in the parlor—she assumed the people who called themselves her parents and aunt were in there talking about her. She quickly headed for the back of the house. At the end of the downstairs corridor, the sound of laughter drew her attention to a room on her left. The long, galley-type expanse appeared to be a kitchen, with many more shiny gadgets and strange boxes. At a chopping table, two Negro women—one of them the maid who had assisted her upstairs—were chatting away as they prepared food.

"What is this?" Melissa whispered to herself. "A kitchen *inside* the house?"

Feeling highly perturbed, she slipped out the back door. She stepped down to an astonishing terrace made from some strange, smooth stone. Staring ahead, she gasped—

Ahead of her, bounded by a small hut, was a gleaming pond lined with this same, amazing stone! She walked toward it, studying its clean, clear water, its long kidney shape, its blue stone apron.

This pool was obviously man-made! But how? She had never before seen such a phenomenon! She examined the furniture positioned near the pool's edge—it seemed to be made of weird straps attached to molded tubes of metal. She picked up a chair and found it to be almost as light as a feather. Astounding!

Hearing the sound of an engine, Melissa left the pool area. She crossed the yard with its strange, short grass and proceeded toward a fence of tall cedar pickets. Peering through a slat in the fence, she spotted a man in the next yard. He was wearing a queer cap, a knitted shirt, and scandalously short pants, and was riding on a horseless engine that swept across his yard, trimming the grass!

"My kingdom!" Melissa cried, turning from the incredible scene. She walked on toward a large building that resembled a carriage house, opened a door, and slipped inside.

She froze in her tracks, staring at three more metal monsters similar to the "ambulance" that had tried to take her away earlier. One of the shiny beasts was painted blue, another was white, and a third green. All had strange black wheels and glass windows tinted green.

Melissa studied the machines warily, half afraid one of them might spring up and devour her. But as the moments passed and no catastrophe befell her, she ventured closer to one of the marvels, studying its interior through the windows. There were two long seats covered in leather, just like in—

"Jumping Jehoshaphat!" Melissa exclaimed. Why, these were carriages! Bizarre-looking carriages! But where did the horses go? There was no place whatsoever to attach their harnesses. Moreover, she had seen no evidence of horses, mules, or oxen anywhere on this property!

She glanced more closely at the interior of the odd conveyance—there was a wheel, like a smaller version of a ship's wheel. Did the wheel steer the carriage? Some lettering on the column of the wheel read, "Power, Ignition, Cruise Control."

"Oh, my!" Melissa cried. This conveyance must also have an engine, much as a train did! It must power itself, just like that bizarre mowing machine next door! It was a horseless carriage!

Yet such phenomena were impossible, weren't they?

Perhaps not in the year 1992. . . . The realization hit her like a massive blow. No longer could she doubt that she had taken a very sharp detour into the future!

She wondered if her parents and Fabian even knew she was missing back in the past. But if what she suspected were true . . .

"Oh, my God, what am I going to do?" she wailed.

Melissa left the carriage house, her overburdened mind spinning with questions. How had she arrived here, in the late twentieth century? And how would she find her way back to the nineteenth century where she belonged?

Oh, heavens, she just didn't know! She was so confused! She had to face the fact that she had no idea how she had gotten here—and that she might well be stuck in the year 1992 indefinitely.

Should she share her dilemma with Jeff or her new "parents"? They did seem such kindly sorts.

She shook her head grimly. No—if she told anyone the truth, they would surely think her deranged, and this time insist she get into one of those shrieking horseless monsters and go off to the hospital, to have those mysterious rays taken, whatever they were. Why, her brain might well be disintegrated before it was all over!

No, she had best keep her peace, investigate her surroundings, and play out the role fate had assigned her. She would get to know these kindly people she was staying with. In time, perhaps she would find the answers she needed.

And if that nice man Jeff Dalton should come

around again . . . She sighed, and then a smile lit her troubled countenance. Would it be such a sin to comfort the poor man now that his real fiancée had disappeared?

Chapter Nine

"Good morning, Mother, Father."

The next morning, Howard and Charlotte Monroe looked up to see their daughter standing in the doorway of the dining room. At once, Howard rushed up and went over to hug her. "Missy, dear, you're up! Are you feeling better?"

She nodded firmly. "I do believe things are clearer now, Father." Tactfully, she added, "And if it would be no great inconvenience, I should greatly appreciate being called 'Melissa.'"

"Oh, of course, dear—er, Melissa."

Charlotte swept over to join them, glancing askance at her daughter's bizarre clothing. Melissa wore a floor-length, sleek black cocktail gown, green suede ankle boots, and a pink cardigan sweater. Her hair was caught up in a prim and uncharacteristic bun.

"My, my, dear," Charlotte murmured. "I must say that's a rather peculiar choice of clothing."

"I'm sorry, Mother," Melissa replied. "This is the best I could do. All of the other garments are truly tawdry."

The two parents exchanged perplexed glances, then Howard took his daughter's arm and led her toward the table. "You must have some breakfast, dear."

"Thank you, Father," she said as he helped her into her chair. "As it happens, I am quite famished."

The parents resumed their seats, and an awkward silence fell as Charlotte poured her daughter a cup of coffee and Howard passed her a basket of muffins.

"So, you say things are clearer now?" Howard asked.

Melissa took a delicate sip of coffee. "Yes, Father."

"Then I must ask . . . Why do you no longer wish to be called 'Missy,' and why aren't you calling the two of us 'Mom' and 'Dad' as you normally do?"

Melissa bit her lip. She had known such questions were inevitable. After all, she knew next to nothing about the woman into whose life she had mysteriously landed—and even less about the astounding year 1992, to which she had evidently been transported.

She folded her hands together primly and said, "I do not wish to alarm you unduly, Mother and Father, but the truth is, following my—er—accident, I do not seem to remember either of you."

"Oh, dear!" Charlotte gasped.

"I'm sorry to hear that, dear," Howard added with concern.

"Nevertheless," Melissa went on, "I have decided to accept you both as my parents. You are such agreeable people," she finished kindly.

Both Charlotte and Howard were too stunned to comment.

"And I need your help," Melissa went on.

"Anything, dear—just tell us," Howard said at once.

Uncertainty etched Melissa's features. "Aside from not remembering either of you, I seem to have lost a few years." She coughed and added under her breath, "A hundred and forty."

"Oh, dear," Charlotte remarked. "You know, we really should take you to the hospital and get that head checked out—"

"Mother, I am not mad," Melissa assured her earnestly. "Please do not commit me to an asylum."

Charlotte's hand moved to her throat. "Why, darling, we would never dream of—"

"I am still rather confused," Melissa forged on. "I need . . ." She frowned. "Books, I think."

"*Books?*" both parents repeated in unison.

"Yes—for the lost years, you see. It has occurred to me that certain of these—historical events— might be recorded in various volumes." Tentatively, she asked, "Is this not true?"

"Of course it is, dear," Howard replied.

"Certainly so," Charlotte added.

"And have we not a library here—somewhere?" Melissa continued with a vague flutter of her hand.

"You mean, you've forgotten that, as well?" Charlotte asked.

"I do know where it used to be," Melissa murmured doubtfully.

"Used to be?" Charlotte repeated.

"Don't worry, dear—I'll get you settled in the library right after breakfast," Howard promised.

Melissa beamed in gratitude and reached over to pat his hand. "Thank you, Father."

"Is there anything else we can do for you?" Charlotte asked.

Melissa smiled shyly. "Well . . . I suppose it would be rather nice to see Jeffrey again."

"He's coming by later this afternoon," Howard assured her. "He must take his mother to church first."

"Oh," Melissa muttered. "Today is Sunday, then?"

"Yes, dear."

"But I thought yesterday was Sunday," she murmured, scowling.

"No, dear, yesterday was Saturday," Howard said.

Melissa's expression grew crestfallen. "And we are not attending services today?"

Both parents exchanged flabbergasted glances, since both Howard and Charlotte were well-aware that nothing short of threats of physical violence had compelled Missy to attend church in years.

Howard cleared his throat. "Well, we thought it best that—under the circumstances—we not attend services today. You know, dear, given your current confusion and all."

Melissa nodded. "Ah, yes, I do see. A prudent decision, Father. Nevertheless, I shall be impelled to spend at least two hours in silent prayer and Bible study."

"*Two hours?*" Charlotte echoed.

"*In silent prayer?*" Howard added.

"*And Bible study?*" Charlotte exclaimed.

Melissa nodded solemnly. "You are both, of

course, quite welcome to join me."

Charlotte and Howard stared at each other in utter mystification.

By nine a.m. Melissa was safely ensconced behind the library doors. Howard led her to the couch and stacked the encyclopedia and year-books on the coffee table in front of her.

All morning long the house rang with the sound of her shrieks. Her hysterical comments ranged from "My stars, electricity!" to "Heavens, men walking on the moon!" to "Forevermore, a dooms-day bomb!" to "Jumping Jehoshaphat, a machine that washes dishes!"

Charlotte and Howard stood in the corridor together, listening in horror and wringing their hands.

"We must do something, Howie," Charlotte confided in a tense whisper. "One would think our library was the site of the Spanish Inquisition. The poor child sounds as if she's about to expire in there."

Howard scratched his head in perplexity. "She only wanted to read some books. She said she's lost a few years."

"It sounds to me as if she's lost her mind," Charlotte replied. "Why, she talks so strangely now, I hardly even know her. This is *not* a girl accustomed to running a ball bearing plant."

Howard mopped his brow with his handker-chief. "It's true the girl's behavior and vocabulary seem—er—eccentric. But surely it's just her con-fusion, Charlotte. Why, even Dr. Carnes said—"

Yet Howard's words were cut short as a par-ticularly harrowing scream rang out. "I'm going in there, Howard," Charlotte declared. "I don't think the Literacy Council ever had this sort of torment in mind."

Yet before Charlotte could reach for the doorknob, Melissa emerged from the room, white-faced and wild-eyed. "I think I understand now, Mother, Father," she said breathlessly.

She slipped to the floor in a swoon.

Melissa drifted toward consciousness. Images swam through her mind—of the Industrial Revolution, two world wars, flappers and nuclear bombs, trains, airplanes, automobiles and space-ships, conditioned air and sewing machines, bra-burning and mini-skirts, computers and junk bonds. Her mind felt like a tiny vessel crammed with more information than she could possibly take in or comprehend.

Then, hearing the sound of sobs, Melissa blinked to gain her bearings and spotted Charlotte weeping in the bedside chair. Her own confusion temporarily forgotten, she quickly sat up. "Mother, are you all right?"

Charlotte stared at her daughter through tears, then abruptly hugged the girl. "Melissa, dear, thank God you're awake! I've been frantically worried about you ever since you fainted downstairs. Your father even went to pull Dr. Carnes off the golf course."

"Oh, dear," Melissa murmured. "I do apologize for causing you any distress or inconvenience, Mother." She squeezed Charlotte's hand. "I'm fine, truly. It was simply the shock of all those . . . years, you see. Please do not fret yourself so on my account."

But Charlotte only sobbed all the more.

"What is it, Mother?" Melissa asked, distraught.

Dabbing at tears, Charlotte confided, "It's just that you're so different now—so confused, and yet so kind, so vulnerable and dear."

"Is that a difficulty, Mother?" Melissa asked.

"A difficulty?" Charlotte repeated incredulously. "The only difficulty is, I like you this way!"

Melissa stared flabbergasted at the bawling woman. "If you like me this way, then why such lamentation, Mother?"

"B-because when you were Missy, you never cared what other people thought—or felt," Charlotte wailed. "Now that you're in—your current state—I feel I should want you back the way you were. Only I don't," Charlotte finished in a torrent of misery.

Melissa patted Charlotte's heaving shoulders. "Mother, you are being unfair to yourself. I really don't want to change back again." Indeed, she realized the truth of the words as she said them—although the statement had a meaning for her that Charlotte might never know.

"Oh, darling!" Charlotte hugged Melissa again. "Do you truly mean it?"

"Yes, Mother, I do."

"We've fought so all your life, and now at last, we're friends!" Pulling back, Charlotte managed a teary-eyed smile. "And it's so remarkable—this change in you has made you look five years younger, just as Agnes said!"

Melissa smiled back guiltily. "I suppose it has."

Charlotte patted her daughter's hand. "Did the books help, darling? Did you find all those years you were looking for?"

Melissa shook her head in amazement. "Carriages with wings, pictures that move, and machines that make indoor weather. This is a most remarkable age, indeed."

Charlotte stared at Melissa in perplexity for a moment, then decided that she must agree.

While Charlotte continued to dry her tears, Melissa turned to the nightstand and picked up the small picture she had examined so closely yesterday. Perhaps now would be a good time to find out more about this "Missy"—and the history of these people.

Extending the photograph toward Charlotte, she said, "Tell me about this, Mother."

Taking it, Charlotte smiled. "Why this was taken of you and Jeff several weeks back, at the opening of a gallery on Beale Street. Don't you remember the occasion, dear?"

"I'm afraid I do not."

"It will come back to you," Charlotte assured her.

"I do hope so." Melissa nodded toward the dresser. "And you must also tell me of the— um—the old-fashioned lady in the photograph— the one who so resembles me."

"Oh, so you noticed that, as well, did you?" Wearing an expression of mild surprise, Charlotte rose, walked over to the dresser, and picked up the faded daguerreotype. "This is Cousin Melissa, of course—a distant relative of ours."

"I see. I was named after her, was I?"

Charlotte's eyes lit up. "So you remember!"

"Well, not exactly, Mother," Melissa hedged. "However, the conclusion seems logical."

"I suppose it does." Staring at the photograph, Charlotte sighed. "You know, the resemblance between the two of you is truly uncanny. Actually, with the way you've been acting and talking ever since your fall, it's almost as if . . ." Abruptly, she laughed and set the photograph back down. "But that would be impossible, wouldn't it?"

Melissa wisely resisted comment on that perilous subject. "Tell me more about Cousin Melissa," she urged.

Charlotte crossed the room and sat down on the edge of the bed. "Well, her family—the Montgomerys—built this house. In the 1840s, I believe."

"I see. Has the family lived here ever since?"

Charlotte shook her head. "No. You must realize that at least seven generations have passed. The family has moved around quite, a bit. Indeed, I believe the Montgomerys left Memphis before the 1860s, and since then the family name has also changed."

"From Montgomery to Monroe?"

"Why, yes."

"And how did that happen?"

Charlotte frowned, laying a finger alongside her cheek. "Actually, I'm not sure. And no one in the family has really kept comprehensive records."

Melissa's bubble of hope burst. "Then you have little knowledge of these Montgomerys who built the house?"

"Not much, I'm afraid. We do have a few old letters written by Cousin Melissa—"

"You do?" Melissa exclaimed.

"Yes, and also some correspondence that the first Montgomery—I believe his name was John— wrote to his wife and daughter—"

"Oh, how fascinating!" Melissa cried.

Charlotte appeared pleased, if somewhat taken aback. "That's about all we have, though, I'm afraid."

"May I see these letters some time?" Melissa asked eagerly.

"Certainly. I believe Cousin Melissa's letters are here in your room somewhere—and I suppose Agnes must have the others."

Melissa was silent for a moment, frowning as she tried to digest all this information. Suddenly, she snapped her fingers and asked, "But if our family has moved around so much, then why are we still living in this house?"

"I take it you don't remember?" Charlotte asked.

"No, Mother."

"Well, soon after your father and I got married in Birmingham, Howard's father died and he inherited a sizable sum. It was his dream to start his own ball bearing factory, and we visited several cities in the south searching for a suitable site. We found a prime location available in Memphis, and, since Howard was aware that his family had originally come from the region of the Chickasaw Bluffs, we decided to settle here. Imagine our joy and surprise when we discovered that the old family plantation home was up for sale."

"I see. So you bought this house?"

"Indeed, we did. We've lived here ever since— and, of course, you were born and raised here, darling."

"How very interesting," Melissa said wistfully. "To live in the very house of one's forebears— I'm sure you felt as if your prayers had been answered."

Charlotte shook her head wonderingly. "I simply cannot believe the change in you. Before, you never took any interest in genealogy—much less in prayer."

"Ah, yes, Mother," Melissa murmured ironically. "It seems that I am rapidly becoming an expert on both subjects."

Chapter Ten

Moments later, Howard Monroe returned with Dr. Carnes in tow. Still wearing his golf clothes and in a foul mood, Carnes trudged up the stairs to Melissa's bedroom. Doctor and patient had a brief, fierce argument about whether or not Melissa belonged in the hospital, and after a dozen firm, polite refusals on the part of the patient, the physician threw up his hands in defeat. He examined Melissa briefly, declared that she "might" live, and left.

Half an hour later, Charlotte came upstairs to inform Melissa that Jeff had arrived and was waiting for her down in the living room. Amid a mood of great excitement on the part of both mother and daughter, Charlotte helped Melissa dress and style her hair.

As Melissa descended the stairs, she felt quite thrilled at the prospect of seeing Jeff again; yet she felt so odd, so exposed, in the strange garments her mother had again insisted she don—this time a straight-lined pale blue skirt that barely covered her knees, a buttoned white shirtwaist, another pair of those bizarre, sheer stockings, and flat leather slippers. Not only that, but Charlotte had curled her hair about her face and shoulders with a weird device called an "electric curling iron." The miraculous gadget did not even have to be heated on a lantern! The heat came from a special cord through which flowed that miraculous force, "electricity." The effect created by the curling device was quite pleasing, yet Melissa felt uncomfortable with her hair styled casually this way, since she was accustomed to wearing a sedate bun.

Melissa arrived at the bottom of the steps, and she paused as she spotted the very same newel button that she and her father had "christened" in this very house only two days ago. She was amazed that the same stone was still here, one hundred and forty years later. Had Missy, too, hit her head on this post when she fell down the stairs? If so, what was the significance? She passed her hand over the polished oval of malachite, but nothing happened.

Frowning, she stepped inside the parlor. Her heart quickened in joy as she spotted Jeff standing near the front window with his back to her. Sunshine outlined his tall, slender profile and danced in his thick blond hair. His beautifully fitted blue suit made him appear all the more debonair and masterful. She wondered at the feeling of instinctive trust, of peace and well-being that washed over her when he was near.

"Jeffrey?" she called out tentatively.

He turned to her joyously, and the light in his eyes was dazzling to her. "Miss—I mean, Melissa, darling." He quickly crossed the room and kissed her cheek. "How are you feeling?"

"Much better, thank you," she replied with a smile. *Especially now that you are here*, she added to herself. "And you?"

"I'm fine, darling. It's you we've all been frantic about." His expression grew deeply concerned as he moved aside a lock of her hair and tenderly touched the still-bulging bruise on her forehead. "Your mother told me you fainted again today, and the doctor had to be called."

"It was a matter of small consequence," she assured him. "The years, you see. Too many at once, I presume—perhaps what you would call an overdose?"

He appeared utterly mystified. "Years? An overdose?"

"I shall explain."

"I hope so." He chuckled and took her hand. "Let's sit down."

The two settled themselves on the antique settee. "First, are you sure you're okay?" Jeff asked anxiously.

"Okay?" she repeated, baffled.

"All right. You know, feeling well?"

"Ah, yes, I am feeling quite okay, thank you," she assured him.

He squeezed her hand. "Are you less confused now, darling?"

She nodded.

"Then tell me about these 'years' you mentioned."

"Well, I did lose quite a few of them—"

"You mean you lost your memory?" he asked, bemused.

"Well, yes, I presume so. However, I am trying

my best to find it." She scowled morosely. "I managed to learn quite a lot in the library today—you know, in the encyclopedias."

Despite himself, Jeff grinned. "I see. And this is what caused you to faint? Too much information at once? Overloaded circuits, so to speak?"

She pondered that a moment, then snapped her fingers. "Oh, you mean like too much current flowing through the curling iron?"

He laughed. "Exactly."

She nodded soberly. "Yes, I presume that is what happened to me."

He smile faded into a worried frown. "You really do have amnesia, then?"

Her eyes grew huge. "Oh, I should hope not!"

"You mean you don't even remember what amnesia is?"

She chewed her bottom lip. "I suppose not. That is, if I do have it, how can I remember it?"

Jeff couldn't help himself. He threw back his head and laughed.

"Have I said something wrong?" she asked, her expression crestfallen.

Jeff took her hand and kissed it. "Of course not, darling. As a matter of fact, you're saying everything right. I shouldn't laugh at your confusion—it's just that I find you absolutely delightful."

"You do? I mean, I am?" she asked raptly.

"You are." He stared at her with concern. "But this amnesia is serious business."

She grimaced. "It does sound serious."

"So you really don't remember me and your parents—or anything else about your life before your fall?"

She sighed. "I'm afraid that pretty much sums up my current mental state, although I am trying most strenuously to get acclimated—especially to all the weird gadgets and whatnot."

He appeared fascinated. "Gadgets and whatnot?"

"Yes. You know, the machine that sweeps the carpets, the water spurting out of pipes into basins, the phones and clocks and blinking lights, and all the rest."

Jeff shook his head in amazement. "Good Lord, you sound as if you've been living in a cultural vacuum! I had no idea your injury was that extensive. Perhaps we should take you to the hospital—"

"No, Jeff, please," Melissa implored. "Dr. Carnes and I have already had this very argument. He couldn't really find anything that much wrong with me—other than my peculiar mental state. And even he conceded that this confusion may soon pass on its own." Biting her lip, she finished, "Besides, I don't think I'm ready to leave the house just yet. There are so many . . . frightening things out there."

He squeezed her hand. "I understand, darling. And I'll help you—in any way I can."

"Thank you, Jeffrey," she said sincerely. "I really appreciate your help, since there is so very much I've forgotten."

Staring into her wide, beguiling blue eyes, Jeff was feeling impulsive. "Have you forgotten this?" he asked intensely, and drew her into his arms.

Prior to this moment, Melissa had been held romantically by only one man—Fabian Fontenot—and Fabian's kisses and caresses had filled her with terror. By contrast, being held by Jeff Dalton was pure heaven. She felt totally at home, safe and confident in his arms, her senses intoxicated by his male scent and her body cradled by his warmth. When his lips tenderly claimed hers, her bliss was complete. She gave herself over to the captivating caress of his mouth and curled her arms around his neck. She heard him groan and felt the pressure of his mouth deepen, until her lips parted to allow his tongue access. He possessed her mouth in a bold, dizzying stroke that left her feeling giddy all over.

Abruptly, he pulled back, staring down into her passion-dazed eyes, his own gaze fervently questioning her. "Well?"

"How could I ever forget that?" she asked breathlessly.

He smiled in joy. "Oh, Melissa, you're so wonderful—so different." Abruptly, a cloud crossed his eyes.

She took his hand. "Jeffrey, what is it?"

His expression deeply abstracted, he got to his feet, shoved his hands into his pockets, and began to pace.

"Please, Jeff, tell me what you are thinking," she implored.

He turned to her with a tight frown. "You know you've changed drastically since you took your fall."

"I know."

"It's almost as if you're a different person."

"I realize this."

Jeff expelled a heavy breath. "The problem is, I like you this way!"

She smiled. "That is what Mother said. But why should this be a difficulty?"

"It's a difficulty because . . ." He clenched his fist and said with self-loathing, "Damn, I'm such a bastard."

"Jeffrey, whyever would you call yourself that?" she cried, aghast.

"Because I don't want you to get well!"

She stared at him, stupefied.

"Don't you understand?" He approached her, speaking through gritted teeth. "When you recover your memory, you'll be Missy again!"

She rose and touched his arm. "No, Jeff, I shall never be Missy again," she assured him gently.

He regarded her in awe and uncertainty. "How can you be so sure?"

She laughed ruefully. "There you will simply have to trust me."

"Trust you? Try adore you," he whispered urgently, pulling her possessively into his arms and kissing her again. She kissed him back eagerly, running her hands over the hard muscles of his back.

Afterward, he stared down at her dazedly and said, "I feel as if I've just fallen down a well."

"Oh, dear."

He grinned. "Metaphorically speaking, that is."

"I'm relieved to hear it."

"It's a great feeling," he added, then chuckled. "Although it's baffling to try to figure out how I could have fallen in love at first sight with a woman I've known all my life."

"In love at first sight?" she repeated in a quivering voice, staring up at him in wonder.

He kissed her forehead. "Let's set a new date for the wedding, darling—right away."

Delight transformed Melissa's face, only to be replaced by sorrow and guilt as she remembered her life in the past—and those she'd left behind.

"Melissa? What is it?" he asked, pulling back.

"I need time, Jeff," she admitted miserably.

"This is all too new to me—and I'm still so confused."

"But you do still want me in your life?" he asked with sudden anxiety.

Melissa spoke straight from her heart. "Oh, of course, Jeffrey. I may not know you that well as yet, but I do like you, trust you . . ." Shyly, she finished, "And need you."

His eyes filled with incredulous joy. "My God, Melissa, to hear you say that you need me!" She felt a tremor course through him as he caught her possessively close. "Don't worry, darling. We'll take it slowly, get to know each other again. We have all the time in the world."

It should have been a moment of sublime ecstasy for Melissa. But, instead, she suddenly felt all color drain from her face as she made a momentous realization. What if she and Jeff didn't have all the time in the world?

While she remained quite baffled by this twentieth century into which she had somehow stumbled, she already loved the new family and fiancé that fortune had presented her with. But fate tended to be fickle—leastwise, the forces of destiny had always controlled her life heretofore with a capricious and even cruel hand.

What if her wonderful new existence here could be snatched away as quickly as it had been given to her?

Chapter Eleven

"Good morning, Mom, Dad."

Sitting at the dining-room table, John and Lavinia Montgomery glanced askance at Missy, who stood in the archway. Both parents struggled to take in their daughter's odd clothing and her equally odd manner of addressing them.

Lavinia rose and hastened over to join the girl. "Are you feeling better now, Melissa?"

"The name is 'Missy,' and yes, things are a bit clearer," she replied.

Lavinia rolled her eyes as she took in her daughter's outlandish choice of attire— a full-skirted ball gown of green watered silk, with a daring décolletage and tight waist. "Isn't that—er—rather a queer choice of dress for morning, dear?"

Missy shrugged, fingering one of the bows on her billowing skirt. "I thought this was what all southern belles wore. Why, in *Gone With the Wind*—"

"Gone with what?" Lavinia repeated in perplexity.

Missy groaned. "Oh, never mind. Just so you know, Mom, I'm not going to change. It was hell getting this prom dress on—not to mention, that torture device of a corset—and I'm not about to go through such agonies again."

For once, Lavinia appeared at a loss for words.

Smiling, John came over to join them. "Oh, let the girl wear whatever she pleases, Vinnie," he chided his wife. "I'm just so thrilled to see her up and about again."

"Thanks, Dad." She glanced about the room, then scowled. "Where's Gran?"

"You mean your grandmother?" Lavinia asked confusedly.

"Yes."

"She had to return to Natchez, dear," John said.

"Too bad," Missy muttered. "It was kind of nice to have one again."

John and Lavinia exchanged glances of utter bewilderment.

Eyeing the breakfast set out on the table, Missy clapped her hands. "Well, how 'bout some vittles around here?" To her flabbergasted parents, she added, "Isn't that what you folks call food?"

"Are you quite sure you're all right?" Lavinia asked worriedly.

"Of course, Mom." Missy started forward, only to do an awkward little dance as she tripped on her hem.

John caught her arm and steadied her. "Easy, my dear. We can't have you taking another tumble."

Missy slanted her new father a look of comprehension. "That's right, Dad. I fell down the stairs yesterday, didn't I? Right before my wedding?"

"So you remember," Lavinia said gratefully.

Missy waved her off. "Do I ever!" Confidentially, she added, "And let me tell you both, that first step's a doozy."

Again, John and Lavinia appeared utterly amazed.

The three settled themselves in at the dining-room table. As Missy took her first sip of coffee and glanced about at the antique furnishings, she realized she was dying for a cigarette. Damn, she'd never get away with smoking here! She was stuck in some provincial outpost of the nineteenth century, and so far, her existence was not nearly as idyllic as that she had read about in history books and romantic novels. Already, she terribly missed her life back in the twentieth century and the many conveniences she'd left behind—even such banal items as toothpaste and toilet paper.

John eyed his daughter as she began to nibble at her breakfast of pancakes and sausages. "My dear, I cannot begin to tell you what a joy it is to see you up and about—and starting to remember things. Only, I must ask, why do you call your mother and I 'Mom' and 'Dad'?"

"Oh, that." Missy took a gulp of coffee. "I hate to disillusion you, Pop, but aside from remembering the fall, my mental state is pretty much a wash-out."

Lavinia gasped in dismay. "You mean to say that you still do not remember us as your parents, or Fabian as your fiancé?"

"Nail on the head, Mom."

"What can we do to help?" John asked with a concerned frown.

Eugenia Riley

"Well—you could tell me a little about our lives here."

"Such as?" John queried.

"What do we do?"

"We raise cotton, of course."

"Oh, yes," she muttered. "That was a really dumb question, wasn't it? I certainly heard that blasted bell clanging at six A.M. this morning, when the hands left for the fields." Stuffing a chunk of sausage in her mouth, she added, "How long have we been living in this museum, anyway?"

"Museum?" Lavinia repeated.

"You know how young people are, Mom," Missy cajoled. "Always criticizing the status quo."

For once, Lavinia looked to John for guidance.

"We've been here ten years," he replied. "Ever since we built the house. Don't you recall that only two days ago you and I had a little ceremony after the craftsman placed the button on the newel post?"

Missy snapped her fingers. "Ahah! The stone was placed there in honor of the mortgage on the house being paid, wasn't it?"

"So you remember!" John exclaimed.

"No, not really." Amid the dumbfounded looks of both parents, Missy turned her attention to Lavinia. "Now—tell me what I did, Mom."

Lavinia appeared highly taken aback. "What you did?"

"Yes. How did I spend my time?"

"Ah, yes. Why, your passed your days as all young ladies do—reading, attending church or charitable organizations, taking piano lessons and knitting with your friends."

Missy wore the repelled expression of someone

112

who had just stepped into horse dung. "You've got to be kidding."

"Of course not."

"You mean I didn't have a job?"

"My dear, it would be most unseemly for a young woman to be employed," John scolded.

"And why not?" Missy countered. "Are you saying that women aren't as capable as men?"

"It's not a question of who is—more capable," John replied tactfully. "But a woman must remember her place."

"Bullpuppy! Give me a break!" Missy declared.

John appeared stunned, while Lavinia drew her napkin to her mouth to cover a snicker.

"So, what's on the docket today?" Missy continued.

"Why, Fabian is planning to come calling on you," Lavinia informed her pleasantly. "The darling boy said that if you were feeling up to it, he might take you for a carriage ride."

Missy slammed her cup into its saucer. "That creep? You can tell him for me to get lost!"

Both parents gasped in horror.

"But that is impossible," Lavinia said at last. "You are engaged to marry him, and we must set a new date for the wedding immediately."

"Get real," Missy snapped to her new mother.

"I beg your pardon?" Lavinia asked incredulously.

Missy thrust her fingers through her hair. "Look, Mom, whether you're aware of it or not, I've had a very rough twenty-four hours. And I wouldn't marry that jerk if he were the next Donald Trump."

"Donald who?" Lavinia echoed.

"Never mind," Missy snapped.

"You do talk most strangely, dear," Lavinia remarked anxiously.

"Well—in whatever language—the engagement is canceled, *finito*, kaput."

There was a moment of stunned silence.

At last Lavinia said in a cold, firm voice, "I'm afraid this will never do, my dear."

"Excuse me?" Missy's tone was also icy.

A look of steely determination flashed into Lavinia's eyes. "Due to your indisposition, Melissa, your father and I have been most tolerant of your—er—unorthodox behavior. But obviously, the time for coddling is past. Make no mistake—you will see Fabian Fontenot today, and you will marry him."

"Dream on!" Missy cried. "And for the last time, Mother, my name is Missy!"

"The contract was made at your birth, *Missy*," John added sternly. "You will not disgrace our family by reneging."

"Damn!" Missy exclaimed.

At once, John Montgomery was on his feet, trembling in mortification as he addressed his daughter. "You will not speak such profanity under my roof, daughter! For heaven's sake, remember your place! You are a lady."

But, as Missy glowered at her new father, Lavinia was chuckling. "Now, John, don't be too hard on the girl. Haven't you noticed the wondrous change in her? Why, she has spirit now!"

"Too much for her own good," John grumbled.

"Think what fun Fabian will have with her," Lavinia added with a smirk. "Oh, I cannot wait to see the fireworks!"

"I'm not going to see him, Mom," Missy insisted.

"Oh, you'll see him, dear," Lavinia assured her.

Missy continued to argue with her new parents throughout the meal. Finally, she threw down her napkin in disgust and stormed out of the room. Out in the corridor, she paused by the newel post, staring intently at the bull's eye of green malachite, the very stone she remembered from her life in the present. How amazing that the button had been attached only the day before yesterday. Had Melissa hit her head on this very post, just as she had back in 1992? If so, what was the significance? Missy ran her fingers over the stone, but nothing happened—although she did seem to glimpse the stone winking oddly.

"Remembering, dear?"

Missy glanced up to see that John Montgomery had joined her. He really was a very dear man, a fine southern gentleman, she mused, noting his charming goatee and the twinkle in his blue eyes. "I'm trying to remember, I guess," she replied with a smile.

He glanced down at the stone. "You know, this bit of malachite is a polished fragment from a genuine Egyptian amulet."

"An amulet," Missy murmured. Abruptly, she snapped her fingers. "But aren't amulets supposed to have—"

"Magical properties?" He chuckled. "Indeed, they are."

Missy felt all color draining from her face.

Missy spent most of her morning exploring the family library. Perusing the handsome floor-to-ceiling bookcases, she found the works of Melville, Hawthorne, Dickens, the Brownings and the Brontes, and other prominent writers of the nineteenth century. But, predictably, there was no hint of the literature of her own world. She spent some time reading genealogical entries in the family Bible. She learned a bit more about the Montgomerys—including the fact that the family had emigrated to this country from England in the early 1800s—but found no answers regarding her own dilemma.

She thought about her new parents, John and Lavinia. A grudging smile lit her face as she remembered her argument with them at breakfast. She considered how different they were from the parents she had left behind. Back at home, she'd always successfully manipulated Charlotte and Howard; hell, she'd gotten away with murder all her life! By contrast, John and Lavinia treated her with loving firmness; she wouldn't be able to pull their strings quite so easily. And yet, through it all, she admired their spirit and respected them for standing up to her.

But if they thought they were going to force her to marry Fabian Fontenot, then they had another think coming! Even though she appeared stuck here for the moment, she had no intention of whiling away her hours with that beast!

This particular resolve proved much more difficult to hold on to than Missy had anticipated. Late that morning, she was lying on the bed in her room, going crazy with boredom, when Lavinia burst in.

"Wonderful news, dear! Fabian has arrived and is waiting for you downstairs in the parlor," she announced cheerfully.

"Tell him he can wait till hell freezes over," Missy replied, just as cheerfully.

Lavinia chuckled. "I expected as much. Consequently, I told the darling boy that if you refused to come downstairs, he should feel free to come up here and fetch you."

Missy sat bolt upright. "You didn't!"

"Indeed, I did, daughter," Lavinia replied. "And I assure you that if you force him to come up here after you, you will not like his methods. Fabian does have quite a formidable temper."

"Damnation!" Missy shot to her feet. "All right, I'll go and see the bumpkin! But only to tell the jerk to go straight to hell!"

Missy tore off toward the door, stumbling twice over her hem. "Hell's bells, Mom, how do you put up with these damned skirts?" she cried, exiting the room and slamming the door.

Lavinia convulsed in laughter.

A moment later, Missy burst into the parlor, pausing in her tracks when she spotted Fabian standing across from her.

He turned and grinned at her, flashing perfect white teeth and looking every bit as devilish and dashing as Clark Gable in *Gone With the Wind*. He wore a long brown frock coat and buff-colored trousers, a silk brocade vest, and an elaborate black necktie.

"Good afternoon, dear Melissa. Feeling better, I presume?" he asked with a touch of cynical humor.

Even though her heart tripped at the sound of his deep, mocking voice and the glint of laughter in his dark eyes, Missy managed to maintain an icy façade. "The name is 'Missy,' and I've had better days, thank you." *Actually, I've had better lives*, she added to herself.

He chuckled and stepped forward. "Now that

I'm here, I think we can manage to improve things a bit."

Missy laughed. "You wish! I only came down here because Mom threatened me with bodily harm—at your hands." Feigning her best southern belle simper, she finished, "And, to tell you, Mr. Fabian Fontenot, to go straight to hell."

He whistled. "My, aren't we feisty today."

"We're also impatient," Missy snapped. "So if you'll excuse me—"

She was turning to leave the room when Fabian grabbed her arm and towed her back inside. "Wait a minute, Missy."

She stared bloody murder at him. "Let go of me, you brute!"

"So you really think you can get rid of me this easily?"

"Hide and watch, buster."

His eyes danced with mischief. "But you're forgetting that I'm so much stronger than you—not to mention older and wiser."

"Hah! Give me a break! If you aren't the most arrogant, egotistical—"

"Now, Missy," he scolded, "continue spouting such treason and I may just be impelled to silence that delectable mouth of yours." He tugged her a few inches closer and stared at her lips meaningfully.

"Damn it, let me go!" She suddenly hated herself for the telltale quiver that shook her voice at his nearness.

He grinned maddeningly. "I'll let you go only if you'll promise not to try to run away again."

"Okay!" she cried exasperatedly.

"Okay?" he repeated perplexedly.

"I agree to your terms, Mr. Fontenot," she said

with haughty formality. "Now get your filthy hands off me!"

Fighting a smirk, he released her. "How is the knot on your forehead?"

"Still black and purple, thank you."

He eyed her ball gown skeptically. "A rather queer selection of attire for a carriage ride—"

"Cut the small talk, Fontenot!"

"Just trying to humor you, dear."

"Then humor me by leaving!" When he only quirked an eyebrow and slowly brushed a bit of lint from his sleeve, she threw up her hands and demanded, "*What* do you want?"

He looked her over lazily. "I should think that would be obvious."

Anger darkened her face. "In your dreams! Now state your business and let's get it over with."

He shook with mirth. "Missy, you're a delight. I can't believe the dramatic change in you. I declare, the fall has definitely brought out your better side—although you do rant out of your head like a harridan, and frankly, my dear—" he stepped closer and scrutinized her face closely—"you look five years older."

Missy made a sound of strangled rage, and the next thing Fabian knew, he was lying flat on his back on the floor. Rubbing a smarting jaw, he stared up at her in stupefaction. He couldn't believe this slip of a girl had actually just knocked him on his heels! "Why you little spitfire. . . ."

She shook a fist at him. "You call me old again, you bumpkin from hell, and it'll be a fine day for the Memphis undertaker!"

He staggered to his feet and stared at her, wild-eyed. "What demon has possessed you? You're behaving like a madwoman!"

"I'm perfectly sane!" Missy snapped. "And I gave you exactly what you deserved."

"Oh, you did, did you?" he shouted.

"Yes, I did!" she shouted back.

"Then perhaps I should give you exactly what you deserve!"

She stepped closer, confronting him eyeball-to-eyeball. "Oh, yeah? So what's stopping you, you big bully?"

Fabian's fury was escalating; he shook a finger at the maddening vixen. "You, woman, are a brat."

"So you've just now noticed that?" she sneered, raising both fists.

Fabian stared at her for a moment, then shook his head in amazement. "I can't believe I'm hearing this."

"Believe it. Then drop dead."

All at once, Fabian laughed, his rage forgotten in his fascination with this headstrong, captivating creature. "You know, I quite like you this way, Meliss—Missy. You're going to be quite a delight to tame and master."

"Master me? You and whose army!"

The laughter faded, but a frightening smile lingered. "Nevertheless, my dear, you are going to be punished for your rash action."

She resumed her previous aggressive stance. "Prepare to hit the deck again!"

This time, it was Missy who didn't know what happened to her. Before she could even think or breathe, Fabian had grabbed her fists, hauled her up hard against his muscled body, and fastened his mouth on hers. A scream of protest was smothered in her throat. At first she tried to fight him, but then she didn't want to.

Fabian Fontenot was a beast, a jerk. He was also, Missy soon discovered, the sexiest man alive. He kissed her as if she were some luscious dish he were devouring—and, for the first time in her life, Missy longed to be devoured!

His mouth was hot, insistent, passionate on hers. He tasted of coffee and cigars, a potent, intoxicating mix, and the scent of him inflamed her. When his tongue stole between her lips, then plundered audaciously deep inside her mouth, a spasm of searing sensuality shot through her from head to toe. It was like nothing she had ever felt before. Her heart was beating madly, her breasts tingled against the crushing pressure of his chest, and the small of her back seemed to burn where his hands tightly gripped her. When she managed to wrench her mouth away his lips followed to claim hers again, stealing her breath away as he deepened the kiss. Feeling his tongue tease and thrust inside her mouth, she could only moan and cling to him.

When he finally pulled back she tottered on her feet, and he chuckled and steadied her. He stared down at her rapt, breathless face with tender amusement. "I presume I've exacted my revenge now—though it seems it wasn't quite punishment for either of us."

At last Missy remembered her righteous indignation and shoved him away. "Why, you bastard!"

His eyes burned with ire. "Melissa, I warn you—"

"Damn it, the name is Missy! And *I* warn *you*! Get the hell out of my sight! If you ever touch me again, I'll—"

"Swoon in my arms, as you so nearly did now?" he supplied ruthlessly.

Missy took a swipe at him, only to have her hand grabbed, her body pulled hard against his, and her mouth claimed once more. When he released her, her expression was dazed, his, inordinately pleased.

"Now," he said, straightening his cuffs self-importantly, "you will go upstairs and change out of that unseemly ball gown into a proper morning frock suitable for my fiancée. Then we shall take our drive about town, have dinner at the Gayoso Hotel, and discuss setting a new date for this wedding forthwith. . . ." He grinned. "Before you compromise my virtue, darling."

Missy was ready to hurl another diatribe at him when he grabbed her face with both hands. She froze at the look of promised retribution in his eye.

"Don't say it, Missy," he warned. "I've tolerated your willful outbursts because I know you've had a bad accident. But my patience is not limitless. If you should malign me again, I assure you that you'll regret it—in full."

Missy opened her mouth to protest, realized her mistake too late, and regretted it not at all as she was thoroughly kissed again.

"Well?" he demanded. "Will you go upstairs and change, or shall I—"

"Yes, Fabian," she muttered, turning and walking dazedly from the room.

Chapter Twelve

"I can't believe this is happening to me," Missy muttered.

She sat next to Fabian in his barouche, which was drawn by a dappled gray horse. She had changed into a fashionable day dress of crisp yellow muslin. A ridiculous little hat with feathers bobbed on her head with each jolt of the conveyance.

While Fabian worked the reins, Missy sat with fingernails digging into the edge of the leather seat. Maintaining her balance was not easy. The carriage rocked, lurched, and creaked on its springs, and the ride was bumpy and miserable. Obviously, these people had never heard of modern suspension systems—or even of automobiles, she mused cynically.

The landscape passing them was alien to her. They were plodding down a plank road past endless cotton fields. Occasionally, they passed another buggy, a farm wagon, or a dray loaded with supplies. The scents of moist earth and manure filled the cool air.

Where in the hell was Memphis? Missy knew she'd just left the home where she'd been born—though a radically different house it was, minus several major remodelings, a four-car garage, six bathrooms, and a modern kitchen—and yet all the familiar landmarks near her home were missing now. She'd spotted no neighbors, no streetlights, no cars, no police cruisers, nothing but endless furrows of dirt. If she still clung to any illusions that she was somehow misplaced in her own time, that fragile hope was rapidly disintegrating.

Fabian seemed to take all in stride as he clucked to the horse and puffed away on a cigar. Missy was tempted to yank the smoke from his mouth, so intense was her nicotine fit at the aroma. Now, it seemed ludicrous to her that she had ever wished to be transported to antebellum times. The elegant dresses she had always thought of as so gorgeous were uncomfortable as hell. And she was stuck in an archaic period without modern conveniences, when woman were the virtual chattels of beasts like Fabian Fontenot.

Missy was forced to confront her own traitorous behavior with him back at the house. Why on earth had she allowed this bumpkin to kiss her? In truth, she hated this man who purported to be her fiancé.

Almost as much as she wanted to jump his bones!

Stifling a sigh of pure frustration, Missy glanced at him, studying his strong jaw and beautifully chiseled mouth, his straight nose and deep-set eyes. His shoulders were broad, his torso lean, his legs long and sinewy. A brazen image suddenly flooded her mind—of those long, muscled legs spreading her thighs widely apart, of him thrusting into her as she moaned in exquisite pleasure . . .

Missy jerked her thoughts away from dangerous territory. Heavens! Why did this man have to be so sinfully handsome? And such a skilled kisser! Missy had to admit that no other man had ever inspired such passion in her. Jeff's kisses certainly paled by comparison.

The thought of Jeff, and the world she'd left behind, brought a wave of melancholy crashing over her. Did Jeff and her parents miss her? Was life even continuing in the world she'd left? She wasn't sure. However, if her theory were correct and she and this "Melissa" had switched places in time, the people she'd left behind might well assume Melissa was her, just as the people here were assuming she was Melissa. What a mind-boggling mess! Certainly, there were differences between her and her distant cousin that her new parents and Fabian had already noted. But both she and Melissa had taken bad falls, which would explain their "confused" states afterward. And, as far as purely physical attributes were concerned, Missy could well understand anyone's mistaking her for Melissa, and vice versa. Back in the present, she had often stared at the daguerreotype of her cousin, and she'd found the resemblance between the two of them truly uncanny.

Had she and this Melissa been switched? If so, how had it happened? Did the "charmed" newel button have any bearing on the mystery? And were she and Melissa now living each others' lives concurrently? This electrifying possibility made her gasp.

"You sound a trifle winded, my dear," an amused male voice interjected. "Reliving our moments of passion, are you?"

Missy stared daggers at Fabian, who was staring back at her with a positively depraved smile. "You wish!" she snapped.

"Come now, you must feel something for me," he teased.

"Try hate at first sight!"

He chuckled. "If you weren't basking in memories of our shared bliss, what, pray tell, brought such a look of breathless fascination to your face?"

"That's none of your damned business."

"Touchy today, aren't we?" Grinning ruefully, he turned his attention back to the horse. "By jove, I don't know what brought about this dramatic change in you—whether it was the bump on your head or that you've simply come to your senses. But I like you this way, my dear. Indeed, I do."

"Well, don't get used to me, buster. I'm not going to be around for long," she snapped back.

All at once, Fabian's attention was riveted on her. "What do you mean by that comment?"

Missy could have kicked herself for speaking without thought. Yet, in a way, it was a relief to hear herself verbalize what she now recognized as the truth—that she wanted to escape this antiquated age in which she was stuck, and the sooner the better. She especially wanted to flee these new, confusing feelings toward Fabian. Missy was used to being totally in charge of her own life and her person—and somehow, Fabian

Fontenot was capable of taking that control out of her hands. This desperately frightened her.

"Well, Missy?" he demanded. "Precisely where is it you're planning to go?"

She shrugged and took a long moment to smooth down her skirts. "Let's just say I'm not planning to marry you."

All at once, his expression grew deadly serious. "Then I'll simply have to change your mind, won't I?" The softness of his tone did nothing to mute the lethal menace radiating from his words.

"Not in this century, you won't," she retorted, and then amazed herself by laughing uproariously.

Fabian frowned at the woman sitting next to him. Missy was laughing uncontrollably, as if she were savoring some private joke that was totally beyond his comprehension. He mulled over the dramatic change in his fiancée. If he hadn't known better, he would have sworn that he was sitting next to a different woman.

That was impossible, of course—wasn't it? Physically, Missy appeared to be the same young lady he'd become engaged to—except that the fall had aged her slightly. Still, the change in her temperament was mind-boggling! Her spirit bore no resemblance at all to that of the meek, mild Melissa he'd known previously. Had the fall brought on a radical personality change—or was she indeed a different person now?

He shook his head at that preposterous possibility. Any fool knew that there was no way this girl could be someone else. And that thought brought to mind a truth he could not deny: He didn't want the old Melissa back; he wanted to keep this new, fascinating Missy.

He stared at her, so beautiful and so proud sitting next to him. This girl he would never take to Africa. This girl he would take to Paris, and feed caviar and champagne—in his bed.

There, especially, he wanted her. Lord, he had enjoyed kissing her! Melissa had always reacted to his advances with fear and revulsion, but not this new Missy! She'd been so passionate, so responsive. He wanted to feel those sweet lips trembling beneath his again, he wanted to make her gasp and pant in desire once more. He wanted to make her give over her beautiful, spirited soul to him—and he would devour every bite!

"Oh, lord!" Missy cried, staring captivated at the passing sights.

They had arrived at Memphis proper, and Fabian was laughing at Missy's unabashed reactions. "Silly girl, your eyes are as big as saucers. One would think you'd never seen Memphis before."

"No lie," she muttered under her breath.

Even though she had previously concluded that she was no longer living in the twentieth century, to have this confirmed so dramatically now was a massive shock to Missy. Gone were the modern streets, skyscrapers, and freeways of Memphis. In the place of the huge modern city stood a small town with dirt streets and mostly clapboard structures. They were now passing down a row of such ramshackle buildings—a feed store, a stable, and a grog shop. Horses were tied to the hitching posts, and on the sagging porches a few old gentlemen, as well as a couple of black men, were lolling about. Wagons and buggies wended past them, stirring up dust in the street, and the air reeked of garbage and sewage.

Incredible! Missy was struggling desperately to take all this in when they turned onto a narrow lane which a sign proclaimed to be "Adams Street"—an area she'd known back in her own time as the "Victorian Village."

"Oh, lord!" she gasped again.

Fabian continued to laugh, while Missy gaped, astounded, at the structures lining the street. The famous Fontaine house was missing, but nearby she spotted the rear, oldest brick section of the Lee house—only the front two sections of the mansion were nowhere in sight! Down the street, workers were just beginning construction on what Missy knew must be the Mallory Neely house.

Missy began to tremble. This was Memphis, all right, but not the Memphis she knew!

In the next block, a sign on a clapboard building proclaimed "Slave Traders," and the half-dozen blacks being herded into the building by a frock-coated gentleman confirmed this. The sight was most sobering for Missy. Of course, she'd been aware that there were slaves back at the plantation, but she'd been too preoccupied by her own troubles to take much note. Now, to see actual evidence that human beings were being bought and sold in this century . . . She was appalled.

They turned onto Front Street, on the bluff just above the river. Missy stared, amazed, at the unfamiliar brick buildings lining the street, at the many conveyances lumbering past, at the boatmen and businessmen trouping by on the boardwalk. She glanced at the landing below, with its row of shacks bounded by various vessels, and spotted a steamboat chugging up the Mississippi in the distance. Nothing was familiar—except for the general contours of the bluff and the river. Still, there was no Mud Island beneath them, no bridges spanning the Mississippi to Arkansas, and no city of West Memphis on the opposite bank.

"Are you all right, Missy?" Fabian asked.

Though white-faced, Missy managed a shrug. "After I hit my head, I suppose I—lost a few things."

Like a hundred and forty years, she added to herself.

Moments later, Fabian led Missy past the elegant columned façade of the Gayoso House Hotel on Exchange Square. Inside the lobby, a crowd swarmed around them—ladies in full-skirted dresses and feathered bonnets, gentlemen in dark suits and planter's hats. Assorted children scurried about, boys in sailor suits, girls in smaller versions of the fashionable frocks of their mothers. Given the crush of people in such a small space, the air was pungent with the odor of unwashed bodies. Hadn't these people ever heard of soap or deodorant? Missy wondered, half nauseated by the stench. She hadn't noticed such unpleasant smells around her parents or Fabian—but this press of humanity was clearly an initiation by fire.

"Where did all these people come from?" she asked Fabian.

"A steamboat must have stopped at the landing," he explained. "And doubtless all of these people have the same idea as we do—to have dinner in the hotel dining room. I do hope we'll be able to get a table." Glancing about, he spotted

130

the maitre d' and snapped his fingers. He grinned as the man approached. "Ah, here comes Jules. We're in luck!"

The maitre d', who was well-acquainted with Fabian and referred to Missy as "Miss Montgomery," led them to a cozy corner table. Taking a sip of water, Missy glanced about at the beautiful dining room, with its high ceilings and crystal chandeliers, its ferns and flowered carpets. Noting the attire of the other diners—particularly the high-collared day dresses of the ladies—Missy realized she would indeed have appeared ridiculous had she gone out in public in the low-necked ball gown, and for a moment she felt grateful toward Fabian for insisting that she change. She studied the snowy white linen on the table, the old-fashioned crystal and sterling, the lovely china plates with gilded edges. This age did have its elegance, she mused.

"You haven't even glanced at the menu, my love," Fabian said.

"I'm not your love," she replied tersely, picking up her menu. "And I'll look at it now."

"Don't trouble yourself," he teased. "I'll order for you."

"You will not!"

He ignored her flash of temper, motioning for a waiter. As the man stepped up, he announced, "My fiancée and I will have the fried chicken dinner."

"Fried chicken!" Missy gasped. "Haven't you ever heard of cholesterol?"

Both Fabian and the waiter appeared bemused. "Frankly, I haven't," Fabian said. "Pray enlighten us."

Missy waved him off. "Oh, never mind." If she

were indeed living in the year 1852, when a dozen minor illnesses might lead to complications resulting in death, she supposed she needn't worry unduly about her arteries getting clogged.

"What would you care to drink, sir?" the waiter asked.

Fabian began, "The lady will have—"

"A white wine," Missy finished.

Fabian raised a dark brow. "My dear, I'm shocked at you. Ladies do not imbibe spirits—and certainly not at this hour."

"Then maybe I'm not a lady," Missy informed him sweetly.

Fabian threw back his head and laughed, while the waiter appeared most ill at ease.

"The lady will have iced tea, and I'll have a mint julep," Fabian said.

"Yes, sir."

As the waiter left, Missy stared daggers at Fabian. "You beast! You get liquor, while I get some insipid tea."

Her remark appeared to fascinate him. The tip of his boot nudged her slipper beneath the table. "If you let me kiss you later, darling, I promise to give you a thorough taste."

As the impact of his remark settled in on her, Missy felt heat rising in her cheeks. Good grief, this bumpkin had made her blush! Never before had any man done this to her—which made his triumph doubly humiliating!

And Fabian was certainly eating it up with his eyes. "Try to control yourself, darling. I know the thought of kissing me fills you with—irrepressible longings—but we are in public, after all. Can you not wait until—"

"Go to hell!" she snapped.

Fabian was still laughing when the waiter brought their drinks.

She sipped her iced tea and eyed him resentfully. "So what do you do, Fontenot?"

"Do?" He appeared confused.

"How do you earn your livelihood?" she simpered poisonously.

"I raise cotton, of course."

She rolled her eyes. "Give me a break. Don't tell me you go out and till the fields?"

"Why, no, but—"

"How else do you occupy your time?"

He grinned. "Let's see . . . I gamble, pursue women—"

"And sip mint juleps?" she finished sarcastically.

He raised his glass in a mock salute. "Indeed."

"Good grief, you're little more than a deadbeat," she muttered in disgust.

"A what?"

"Oh, hush and drink your julep."

The meal was surprisingly delicious. The chicken—fried to perfection—tasted more like chicken than anything Missy had ever eaten before. The gravy was thick and mouth-watering, the green beans fresh and flavored with bacon, the potatoes fluffy and hot. And the biscuits . . . so light and sweet, they melted in her mouth!

Missy devoured every bite. She even grabbed a chicken leg that Fabian showed no interest in eating. Once he had finished his meal, he propped his chin in his hand and stared at her in fascination.

"Haven't you heard that ladies don't gorge themselves in this manner?" he asked mildly.

"I've already told you, I'm not a lady—and furthermore, you're not my mammy," she snapped back.

"You'll get fat," he warned, winking at her solemnly. "Of course, I want you fat—at least once annually—but I'll never tolerate permanent gluttony."

Missy tossed down her fork. "Look, you idiot, I've already told you I'm not going to marry you—and that goes double for having your children."

"Don't you want my children?" he asked, feigning a wounded air.

She was afraid to comment on that loaded subject. "Don't you think you're putting the cart a bit ahead of the horse?"

"Ah, yes. First I must convince you to accompany me to the altar."

"You and Patton's Third Army!" she scoffed.

"Patton's what?"

"Never mind."

He shook his head. "I'll be deuced if you haven't turned into a battle-ax."

Rather than becoming insulted, Missy turned thoughtful. "What was I like before?"

He appeared amazed. "You mean you actually don't remember?"

"A lot of things have been—well, fuzzy since the fall."

He leaned back in his chair, his mouth tight. "You were a very meek and mild young lady—and you bored the living hell out of me."

"Then why were you going to marry me?"

"Honor, my dear," he replied solemnly.

"You have honor?" she scoffed, and then regretted it immediately when she spotted the ire rising in his face.

"Southern gentlemen take their honor quite

seriously," he informed her in a voice so frigid, it sent a chill up her spine. "Indeed, if you were a man and had cast aspersions on my character that way, I would call you out—"

"Oh, for Chrissakes!" At the look of naked rage in his eyes, she held up a hand. "Very well, you have honor. Good grief, Fabian, the way you're carrying on, you'd think I had called you gay."

"Gay? But I try to be gay as often as possible—"

Missy rolled her eyes. "Fabian, believe me, you are *not* gay. Not that I have anything against people who are, but you definitely are not—"

"I'm as gay as the next man," he cut in irately.

"Fabian, you don't know what you're talking about," she insisted.

"Are you calling me a stick-in-the-mud, woman?"

She glanced at him in mock horror. "*Moi?* Never."

He appeared only slightly mollified. "How did we get off on this tangent, anyway?"

"I cast aspersions on your honor." Before he could become indignant again, she rushed on. "Look, for the record, I'll agree that you are honorable, even pleasant at times—if not truly gay. Now tell me more about why you were marrying Melissa."

He regarded her with a perplexed smile. "You mean you, of course?"

"Right. Why were you marrying me?"

He sighed. "Because the contract was made between our families at your birth." He frowned. "You mean to say you don't remember that, either?"

"No, though Dad mentioned it this morning."

135

She shook her head wonderingly. "I can't believe it. An arranged marriage."

"Why so astounded?" he queried. "Such contracts are not uncommon. You see, my family owns the plantation next to yours, so this seemed a logical match. Indeed, I felt even more obliged to honor the contract after my parents died in the yellow fever epidemic two years ago."

"I'm sorry," Missy muttered, only half hearing his last words. So Melissa and Fabian had planned to marry for the sake of expedience, just as she and Jeff had back in the present! The realization was quite jolting.

"Our marriage was to be a merger, then?" she asked.

"An odd way to put it."

"But accurate."

"Perhaps."

"So . . . We set a date for this marriage—and then what?"

"You took a tumble down the stairs right before the ceremony, and woke up talking and acting like an entirely different person." Finishing his statement, he regarded her with sudden uncertainty.

She found his scrutiny unnerving. "What is it?"

"I just had a thought—a terrible thought," he murmured.

"What?"

He reached out and stroked her cheek with an odd tenderness. Unbidden, a shiver of longing rippled over her.

"Don't change back again," he whispered intensely. "Don't ever change back."

Staring into his dark, mesmerizing brown eyes, Missy found breathing difficult. While it went against the grain for her to agree with Fabian Fontenot, she was not about to become the reincarnation of her distant cousin, Mealy-Mouthed Melissa.

"You can bank on it," she muttered.

An hour later, Fabian was escorting Missy up the fragrant path toward the Montgomery mansion. The advent of spring was evident in the many blooming plants and trees gracing the grounds.

"By the way," Fabian said, "I accepted a dinner invitation for us at the Sargeants' tomorrow."

"Gee, thanks for asking me!" Missy retorted sarcastically. "And just who are the Sargeants?"

He appeared flabbergasted. "Missy, I'm shocked at you. Lucy Sargeant is one of your best friends. She and Jeremy are part of a couples group we belong to. We all meet for dinner each fortnight. Don't tell me you've forgotten that, too?"

"So it appears."

"No matter. Perhaps during the evening we can discuss a new date for our wedding."

Missy whirled on him. While she had to concede that she had enjoyed their lively banter at lunch, now he was acting like a jerk again. "You really don't listen, do you?"

"You're marrying me, my dear," he said in a tone laced with steel. "Never doubt it."

She laughed bitterly. "And you had the gall to say you didn't want me to change back again, when what you really want is a weak-spined little woman you can order about, like your precious Mel—like I used to be!"

He grinned lazily and reached out to toy with one of her blond curls. "Oh, I do not mind your spirit, my dear, as long as you recognize who's wearing the pants."

She yanked herself free from his touch. "You can take your damned pants, stuff them in your big mouth, and gag on them!"

He ignored her flash of mettle. "You'll be ready tomorrow evening at five, then?"

"Sorry—I have other plans."

Now, she had incited his anger, and he gripped her by the shoulders. "You would betray me with another?"

"I'll certainly try my best."

"Why, you witch!" He shook her slightly. "You will be ready—precisely at five tomorrow—or you will suffer the consequences."

"What consequences?"

"The consequence of a very sore derriere."

"When rockets fly to the moon," she scoffed.

"When rockets what?" he asked exasperatedly.

"Never mind!"

For a moment they glared at each other. "A lady would obey her fiancé," he gritted at last, a muscle working in his jaw.

"For the last time, Fontenot, I'm not a lady—or your fiancée!"

"If you continue to defy me so brazenly, I'll consider that my license to consider you a woman of loose morals."

Missy convulsed in laughter. "Get the hell out of here!"

"And I'll treat you accordingly."

"You'll do nothing of the—"

The rest of her protest was smothered by a punishing kiss. Fabian held her so tightly, she could not breath, as his lips, his tongue, did unspeakably erotic things to her mouth, to her senses. Thrust, retreat, thrust deeper, linger, tease . . . Her sob of outrage became a moan of pleasure, followed by a soft cry of surrender, an inarticulate plea for more. . . .

"Well, Missy?" he demanded, his mouth lingering a mere hair's breadth above her own.

Missy's head was spinning as she panted for breath; her fingernails were digging into the cloth of Fabian's frock coat. Luckily, she remembered in the nick of time that people knew very little about birth control in the nineteenth century. Otherwise, she would have continued to provoke him—just to have the mind-blowing thrill of being ravished by him right there on the garden path.

"I'll be ready at five," she muttered, moving past him like a sleepwalker.

Chapter Thirteen

"But, Melissa, darling, you have to leave the house sometime."

The following morning, Melissa sat in the parlor with Jeff. He had just asked her to go out for a drive around the neighborhood.

Wringing her hands, she stammered, "I—I appreciate your wanting to take me to see the sights, Jeff, but I'm still . . . well, very confused and frightened. I've lost all these years, you see."

His gaze was filled with compassion. "You still don't remember anything, do you, darling?"

"No. Not much, at any rate. . . ." She bit her lip. "However, I have been reading—history books, that sort of thing."

"Oh, yes," Jeff said with concern. "Charlotte mentioned that you've been spending a lot of time screaming in the library."

"I'm afraid that . . ." She glanced away uneasily. "Well, the books have been little comfort."

He reached out to stroke her cheek. "I'm sorry,

darling. Tell me what you have learned."

"I've learned that we live in an age of miracles—of horseless carriages and winged chariots."

"Horseless carriages and winged chariots?" he repeated, amazed. "My, what a quaint manner of speech you've developed." Catching her sudden, dismayed expression, he added, "I'm sorry. Go on."

Melissa's expression grew turbulent. "I've learned that we live in an age of violence and addiction. That we have produced poisons that are slowing destroying our planet and bombs that could end civilization in an instant." Staring at him in anguish, she finished, "It's a frightening world, Jeff."

"I know," he commiserated. "But the picture is far from entirely bleak. We've done much to eliminate disease and human suffering." He smiled at her tenderly. "There are good people in this world."

"I know," she whispered back. "And I feel so blessed to know one of them."

"Oh, Melissa!" Jeff's heart welled with joy as he leaned over to kiss her. She kissed him back eagerly, relishing the closeness, the heat of his warm lips.

Yet after a moment, he pulled away. He stood and walked off toward the window.

"Jeff, what is it?" she asked.

He turned, shaking his head incredulously. "My God, the change in you . . . ! I feel as if I'm losing my mind!" Then, staring her straight in the eye, he amended, "No, I'm losing my heart."

"As I am," she added fervently.

"Oh, darling!" He returned to her side, taking both her hands in his. "Someday soon, I'm going to tell you a story."

"Why can't you tell me the story now?"

He reached out to brush a lock of hair from her eyes. "Because you're still so confused. We must find all those years, mustn't we?"

She nodded. "But can't you even tell me what the story is about?" She smiled shyly. "I love stories, you see."

Jeff's expression grew wistful. "It's about a man who was all smiles on the outside, but dead on the inside. Until an unforeseen accident brought a wondrous change into his life."

Melissa blushed in pleasure. "It sounds like a wonderful story."

"Oh, it is." He pulled her to her feet. "But we'll save it for another day. Now, darling, we're going for our drive."

Melissa hesitated, her mind searching desperately for an avenue of escape. "Mother mentioned that you were coming here from—from your place of employment. Are you certain I am not taking you away from your duties?"

He shook a finger at her. "Good try, but it won't work. The nice thing about being owner of a business is that I can take a day off once in a while. We're going on our drive—and for a nice lunch—and that's final."

Her anxious gaze entreated him. "But, Jeff, you know how those horseless monsters frighten me. I've seen them from my window—whizzing by so fast. Mother and Father have several of them, but I'm too afraid to get into one."

"Aha!" he cried. "So you have left the house!"

"I only ventured as far as the carriage house," she admitted.

"Carriage house? You mean the garage?"

"Yes."

He squeezed her hand. "You're simply going to have to trust me. Will you do that much?"

Melissa's expression grew radiant. "With my life."

Outside the house, a wonderful surprise awaited Melissa: at the curb was parked a horse and carriage, with a straw-hatted driver awaiting them on the front seat.

With a cry of joy, she turned to Jeff. "Oh, Jeff! A carriage! You mean to say you still use such conveyances in this age?"

"I beg your pardon?" he asked perplexedly.

She shrugged. "Never mind. It is of no consequence."

Though his expression was bemused, Jeff led her toward the rig. "I've noticed how cars—how so many things—frighten you since your fall. A friend of mine runs a sightseeing service downtown, so I arranged to hire one of his carriages and drivers for the day. Who could object to an old-fashioned horse-and-buggy ride?"

Melissa clapped her hands. "Who, indeed? Certainly not I!"

Yet as they neared the carriage, a bright red sports car zoomed by in the street, and Melissa dug in her heels.

Jeff touched her arm, studying her wild-eyed countenance with concern. "Darling, why do cars—and everything else—frighten you? You've been around these things all your life—"

"It's the years, Jeff," she said lamely. "The lost years."

"Still, the way you speak, the way everything overwhelms you, it's almost as if you're accustomed to living in another time."

Melissa hesitated a moment, then said solemnly, "Perhaps I am."

But Jeff only laughed. "Oh, darling, you're such a delight. On top of everything else, you've developed a sense of humor!"

He was still chuckling as he helped her into the carriage.

"Oh, my," Melissa said.

They were now plodding down the strange, smooth gray streets in the open carriage, and Melissa was craning her neck at the passing sights. As they turned a corner, she spotted several more bizarre-looking houses, squat and squarish, fashioned of brick, wood, and some strange roofing material that she'd never seen before. Outside one house, three young girls dressed in boys' clothing were propelling themselves about on amazing three-wheeled conveyances.

Then her head turned at the sound of a very loud music box, and she watched a huge white wagon—she believed it was called a "truck"—glide down the street. The word "ice cream" was emblazoned on its side. As it stopped, the three small girls rushed up to it with coins in hand.

Melissa stared at Jeff in disbelief. "Forevermore—ice cream delivered to one's home?"

"Melissa, you're incredible," he replied, then called out to the driver, "Hey, Bill, let's stop a moment."

The carriage halted, and Jeff offered Melissa his hand. "Want to come see the ice cream truck?"

She shook her head vehemently. "I can see it quite well from here, thank you."

Chuckling, he said, "Okay. Just wait here a minute?"

"I wouldn't dream of budging."

Melissa sat tensely, watching Jeff climb out of the carriage and cross over to the truck. He spoke briefly with the white-uniformed driver and handed the man some money. A moment later, he returned with three small items, handing one up to the driver before he hopped back into the carriage.

"Here, darling," he said, placing in her hand one of the objects, which was something very cold on a stick, the frigid part wrapped in colorful paper.

"Thank you," she murmured, perplexed. "What do I do with this?"

Jeff laughed. "First you unwrap it, darling."

Melissa pulled off the wrapper and gasped. She was staring at a thick shaft of frozen confection, composed of many different layers and rainbow colors. "It's the most wondrous thing I've ever seen!"

Jeff laughed, and realized that, for once, he was tempted to say something very wicked. As the carriage continued down the street, he watched Melissa's reactions closely as she stared captivated at the ice cream. "Er—darling . . ." he murmured at last.

"Yes?" she asked intently.

"You're supposed to eat it." When she merely stared at him blankly, he explained, "It's ice cream. You eat it."

"Oh." She stared at the shaft in perplexity. "How?"

Now Jeff's voice did drip with wickedness. "You lick it."

"Oh." She continued to scowl at the confection.

Jeff convulsed in laughter. "Here, I'll show you how."

He took her hand and stared down into her gorgeous blue eyes. His voice trembled as he whispered, "Lift the ice cream to your mouth, darling . . . That's good. Now stick out your tongue . . . Run it over the shaft of . . . My God, you're an angel!"

The rest of Jeff's instructions were lost in a devouring kiss that left both of them wet and sticky.

They stopped at an eatery at one corner of a huge collection of buildings Jeff referred to as a "shopping center." They entered the establishment through an astounding door fashioned of glass.

Melissa was fascinated by the interior, which was dark and elegant, with mysterious, soft lights recessed in the ceiling. As was true back at the house, the walls seem to ooze sound—a woman was wailing a haunting song to the beat of a moody, rhythmic accompaniment.

Once they were seated, Melissa glanced uncertainly at Jeff. "The woman singer is not trapped behind the walls, is she? It's a hi-fi system, correct?"

He chuckled. "What delightful, outmoded things you say! The music is stereo, and it's called a sound system. It comes from speakers." He pointed at a black box in the rafters above them.

Frowning, she craned her neck. "I see. But how does the sound get to the speakers?"

"Electricity, darling."

"Aha!" She snapped her fingers. "I read about that, also. Electricity is what powers the lights, the curling iron, and the TB—"

"TV." Jeff was shaking his head as the waiter deposited their menus. "What would you like for lunch?"

"Lunch?" She frowned. "You mean dinner."

"No, darling, that is tonight."

"But that is supper."

He shrugged. "Whatever you say. Just tell me what you're hungry for."

"Ice cream," Melissa said, and Jeff's laughter could be heard all the way across the restaurant.

"Shall I order for us?" Jeff asked, as the waiter took out his pad.

She nodded. "That would be splendid."

"You'll want to begin with your usual white wine, I presume?"

Melissa was aghast. "Jeffrey! Ladies never drink spirits."

Both Jeff and the waiter appeared fascinated. "Then what do ladies do?" Jeff couldn't resist asking.

"Why, they care for their homes and husbands, have children, do charity work, and attend church," Melissa replied stoutly.

"May I marry her, sir?" the waiter asked.

Jeff grinned at the young man. "No, I'm going to."

Jeff ordered for them both, and the waiter was still chuckling as he left.

Jeff propped his chin in his hand and stared at Melissa.

She was slightly unnerved by his intense scrutiny. "Is something wrong?"

"I'd say everything's perfect. Only . . ."

"Only?"

He gestured in amazement. "I just can't believe

147

how different you are! Your mannerisms and speech, your gentleness, the way you're always thinking of others. It's almost as if a totally different woman got up from that fall on our wedding day."

Melissa was pensively silent for a long moment. "Tell me what I was like—before."

Jeff's expression was abstracted as he waited for the waiter to deposit their drinks. "Now that you've changed, I hate to criticize—"

She reached out and touched his hand. "I must know the truth."

He nodded. "You were very hard-charging and ambitious. You worked like a demon at your parents' ball bearing plant—"

"I did? You mean I was one of those—blue-stockings?"

"You mean women's libbers?"

"Ah, yes."

"You were quite liberated. You were also—"

"Yes?"

He squeezed her hand. "I'm sorry, darling. There's no other way to put it. You were very selfish and self-centered."

She nodded. "I believe you. But, if I was like that, why did you want to marry me?"

"Our families wanted the marriage," he said grimly. "It was a merger—Monroe Ball Bearings and Dalton Steel Tubing."

"Then you agreed to marry Miss—er, me—in order to please your parents?"

He sighed. "Actually, there's only Mom left now. Dad died a year and a half ago."

She gasped in dismay. "Oh, I'm so sorry, Jeff. I—I should have remembered."

"It's not your fault you don't remember."

"So you planned to marry me to please your mother?

He avoided her eyes and spoke grimly. "To tell you the truth, Melissa, I really didn't care who I married."

"Does this have to do with the story you mentioned earlier?"

He smiled ruefully. "You're very perceptive. Something happened six years ago, and I felt as if my life had ended."

"Oh, Jeff! I'm so sorry!"

"Don't be." He stared at her earnestly. "For now, I owe everything to you. You see, three days ago you fell down the stairs, woke up a different woman, and resurrected a dead man."

"Oh, Jeff! You mean—"

"I mean, darling, that the change in you has given me a new lease on life."

"Oh, I've never heard anything so sad—or beautiful!" Melissa said, dabbing at a tear. "Will you tell me this story—soon?"

"You really want to know? Missy didn't—I mean, you never asked before."

She smiled radiantly. "But didn't you say I'm a different woman now—in spirit, of course?"

"Indeed, you are."

"So, will you tell me?"

He nodded. "Yes, darling. Soon."

They exchanged shy glances during the meal, which Melissa enjoyed tremendously. Jeff had ordered her a pie called a "quiche," which she found rich and delicious.

As the waiter was taking away their plates, Jeff snapped his fingers and stared at Melissa in amazement. "I knew there was something else different about you! You don't smoke anymore."

Melissa blushed to the roots of her hair. "Why, Jeffrey! I'm stunned. A lady never smokes."

"Are you certain I can't marry her, sir?" the waiter interjected with a grin.

"Out of the question," Jeff informed him. "But you can bring us some dessert." He winked at Melissa. "What do ladies like for dessert?"

"They love ice cream."

Jeff stared at her with the eyes of a drowning man.

Half an hour later, Jeff and Melissa were back at the house, standing next to the newel post, kissing.

"Melissa, marry me," he whispered passionately, kissing her cheek, her hair. "I want you—need you in my life so much."

Sadness filled Melissa's heart as she withheld the very promise she so longed to give. "Jeff, I need more time. I can't marry you until things are—clearer."

"I know I must seem impatient, even impetuous," he whispered intensely. "I can't even fully describe my feelings. It's just that every time I'm with you, I'm in heaven."

"I am, as well," she replied ardently, kissing him back and clinging to him.

Melissa reveled in Jeff's nearness. She already knew that she loved this kindly, tender man. Yet being with him was also tearing her apart. She wasn't sure just how she'd gotten here, or how she might make her way back to her own time. Nevertheless, how could she turn her back on the promises and obligations she'd made in the past—even if she truly didn't want to return to those she'd left behind there?

Chapter Fourteen

"Dulcie, I'm sorry I threw the chamber pot at you the other day," Missy said.

Missy sat on her bed, watching her maid dust the room. Over the past couple of days, she had become better acquainted with the young black woman, and she now deeply regretted her temper tantrum when she had first arrived here.

At the dresser, Dulcie, a slim, pretty young woman in cottonades, whisked her feather duster to and fro. "That all right, Miss Montgomery. You confused after your fall. Your aim wasn't no good, anyhow. 'Sides, I say if you is throwing chamber pots, it better before than afterwards."

Missy considered this a moment, then burst out laughing. "Dulcie, you have a wicked sense of humor! And I say you should have thrown that pot right back at me."

All at once, Dulcie turned serious, shaking her head vehemently. "Oh, no, miss. That ain't allowed."

Missy frowned. "Because you're a slave. How does it feel to be kept in bondage?"

Dulcie shrugged. "I ain't never thought about it much. Your ma and pa, they good to us."

"It's not the same as being free."

Dulcie didn't respond.

"I must speak with Dad about this," Missy mused aloud.

Dulcie turned. "Are you going to supper with Mr. Fabian?"

"Him!" Missy groaned. "I wish that jerk would get lost!"

Dulcie giggled. "Miss Montgomery! You talk more strange than the conjure woman castin' her spell!"

Dulcie was still laughing as she left the room.

Afterward, Missy paced, thinking grimly of her date with Fabian in a few hours. This trip to the nineteenth century had been a nice little diversion, but now it was time to get out of here—before that beastly, sexy Fabian took complete charge of her life! And here she was, thinking of trying to free the slaves. Certainly, that would be a noble pursuit, but she simply couldn't afford to become caught up in the lives of the people here.

But how could she leave the nineteenth century when she wasn't even sure how she had gotten there in the first place?

She knew, of course, that her trip through time had something to do with her fall down the stairs, and she suspected the "charmed" newel button had also played a role. But what, precisely, had impelled her to go spinning off to another time?

She left her room and crept down the stairs, carefully examining each step for a hidden door or some other otherworldly quirk. She carefully relived the moments of her accident back in the present, but could discern no answers.

At last, she arrived at the newel post where she'd hit her head. Again, she stared at the green malachite stone, and again, she discerned that odd, winking light.

Suddenly, Missy sucked in her breath violently. As she watched, mesmerized, the concentric circles in the stone began to part like ripples in a stream, and she saw a hazy vision of the woman she had come to know as "Melissa" standing in her own house back in the present—and kissing her fiancé, Jeff!

Missy gasped, utterly electrified.

"Oh, what am I going to do?"

After Jeff left, Melissa felt filled with love, confusion, and despair. She wanted to be with Jeff and her new parents, but she still felt great guilt about those she'd left behind in the past. She knew in her heart that the only honorable thing would be to go back to the place where she belonged.

But how could she return to the past, when she still had no idea how—or why—she'd been propelled to the 1990s in the first place?

She did know that both she and Missy had disappeared after they fell down the stairs on their wedding days. Had Missy taken a flight through time then, just as she had?

Again, she wondered if the "charmed" newel button had any bearing on the bizarre happenings. She stared intently at the malachite stone. To her shock and amazement, she saw a blurry image of her namesake Missy standing in her own home, in the past.

"So that's it! That's it!"

Long after the images disappeared, Missy stared flabbergasted at the newel stone. Now at last she understood everything. Bizarre as it all seemed, she and this Melissa *had* replaced each other in time, and they were now living each other's lives concurrently, one hundred and forty years apart! She presumed the "switch" had occurred when they simultaneously took their tumble down the stairs and hit their heads on that crazy newel post.

But *why* had the switch occurred? Why?

I wish I were anywhere but here . . .

"Oh, my God!" Missy cried, feeling thunderstruck as she recalled the very wish she'd made on her wedding day. Holy cow, had she caused this to happen?

Missy raced back to the newel post. "I wish I were anywhere but here, I tell you! I wish I were anywhere but here!"

Nothing happened.

"I want my life back!" she cried desperately. "Living in the past is a crock and should be reserved for the history books!"

Again, nothing happened, and suddenly, Missy remembered the old adage, "Be careful what you wish for . . ."

She slid to her knees, sobbing.

"Oh, dear," Melissa muttered. "Oh, dear."

At last she understood the bizarre mystery. She was here with Jeff and Missy's parents, while

Missy was living in the past, with Fabian and her own parents.

It occurred to her suddenly that, just as everyone here was assuming that she was "Missy," everyone in the past must be assuming that Missy was actually herself.

She wasn't even missed! There was no reason for her to return—

But there *was* a reason, she realized with a sudden wave of melancholy. The woman who had taken her place in the past looked deeply troubled.

Did "Missy" want her old life—and her fiancé—back?

Chapter Fifteen

"Missy, dear, why are you talking to the newel post?"

Missy turned to watch Lavinia sweep in the front door. Arriving at Missy's side, the matron glanced askance at her daughter's red eyes and swollen face. She reached out to touch the girl's trembling chin.

"What is it, my dear?"

"I was just—remembering the other day when I fell, and thinking about the confusion I've felt since then," Missy replied, trembling. "I'm sure it all has to do with my hitting my head on this newel post."

"I see." Lavinia fought a smile. "But do you really think talking to a post will help?"

"Guess I'm feeling desperate," Missy muttered.

Lavinia chuckled. "My, what odd things you say these days." She squeezed Missy's hand. "I wouldn't worry unduly about such matters, daughter. Who's to say that this confusion has not benefited you immensely? As a matter of fact, your father and I like you much better now that the fall has brought out your better side."

"I like you both, too," Missy admitted with a wan smile.

"Now, chin up, daughter," Lavinia continued briskly. "We must get you upstairs and changed. Fabian will be calling shortly, to take you to the Sargeants' dinner party."

"I'm *not* going out with him, Mom," Missy insisted.

"But of course you are, dear," Lavinia maintained stoutly, tugging the girl up off the stairs.

"The man is a creep!"

"Nonsense. The man is a prince."

"Well, if you're so enamored of him, why don't *you* take him?"

"Don't tempt me, dear."

Up in her room, Missy ranted, raved, and pleaded with Lavinia, all to no avail. The matron ignored her daughter's histrionics and calmly went about selecting Missy's clothing for the evening. Moments later, Missy sat pouting at the dressing table as her mother styled her blond hair in loose ringlets atop her head.

She couldn't believe she had let this woman talk her into going out with Fabian! Again, she marveled at her inability to manipulate her new parents in the past. In the few days she'd been here, she'd found John and Lavinia to be every bit as strong-willed and resourceful as she was. And she continued to feel a grudging respect for them for not putting up with her own willful behavior.

"There," Lavinia said as she finished. "What do you think?"

"It's looks great, Mom," Missy conceded sulkily.

Lavinia slanted her a look of reproach. "Now, my dear, won't you be happy to see your friends again?"

"Friends? What friends?" Missy asked blankly.

"Why, your three best friends, Philippa Mercer, Antoinette McGee, and Lucy Sargeant. Don't you even remember them?"

" 'Fraid not."

"Oh, dear. But you will be glad to see Fabian?"

Missy shot to her feet and threw her mother a glowering look.

Lavinia shook a finger at her. "You're going tonight."

Watching her mother stride off to the bed to fetch her frock, Missy asked nastily, "And if I absolutely, categorically refuse?"

Lavinia's lips were twitching as she turned. "You're welcome to stay here and help me hostess the Hospital Auxiliary meeting."

"Hospital Auxiliary?"

"Yes. Tonight, the priest from Calvary Episcopal Church is stopping by to lead us in prayer. Afterward, we're rolling bandages."

"Oh, for heaven's sake!" Missy threw up her hands. "I'll go out with the beast!"

"Splendid." Lavinia carefully pulled the tailored frock of green silk over her daughter's head. Once every fold was in place, she clapped her hands. "There! How beautiful you look!"

Missy was reluctantly admiring her reflection in the pier mirror when a knock came at the door.

"Come in!" Lavinia trilled out.

Dulcie slipped inside the room. "Mr. Fontenot here, mistress," she said to Lavinia.

"Thank you, Dulcie." Lavinia handed Missy a large blue bag with a handle. "Don't forget your knitting, dear."

"*Knitting?*"

"Why, yes. You and the other ladies have needlework to complete for the church bazaar."

Missy was so stunned, she could only stare at Lavinia.

"I'm not knitting tonight, and that's final!"

"But what will you do while the other ladies knit?"

"Get drunk."

"Why, Missy! What a scandalous thing to say."

Down in the foyer, Fabian Fontenot chuckled as he watched Missy and Lavinia come down the stairs, arguing every step of the way. Lavinia was trying to foist the knitting bag off on Missy, who was equally determined to fend it off.

My, though, his fiancée looked like an angel tonight with her lush curls piled atop her head, and wearing that lovely, shimmery green silk frock that hugged her curves so divinely—even if the words spewing from her outspoken little mouth were hardly angelic!

"Mom, this is ridiculous!" Missy argued as the two women continued downward. "I don't even know how to knit!"

"You've forgotten? I'm sure the other ladies will teach you."

"When Memphis slides into the river they will!"

"Now, Missy!" Lavinia scolded. "This outburst is most unladylike." Spotting Fabian, she smiled. "Why, hello, Fabian darling. If you don't look the very devil tonight!"

"Thank you, Lavinia," Fabian said, grinning, as the two women arrived at his side. "I do take it you were complimenting me?"

"Of course, you sly rascal," Lavinia assured him, tapping his arm with her beringed fingers. She nodded toward Missy. "Doesn't your fiancée look enchanting tonight?"

"I'm not his fiancée!" Missy snapped.

"Indeed, she does," Fabian rejoined, ignoring Missy's protest.

"And furthermore, I'm not knitting," Missy added vehemently.

Lavinia rolled her eyes toward Fabian. "Fabian, dear, make this wayward girl see reason."

He stroked his jaw. "Perhaps we could dispense with the knitting for one night?"

Lavinia looked taken aback for a moment, then shrugged. "Very well, Fabian, whatever you say."

He extended his arm to Missy. "Shall we go?"

"Why not?" she asked nastily.

They strolled outside into the coolness of late afternoon. Fabian led Missy toward a large coach awaiting them at the end of the path. A driver in livery opened the door, and Fabian assisted Missy into the conveyance. Settling herself onto the leather seat opposite him and smoothing her skirts about her, she was struck by how ungodly handsome he looked tonight. Before, she'd been too busy arguing with Lavinia to really notice how debonair he appeared, in his black velvet tailcoat, dark trousers, white ruffled linen shirt, and silk necktie. His thick dark brown hair gleamed, even in the fading light, and Missy's heart quickened at the beauty of his deep-set eyes, the classical perfection of his nose, the strong line of his jaw, especially with that sexy shadow of whiskers—

Too bad he was such an insufferable brute!

"Well," he said as the carriage rattled off. "Aren't you going to thank me, Missy?"

"Thank you for what?"

"For coming to your aid regarding the knitting?"

"Hah! Should I thank you for being sensible, when everyone else here is hopelessly provincial?"

He whistled, then grinned. "So you find me sensible now? I must say that's quite an improvement."

"Don't get your hopes up, buster. Just because you showed one moment of intelligence doesn't mean I've changed my mind about you."

"But you're accompanying me tonight," he teased.

"Only because Mom backed down on the needlework. It's bad enough to have to spend an evening with you. But that knitting business was definitely a deal-breaker."

He laughed. "My dear, you do say the most outrageous things." His voice hardened slightly, as did his eyes. "I can't wait to smother such treasonous remarks before they leave those ruby lips."

Fighting the surge of sheer sexual longing that swept her at his words, Missy retorted, "You and—"

"Patton's third army?" he supplied.

"You've got it."

"I must meet this Patton some time."

"Believe me, the two of you have much in common."

They fell silent, and Missy stared out at the shadowy landscape as they passed. They were plodding down a crude dirt road—this time, past dense thickets of oak and pine. She realized that this was the first true forest she'd seen since she'd arrived here.

Missy snapped her fingers. "I knew something was missing!"

"What is missing?" he asked in perplexity.

"Where in the hell is the kudzu?"

"The *what*?" he asked.

"The kudzu, you idiot."

"I've never heard of such a thing. What is this kudzu?"

"Are you from outer space?" she asked incredulously. "Kudzu is the vine that is strangling the entire South!"

He chuckled. "I assure you, my pet, that the South is quite unmolested by your mysterious vine."

"I'm not your pet!"

Devilishness danced in his eyes. "Let me see—you're not my dear, my darling, or my pet. What, pray tell, may I call you, then?"

"Ms. Monroe, thank you."

"Ms. Monroe? What is this Ms.?" Fabian appeared utterly mystified. "And may I remind you that your name is Montgomery?"

"Oh. Guess I forgot."

"You seem to have forgotten much." He scowled at her fiercely for a moment, started to say more, then clamped his mouth shut.

Missy was staring at the landscape again. "What exactly is tonight about?"

"You mean you don't remember that either?"

She glared at him.

"Very well," he said tiredly. "For over a year now, you and I have gotten together each fortnight with three other couples who are our closest friends."

"And how do we all pass the time?" she sneered.

"First, we dine together, then the gentlemen excuse themselves for brandy and cigars while the ladies chat."

"You mean, we spend the balance of the evening segregated?"

"Normally, the gentlemen rejoin the ladies later on. Sometimes we play whist, or dance the quadrille—that is, when Lucy Sargeant's mother is there to provide piano music. However, tonight, the gentlemen will leave early for a political meeting, while you ladies will remain behind to do your needlework for the church bazaar."

Missy was almost too appalled to speak. "You *must* be joking!"

"Not at all."

"Holy cow," she groaned. "I've died and gone to Boston."

Chapter Sixteen

Toward twilight, they reached the end of the dirt road, the coachman halting the carriage before a well-lit Greek Revival mansion, which stood in the moss-draped splendor of dusk, high on a bluff above the Mississippi. A gasp of recognition escaped Missy as she realized that she had seen this house before. Indeed, she had been inside! While the paint looked much fresher and the greenery and outbuildings were unfamiliar, this was clearly the summer house owned by Jeff's family back in 1992!

"I know this place!" she cried.

Fabian chuckled as he swung open the door and stepped out. "I'd say it's about time you recognized something," he muttered.

"Whose house is it?" she asked as he helped her alight.

He rolled his eyes and led her toward the path. "So much for recognition. This is the home of

Jeremy and Lucy Sargeant, our hosts for the evening. You see, we rotate houses each time the group meets."

"Do we?" Missy asked with a touch of impertinence. "And where do we entertain when it's our turn, Fabian?"

"At your family home—or mine," he replied. "We're the only ones among the four couples who are still unmarried." A determined note entered his voice. "But that will be remedied soon enough, my love. Once we're married, we'll host the group together at my family's home—until we can built our own."

"Huh!" she scoffed. "And what do your parents have to say about your commandeering their house for the evening?"

All at once, Fabian stopped in his tracks, a mask covering his features. "Nothing," he replied in a cold, clipped voice. "My parents are deceased. Don't you remember my telling you yesterday? I lost both my parents in the yellow fever epidemic two years past, and I currently share my home with my grandparents."

Instantly contrite, Missy touched his sleeve. "Fabian, I'm sorry. I do remember, now that you mention it. I spoke without thinking—"

"I'll be deuced if you haven't forgotten everything!" he cut in exasperatedly. "For heaven's sake—you went with me to the funeral, Melissa!"

For once, she didn't have the heart to correct him for not calling her Missy. "What can I say? Again, I apologize."

Grimly, he led her up the steps and rapped on the door. "If you didn't look so much like yourself, I'd swear you were someone else."

They waited in tense silence until a slightly built man with thinning brown hair and a stiff smile opened the door. "Fabian, Melissa, how good to see you both again."

"Missy, do you remember Jeremy Sargeant?" Fabian asked, ushering her inside.

"How do you do, Jeremy?" Missy said, extending her hand.

Jeremy took and kissed her gloved hand. "How are you feeling, Melissa, dear?"

"I'd feel much better if you called me Missy," she replied.

At her flash of spirit, Jeremy glanced confusedly at Fabian, who merely shrugged and offered the other man a forbearing glance.

"Certainly, then—er, Missy," Jeremy said, coughing. "Why don't we join the others? Everyone has been most concerned about you."

As their host led them down the hallway, Missy glanced at the Oriental runners, the marble-topped tables, and the gilt-edged mirrors. Heavens! This house certainly looked far different from the rather threadbare, sparsely furnished summer home she remembered from the present. Being here now gave her a weird sense of *déjà vu*, similar to what she felt while she was at the plantation house.

Jeremy ushered them into a parlor filled with ferns, chandeliers, plush rugs, and elegant Chippendale pieces. Three women in sumptuous tailored gowns rustled themselves up from the silk damask settee, while two men sauntered over from the sideboard to join them.

"Melissa!" the three women cried in unison.

"It's Missy now," both Jeremy and Fabian corrected in unison.

At the admonishment, the women paused and regarded Missy warily.

Fabian stepped forward. "Ladies," he explained sheepishly, "I'm afraid Missy has suffered from some—er—memory lapses since her fall. I must apologize that she doesn't remember you." Catching Missy's eye, he nodded toward each woman in turn. "My dear, may I present your three best friends—Lucy Sargeant, Philippa Mercer, and Antoinette McGee."

Studying the three, Missy was not impressed. Philippa was a raw-boned brunette with a pinched frown; Antoinette was a flighty-looking redhead with buck teeth; Lucy Sargeant was a petite little blonde, who appeared shy and innocuous as a mouse.

What a bunch of ninnies!

"Nice to meet you all," she said dully.

The three women exchanged perplexed glances, and then, one by one, greeted her.

"We're so sorry about your accident, dear," Lucy said earnestly, pecking Missy's cheek.

"You're looking so much better now," Antoinette added with a giggle, touching Missy's hand.

Philippa kept her distance. "Glad you didn't let the fall keep you down," she said archly, and everyone laughed.

The two other men, to whom Missy was introduced next, didn't fare much better in her mind. Charles Mercer, pot-bellied and balding, greeted Missy with a wrenching handshake, a sly wink, and a sultry, "Why, hello there, again, little lady."

"I'm no one's little lady," she retorted.

While Charles stepped back in shock, Brent McGee—an obvious lecher with his black hair and still-blacker eyes—roved his salacious gaze over Missy, took her hand, and slowly kissed it. "Why, Melissa is obviously her own person—aren't you, my dear?"

Missy snatched her hand away. "The name is Missy—and as for being my own person, why don't you explain that to Fabian?"

Amid shocked murmurings, Jeremy Sargeant clapped his hands. "Well, aren't we all relieved to see Missy doing so well?" He smiled at her. "Lucy and I have been praying for you, dear."

"Oh, brother," she groaned.

"Shall we dine?" Lucy added nervously.

The eight adjourned to the dining room and took seats at the elegantly set Empire table. While everyone sampled the first course of cream of corn soup, the ladies began to test the waters with Missy.

"Is it true that you don't remember anything, dear?" Lucy asked.

Missy shrugged. "That depends on which century you're talking about."

While Lucy struggled to digest this, Philippa stared at Missy pointedly and said, "You look five years older now."

"And you look like Methuselah," Missy snapped back.

Antoinette giggled. "Why, Missy has spirit now—how queer!"

"At least I'm not a ditz like you," Missy replied.

Wearing dumbfounded expressions, the ladies desisted from further queries and began to converse quietly among themselves. Bored with the company, Missy turned her attention to the main course of duck with dressing, wild rice, and corn fritters. While the other ladies picked at their fare, Missy ate her food with great gusto, prompting more than one mystified stare from the others.

She kept only half an ear on the conversation, but grew increasingly irritated when it dawned on her that there was a complete division of the sexes at the table. The women were chattering about such inanities as recipes for stewed okra and the latest fashions in *Godey's Lady's Book*, while the men discussed the more important topics of gambling, horse racing, local and national politics—and, most particularly, cotton prices.

Missy soon tuned out the women and focused on the men. She nibbled her pecan pie and listened intently as they discussed the Compromise of 1850 and the recent "states rights" conventions prompted by the controversial measure.

"I say, if slavery is ever abolished in the South, Tennessee should secede from the Union," Charles Mercer declared.

"I second the motion," Brent McGee added fervently.

"But wouldn't such a move prompt a conflict with our neighbors to the north?" Fabian asked wisely.

"If those cravens dare try to stop us, they'll rue the day!" Charles declared, pounding a fist.

"If you guys go to war over this slavery business, you're going to get the pants beat off you," Missy suddenly announced.

Total, amazed silence fell in the room.

At last, Fabian coughed and said, "Missy has been a bit outspoken since her fall."

"Indeed," Jeremy Sargeant said coldly.

With a condescending smile, Charles Mercer reached across the table to pat her hand. "Now, little lady, you just let us menfolk handle such serious matters."

Missy shot to her feet. "I'm not your little lady, you overblown boor, and furthermore, you put your slimy hands on me again and I'll deck you!"

While the other women gasped, Charles paled visibly and turned to Fabian. "Deck? What is this decking business?"

"I don't think you want to know," he replied ruefully. To Missy, he added in a soft, menacing tone, "Please sit down, my dear."

Glaring at him, she complied.

"Charles, you mustn't be cross with Melissa," Lucy put in kindly. "She's not herself these days."

"I'm every bit myself, and I don't need you defending me!" Missy retorted.

Amid scandalized comments, Fabian said, "Gentlemen, I think it might be wise for us to adjourn to the study for brandy and cigars."

"Agreed, Fontenot," said Charles Mercer.

"Amen," Jeremy Sargeant added.

Watching the men get to their feet and troupe out of the room, Missy tossed down her napkin. "What a bunch of wimps!"

"Wimps? What is this wimps?" Philippa asked.

"I'm saying they're a bunch of cowards for not staying and finishing the argument with me."

"But Missy, dear, a true gentleman never argues with a lady," Lucy pointed out tactfully.

"And why not?" Missy demanded.

"Besides, they must leave soon for their political meeting," Antoinette added, giggling nervously.

"And you women just let them desert you?" Missy demanded.

"You certainly did everything in your power to hasten their departure," Philippa pointed out cattily.

Missy was tossing Philippa a sneer when Lucy said placatingly, "Now, ladies, we must be kind to dear Mel—Missy. We must remember that she has suffered a terrible fall, that she isn't herself—"

"For the last time, I'm myself, and don't any of you forget it!"

"But you've forgotten some things, haven't you, Missy?" Lucy continued patiently.

"Such as?"

"Such as the fact that the three of us are your very best friends. Why are you so angry at us?"

Missy was silent for a moment, feeling guilty. She had to admit that Lucy was really very sweet, even if these other two dingbats were getting on her nerves.

"I have a feeling you've also forgotten that we all were planning to do our needlework for the church bazaar after supper," Philippa added imperiously.

Missy flung a hand to her breast and feigned a horrified look. "*Moi?* How could I?"

"If you've forgotten how to knit, I'd be happy to teach you again," Lucy offered.

Missy ground her teeth.

Rising, Lucy asked, "Ladies, shall we adjourn to the parlor?"

"You mean we're not going to join the men?" Missy asked.

"That would not be our place," Philippa informed her crisply.

"So what, *pray tell*, is our place?" Missy queried sarcastically.

"To obey our husbands," Lucy said.

"And have their children," Antoinette added.

"And make a contribution to the community," Philippa finished.

"Give me a break," Missy groaned. "You people are hopeless."

Philippa sniffed disdainfully. "Shall we, ladies?"

Watching the three women head for the door, Missy said, "You others suit yourselves, but I'm going with the men to their meeting."

The women froze in their tracks, like so many bug-eyed statues.

"But, Melissa," Philippa said finally, "that is not *your* place, either."

Missy surged to her feet and charged past the other woman. "Don't you dare try to tell me my place, you self-righteous prig!"

Amid a chorus of shocked gasps, Missy stormed from the room.

Chapter Seventeen

Missy walked down the house's central corridor until she spotted a room with curtained French doors. Gazing inside, she spotted the men milling about, smoking cigars. They were obviously about to leave for their meeting.

Thrusting her chin high, Missy entered briskly.

Four men with utterly stunned faces turned to stare at her.

"May I join you, gentlemen?" she asked sweetly.

Charles Mercer turned grimly to Fabian. "Fontenot, kindly instruct your fiancée regarding her place."

At Charles' words, Missy attacked him directly. "Don't you dare lecture me on my place, you braying jackass! I've had quite enough of that from the three Knitting Ninnies in the other room. My *place* is wherever I choose to be. And,

173

at the moment, it's right here!"

While three of the men regarded her in white-faced silence, Fabian moved to her side and whispered sternly, "May we have a word in private?"

She glared at him. "Very well. But it won't change anything."

He pulled her resisting body out into the hallway. Shaking a finger at her, he said, "Missy, the other gentlemen and I are about to leave for our political meeting. Kindly rejoin the ladies."

"No. I want to come with you."

His face darkened in anger. "That's out of the question."

"You coward!" she scoffed. "You're just afraid that I'll be smarter than the other chauvinists at your meeting. But then, you wouldn't dream of admitting an addle-brained female, would you?"

"Missy, you're being impossible!"

She dug in her heels. "Look, either I'm going with you, or we may as well go home."

Staring at the feisty, infuriating young woman, Fabian found himself fighting a grin. "You don't seem to understand," he said at last. "The other gentlemen won't admit you to the meeting."

She smiled back coyly and fingered the watch fob dangling on his brocaded vest. "They would if you asked them to."

"Aha! So now you're resorting to feminine wiles?"

She slanted him a sultry yet determined look. "Fabian, either you convince them to let me go along to the meeting, or I promise to ruin the evening for everyone."

"Damn it, Missy!" he exploded. He began to pace, tossing her frequent, furious glances.

"Well, Fabian?"

"You know this is highly improper," he informed her. "The meeting is to be held at a tavern."

"What kind of meeting is *that*?" she scoffed.

"The Memphis Board of Health," he informed her.

"The Board of Health, my butt!" she jeered. "Actually, I would *love* to offer my two cents' worth on the state of local hygiene."

"If you're wise, you'll keep your mouth shut."

"No promises. And it sounds like you're wavering, Fontenot."

He groaned. "Very well. I'll convince the others to let you come along. But my cooperation will not come without a price."

She tossed her curls. "If you think you can intimidate me with threats of savage male retribution, forget it."

Yet as Fabian led her toward the study, his frightening smile gave her second thoughts.

The other men protested, expostulated, hemmed and hawed, and finally grudgingly consented to allow Missy to come along and sit in at the meeting. Jeremy, Brent, and Charles left for town in the Sargeant carriage, while Missy and Fabian followed in his coach. They passed the trip in stony silence.

At last, both conveyances stopped before a poorly lit tavern on Front Street. Spotting a bell hung above the door of the ramshackle structure, Missy wondered if this were the famous Bell Tavern.

"A political meeting in a dive like this?" she sneered to Fabian.

He shrugged. "They've reserved a back room for us."

175

She rolled her eyes as he helped her out. With their grim-faced companions, they entered the smoky tavern, which was filled with unwashed, slovenly hooligans Missy was certain qualified as "river rats." The atmosphere was loud and rowdy, and a couple of slatternly barmaids, as well as several jaundiced rivermen, stared rudely at her as she crossed the room with the men.

In a well-lit and passably neat back room, Missy was introduced to two more gentlemen— Mark Davis and James Henderson—who comprised the balance of the committee. Both men greeted Fabian with raised brows and Missy with stiff courtesy.

Once all were seated at the round table, the chair, James Henderson, brought the meeting to order. "Mr. Fontenot," he began stiffly, "would you care to introduce your *guest* to the board?"

Fabian coughed. "Gentlemen, I beg your indulgence. My fiancée was so fascinated by the workings of the Board of Health that she begged to come along and sit in tonight."

"Well, I presume that is acceptable," Henderson said pompously. "Welcome, Miss Montgomery."

"Thank you," she muttered, restraining herself just in time to keep from correcting him and demanding that he call her "Ms. Monroe."

"Tonight, we must draft our recommendations for the Mayor and aldermen," Henderson continued. "Since Dr. Fletcher is with a patient at the moment, we'll simply have to muddle through on our own." He nodded to Jeremy. "Mr. Sargeant, will you take notes?"

Jeremy pulled out a pencil and several sheets of parchment.

"Given the many deaths from the cholera epidemic last season and the sporadic incidents of yellow fever," Henderson went on, "the aldermen have asked us to suggest ways to contain any possible epidemics this year."

"There's really little we can do other than to quarantine the sick to stop the spread of the malaise," Charles Mercer put in."

"I agree," Brent McGee added.

"If we clean some of the riffraff out of the harbor district and Pinch, things would be considerably improved," Jeremy put in self-righteously. "Those scum are the ones spreading this pestilence."

Several men nodded, while Missy listened in amazement.

"Then we can draft these recommendations and proceed with our more important business?" Henderson asked.

Just as all were murmuring their assent, Missy sprang to her feet. "Wait just a minute here. Are all of you nuts?"

There was a moment of stunned, cold silence in the room, then Chairman Henderson said, "Young lady, you are out of order."

"Too bad! I'm going to be heard out!" Missy declared.

Henderson glanced meaningfully at Fabian. "Fontenot?"

He shrugged. "James, if I could stop her, I would."

Henderson directed a frigid glare at Missy. "Very well, young lady, you may speak."

"Thank you," Missy retorted, eyeing the assemblage with contempt. "First of all, you dopes, I must educate all of you. Quarantining the sick will have little effect in containing the epidemics, since yellow fever is spread by mosquitoes and cholera by contaminated drinking water."

Whatever response Missy had expected from her remarks, she was totally unprepared for the explosive laughter that rocked the table.

"That's the most absurd thing I've ever heard," Charles said.

"Water and mosquitoes—ridiculous," Brent added.

"And you're keeping us from our important business," Jeremy reproved.

Missy pounded her fist on the table. "Look, you morons, I'm trying to save lives here! If you want to curtail the epidemics, you must first clean up the garbage and sewage in the streets, fill in the bogs, and establish a public water and sewage system."

The men were still shaking with mirth. "How could such steps have any effect in halting the epidemics?" Mark Davis asked.

"Try it and watch," Missy snapped. "Everyone knows that the first step toward preventing illness is proper hygiene—private and public."

Brent McGee was shaking his head. "Silly girl, there's no connection between garbage and disease."

For once, Missy was rendered speechless.

"Besides, epidemics are the will of the Almighty," Jeremy added.

"And you're keeping us from our more important business," Fabian reproved.

Missy whirled on him. "*What* more important business?"

He drew out a pack of cards and grinned.

Missy threw up her hands as realization dawned. "Why, this meeting is nothing but a

sham! You guys are just a bunch of hypocrites—
and hedonists! Well, see if I care when this summer you're all dropping like flies from the fever."
She collapsed into her chair, appearing at a loss,
then glanced about the table uncertainly. "Will
you deal me in?"

That comment brought down the house.

More hemming and hawing followed, but the
men were ultimately persuaded to deal Missy in.
She couldn't believe the elaborate ruse they had
created to cover their backroom poker game. They
were like a group of naughty schoolboys sneaking
off to make mischief.

She laughed over the fact that they were playing for matchsticks. "Don't tell me all you he-men
are afraid of losing a few bucks?"

At her jibe, several of the men colored in outrage, while Charles haughtily defended, "Jeremy
has religious scruples against gambling."

With lips twitching, Missy turned to him. "You
have moral objections to gambling, but not to the
evils of poker?"

Jeremy drew himself up with hauteur. "A game
of cards, in and of itself, seems harmless enough."

Missy waved him off. "What a bunch of wimps!"

Charles looked to Fabian. "What is a 'wimp'?"

"I don't think we want to know," he replied
ruefully.

"Gentlemen," Missy declared, "no game is worth
the gamble unless the stakes are high enough."

Fabian glanced sharply at her. "Ah, yes, my
dear. It seems you have gambled with *very* high
stakes tonight."

Ignoring his veiled threat, she continued crisply, "I say we play for money."

Chairman Henderson coughed. "Well, Jeremy?"

"Let it be as the *lady* wishes," he pronounced tersely.

Henderson nodded to Missy. "Would you care to make the first bet?"

"Of course." Her face went blank, then she glanced at Fabian. "Fabian, honey, be a doll and lend me some money."

All six of the men roared with laughter.

In due course, Fabian was persuaded to bankroll Missy, and she proceeded to horrify and infuriate every male present by winning five straight hands of five-card stud—and at least five dollars off each gentleman. To add insult to injury, when the barmaid brought in beer, she shocked all of her companions by pouring herself a mug. She downed the beer neatly, amid the amazed glances of the men.

When she turned to Mark Davis and asked for a cheroot, Fabian had obviously had all he could endure. He shot to his feet, pulling Missy up with him. "Gentlemen, if you'll excuse us, my fiancée needs to go sit with her ailing mother."

"My mother is perfectly—"

"Good night, gentlemen," Fabian added, yanking Missy out of the room and back through the tavern.

Within seconds, they were outside, the door banging shut behind them as they headed for the coach.

"What was the meaning of that?" Missy demanded, trying to wrench his fingers from her arm. "Just when I was starting to have some fun, you had to spoil everything!"

"Fun, my hat!" he scoffed, pulling her toward the carriage. "I've had quite enough of your disgraceful behavior!"

"*I'm disgraceful?*" she practically shouted. "You and your friends are the ones who sneaked off for some sleazy backroom poker game, under the high-minded guise of a political meeting!"

"The other gentlemen and I had no desire to spend the evening holding skeins of yarn!" he retorted.

"And you think I did?"

They had reached the coach, and he all but propelled her inside. He barked out a command to the coachmen and got in across from her.

As they rattled off, she argued, "You're just mad because I won—and because I have twice the brains of your inane committeemen."

"Hah! Little girls who show off get taken home—to bed."

While the word *bed* gave her a certain decadent thrill, her fury was still escalating. "How dare you insinuate that I'm a child!"

"How dare you act like one!"

Once they had exhausted their various insults, they fell into a stormy silence. Back at the plantation house, Fabian's ungentle hands pulled Missy from the conveyance. Then, as they started down the path, he surprised her by making a quick detour, towing her off into the trees.

"Where are you taking me?" she demanded.

"To a place of seclusion," he gritted back. "You and I are having ourselves a little chat."

"Baloney!" Missy scoffed.

"What do you mean by 'baloney'?"

"It's what you're full of, buster! You're still mad because I bested you and your insufferable friends!"

He made no further comment, though his fingers tightened on her wrist. A moment later, he flung open the door to a small hexagonal building and propelled her inside.

"Where are we?" Missy asked, wrinkling her nose at the musty smell and blinking to adjust her eyes to the darkness.

Fabian slammed the door shut, and Missy watched his shadowy form advance on her. "We're in a *garçonniere*."

"A *what*?"

"In one of your parents' guests houses."

"Oh."

The room they were in seemed very small. As Missy's eyes began to adjust to the darkness, she spotted a daybed nearby, as well as a table and chairs, and a tightly wound spiral staircase curling up into the darkness of what she assumed was a sleeping loft.

"So," she taunted, "are you going to sweep me off up those stairs and ravish me, now that you've abducted me?"

"Don't tempt me!" he snapped.

She expelled an exasperated sigh and crossed her arms over her chest. "All right, Fontenot. Why don't we just have it out, now that I've stepped all over your silly macho pride?"

He took a menacing step toward her, and, even in the scant light the hard glitter in his eyes was unnerving to her. "You really like to provoke me, don't you, Missy?"

"So what if I do?" She shrugged with bravado. "Now, aren't you going to follow suit like every other bumpkin tonight and tell me I've forgotten my place?"

"Oh, I've a place in mind for you," he said in a soft voice that sent a chill coursing through her.

"And where is that, *pray tell*?" she mocked.

He stared her straight in the eye. "In my bed, with me buried to the hilt inside you."

She stared back at him, electrified, a hot spasm of desire seeming to implode inside her at his audacious words. Before she could even think, he grabbed her about the waist, pushed her down onto the daybed, and pinned her there with his hard, aroused body.

At last she remembered herself. "Let me go, you brute!" she screamed, beating on his chest.

He easily grabbed her wrists. "You like crude talk, don't you, my dear? You enjoy shocking and titillating others. Well, maybe that's a game two can play—"

"Get off me, you big oaf!"

"But don't you want to know more about the place I have in mind for you?" he taunted ruthlessly.

"Spare me the revolting details!"

"Ah, but that's what makes the game truly fun." He leaned over and nibbled on her ear, and despite herself, she froze. Fiercely, he whispered, "Your place is clawing and panting beneath me—"

"Shut up!"

"With your legs wrapped tightly about my waist."

Missy was as scandalized as she was aroused. "Why, you—"

He grabbed her face and began nipping at her trembling mouth. "Your place is moaning into my mouth and begging me for more."

Now Missy was too fascinated to speak.

He spoke with increasing passion. "Your place is with me, you little brat—with me loving you and making love to you until you can't move from my bed—"

"No," she denied weakly.

She tried to turn away, yet his hands held her head, forcing her to meet his burning gaze. "I told you, Missy, that my cooperation comes with a price tonight. Prepare to pay it."

And Fabian smothered her feeble protest with his demanding mouth and thrusting tongue.

All the fight in Missy died, drowning in the torrent of desire sweeping over her. Fabian's kiss was hot, hard, rapacious, as unyielding as the stiff manhood pressing into her so brazenly. Inside, Missy was on fire, the core of her aching for his thrusting heat. Soon she was reduced to mindless whimpers. She curled her arms around his neck and kissed him back.

He pulled back and stared down at her. "So you're enjoying our coarse little conversation, are you?"

Fabian hardly got the response he'd anticipated; even in the throes of passion, Missy was all rebel. "If you think you're shocking me, Fontenot, dream on."

Something violent flared in his eyes, and the next thing she knew, he was unbuttoning her dress.

"Damn it, Fabian, stop it!"

He chuckled and continued.

"I said stop it!"

"Do I hear a note of panic?" he taunted. "Or is it a gasp of desire?"

When he pushed her stays aside and fingered her taut nipple through the sheer cloth of her chemise, Missy did panic—but only because it felt too good!

"Don't, Fabian!" she begged breathlessly.

"Don't?" he mocked, still fingering her nipple.

"Please . . . I'm not ready for this."

His face dipped down, his teeth tugging on her turgid nipple though the tormenting veil of cloth. "But of course you are."

"Oh, God!" she cried.

"Kiss me," he demanded.

Missy lost it then, pulling his lips down to hers, slamming her mouth against his and sucking his tongue into her mouth.

"Good Lord, woman!"

"Talk dirty to me some more," she purred shamelessly, kissing him again.

She heard him groan, felt the tremor that seized him. She heard a tiny rip, and the next thing she knew, his hot mouth took her nipple greedily—and she was losing her mind.

"Fabian, I can't stand it!" she gasped, raking her fingers through his hair and pulling his face tighter against her as his tongue flicked tormentingly against her nipple.

"Your breasts are perfect," she heard him murmur.

He took his time, kissing and sucking on each breast in turn. She was writhing beneath him in an agony of need when she heard the rustle of her petticoats and felt his hand slide up her leg.

"Fabian!"

"Shhhh!" he murmured, moving his mouth to hers again.

As his tongue performed a slow, riveting dance deep inside her mouth, his fingers found the slit in her pantalets and he began to stroke her—gently, exquisitely. Missy wrenched her mouth from his, gasping for air and tossing her head from side to side. He watched her reactions avidly. When she sobbed and bit her own lip, he kissed her again, whispering, "Bite me—don't mar that beautiful mouth."

She kissed him with such blazing hunger that tears sprang to her eyes. He slid a finger inside her, deepening the unbearable eroticism. At the moment of her climax, she did bite his lip, though not hard enough to draw blood. He prolonged the exquisite moment until she thought she might faint. She heard his satisfied growl as she sobbed and panted into his mouth.

"Are you all right?" she heard him ask.

"Yes . . . Oh, yes."

She heard him whisper, "Next time, I'm taking you with my mouth, and then . . ."

The rest of his sentence curled her toes. She could only cling to him in delirious delight.

They lay coiled together for a long moment, letting their heartbeats return to normal. Then Fabian sat up, his expression oddly remote as he helped Missy straighten her clothing.

He stood and extended his arm. "Shall we go, my dear?"

Missy blinked at him uncomprehendingly. She couldn't believe the sudden change in him—from passionate lover to stuffed shirt! How could he act so unaffected, after they'd just writhed together like a couple of cats in heat? She was trembling all over, turned inside out emotionally, having just experienced the most intense, the most incredible—and the only—climax she had ever known in her life! Now, shameless hussy though she doubtless was, she wanted nothing more than to tug him back down on the daybed and find out what dying of pleasure was truly like.

But Fabian . . . He was standing there emotionless, staring at her with the unfeeling eyes of a stranger! Damn him, why had he done this then? To punish her? To degrade her?

"Fabian," she managed at last. "What's wrong?"

"Nothing," he replied flatly. "It's simply time to take you back to the house."

He was unreachable! She had no choice but to rise on her wobbly legs and leave the guest house with him.

Outside, the cool night air felt like ice on her burning face. As they proceeded back toward the path, she heard him clear his throat. "There's no question, now, that we shall marry at once."

"What?" she cried, stopping in her tracks and glaring at him.

"We've gone much farther than an affianced couple properly can," he continued arrogantly. "We'll marry within a fortnight."

"We will not!"

He shook a finger at her. "Missy, I've been most tolerant of your unseemly behavior tonight. But I've had quite enough of your willfulness!"

"Too bad! You're such a typical male!"

"Meaning what?"

"Meaning that you seduced me just now only to drive home your point!"

He considered that, then grinned at her lecherously. "Well put."

She slapped him, then hated herself because her trembling hand packed little punch. "You jerk! You think you can solve everything with just a little sex!"

"A little sex?" he roared. "Where on earth, woman, did you learn this loose manner of talking? It's enough to make me wonder if you've been unchaste—"

"Unchaste? Why you pompous ass! You've no

187

doubt rutted like a charging stag in every bordello on the Mississippi. Furthermore, I'm not the only one who just got her jollies in that—that gargoyle—"

"*Garçonniere*."

"Whatever." Her mouth twisted into a sneer. "A few moments of pleasure in bed do not a marriage make!"

"Damn it, woman!" Fabian grabbed her by the shoulders and spoke with barely suppressed violence. "You're marrying me if I have to beat the stubbornness out of your hide first."

Missy was at her wit's end. "Oh, this is ridiculous! We fight like cats and dogs and hate each other's guts. Why on earth would you even *want* to marry me?"

"After that, you can ask?"

"Oh, you—you cad! You only want a bedmate!"

He grinned. "I'd say a bed would be a very appropriate place to begin our marriage."

She yanked herself free of his grip. "For the thousandth time, you blockhead, I'm not going to marry you!" Suddenly, she smiled, as a deliciously wicked idea occurred to her. She looked him over insultingly. "However, I might be amenable to a discreet little affair."

Fabian was so affronted, he actually trembled before her. Then her own words came back to haunt her.

"In your dreams, lady," he snapped, grabbing her arm and dragging her off to the house.

Chapter Eighteen

Missy stormed back inside the house in a fine rage. She paced over to the newel post and glared at the stone.

"I want my life back, do you hear me?" she yelled at the button of green malachite. "Give me my life back!"

Suddenly, as if in answer, the circles on the stone began to part. As Missy watched in awe, she again saw an image of Jeff and Melissa, passionately kissing in the present.

"Damn it, not again!" she cried. "Melissa—or whatever the hell your name is—do you hear me? You can have Jeff, but I want my life back!"

Jeff ended the kiss reluctantly and stroked Melissa's cheek tenderly. "Did you enjoy the movie tonight, darling?"

"You mean the one on TV?" she asked tentatively.

189

He chuckled. "On the VCR."

She nodded. "Oh, yes. *Gone With the Wind*. I cannot believe this miracle of moving pictures. It was such a fascinating story. . . . and so very sad. It's difficult for me to believe that all this will really happen to the South."

He paled visibly. "What do you mean, 'will really happen'? The Civil War happened a hundred and thirty years ago! Sometimes, Melissa, you scare me to death!"

Realizing her error, Melissa didn't respond at once. Should she tell Jeff the truth—that she now knew she had been "switched" with his real fiancée? It seemed the perfect opportunity.

Only, if she did, wouldn't he think her mad?

"Melissa, please, tell me what you meant!" he implored.

She glanced at him contritely. "I apologize, Jeff. You're correct that the Civil War occurred over a century ago. It's just . . . well, I'm still confused over the lost years."

He sighed, regarding her worriedly. "I sense that there's more to it than that. Sometimes, Melissa, if I didn't know better, I'd swear you were someone else!"

She was miserably silent.

"I'm sorry," he quickly added. "I know you're still confused, and you don't need me aggravating the situation." Before she could protest, he pressed a finger to her lips. "Darling, there's a place I want to take you tomorrow. Will you come with me?"

"In the carriage?" she asked hopefully.

"In my car," he replied firmly.

She bit her lip. "Oh, Jeff, I'm not sure."

"Sweetheart, you're making such wonderful progress. I think you're ready for a car ride now.

And the place I want to take you to—it's off a busy highway, and traveling there in a carriage would be downright dangerous."

"Well . . ."

Fervently, he whispered, "I want to tell you my story."

Her gaze flashed joyously up to his. As she glimpsed the mingled hope and uncertainty in his eyes, her fear at once took a back seat to the bliss that he was opening up to her. "Of course, then, darling!"

"Oh, you angel!" he breathed.

But as he kissed her again, sadness welled within her. Jeff was now willing to share more of his life with her. And Melissa knew that in all conscience she must also find the right moment to share the secrets of her heart with him. . . .

As the images of Jeff and Melissa faded, Missy was so exasperated that she stamped her foot. "Damn it to hell, will you listen to me?"

"Daughter, why are you ranting at the newel post again?"

Missy glanced up to see Lavinia descending the steps in her lacy wrapper; she was staring at her daughter in utter stupefaction.

"Oh, hi, Mom," she said morosely. "Guess I'm still trying to figure out how I lost my memory."

Lavinia tossed the girl a sympathetic smile. "Is that why you were yelling that you wanted your life back?"

"Yeah, I guess so," Missy muttered guiltily.

"Don't change too much, dear," Lavinia advised. "You're quite delightful just the way you are."

"Sure, Mom."

"So—how was your evening with Fabian?"

Missy waved her off. "Don't talk to me about that bastard!"

Lavinia was aghast. "Bastard? Why, Missy Montgomery, I'm shocked at you! You know perfectly well that Fabian's parents were properly married. How dare you cast aspersions on their memory this way! Why, you attended their funeral—"

"I know, Mom, and I'm sorry." To her surprise, Missy found she did feel genuinely contrite, especially as she remembered Fabian's obvious pain over his parents' deaths.

Lavinia seemed appeased. "Very well. Let's get you off to bed."

"Sure, Mom." Missy hugged her impulsively. "You know, you're really a good mother."

Lavinia beamed. "Why, what a lovely thing to say!"

"It's true. You don't put up with any of my sh— any of my nonsense."

"Thank you, darling."

The two went off up the stairs arm in arm.

Back in her room, Missy sighed as she spotted Dulcie sitting in the bedside chair and mending one of her chemises. "For heavens sake, Dulcie, it's so late! You should be in bed, not waiting up for me!"

Dulcie appeared hurt as she laid aside her sewing. "Don't you want me waitin' up for you, Miss Montgomery?"

"It's very kind of you—but my point is, what about your own life?"

Dulcie stared at her confusedly.

Missy waved her off. "Never mind—look, I'm not trying to make you feel bad."

Tentatively, the girl rose. "You want me to help you undress?"

Missy smiled. "Sure. Thanks."

The girl stepped forward. "You have a good time with Mr. Fabian?"

"Don't ask!"

As Dulcie helped her dress for bed, Missy reflected on the oppression of the women here—not just Dulcie, but her three female companions tonight. Why was it that none of them even questioned their plight? It made her burn to change things—

Almost as much as she yearned to strangle Fabian Fontenot! She thought about him after Dulcie left, as she lay alone in the darkness. Oh, the things he had made her feel tonight—incredible anger, unspeakable passion, mindless ecstasy. . . .

Slamming that dangerous mental door, she turned her thoughts to Melissa. Her cousin was obviously having a grand time jumping all over Jeff back in the present, and seemed blissfully unaware that *she* was miserable here, stuck with the jerk Melissa had left behind in the past.

Actually, the poor girl had likely fled for her life!

Now, Missy wasn't sure she'd ever figure out how to get out of here, to get her old life back, unless it was to fall back down the stairs again, and risk breaking her neck.

The thought brought a chill washing over her. Was that how she'd gotten here in the first place? Had she and Melissa both died in their falls, and replaced each other due to some freaky reincarnation or something?

Oh, it was all too confusing! But the fact was that for now, she did appear to be stuck here.

She liked her new parents, much as she didn't like some of the feelings she was having to deal with—her debilitating lust for Fabian, her guilt over her own actions, her desire, for once in her life, to think about the feelings of others, her regret that she had acted rather bratty tonight—

What had come over her? She was going soft! She had taken Melissa's place, and now she seemed to be taking on part of her psyche! Missy usually took pride in her own self-centeredness—so why was it that tonight she did feel rather ashamed of some of the things she'd said to Fabian, her friends, and her mother?

Lord, she had to pull herself together! For one thing, if she didn't gain control of her raging libido soon, she would surely dissolve in a puddle the next time the beastly Fabian touched her.

And, as long as she was still trapped in this provincial outpost of the past, she might as well educate these people. That would mean giving the females around her a few stout lectures.

And Fabian Fontenot could use some straightening out too!

Fabian's mood was grim as he rode away from the Montgomery estate. He was at the limit of his patience with Missy, and it scared him to death that he was now head-over-heels in love with the little hellion.

How dare she welcome his advances tonight, then tell him she was exploiting him to assuage her own sexual appetites! How dare she presume to take advantage of *him* in a tawdry little affair!

Suddenly he grinned as a delightfully wicked idea occurred to him. Why not give the vixen precisely what she wanted—and deserved? She might have bested him at poker tonight, but she'd evidently forgotten that he, in reality, held all the cards. The little spitfire would soon have her hand called—in full.

He laughed. Ah, it was perfect! Little girls who played dangerous games such as Missy did got bedded thoroughly—and made thoroughly pregnant—and then were summarily dragged off to the altar.

Chapter Nineteen

"Melissa, you have to get into the car sometime," he reasoned.

The next afternoon, Melissa stood outside the house with Jeff. The afternoon was crisp and cool. She wore a printed sun dress and a sweater, he a sports shirt, blazer, and slacks.

He had been trying for ten minutes to coax her into his car. Yet Melissa had remained frozen in place, staring in trepidation at the gold monster parked at the end of the walk.

She wrung her hands. "I did so enjoy the carriage ride the other day, but I'm still frightened of these—beasts. They zoom by at such incredible speeds—"

"We'll go slowly, darling—twenty miles an hour, if you prefer—"

"Twenty miles an hour? Well, I suppose I've heard of trains going faster, though I've never been on one."

Jeff shook his head. "What outlandish things you say. Come on, now, don't you want to see my favorite spot out on the bluff?"

"Well . . ."

Her moment of indecision was ample encouragement for Jeff; he caught her hand and tugged her gently over to the curb, opening the door to the slick-looking machine.

Melissa chewed her bottom lip as she stared at the interior with its many frightening dials, whatnots and buttons. "What do I do?"

He laughed. "You get in, darling."

Gulping, Melissa climbed in and sat down gingerly. After shutting her door, Jeff went around to his side and slipped in beside her. A bell began ringing, and she jerked toward him.

"What is that sound?"

"Only a warning that the key is in the ignition."

"Oh. I see—I think." Then she gasped as a strap came down and wrapped itself, snakelike, around her.

Jeff chuckled at her unabashed reaction, reaching over to secure the strap. "Automatic seat belts. Don't you remember?"

She shook her head violently.

Melissa hung on to the seat as she watched Jeff turn a key and felt the entire car throb to life. "What is happening now?"

"Just the engine, darling. It's what powers the car." He winked at her. "You know, like a train."

Wide-eyed, she nodded.

Melissa was as tense as a woman sitting on a block of ice as Jeff put the car in gear and eased away from the curb. "Relax, darling, I'm not going to let anything happen to you."

She gulped as she watched the street and houses whiz past them. "We're going so very fast!"

"Twenty miles an hour?" he teased. "If I go any slower, I'll get a ticket."

"A ticket to what?"

He laughed again.

As they drove along, Jeff gradually increased his speed. They came out onto a street Melissa remembered from their carriage ride the other day, passing the odd stores and restaurants that flanked them on either side. They continued on for a few more minutes, past blinking lights and tall poles draped with weird lines. Melissa had learned that some of these wire cables carried the mysterious current called electricity, while others relayed peoples' voices from one house to another on the miraculous "phone."

Melissa heaved a sigh of relief as Jeff turned them onto a near-deserted two-lane highway bounded by forest.

"This road circles the city," he informed her, "and takes us out onto the bluff. We're going to a summer house my mother owns."

"Will your mother be there?"

"No, darling, but she does want to see you again as soon as possible. She's been quite worried about you since your fall. As a matter of fact, I told her we would stop by after our drive and take her out for a bite to eat. Is that okay with you?"

She nodded. "That would be most kind of you, Jeff. You are a devoted son, and I really would like to meet—er—see your mother again." Suddenly, she frowned. "But do you mean to say you're taking me to this summer house alone, without a chaperon?"

He tossed her a bemused glance. "You say the oddest things."

"I'm sorry."

"Don't be." He grinned. "By the way, have you thought about what you want to do about work?"

She paled. "Work?"

"Yes. When I came to pick you up your mother mentioned that George Schmidt has called several times to find out if you're coming back to the plant. I promised Charlotte I'd ask you about it."

"What is this plant?"

"Monroe Ball Bearings, of course."

"I see. And what did I do there?"

"You ran the place, of course. So, do you want to go back?"

She shook her head. "No, I think we must let George do it."

Jeff threw back his head and laughed. Then, noting her confused expression, he teased, "Don't you understand why that's funny?"

She shook her head solemnly.

Still chuckling, Jeff maneuvered the car around a curve.

Melissa glanced at the forest of pine and oak they were passing. Everything was covered with a thick green vine. "What is this ivy climbing all over the forest?"

"Ivy?" he repeated in amazement. "Don't tell me you've forgotten about kudzu?"

She sighed. "I presume I have."

Jeff proceeded to lecture her on kudzu: that it had been brought over many years before to prevent soil erosion and was instead doing its best to choke out all remaining vegetation in the South.

By the time he finished Melissa was feeling a little more comfortable riding in the car. She did love being with Jeff, although she still wished she could figure out how she'd gotten to the year 1992 and whether she'd be allowed to stay. She'd done what investigating she could on her own. A couple of days ago she'd found in a dresser drawer her very own ancient letters that her new mother had told her about. She'd felt both unnerved and moved to read the half dozen letters she'd sent her parents while staying with her grandmother in Natchez when she'd been thirteen. Then, yesterday, Aunt Agnes had brought over nine letters her father had sent to her and her mother when he'd been in the east buying a new cotton gin. Her father's letters in particular had filled her with poignant emotion and bittersweet regret. While she would treasure all of the letters, unfortunately none of them dated to the time after she had left the past, and thus they could offer no answers now.

Melissa tensed a bit as Jeff turned the car onto a gravel road. At the end of the narrow lane she spotted a familiar Greek revival mansion, now a graying spectre, standing at the edge of the river bluff with a curtain of greenery draped about it.

"I know this house!" she cried without thinking. "It's the home of Jeremy and Lucy Sargeant. Lucy is my best friend!"

All at once, Jeff braked the car and stared at Melissa, white-faced.

"Jeff, what's wrong?" she asked.

"You're scaring me to death, Melissa."

"What do you mean?"

"I once went to the library and researched the background of this house. It was built by James

Sargeant and given to his son Jeremy on his marriage—in the year 1848."

Melissa felt all color draining from her face. "Oh. I see."

"Jeremy married a woman named Lucy," Jeff continued anxiously. "And now you're saying she is your best friend?"

Melissa stared out the window at the deserted house and bit her lip. Should she tell Jeff the truth? Now seemed the perfect opportunity—and yet, some part of her still feared his reaction, and warned that she might not know him quite well enough yet.

She glanced at him apologetically. "Jeff . . . I'm still very confused. I'm sure that I, too, must have been aware of who built the house. Didn't you mention it to me before?"

"Well, I suppose I might have, but—"

"Then after my fall, things became . . . well, so very muddled."

He appeared unconvinced. "I hope that's all there is to it. For a moment there, I almost thought you'd somehow appeared here from another century. But that would be quite impossible, wouldn't it?"

Melissa nodded, glad she hadn't told him the truth.

He got out and helped her out of the car, and they walked over to the old house. Blooming dogwood and azaleas lined the path, and the scent of spring greenery was thick in the air.

"Oh, Jeff, I want to see the inside!" she cried.

"Of course you will."

On the front porch he took out a key, unlocked the door, and creaked it open. "The house has been in my family for generations," he explained.

"But I'm afraid my folks pretty much lost interest in it long ago. We've kept on the electricity and water, and an occasional family or business guest will stay over here. But otherwise, the house is left deserted."

Melissa glanced from the parlor on one side to the dining room on the other. She knew every inch of this house—although the rooms looked vastly different now, with their faded wallpaper and drapes, the sparse, austere furnishings, the threadbare rugs and scarred floors.

Watching her reactions, Jeff said, "I wanted us to fix the place up and make it our home after we married, but you objected."

"I did?" Melissa asked incredulously. "Whyever would I object?"

"You liked the design, but found the location too isolated," he said with a trace of bitterness. "You wanted to build in town."

"Then I must have been out of my mind," Melissa said firmly. "Jeff, let's fix the place up!"

His face lit up. "Are you kidding me?"

"Not at all!"

A shadow crossed his eyes. "But what if you change your mind again once you regain your memory?"

"I promise you, I won't change my mind." Observing his continuing frown, she added, "What is it? If we can't afford the restoration—"

"Don't be silly. My mother wanted to finance the remodeling as a wedding gift."

"How appropriate. Jeff, the house deserves to be fixed up. It's really a sacrilege to leave it in this state."

He stared at her intently. "And then what, Melissa?"

"What do you mean?"

"Who's going to live here?" he asked seriously, pulling her into his arms. He leaned over, tenderly kissing her cheek, and she shivered with delight. "The poet said, 'Come live with me and be my love.' Will you, Melissa?"

"Oh, Jeff," she said in anguish. "I wish I could."

He caught her face in his hands. "What's holding you back? Please tell me the truth; I can bear it. If you don't love me—"

She placed her fingers over his mouth. "Jeff, how could I not love you? I simply must wait until things are clearer."

He sighed, managing a resigned nod. "Come with me. There's something else I want to show you."

He led her down the hallway and out the back door. Near the edge of the bluff stood a delicate gazebo, with roses climbing its trellises.

"Oh, Jeff! How delightful!"

They went into the lacy enclosure and sat down together, holding hands. For a moment, both inhaled the luscious scent of the flowers and stared at the magnificent river below them as it slapped against the muddy banks.

At last, Melissa asked, "Jeff, are you going to tell me your story now?"

He glanced at her in pained uncertainty.

She took his hands. "Isn't that why you brought me here today? And don't you think it's time?"

He nodded. "You're right. You see, I once loved a woman, and she died."

"Oh, Jeff, I'm so sorry."

With a faraway, wistful light in his eyes, he began, "Her name was Abbie, and we grew up together. . . ."

Over the next half hour, Jeff spilled out the entire story of his relationship with Abbie—how they'd fallen in love, how they'd become lovers for only one brief, exquisite night, how she had died, how his soul had gone with her. . . .

By the time he finished in a broken voice, Melissa was in tears. "Oh, Jeff, that's the saddest story I've ever heard! To think that she was killed by a drunken driver! You must have been shattered!"

"I was."

She shook her head, her expression deeply troubled. "There are so many evils in this age."

"I know. But, darling, there is good, too." He gazed at her tenderly. "Don't you understand? It's over now."

"Over?"

"Not that I'll ever forget Abbie. In a way, I'll always love her. But I found a second chance at life—and love—when I found you. And I know Abbie would have wanted this for me."

"Oh, Jeff!" Trembling, she fell into his arms.

He stroked her back. "Only, my darling, I'm so afraid."

"Afraid? Why?"

He spoke with a catch in his voice. "Since your fall, you've been like a new woman, a woman I've come to love with all my heart. But there's also something about you that's so elusive. Why do I have this feeling that at any moment I could lose you? What will I do if you revert to your old self again?"

"I've told you, Jeff, I won't."

"Then why can't I shake this fear?"

Melissa couldn't answer him, as tears again welled in her eyes. Oh, he was so perceptive! Jeff had sensed her very own fears. She, too, loved him now with all her heart, but how could she promise him she would stay, when she wasn't even sure how or why she'd gotten here—or when she might be snatched away again?

And the memory of Missy's tortured face in the newel button continued to haunt her. Melissa felt torn in two. She couldn't bear the idea of hurting Jeff. But how could she seek her own happiness at another's expense?

Chapter Twenty

"Now, ladies, come to attention."

Missy stood in the parlor of the Sargeant home, with her three "best friends," Lucy Sargeant, Antoinette McGee, and Philippa Mercer, gathered about her. The other ladies sat on side chairs with their needlework in their laps, while Missy stood at the center of the group, frowning formidably.

"What is it you wish to tell us, Missy?" Lucy asked politely.

"First of all, you may as well put away that knitting, because we aren't finishing those afghans today."

There was a collective gasp of horror.

"Missy, what are you talking about?" Philippa asked archly. "I swear, your nature has taken quite a disagreeable turn ever since you took that fall. You know these afghans and shawls are all promised for the church bazaar on Saturday."

"To heck with the church bazaar." Taking in their mortified expressions, Missy continued,

"Look, if the three of you want to knit after I'm finished, fine. But I will be heard out."

"I don't mean to be rude, dear, but if you did not wish to sew with us, why did you come here today?" Lucy asked.

"Because my harridan of a mother insisted!" Missy cried exasperatedly. "If I'm stuck with you three ninnies as friends, then there will have to be some changes."

Philippa drew herself to her feet. "I think we've tolerated your abusive tongue quite enough, Missy Montgomery."

"Oh, yeah?" Missy retorted.

Antoinette giggled. "Oh, let her finish," she said, waving Philippa off. "I think it's amusing."

With a noisy harrumph and a rustle of her skirts, Philippa resumed her seat. "Very well, Missy. Speak your mind."

Missy paced for a moment, hands tightly clasped behind her back, then turned to face the others. Staring at their expectant faces and feeling a needle of conscience, she said, "First of all, I think Philippa made a valid point just now."

"She did?" Philippa echoed. "I mean, I did?"

Missy nodded. "It's true that I have acted rather bratty toward you all—especially the other night— and for that, I apologize. After all, I was with that beast, Fabian Fontenot, so how can you blame me?" When no one responded she finished under her breath, "Besides, I've had a rather rough hundred and forty years."

"A hundred and what?" Philippa asked.

Shaking her head, Lucy added, "Just what are you saying?"

"I'm saying that it's not your fault you are the way you are," Missy explained. "But if you refuse to change . . ." She shook a finger. "Ah, then that *will* be your fault!"

"Change how?" Antoinette asked.

Missy threw up her hands. "Isn't it obvious? I can't believe the three of you tolerate bondage at the hands of your husbands!"

"*Bondage!*" the three cried in unison.

"Yes, bondage!" Missy declared passionately. "You have no rights. You can't vote, serve on a jury, or even go out by yourselves, without some manservant along to protect you. You're often segregated from the men at social gatherings, as if you're some kind of outcasts. Your opinions are never taken seriously. Your husbands treat you in every way as intellectual inferiors—"

"But that's not true, Missy," Lucy defended fervently. "It's just that our interests are different—"

Missy rolled her eyes. "Ah, yes. Your hallowed interests! Having babies, running households, and obeying your husbands?"

Three heads bobbed in agreement.

"Well, you tell me something then," Missy continued angrily. "Where is it written that a woman can't do anything a man can? Tell me, were all of your born with "baby-makers" stamped on your bellies?"

The others were so astonished, they could only stare at Missy.

"But, Missy," Antoinette defended at last, "we're all happy with our lives."

"Are you, indeed?" she challenged. "So there's nothing at all about the black-eyed lech that you'd want to change?"

Antoinette's expression went utterly blank.

"She's talking about Brent," Phillipa explained to Antoinette.

"Oh," the latter said.

"Well? Isn't there something about darling *Brent* that is not quite to your liking?" Missy demanded.

Antoinette bit her lip. "Well . . . I dislike the way he flirts with other ladies—"

"Aha!"

"And, at times, I do feel resentful when I've had a really trying day—sometimes the baby gets colicky, you see—and Brent wants . . ." Her voice trailed off and she blushed vividly.

"What did I tell you?" Missy asked triumphantly. "So Casanova wants to cut a rug, and you're too tuckered to tango?"

Antoinette nodded, wide-eyed, while Lucy confided to Philippa, "My stars, I have no idea what she's talking about."

Philippa replied behind her hand, "Whatever it is, I'm sure it's filthy."

"So cut the jerk off," Missy advised Antoinette.

Antoinette eyes were huge as she raised a hand to her breast. "Precisely *what* are you suggesting I should cut off?"

Missy waved her off. "Oh, for heaven's sake, you'd think I was suggesting castration! I mean, try separate bedrooms for a change. Think about your own needs and don't let him use you."

"But, it is a wife's duty to sate her husband's—er—lusts—"

"Bullpuppy! What about a husband's duty to his wife?"

"Our husbands do their duties," Philippa put in archly, "by furnishing us homes and providing for us."

"I'm not talking about a roof over your head and three squares a day," Missy said heatedly.

"I'm talking about his respecting you as a person, an individual."

The three women exchanged lost looks.

"Good grief, you people are hopeless," Missy said, gesturing her frustration. "I've never heard of such antiquated outlooks!"

"I assure you, our thinking is perfectly modern, and we are indeed content with our lot," Philippa declared.

"Oh, yeah?" Missy turned on her. "So there's nothing about good old Chucky-poo you would change?"

Now Philippa glanced away in extreme discomfort.

"Come on, now, I dare you to tell us!"

"Well . . ." Grudgingly, Philippa admitted, "Charles does ask me to fetch his boots quite a lot."

"Right before he asks you to kiss them?" Missy supplied.

Everyone laughed.

"One time," Philippa continued with some resentment, "when Charles asked me to pull them off, he pushed on my—well, my nether regions—so violently that I went crashing into the fireplace. I had a huge goose egg on my forehead as a result, and he had the gall to call me a clumsy ox."

"See what I mean?" Missy cried. "These men have no respect for you, and it's at least partially your fault for tolerating their unacceptable behavior."

"Then what should I do?" Philippa asked.

"The next time he asks you for his boots, bash him over the head with one, and let him see what a goose egg is like!"

Despite herself, Philippa smiled.

Missy turned to Lucy. "Now you. There must be something Jeremy does that offends you."

"Oh, never!"

"Come on, Lucy," Philippa chided. "The rest of us have confessed, so you must, as well."

Lucy bit her lip. "Well . . . Jeremy does go to his theology study group at least four nights a week—"

"Four nights a week!" Missy echoed.

Lucy nodded miserably. "I've asked him to take me along, but he insists that the discussion would be—totally beyond my capabilities to understand."

"Oh, of all the insufferable arrogance!" Missy declared. "And I bet no woman is ever allowed to join the group?"

"Quite true." Taking out her handkerchief, Lucy began to sniff. "The most difficult part for me is that the group is currently discussing predestination—and I do so want to understand predestination!" She burst into a torrent of violent weeping.

Missy patted her heaving shoulders. "My advice to you is to go on strike."

"On strike?" Lucy repeated confusedly.

"Yes. Quit being his wife entirely until he starts taking you along to group study. That'll fix his wagon."

Lucy paled. "Oh, but I wouldn't dream—"

"Look," Missy cut in heatedly, "I can't help any of you if you're going to wimp out on me like a bunch of hot-house flowers—"

"Who said we wanted your help?" Philippa cut in with sudden acrimony.

Missy laughed. "You know, that's a good question." She folded her arms over her chest and stared at all of them in challenge. "Do you want my help or not?"

There was a long moment of silence, a few murmurs of indecision, then all three said in unison, "Yes."

"But we must know what it is you are proposing," Philippa said.

"I'm proposing that you become your own people."

Total silence.

Missy felt as if she were indeed lecturing a group of potted plants. "Look, isn't there anything any of you have ever wanted—I mean, beyond being wives and mothers?"

More silence.

"Who says a woman can't be anything she wants to be?" Missy elucidated. "Why, any of you could become Mayor of Memphis, or President of the United States."

"But how can we," Lucy pointed out, "when, as you said, we can't even vote?"

"That's precisely my point," Missy cried, gesturing vehemently. "Why aren't you working to change things?"

"You want us all to become bluestockings?" Philippa asked.

Missy shrugged. "If that's what you want to call it. I call it pursuing your own destiny." She turned to Antoinette and said, "Now, tell me what you want—and I mean, *really* want out of life— besides sating good old Brent's lusts."

Antoinette blushed vividly, then admitted, "Well, I've always yearned to sell hats—but Brent has told me it's unseemly for a woman to be a shopkeeper."

"Then to heck with Brent." She turned to Philippa. "And what is your dream?"

"Actually . . ." Philippa took a deep breath, then confessed, "I've always loved to ride, but Charles says it's unladylike. My real dream, however, is to raise thoroughbred horses, then race them here, and in Natchez."

"So, do it!"

Philippa blustered, "But that would be a scandalous thing for a lady to—"

"Why? Why is it scandalous for a lady to race horses? Would it be scandalous for a man?" When no one answered Missy finished, "Do you see my point now?"

The other three mulled this over, then murmured agreement.

Missy turned to Lucy. "And what is your goal?"

"Come on, you can tell us, Luce!" Philippa encouraged.

"Well . . ." Lucy managed a shy smile. "I've always wanted to paint—you know, the Holy Virgin and all the saints. But Jeremy says my desire is pure vanity, and that it would take me away from my more important wifely duties."

"What a sanctimonious prig!" Missy said disgustedly. Before the others could protest, she continued, "Look, ladies, we have only one life to live—" she paused, perplexed—"*I think.* So all of you should go for it."

"Go for it?" Antoinette echoed.

"Follow your dreams."

The ladies considered this a moment, then nodded.

"And what about you, Missy?" Lucy asked.

"What do you mean?"

"What is your heart's desire?"

Missy mulled over that. "You know, I'm not really sure. But for now, I think I'll stick with educating Mr. Fabian Fontenot."

Everyone laughed.

Missy left shortly thereafter, and the other three women put their heads together.

"What's she's suggesting is treason," Antoinette declared.

"Utterly scandalous," Lucy added.

"Let's do it," Philippa said.

The three giggled conspiratorially.

"You know, Missy has really changed," Antoinette remarked.

"Indeed, I don't know her anymore," Lucy concurred.

"Ah—but for once, aren't we all glad we know her?" Philippa asked.

Everyone agreed.

At five o'clock that afternoon Missy was summoned to the parlor of her parents' home to face a fuming Fabian Fontenot. She entered the room to find him pacing the Persian carpet in a fine temper, his expression turbulent and his jaw set hard as granite.

"Hi, Fabian, honey," she called out.

He whirled to face her with eyes blazing. "Missy, you will call off this madness at once!"

"What madness?" she asked innocently.

"You have all of my male friends furious at me because you've organized their wives into mutiny!"

"Have I?" she simpered, batting her eyelashes at him. "Just little ole me?"

He advanced on her furiously. "Do you know

that at this very moment Lucy Sargeant has locked herself in the attic and is painting cherubs, Antoinette McGee is out scouting locations for her new millinery shop, and Philippa Mercer is packing to leave for Kentucky, there to buy herself a pair of blooded horses!"

"Bravo!" Missy said, clapping her hands.

A muscle jerked in his cheek. "You will stop this nonsense posthaste!"

"You mean you object to our little consciousness-raising session?"

"Consciousness *what*?"

"All right, call it goal-setting." She winked at him mischievously. "Do you want to know what my goal is, Fabian?"

"Pray enlighten me."

She stared at him meaningfully. "I'm going to tame the savage beast."

"When hell freezes over, you are."

"Hide and watch," she said smugly. "As for freezing over hell, the other ladies and I will take that up at our next session." She tossed her curls and turned to leave.

He charged after her, grabbing her arm. "Listen to me, you little termagant! There will be no more *sessions*. You will convince these three women to honor their places and leave off this lunacy, and then you will never again provoke them to such treason."

His audacious words made something snap in Missy, and she shoved him away angrily. "Look, you big jerk, get this through your thick head! I'm going to do precisely as I please, as are my friends, and you can drop dead!"

"Why, you little brat!" Fabian was livid, shaking a finger at her. "You play the game without rules.

You forget you are outmatched. You forget I've had it in my power to win all along."

"Hah!"

"What was it you said, Missy? 'Hide and watch'?"

He turned on his heel and strode from the room.

"And don't come back!" Missy yelled after him.

Afterward, Missy flounced down on the settee, wondering why she wasn't laughing her head off in jubilation. She'd won, hadn't she?

Then why did she feel instead that she'd also lost something important, and that only time might reveal the true depths of her own defeat?

Chapter Twenty-one

Melissa sat on a chair in her bedroom, knitting an afghan. Across from her, sprawled on her bed, were three young women her mother had just introduced to her as her best friends—Lisa, Michelle, and Jennifer. All were attractive, unmarried, and in their mid-twenties. Lisa, a brown-eyed blonde, was perusing a fashion magazine; Michelle, a vivacious redhead, was painting her fingernails; Jennifer, a brunette, was flipping channels on the TV with the remote control.

Lisa glanced up from her magazine, smiling at Melissa. "We're all so glad to see you doing better, Missy."

"Thank you most kindly," Melissa said as her knitting needles clicked. "And if it is not a hardship, I would greatly prefer being called 'Melissa.'"

The guests exchanged confused glances, then Michelle said, "Sure, Miss—er, Melissa. What's that you're crocheting?"

Melissa smiled. "I'm knitting an afghan for Mother. I've noticed that sometimes she takes a chill in the evenings, when she sits in the parlor with Father."

The others could only shake their heads.

"You never knitted before," Jennifer remarked. "Is it true you don't remember anything since your fall?"

"I'm afraid that pretty much sums up my mental state."

"You're so different," Michelle said.

"Indeed, others have said the same thing."

"So the wedding to Jeff is on hold?" Lisa asked.

"On hold?" Melissa repeated.

"Postponed."

"Ah, yes. For now."

"Did you forget him too?" Jennifer asked.

"I fear I didn't remember him—at first. But Mr. Dalton and I are making remarkable progress in getting to know one another."

The three visitors rolled their eyes, then convulsed into giggles.

"Gee, Melissa, you talk so weird now," Michelle said.

"Have you been able to jump Jeff's bones yet?" Lisa added.

Stunned, Melissa glanced up. "I beg your pardon?"

Lisa smirked. "You know, have you gotten Jeff into the sack?"

Melissa was appalled. "I would never dream of jumping on Mr. Dalton's bones—much less of putting him in a sack." Then her expression grew bewildered as her three friends all but split their sides laughing.

"Melissa, you're a hoot," Michelle said.

"What does Jeff's mother think of this change in you?" Jennifer added.

"Irene and I are getting along quite well," Melissa replied.

Lisa, meanwhile, was scowling as she flipped her mane of long blond hair. "Hey, guys, do you think I should get a perm?"

"A perm what?" Melissa asked.

"A perm wave, you ninny," Lisa teased.

Melissa remained baffled. "I think one should always hesitate to do anything permanent to one's hair."

Lisa shrugged and went back to her magazine.

"Do you think I should move in with Jason?" Michelle asked.

Melissa stared at her. "Move in where?"

"To his apartment."

"Do you mean, should you marry your young man?"

Michelle chuckled. "No, silly. I mean, should we shack up together?"

Melissa gasped. "You mean both occupy the same shack? Without benefit of marriage?"

"That's what makes it fun," Michelle said with a wink.

"Surely you jest!"

"Not at all."

"You mean you propose living in sin with your fiancé?"

Melissa's question prompted gales of ribald laughter from the others.

"Melissa, you're hysterical!" Michelle declared.

"I should hope not," Melissa said soberly. "Moreover, how can you expect this Jason to respect you if you throw yourself at him?"

Michelle waved her off. "Get out of here!"

"Where do you wish me to go?" Melissa asked, then was flabbergasted when it was again many moments before the others regained their composure.

Staring at the three giggling women, Melissa decided it was time she took charge of things. She cleared her throat and smiled at them. "Since I don't remember any of you, why don't you tell me a little about your lives?"

"Such as?" Lisa asked.

"What all of you do with your time."

The three considered this a moment, then Lisa said, "I live on a trust fund and travel a lot."

Jennifer said, "I work in my father's brokerage firm—when I want to."

Michelle said, "I'm planning my wedding."

Lisa winked at Melissa and added, "Yeah, and Shelley's been planning that little *soirée* for three years now."

Melissa nodded meaningfully. "I understand, then. It's easy to see what your problem is."

"*What problem?*" the three asked in unison.

"None of you has any meaningful endeavor to occupy you."

"What do you mean by 'meaningful endeavor'?" Jennifer queried.

"You all live your lives for yourselves, instead of thinking of others," Melissa explained.

Michelle glanced askance at Lisa. "Is she for real?"

Lisa shrugged. "Who knows?"

"Given the fact that all of you are at the age of spinsterhood, I'm really shocked that you aren't already married and in the family way by now," Melissa scolded.

"*In the family way?*" the three echoed.

"Indeed. Beyond that, consider all the time, talent, and resources you are wasting. Why, you could spend your time helping the poor, or volunteering at the hospital, or attending Bible study."

The others were too amazed to comment.

"I sense an unhappiness in you all," Melissa continued. "And I fear the situation will continue until you begin to make a contribution to the world around you, instead of just thinking of yourselves."

"Look, Melissa, not everyone likes knitting or Bible study," Michelle pointed out. "You certainly didn't before your brains got jostled."

"Then perhaps you have not found the right niche where you can make your own contribution," Melissa said. "One thing I have noticed about this cen—this time in which we live—is that many people are quite self-absorbed. This does not make for the happiest life, I feel."

This time, there was no laughter, as the three others frowningly considered Melissa's words.

"You know, Melissa, I kind of like the change in you," Jennifer remarked. "It looks like the fall has made you reconsider your own life, and that's to be commended."

"Thank you," Melissa replied.

Michelle said, "But don't forget that your three best friends still have something to offer to you."

Melissa smiled at them sincerely. "Oh, my dears. Did I ever say you didn't?"

"Then tell us why you don't wear makeup—or low-cut blouses—any more," Lisa said.

Melissa's mouth took on a stern set. "Why, such are the accouterments of creatures of the streets."

That comment brought down the house. While Melissa stared at the others, mystified, her friends rolled about the bed, shaking with merriment until tears sprang to their eyes.

A moment later, a still-giggling Lisa came over to Melissa's side. "Come on, silly, let us make you up. I've some great ideas for highlighting your eyes."

"I'm afraid that's out of the question," Melissa said primly.

Lisa shook a finger at her. "Here, you want to give us all this grandiose advice, but you won't take ours in return?"

"Well . . ."

Sensing eminent victory, Lisa took Melissa's knitting and set it aside, then tugged the other girl to her feet. "Come on, Jen and Shelley, this is going to be great fun," she called to the others as she led Melissa to the dressing table.

Within seconds, Melissa was seated, and the others were swarming about her, giggling and grabbing cosmetics.

"I get her eyes," Lisa said.

"I'll do her lips," Michelle added.

"And I'll apply the blusher," Jennifer said.

"Try not to make me look too much like a doxie," Melissa implored.

"Get out of here!" Lisa exclaimed. Then, as Melissa started to rise, she grabbed her shoulders and pushed her back down. "Oh no you don't!"

"Will you kindly make up your mind?" Melissa asked exasperatedly.

Lisa winked at Melissa as she picked up the eyeliner. "Before you know it, kid, you're going to look like a different woman."

"That's what I'm afraid of," Melissa said morosely.

Lisa was flipping her hair again and staring into the mirror. "And then you and I can talk about going to Sidney's for a perm."

"Oh, dear," Melissa said.

Chapter Twenty-two

Missy found the next gathering of the couples group to be a dismal event, indeed.

Fabian was still furious at her following their recent showdown, and he hardly spoke a word to her from the time he picked her up until they arrived at their destination. The supper, originally scheduled to be held at the Mercer home, had to be shifted to the Sargeant home again. When Charles Mercer had been unable to talk Philippa out of her wild scheme to go to Kentucky to buy thoroughbred horses, he had finally thrown up his hands and accompanied her.

Supper in the Sargeants' formal dining room was awkward, not just because the Mercers were missing, but because, like Fabian and Missy, the other couples were not speaking to each other. The three men conversed over the women's heads, involving themselves in a heated discussion on whether or not the Pacific railroad would ever make its way through Memphis. The women murmured about the church bazaar to be held on Saturday and exchanged sympathetic glances.

Over coffee and apple pie, Jeremy announced, "Ladies, if you will excuse us, the other gentlemen and I shall adjourn for brandy and cigars."

The three women exchanged meaningful glances, and then Lucy said, "I'm sorry, dear, but the other ladies and I choose not to excuse you."

There was a moment of stunned silence, then Fabian turned to Missy and inquired icily, "Is this new rebellion your idea?"

"Of course, sweetie."

As Fabian glowered at Missy, Jeremy slanted a stern glance at his wife. "Lucy, I'm shocked at you. I think you're being quite rude to the gentlemen present."

While Lucy bit her lip in uncertainty, Antoinette said petulantly, "But Jeremy, isn't it rude of you and Fabian and Brent to desert the three of us? Are you going to stay angry at us forever?"

"Bravo!" Missy put in, winking at Antoinette.

"We men have business to discuss," Brent informed Antoinette exasperatedly. "And don't you women have needlework to complete for Saturday's church bazaar?"

"Everything is in readiness for the bazaar," Antoinette returned forthrightly. "I'm even donating six hats from my new shop."

"Why don't you donate the entire shop?" Brent sneered. "Besides, I can't believe you ladies don't have something you can do—"

"But we don't, Brent," Missy simpered. "Indeed, the three of us rushed about like ants before a thunderstorm, just so we could have the thrill of spending the evening with you gents."

Fabian rolled his eyes.

Brent looked at Missy with sudden interest. "And what, pray tell, do you ladies have in mind to pass the balance of the evening?"

"Oh, perhaps a few games of whist, a bit of dancing, a snifter or two of brandy," Missy replied, deliberately batting her eyelashes.

As Brent stared back at her with avid interest, Jeremy cleared his throat and said, "Brandy for ladies is out of the question."

Missy tossed Jeremy a disgusted look. "What a pompous windbag you are."

Sensing an imminent confrontation, Lucy hastily put in, "Couldn't we all study our Bibles?"

Jeremy shook a finger at his wife. "I've told you before, Lucy, that I am not going to allow you to finagle your way into my theological study group. I find these machinations contemptible—"

"Oh, let her speak!" Missy defended, glaring at Jeremy.

"May we study the Bible, then?" Lucy asked Missy. "I would so like for us to discuss St. Paul's letter to the Thessalonians—"

"There, I think you'd better lighten up," Missy advised.

"Oh," Lucy murmured.

"We can talk about the Spring ball Missy's parents are giving in two weeks," Antoinette put in. "I bet Mr. and Mrs. Montgomery will announce a new wedding date for Missy and Fabian then."

"They'll do no such thing," Missy assured her.

"Anyway, who cares about the ball?" Brent asked.

"I'm having a new dress made," Antoinette replied, pouting.

"Who gives a fig about your new dress?" Brent

continued with growing frustration. "Your mindless simperings only prove that gentlemen and ladies have nothing in common."

Missy flashed her dazzling smile at Brent again. "Are you certain we have nothing in common?"

While Brent stared at Missy in fascination and Fabian ground his teeth, Lucy said, "You know, we do have a problem with regard to Saturday's bazaar. With Philippa gone to Kentucky, we'll need someone else to be in charge of her baked goods booth."

A delicious idea sprang to Missy's mind, and her eyes lit up with mischievous pleasure. "Why don't you three men do it?"

Comments of outraged male pride greeted her suggestion.

"That's out of the question!" Jeremy said.

"Ridiculous!" Brent concurred.

"Amen," Fabian added.

"But don't you three wish to make a contribution to the church building fund?" Missy pursued innocently.

"We're going out to the bluff early Saturday morning to help construct the booths," Fabian informed her. "That will be ample contribution."

"So you three get to eat barbecue and flirt with the ladies while the three of us toil away in our booths?" Missy protested.

"Selling afghans and lace doilies is women's work," Fabian gritted.

"And I say that a true man is confident enough about his masculinity to do anything necessary," Missy shot back. She turned to Brent and patted his hand. "What about you, Brent? You strike me as a man who's very confident about *his* masculinity."

While Brent gulped and stared at Missy greedily, Antoinette protested, "Missy, I'd appreciate it if you'd take your hands off my husband."

Missy did so at once, laughing. "Did I make you jealous, Antoinette?"

"I think that's beside the point," she said archly.

"Then what is the point?"

"The point is, you said we should be more aggressive—"

"*Assertive*," Missy corrected.

"Whatever. And I don't like you flirting with my husband."

Missy chuckled again. "You're right and I apologize." She winked at Brent. "I shouldn't flirt with your husband, even if he is a lecher—"

"That may be true, but he's my lecher."

As all three men present looked on, flabbergasted, Missy continued, "Again, I agree. Actually, I only had in mind provoking Fabian. But he's so moody and blockheaded, I don't think I could get through to him if I hit him over the head with a bale of cotton."

Suddenly, Fabian shot to his feet, shaking a fist at Missy. "Enough, Missy! We're leaving!"

She rose, too, facing him down defiantly. "So you have a voice, after all?"

"Yes, and as usual, you aren't listening to it. I said we're leaving—so go fetch your wrap!"

"Oh, you're such a typical male!" she retorted with an exasperated wave of her hand. "Just walk out, instead of facing up to an issue!"

"What issue?"

"That women and men are equal, damn it! That there's no reason why a woman can't become

228

involved in business or politics, no reason why a man can't be in charge of a pastry booth—"

"Damn it, Missy! Brent, Jeremy, and I are not selling pies!"

"Are you saying men can't sell pies as well as women can?" Missy challenged.

"No! I'm saying that selling pies is women's work!"

"That's just what I mean! You're all a bunch of provincial bumpkins! You're thinking's so narrow, I could use your damn head to thread a needle!"

"I think we've all heard quite enough," Fabian said, advancing toward Missy, his features white and his eyes glittering with rage.

"You just want your mealy-mouthed Melissa back!" she accused.

"Perhaps I do," he retorted.

"I think we should all like Melissa back," Jeremy added, getting to his feet.

Brent rose as well. "I concur. We're all quite tired of this women's federation—"

"Liberation," Missy corrected.

"Whatever you call it, we've had enough!" Fabian declared.

Now Lucy rose to defend her friend. "I can't believe the terrible things you gentlemen are saying to Missy," she scolded in trembling tones. "You're being cruel and ungentlemanly."

Antoinette bobbed up next, wrapping an arm protectively about Missy's waist. "I agree. Furthermore, Lucy and I like Missy just the way she is."

"Have you thought of the terrible things she's said to *us*?" Brent demanded.

"Well, maybe it's time," Antoinette argued.

"Before Missy—changed—we women never knew that we'd drawn the short lot in life. But Missy has helped us to see our existence in an entirely different light. Why is it that you men get to go out in the world, to have businesses and vote and have all the fun, while we're supposed to stay at home, rear children, and knit?"

"That's just the way things are," Brent blustered.

"Well, they don't have to stay that way," Missy shot back.

The two sides squared off, glaring at each other. The three men consulted among themselves for a moment, while the women watched warily.

Fabian stepped forward with a glint of challenge in his eyes. "So, you women truly think you're our equals?"

"Actually, we're your superiors," Missy informed him. "We live longer, we're more intelligent, and we're less inclined to let our emotions rule us."

"Is that so?" Fabian replied with an unnerving calm. "Then if you're so confident of your superiority, you won't object to a simple wager?"

She glanced at him suspiciously. "What wager?"

"You say you're more intelligent than we are. Would that apply to business matters?"

"Certainly."

"In that case, Jeremy and Brent and I agree to sell pies."

"What?" Brent cried.

"Fontenot, surely you jest!" Jeremy added.

He turned to the others. "Not at all, gentlemen, and if you'll simply trust me a bit, I think we can end this little—war of the sexes."

The two men nodded wearily, while Missy

laughed and said, "Fabian, I hate to disillusion you, but the war between the sexes is never going to end."

"This war will," he said meaningfully. "Because my wager is that Jeremy, Brent, and I will be able to make more money on Saturday selling pies than you three will with your needlework."

"Hah!" Missy cried. She turned to the others. "Shall we take them up on it, ladies?"

"Certainly," Antoinette said.

"I think we should," Lucy added.

"What do we get if we win?" Missy demanded with a smirk.

Fabian chuckled. "Ah, you don't miss a beat. If you win, Brent, Jeremy, and I will promise to quit harassing you concerning your—er—unorthodox attitudes and activities of late."

"Oh, I love it!" Missy cried, clapping her hands. Then she caught the wicked glint in Fabian's eye. "And if you three win?"

He glanced at Antoinette and Lucy. "You two will become dutiful wives again, never questioning your husbands' absolute authority."

Both women glanced toward Missy for guidance. "Should we?" Antoinette asked.

She shrugged. "Why not go for broke?" To Fabian, she said, "They accept your terms."

"Splendid." Staring at Missy, he rubbed his hands together and smiled nastily. "And as for you . . ."

Easily anticipating his next words, she stared him in the eye. "I'm not going to lose."

"But if you should . . ." he drawled.

"*If* I should?" she inquired icily.

A devilish smile lit his countenance. "You will marry me."

*   *   *

You will marry me. Fabian's words haunted Missy as they rode home. Although the journey passed in silence, Missy could almost feel his dark gaze boring into her from the opposite seat.

"Did you enjoy airing our dirty laundry in public tonight?" he asked mildly.

"Eminently," she snapped back. "Besides, since all the couples are dealing with the same issues, I'd call it collective dirty laundry."

He chuckled. "Ah, but it's you, Missy, who stirred up this tempest in a teapot in the first place."

She shrugged. "So it is. And you're mixing your metaphors."

"Looking forward to Saturday?" he added casually.

Missy laughed. "You and your friends are going to lose."

"Are we? But that would seem to negate your argument. If women and men are equals, then the three of us should be as successful at selling pies as any three women."

"I said that we're your superiors, Fabian," she pointed out.

"So you did. We'll see what Saturday brings."

She was quiet a moment, feeling unnerved by the tension between them, the intimacy of the dark coach. At last, she dared to ask, "Why did you make my marrying you your prize if I should lose?"

"Because it's what I want."

"But why?"

He looked her over slowly. "Perhaps because I prefer to make you my bride before I seduce you."

As much as he maddened her, longing swept over her at his words, leaving her all but debilitated in its wake, her pulse racing and her palms sweaty. Nonetheless, she was determined to hold her own. "Sex again," she uttered in a trembling tone. "Other than that, you—you hate me, Fabian."

"Do I?" he asked with an odd trace of compassion. "Do you really think that's all I see in you?"

"Yes." She was astonished to find herself on the verge of tears. "You've been very cold to me lately. I think the only reason you want to marry me is so you can punish me for the rest of my life."

"I would like to punish you," he murmured. Abruptly, he reached out, pulling her across the carriage into his lap.

"Fabian, no, don't," she protested weakly, hating herself for the way she quivered at his nearness, the way her heart was hammering in wild anticipation.

"I would like to punish you," he repeated in his deep, mesmerizing voice. "But in my bed."

Missy's world spun out of control as Fabian's mouth descended on hers. The heat of his lips on hers felt so right, so thrillingly provocative. She realized with awe that she had actually missed his kisses, that the estrangement between them had hurt.

Oh, Lord, she couldn't let this happen! She was getting in too deep! He smelled so good and felt so good—and she felt so cherished and needed, cradled close to him this way.

Mercy, what had happened to her pride, her independence? She was growing as spineless and weak-willed as some of the women she had scoffed at.

Then he began to nibble on her lower lip, and her resolve crumbled. She gasped in pleasure, running her fingers through his thick, silky hair.

"When I kiss you until you beg for mercy, will that be punishment, Missy?" he whispered. "When I drive into you until you sob in pleasure, will revenge be mine?"

She clung to him, sobbing in sheer frustration. "I won't be Melissa," she whispered vehemently. "I won't."

He chuckled, a deep sensual rumble. "Oh, my sweet darling, is that what's troubling you? Do you really think I want your former insipid self back?"

"You want to tame me into a dutiful little wife," she argued. "You want me to obey you, just as you want Antoinette and Lucy to obey their husbands."

"I don't think I ever need worry about your becoming a docile, subservient mate," he teased, his mouth against her wet cheek. "Don't you understand? All the joy is in the battle, love, even though I shall win."

Missy tried to argue, but Fabian's kiss smothered her protest. He shifted her onto the seat next to him; his hand moved boldly to her breast, and riotous desire raked over her. Her hand moved inside his coat, her fingers feeling the muscled contours of his chest through his shirt, and then moved lower, until she touched his maleness— hard, warm steel that pulsed against her fingers.

A sob of pure frustration rose inside her, even as unspeakable desire twisted deep in her gut. Oh, God, she wanted him so! She wanted to lose to him, she wanted him to force her into marriage. And she needn't worry about his big mouth, because she would be too busy kissing him senseless for him ever to utter a word.

Then, as the coach stopped, he wrenched his mouth from hers. "Hey, easy, darling," he teased. "We'd best get you inside."

He spoke in the confident tones of a man who had decided that victory was imminent and wanted to savor it in full. This reality both troubled and exhilarated Missy as he led her to the door.

Seconds later, as Missy entered the house, she paused by the newel post and once again saw an image of Melissa and Jeff kissing ardently in the present. She felt as if her life were slipping away from her—in both centuries!

"Damn it, Melissa, will you get a grip and control yourself?" she hissed to the button. "Somehow, I'm going to find my way back to the twentieth century and get my own world back! Do you hear me? You can't have my life, I tell you!"

The images faded. Missy knew her words should have brought some sense of vindication; instead, she was left wondering why bitter tears stung her eyes.

Chapter Twenty-three

"Oh, dear," Melissa said.

Jeff had just dropped her off from their date, and she stood staring into the newel button. She spotted Missy glaring at her formidably and spouting words Melissa could not hear—though their import was quite clear.

During the past few days, she had spotted Missy's angry countenance several times, the visions reminding Melissa that she was living a life that did not really belong to her.

Now, the images faded and Melissa shuddered.

Heavens, Missy had looked so unhappy! Melissa knew in her heart that she needed to tell Jeff the truth, to see if somehow they might release poor Missy from her purgatory.

But that might mean that she would need to go back to the year 1852, and she didn't want to go! Still, Melissa's sense of altruism demanded that she do something to help her cousin. And, looking beyond the question of Missy's fate, was she being fair to Jeff to go on seeing him, to keep nurturing a love that time might snatch away?

Dear Jeff. The two of them continued to spend every free moment together out at his family's summer house. They sat in the gazebo together, holding hands, kissing, and staring into each other's eyes. They read poetry together, got to know each other better, and fell more deeply in love.

Was that love doomed? How Melissa wished she knew!

The next afternoon, Melissa sat with Jeff in the gazebo behind his parents' summer house. She wore a new spring outfit—a lacy, long-sleeved blouse, a calf-length, floral-printed skirt, and a pair of soft leather boots. While Melissa was still too frightened to go "into town" and confront the massive steel-girded skyscrapers of Memphis proper, recently, with the encouragement of her mother and friends, she had begun to visit the amazing "shopping malls" of suburban Memphis. With help from the others, she had set a new style for herself, buying dresses, blouses, and skirts with delicate, feminine lines. While she had refused to have her hair "permed" as Lisa had wanted, she now styled her blond tresses down and fashionably curled. She had even started wearing light makeup. When she had asked Jeff if he approved of the changes, he had grinned and informed her that anything she wanted to do was fine with him, that she would look gorgeous wearing an old gunny sack.

Now, she feasted her eyes on him, looking so handsome in his sky-blue knitted shirt and tan slacks, with the sunshine of the perfect spring day gleaming in his thick hair. He sat with a stack of leather-bound books in his lap. He had been reading her love poems all afternoon.

How she adored him! But would her blissful existence with him soon be shattered?

He glanced up, noting the anxious look in her eyes. "What is it, darling?"

Melissa got up and walked over to stare out at the Mississippi. She watched a barge float down the gleaming river and inhaled the scent of wet earth that laced the air. Not ready to confront her deepest fears, she began by discussing other troubling issues.

"I've been reading a lot lately—you know, about the lost years."

"Ah, yes."

She turned to him. "It's such a strange, violent world in which we live, Jeff, with despots gobbling up their neighbors, and people murdering each other just to get a few dollars so they can snort rocks—"

"Ah, you mean cocaine?"

She nodded morosely. "It's unthinkably evil."

He rose and walked over to join her. "I know, darling. But have you thought that we might make this world better?"

She stared at him with forlorn hope. "Do you think that's possible?"

He caught her in his arms, and his voice trembled with his heartfelt words. "A year ago, I would have said no. But since I've found you—I mean, since you've changed . . . Now, I think anything's possible."

Joy welled within her. "Oh, Jeff, I feel the same way! I would so love to make a contribution to this world. You know, we could become missionaries." She hesitated. "I mean, if you should want to." *And if I'm allowed to stay here*, she added to herself with a surge of melancholy.

He smiled down at her. "Darling, I think that's a wonderful idea. Or we could join the Peace Corps—or just help out where we're needed in our own community."

"Yes, I think that would be excellent."

"Then you're sure you won't want to return to work?"

"Yes, I'm sure. As I said, we must—"

"Let George do it?"

She nodded.

Chuckling, Jeff led her back to their bench. He opened the book of Shakespearean sonnets and quoted, "'Shall I compare thee to a summer's day? Thou art more lovely, and more temperate.'"

She smiled. "You exaggerate, of course."

He gazed at her tenderly. "Not at all. I used to write poetry myself, all the time." Abruptly, he glanced away.

"For Abbie?" she asked gently.

His anguished gaze met hers. "Yes. I'm sorry to bring it up."

"No, don't be. I think it's lovely that you wrote poems for her. And you'll write them again one day."

He spoke with great emotion. "I already have."

Her entire face lit up. "You're written a poem?"

"Yes," he said hoarsely. "For you."

Melissa clapped her hands. "Oh, I must hear this!"

"Are you sure?" he asked tentatively.

"Jeffrey Dalton, don't you dare keep me in suspense for one more instant!"

He smiled and pulled a crumpled sheet from his pocket. "It's called *My Melissa*."

"Oh, I love it already," she said. "Do read it, pray."

Jeff stood, smiled at her lovingly, and read aloud:

My Melissa
by Jeffrey Dalton

You came to me one morn,
Like the answer to a prayer,
By fate, you were reborn,
My Melissa, gentle and fair.

You soothed a soul of deep, dark gashes,
You touched a life of guilt and despair,
You rose from your own ashes,
You taught me how to care.

From numbness, you brought feeling,
In darkness, you found light,
With a heart of love and healing,
You have taken away my night.

When he finished, she was in tears. "Oh, Jeffrey! That's the dearest poem I've ever heard!"

He sat down, pulling her into his arms. "And it's written for the dearest woman I've ever known."

For a long moment, they held each other close and shared their joy. At last, Melissa wiped her tears and said, "Your verse is wonderful. It reminds me of the beautiful love poems of Elizabeth Barrett Browning. You know, I thought it was so romantic when she eloped with Robert

Browning. Why only last year, I read her newest, *Sonnets From the Portuguese*. It was quite splendid—"

"Melissa!" Suddenly, Jeff was standing, staring at her white-faced and wild-eyed. "Elizabeth Barrett Browning's sonnets were first published in 1850! What on earth are you talking about?"

She glanced away miserably. "I'm sorry, Jeff. You know I've been so confused since my fall—"

"There's more to it than that," he insisted. "There's something you're not telling me! Ever since your fall, you've been so different! If I didn't know it was impossible, I'd swear you're someone else!"

Melissa hesitated for a long moment. She knew that here, at last, was the perfect opportunity to tell Jeff the truth. Besides, he had bared his soul to her, sharing his deepest thoughts, feelings, and fears, and it was high time she reciprocated by sharing with him all the secrets of her own tormented heart.

She stared him in the eye. "It's not impossible, Jeff. The truth is, I am someone else."

He laughed. "You're joking."

She gazed at him earnestly and slowly shook her head.

He stared back. At last, in a voice edged with panic, he said, "Oh, my God, it's true! You really think you're someone else!"

"Not think," she corrected. "I *am* someone else. And I think you'd better sit down."

He did, shaking his head in stupefaction and eyeing her warily. "I realized there was more to this confusion of yours than you were letting on. But this! Damn it, I knew I should have insisted you go to the hospital—"

"Jeff, it has nothing to do with the hospital, or with X rays," she put in firmly.

He sighed, staring at her with compassion. "Very well. So tell me, who do you think—I mean, who are you?"

Melissa drew a deep breath. "I'm Melissa Montgomery, a relative of the young woman you knew as Missy."

He appeared highly skeptical. "Missy's relatives, the ones who owned the house originally, were called Montgomery."

"That is my family."

"My God! And you're trying to tell me that you're not Missy Monroe at all, but some distant cousin of hers?"

"That is correct."

"But that is ridiculous!" he cried. "You look too much like Missy to be anyone else!"

"Jeffrey, I assure you, I'm telling you the truth."

He shook his head disparagingly. "Melissa, you can't possibly be someone else. Why, the resemblance would be so uncanny that . . ." Suddenly he paused, staring at her intently. A look of terrible uncertainty crossed his eyes. "Though now that I think about it, there are some minor physical differences, ever since your fall. The way the lines have disappeared from around your eyes, for instance."

She nodded. "That's because, ever since my fall, I've been someone else. I'm five years younger than Missy. She was twenty-five, and I'm only twenty."

He continued to appear baffled. "So, you're saying you're some distant relation from . . . where?"

She drew a bracing breath and blurted, "From one hundred and forty years in the past."

Jeff shot to his feet. "You're got to be kidding me!"

She shook her head again.

He gestured his exasperation. "But this makes no sense! You couldn't possibly have come here from one hundred and forty years in the past! How would you have gotten here? Besides, if you are indeed someone else, then where is Missy?"

Melissa bit her lip. "As nearly as I can figure, she took my place, in the year 1852."

"*What?*" he cried.

"Jeff, please sit down and let me explain."

"Melissa, I can't believe this! You must surely have suffered some serious mental injury in your fall—"

"Jeff, I assure you, my mind is perfectly sound. Will you just try to believe me for now—if only for the sake of argument?"

"Very well." Groaning, he sat down.

She stood and began to pace. "Until a few weeks ago, I was living in the year 1852. I lived in the house the Monroes live in today. Only the grounds were much larger then, many hundreds of acres. We lived on a cotton plantation."

Jeff's expression was amazed. "That's true. The house where Missy—you—live was once part of a plantation. But Missy—you—would have known that."

She sighed. "At any rate, I was to marry a man I did not love—a man my parents had chosen for me. On the morning of the wedding, February 29—"

"You're saying, February 29, 1852?" he cut in.

"Yes."

"But February 29 was the day Missy—er, you and I were to marry!" he exclaimed.

"Precisely. As it happens, both 1852 and 1992 are leap years."

"I'll be damned," he muttered.

"I believe Missy and I were wearing essentially the same wedding gown, as well."

Jeff snapped his fingers. "That's right. Missy had planned to wear a replica of . . . was it your dress?"

"Yes." She wagged a finger at him. "And you're beginning to sound as if you believe me, Jeff Dalton."

He crossed his arms over his chest and set his chin stubbornly. "Strictly for the sake of argument."

"Very well. Anyway, on the morning of the wedding, I was feeling quite morose. You see, my fiancé, Fabian Fontenot, had told me our wedding trip would be a safari to Africa, where we would be hunting elephants—"

"The man was taking you elephant hunting on your honeymoon? What a jerk!" Jeff cried.

Melissa had to repress a smile as Jeff became increasingly caught up in her tale. "Well, yes, Fabian was quite strong-willed. At any rate, I knew that I would displease him as his wife—"

"He was an idiot, too, then."

She smiled. "But we were both prisoners of honor and the marriage contract our families had signed at my birth. On the morning of the wedding, I stood at the top of the stairs and thought 'I wish I could be anywhere but here . . .' The next thing I knew, I stumbled on my hem, tumbled down the staircase, and hit my head on the newel post. Then I awakened here, in the twentieth century."

"You stumbled down the staircase?" Jeff repeated incredulously. "But that's what happened to Missy!"

"I know. I think that's the moment when she and I switched places in time."

He shook his head. "This is simply outrageous."

"I think it was the newel button that made the switch happen."

"The newel button?" he asked in bewilderment.

"Yes. It was attached to the newel post on the day before my wedding was to have occurred in the past—and I've noted the same stone is still there today."

He frowned thoughtfully. "You're talking about that oval of green malachite?"

"Yes."

"And you're saying it was originally attached to the newel post in 1852?"

"Indeed."

"How fascinating," Jeff said. "But why is this significant?"

"You see, my father in the past—John Montgomery—explained to me that the button was a fragment of a genuine Egyptian amulet. It was supposed to have possessed magical properties. So, when Missy and I both hit our heads on the button . . . Well, I think that's when the switch occurred."

"My God, that's the most uncanny thing I've ever heard!"

"Do you believe me, Jeff?"

He got up and began to pace, his expression deeply abstracted. After a moment, he turned to her, his features creased with tension and uncertainty. "I must be honest. On the one hand, I find it most difficult to believe you. Yet on the other hand, how else can I explain this incredible change in you? You're nothing like Missy in temperament. It is truly as if you're a different woman." He hesitated a moment, then added, "Now it seems that maybe you are."

"Oh, Jeff, it would mean so much to me if you would believe me!" she cried. "Please don't think me insane."

He caught her in his arms. "I could never think that, darling. Confused, perhaps, but not insane. Nevertheless, the fact remains that, even though you may think you're someone else, you're still Missy's spitting image. I just wish there were some way I could know for certain if this bizarre story is true."

Melissa bit her lip. "Wasn't there anything that would have distinguished Missy from me? A birthmark, perhaps?"

He snapped his fingers. "You know, she did have a rather large mole inside her right thigh."

Melissa's face flamed. "Jeffrey Dalton, however did you gain access to that intimate region?"

He chuckled. "We went swimming together a number of times, and Missy—I mean, you—were quite a believer in skimpy bikinis."

"Bikinis?"

"Bathing suits."

"Oh."

He glanced downward. "Well, Melissa?"

She hesitated a moment, and then, with her face bright as an apple, she raised her skirts high. He perused the area with all the speed of true gallantry, then glanced up at her in astonishment as she smoothed down her skirts.

"I'll be damned—there's not a mole or birthmark anywhere on you." Hastily, he added, "Of course, you could have had it removed."

"But wouldn't that have left a scar or some other sort of mark?" she asked wisely.

"Correct." He gulped, staring at her as if he'd never seen her before. "My God, it's true! You *are* someone else. How could this have happened?"

She shook her head in amazement. "I wish I knew. I really know little about such matters—traveling in time and all. But, considering all the fantastical inventions of the twentieth century . . ." Twisting her fingers together nervously, she continued, "I've tried to learn all I can, Jeffrey, but I still have so far to go. And I did wonder if perhaps mankind has discovered a way to travel through time?"

Jeff laughed. "Not yet, darling, though various scientists and philosophers have espoused their theories."

"I see. I think."

He stroked his jaw. "Actually, so far, man has traveled through time mostly in literature—in works by H.G. Wells, Mark Twain, and so forth."

"I must read these books."

"You must." He stared at her with new doubt. "Melissa, are you quite certain you came here from another century? I mean, I'm beginning to believe you're someone else, but this business about traveling through time is pretty outlandish. Are you sure you didn't just come visiting here from another state or something?"

She laughed. "No. I swear I came here from another Memphis, Tennessee—the Memphis of 1852. In fact, when we return to the house, I'll show you something that I think will prove this to you conclusively."

He sighed. "Very well, darling. I'll try to keep an open mind."

"Thank you, Jeff."

He regarded her with love and wonder. "I can't believe you're truly someone else."

"I am."

Abruptly, he laughed. "Do you know what the best part is?"

"What?"

"Now I never have to worry about you reverting back to your old self, about losing the wonderful new woman you are."

Suddenly, her expression clouded.

"Melissa? What is it?"

She gazed up at him, her expression miserably torn. "But I haven't told you the entire story, Jeff. About why I know Missy has taken my place in the past."

He nodded. "Ah, yes. Please continue."

"I've seen Missy's face in the newel button."

"You've seen her face?" he exclaimed.

"Yes!" she cried wretchedly. "She's living my life now, while I'm living hers—"

"You mean like two dramas being enacted simultaneously, only one hundred and forty years apart?"

"Yes. That is it precisely."

"This is unreal!"

"Oh, it is very real, all right." Abruptly, Melissa burst into tears. "You see, Missy *hates* being me! In truth, I've never seen a more unhappy woman, and I feel the only honorable thing to do is to try—somehow—to switch places with her again."

"No!" Jeff cried, his eyes suddenly anguished as he hugged her tightly to him. "I won't let you do this! I'm not sure just how you came to me, Melissa, but I do know that you've made my life worth living again. Now that I've found you, I won't lose you!"

"Jeff . . ." In a small voice, she said, "We may not have a choice."

"I refuse to believe that!" He caught her face in his hands. "There's still so much about this that confuses me. But don't you understand that there must be a purpose behind all this—that we must have been meant to find each other at this moment in time? Missy and I were never well-suited, just as you and this Fabian obviously weren't. Yet you and I are perfect for each other!"

"I realize that," Melissa said, shuddering. "It's true that I may have found my heaven—but Missy has found her hell. She appears to be no more content with Fabian than I was. I can't seek my own happiness at her expense. She's miserable, Jeff."

Jeff laughed bitterly and clutched Melissa close, his eyes crazed with worry. "Missy will always be miserable about something."

Chapter Twenty-four

As he drove Melissa home, Jeff's thoughts were turbulent. The things she had just told him boggled his mind, to say the least.

Was she insane? Had the fall on their wedding day given her permanent brain damage?

Well, if she were brain-damaged, then that was precisely how he wanted her! He realized now, as never before, that Missy had never been right for him, that he'd never loved her, that he'd been like a zombie trudging through life.

Until his wonderful Melissa had come to him! Could what she had said possibly be true?

Jeff was very metaphysical in his thinking. He had always acknowledged intellectually the possibility of time travel. But to be confronted with someone who claimed she had actually traveled through time—to have her insist she had been switched with his real fiancé—it defied belief!

Yet, in another way, Melissa's claims made eminent sense. How else could he explain the dramatic change in her? The sudden sweetness, kindness, and evenness of her nature? Her quaint and decidedly old-fashioned mannerisms and speech? The slight differences in her appearance, which had become increasingly apparent following her disclosures: the tiny lines that had somehow vanished, the deeper blue of her eyes, the slightly fuller lips, the more pronounced widow's peak along her hairline?

Nevertheless, if this woman were not Missy, she still looked enough like Missy to be her identical twin! All in all, he remained very confused, but one thing he did know—he couldn't bear the thought of losing her! If her claims were true and she and Missy had switched places in time, then it followed, just as she had said, that they might at some point switch back again. This he would fight with all his being.

As they pulled into the driveway of the Monroe house, she turned to him with a tentative smile. "Could you wait for me behind the house? I need to go get something—something I must show you—and I'd prefer that we not be overheard."

"Of course, darling," he said, feeling baffled, yet intrigued.

A few minutes later, Melissa joined Jeff on the patio, sitting down in the chair next to his. She handed him an old daguerreotype and said simply, "Here. This is me."

Jeff glanced, electrified, at the ancient-looking picture of Melissa in her wedding gown. "Good God, you're right! This is you! But how can this be? This picture is so old and faded. It looks like something out of the nineteenth century."

"It is," Melissa interjected. "Turn it over and

read what's written there."

His features pale, Jeff turned the picture over. On the back, someone had written, in elegant, washed-out script, "Melissa Montgomery, February 29, 1852."

"My God!" he cried.

"Do you believe me now?" she asked.

"Good heavens, how could I not?" With eyes filled with wonder, he continued, "You know, now that I think about it, I remember Missy mentioning this picture, when she told me she was planning to wear a replica of your wedding dress. She even mentioned the resemblance, although she never actually showed me this. Good grief, the two of you are like twins!"

"I know," Melissa said.

"So you and she did change places?"

She nodded solemnly.

"This is simply amazing! You and Missy were scheduled to be married on exactly the same day, in the same house, in the same wedding dress—"

"At the same hour," she provided.

"Only one hundred and forty years apart!" Jeff finished.

"All true."

"And from what you've already told me, you both took a tumble down the stairs, presumably at the same moment—"

"True again."

"And you think that's when this amazing switch occurred?"

"Yes. I think it had to do with the newel button."

He scowled. "Should we take a look at it?"

She bit her lip, then nodded. "While I was in the house, I noticed that Mother and Father are out.

I suppose it will be safe for us to talk there."

Jeff squeezed her hand and gazed at her tenderly. "You don't want them to know about this, do you?"

She shook her head vehemently. "Can you blame me?"

"Not at all," he said feelingly. "Telling Howard and Charlotte would only worry them to death—and I doubt they'd even believe you."

"But you do, don't you?" she asked hopefully.

"Yes, darling, I do," he answered straight from his heart.

Inside the house, Melissa went upstairs to put the picture away while Jeff stood at the bottom of the stairs, scrutinizing the newel button. The malachite bull's eye was unusual, with its deep green color and odd concentric circles, but he could spot no images floating about in it.

When Melissa rejoined him, he asked, "So you've seen Missy's face in this stone?"

"Indeed." She glanced at the polished button. "Sometimes the circles will begin to ripple and part, and that's when I can see her. She's in my house, in the year 1852—and as I've already told you, she's wretchedly unhappy."

"Hmmmmm." He stared intently at the stone. "I can't see anything now."

"She isn't always there," Melissa explained. "Indeed, my sightings of her are quite rare, and I've never seen her when anyone else was nearby."

"I suppose that makes sense. Whatever this bizarre phenomenon is, it's likely shared only between the two of you."

"I suppose."

He took her hand. "Let's go sit in the living room."

They sat down on the sofa together, both wearing troubled expressions. "Tell me more of the life you left behind," Jeff said at last.

"Well, I was born in the year 1832," she began.

He shook his head in amazement. "Go on."

"Memphis was only a tiny river town then," she explained. "In fact, it was still relatively small when I left it. My parents were John and Lavinia Montgomery. I grew up with them on a cotton plantation east of town."

"In this house," he supplied excitedly.

"On this land," she replied. "Actually, my first ten years were spent in a modest old cottage. This house was built in 1842. In fact, as I told you earlier, the day before my wedding was scheduled, my father had a workman place the newel button on the newel post, in honor of the mortgage on the house being paid."

"Ah, yes. A fascinating custom. But we're getting ahead of ourselves. Tell me of your upbringing."

She laughed. "My childhood was quite dull by today's standards. I spent almost my entire life on the plantation. A governess taught me the rudiments of reading and writing, and also sewing, knitting, decorum, and all the ladylike skills. The best times were when relatives came visiting, or we went to see them." She smiled wistfully. "One time, we even took a steam packet all the way to St. Louis. Another time we went to New Orleans for Mardi Gras. By the time I was twenty and preparing to marry Fabian, most of my free time was taken up with church and charity work."

Jeff chuckled. "How times have changed. What about your relationship with your parents? What was that like?"

Melissa sighed. "My parents are—were—quite spirited and outspoken. I must confess that they shocked many a Memphian with some of their public arguments."

"How amusing."

"And I must also confess that they seemed disappointed in me as their daughter."

He was crestfallen. "Disappointed? But why? You're an angel!"

She smiled. "I may be an angel to you, but I fear my parents found me lacking in spunk. I think they would have preferred—well, a daughter like Missy."

"And now they have her," he said with a rueful chuckle.

"So it appears. I think the biggest joy of their lives was knowing they were gaining Fabian Fontenot as a son-in-law."

"Oh, yes. Tell me about this marriage contract business again."

"The contract was made at my birth between Fabian's family and my own. It was considered a sacred trust. You see, Fabian's parents were French immigrants and quite steeped in Old World traditions. I think their deaths in a yellow fever epidemic made Fabian all the more determined to honor the contract—you know, out of guilt. The Fontenot plantation bordered our own, so there were practical reasons to join the two estates, as well."

Jeff's expression was stunned. "Why, that's just like Missy and me! We were planning to marry largely due to the urging of both our families, and to merge my family's business, Dalton Steel Tubing, with her family's enterprise, Monroe Ball Bearings."

She nodded. "The similarities are quite astounding, I must agree. Anyway, except for the contract, I never would have married Fabian. As I explained, we were quite ill-suited. I may have been resigned to my fate, but Fabian despised the idea of me as his wife."

"The son of a bitch! How could he not adore you?"

She slanted him a half-amused, half-beseeching glance. "Jeff, you must understand. Fabian was very arrogant and strong-willed. I was totally outmatched by him. He used to treat me quite badly, but I know he felt guilty afterward. He wasn't really an evil man—I think it simply drove him quite past his patience that I gave in to him on everything. I suppose I'm what you would call in these times a pushover."

"You are not!" Jeff defended indignantly.

She couldn't suppress a giggle. "And you are most kind. My point is, however, that Fabian needed a woman who could stand up to him and put him in his place."

All at once, Jeff was on his feet, his eyes alive with humor and realization. "And now he has Missy!"

"I suppose he does."

Jeff rubbed his hands together. "Oh, this is so delicious, I just wish I could be there to watch the fun!"

"What do you mean?"

Turning to her, he laughed. "Can't you see it, Melissa? A modern, liberated woman matched up with a male chauvinist pig!"

Melissa paled. "I would not go so far as to call Fabian a pig!"

He flashed his charming dimples and shook

his head. "No, you don't understand—that's just a figure of speech for a very domineering, macho type man." He began to pace, his expression filled with triumph and delight. "I just love it! It's too perfect!"

"Love what?"

He spoke with increasing animation. "Don't you understand, darling? Here, we had four people whose lives were all wrong—two couples who were marrying for the worst of reasons. Then fate stepped in and set things right!"

She appeared skeptical. "You're going to have to explain that a bit more, Jeff."

"Okay. You had the wrong parents, didn't you?"

"Well, perhaps."

"And the wrong fiancé?"

"Oh, definitely."

"But you love Charlotte and Howard, don't you?"

"They are quite dear."

"And they love you?"

"Yes."

He stepped over and grasped her hands. "And the two of us? We're perfect for each other, aren't we?"

She smiled dazzlingly. "Oh, yes."

"Now let's move on to Missy. Do you know that she and Charlotte and Howard never got along?"

"No—but it does stand to reason. Charlotte and Howard are both so conservative, traditional, and soft-spoken, and, from what I've gathered about Missy, she's evidently quite the rebel."

"True. Missy drove them up the wall."

"Oh, dear."

He chuckled. "I'm speaking figuratively, darling."

"I'm relieved to hear it."

"As for Missy and me, I think she was just like your Fabian. She hated the fact that she could always push me around—when the truth was, I just didn't care." He stared her in the eye and added in a fervent whisper, "Not then."

"So what is your point?"

His eyes gleaming, Jeff concluded, "The point is, you and Missy both had the wrong parents and the wrong fiancé, and now you both have the right parents and the right fiancé."

She considered this for a moment in frowning silence. "I suppose that's true of me, Jeff—but Missy is not happy! If you could have seen her face—"

He waved her off. "A minor inconvenience. She'll get over it."

Yet Melissa shook her head sadly. "Jeff, I love you dearly, but you must understand that there can be no love without honor."

"What do you mean?" he demanded tensely.

She stared at him with a terrible fatalism. "I'm saying that, whether I was unhappy in the past or not, in my mind, John and Lavinia Montgomery are still my parents, and Fabian Fontenot is still my fiancé."

"No!" he cried.

Though tears were now welling, she forged on. "And if Missy wants her life back, it should be hers to reclaim."

He pulled her to her feet and spoke with fierce emotion. "Darling, you cannot mean this! Say no to this insanity! Doesn't our love mean anything to you? You would sacrifice the rest of your life— our lives together—for her?"

She gazed up at him with love and heartache.

"That's just my point. It's not my life in the first place—it's hers."

He drew his fingers distraughtly threw his hair. "But you don't even know *if*—much less, *how*— you might switch places with her again!"

"That's true. But if Missy wants this, I must try. I must leave it up to her to let me know how the switch will be accomplished."

Suddenly Jeff smiled as new hope dawned. "There's another possibility."

"And what is that?"

"Missy could decide she likes living in the year 1852. She could decide to stay there."

Melissa appeared skeptical. "At this point, I consider that unlikely."

He gripped her by the shoulders. "But what if she should change her mind? If she should decide, like you, to adopt her new parents and fiancé?"

Melissa mulled this over. "If everyone were happy, including Missy, then I suppose I could stay here honorably."

Jeff expelled a relieved breath, then snapped his fingers. "You know, we may have the advantage, being here in the present."

"What do you mean?"

"Well, in the past, Missy can't really see the future—that is, the future happening to us here after she left 1992. We, on the other hand, can look back to the period in which she is now living."

"I'm not sure I see the significance," Melissa murmured.

"Won't there be records, something to show whether or not Missy actually remained in the past?"

Melissa considered this, then shook her head.

"If what we suspect is true and Missy has taken my place, then what possible help could records be? How can we know for certain whether or not the two of us ever switched back again? If, for instance, a record should refer to 'Melissa Montgomery,' how can we know if it's me—or Missy posing as me?"

"Damn. I see your point."

"Besides, soon after I arrived here, Mother told me the Montgomery family left Memphis before the 1860s."

Jeff snapped his fingers. "I wonder if Missy warned them about the war!"

"What do you mean?"

"Well, Missy would know all about the history of the intervening years. If she stayed in the past, I'm sure she would have warned your family about the Civil War. In fact, knowing that your family moved away before 1860, I'm now convinced of it! This must mean that Missy is the one who stayed!"

Yet Melissa shook her head. "Not necessarily."

"Why not?"

"Well, if I went back again—knowing what I now know—I would do precisely the same thing."

He groaned. "You're right again. Still, there must be something—"

Melissa shook her head. "Mother said there are almost no family records in existence, and she and Father returned here to Memphis only after they married some twenty-odd years ago. The family does own a few old letters that my father and I once wrote—in fact, I was able to read them recently—"

"You were? I must see them!" he cried excitedly.

She nodded. "Of course. I'm sure you'll find them interesting, but unfortunately, all were written before Missy and I were switched." She drew a shuddering breath. "I know of no way to find the answers we seek."

Jeff sighed and clutched her close. "Somehow, darling, we will."

Later, as Jeff drove home, he remained consumed with turmoil. He'd been presented with all but conclusive proof that the woman he now knew as Melissa had actually switched places in time with his real fiancé, Missy Monroe. His mind remained both boggled and tormented. The agonizing question was, would lovely Melissa be allowed to stay here with him?

While Melissa seemed to put little faith in records—obviously having come from an era when most vital statistics were kept in family Bibles—Jeff knew that somewhere there had to be more information on the Montgomery family in the 1850s, and some records concerning whether Missy—or Melissa—had remained in the past. Not only that, but if he knew Missy, she would have left her own indelible mark on any age in which she might have lived. If she had stayed in the past, somehow, proof must exist.

His mother was friends with a prominent local genealogist. He must put Mildred Reed to work on this at once, perhaps under the guise of wanting to surprise Melissa with some information on the history of the Monroe/Montgomery family.

Should he tell Melissa of what he was planning to do? He shook his head grimly. Already, just as Melissa had said, he very much feared that any truths he uncovered might be of little comfort to either of them. And if the news he discovered was bad, he wanted to reserve for himself the option of withholding the truth from her. If that was being selfish, he simply loved Melissa too much to care.

Chapter Twenty-five

The day of the Presbyterian church bazaar
dawned brisk and cool. Because Fabian had
gone out to the bluff early to help the other men construct the booths, Missy traveled
to the event with John and Lavinia in their
barouche.

The bazaar was held in a small, grassy park
off the public promenade overlooking the Mississippi. As the three entered the clearing—Missy
carrying a stack of knitted goods and John and
Lavinia bearing boxes of donated knick-knacks—
they were greeted by the sounds of hammers and
shouting as the men put the finishing touches
on the dozen or so booths, decking them with
bunting. The scene was colorful, with the booths
arranged in a pleasing semi-circle, and a super-
vised play area for the children established off to
one side, complete with pony rides and a metal
tank for launching toy boats. Other volunteers

were already arriving with donated goods that ranged from covered dishes for the noonday meal to canned goods, hand-sewn items, and gewgaws.

"Everything is proceeding nicely," Lavinia commented as she looked over the bustling scene. "The day's receipts will make a fine contribution to the church building fund."

"And what a fine-looking couple of salesladies you two will make," John added with a twinkle in his eye, admiring his wife and daughter in their matching braided, navy blue jackets and skirts, and their jaunty feathered hats.

"Ah, there are Eleanor and Grace," Lavinia declared with a smile, waving toward two ladies who were working at a booth beyond them. She turned to Missy. "Will Fabian be fetching you home?"

"I'd prefer to ride back with you two."

Lavinia laughed. "That darling boy will never tolerate such treason."

"We'll see," Missy replied enigmatically.

"If you'll excuse us then, dear?" John added. "We'll come see how you're doing later."

"Sure—have fun," Missy replied.

As John and Lavinia went off to the booth Lavinia would staff with her friends, Missy joined Antoinette and Lucy at the booth the three ladies would be in charge of at the center of the park. Next to their booth was the one Fabian, Brent and Jeremy would man—it was curiously vacant at the moment, except for a few pies and cakes that had already been set out.

"Good morning, ladies," Missy said gaily as she slipped behind the counter. She set down her pile of knitted and crocheted articles, all of which had been made by Melissa prior to their switch.

"Everything looks in readiness. But—where are the men?"

"That is odd," a frowning Antoinette informed her. "They finished their work on the booths, then disappeared."

"I'm quite baffled," Lucy added.

"Hmmm," Missy murmured. "They're never going to win today if they walk off the job—unless they have a trick or two up their sleeves that we aren't aware of."

The men's absence was soon forgotten as the three women busied themselves arranging their goods with as much eye-appeal as possible, dangling potholders and samplers from the vertical supports and draping their most colorful afghans across the front of the booth.

Shoppers had started arriving—fashionably attired couples and entire families—when the men reappeared, not even glancing toward the ladies as they strode to their booth bearing boxes crammed with pies, cakes, and cookies.

"What on earth . . . ?" Missy muttered, watching the procession.

As the three women looked on, perplexed, the men made at least half a dozen additional trips to the booth, carrying still more boxes overflowing with baked goods.

"Where did they get all that?" Antoinette cried.

"I would wager they bought out the bakery in town," Lucy put in suspiciously.

Setting up their booth, the men continued to ignore the women. By now, the park grounds swarmed with shoppers. While the women's booth drew half a dozen or so browsing ladies, the men's booth soon became a mob scene.

When traffic fell off at the ladies' booth, all

three stared at the men's booth in perplexity.

"What do you suppose they're doing over there?" Antoinette asked, chewing her bottom lip.

"They're bound to be ahead of us on receipts already," Lucy fretted. "Just look at all those people in line!"

Missy nodded grimly. "You two watch the booth," she said. "I'm going to go see what's going on."

Missy maneuvered herself around the crowd and approached the booth from its blind side. "Yes, Mrs. Topp," she could hear Fabian saying graciously to a lavishly dressed matron. "You may have this cake for twenty-five cents."

"Oh, my!" the ecstatic woman exclaimed. "The bakery on the square charges at least triple that amount for such a fine cake!"

Fuming, Missy went around to the back of the booth and entered through a parting in the curtains. She spotted Fabian's towering figure at once; he stood with his broad back to her, dressed in an elegant black frock coat and matching trousers. Jeremy and Brent flanked him on either side. All three were grabbing money and handing out baked goods as fast as they could.

Setting her mouth with determination, Missy stepped forward and tapped him on the shoulder. "Fabian, I must speak with you."

If he was surprised by her sudden appearance, he did not show it, merely tossing her a forbearing glance. "Sorry, Missy, but as you can see, I'm quite occupied at the moment."

Not bothering to argue with him, Missy grabbed his arm and towed him out of the booth.

"Damn it, Missy, what's the meaning of this?" he asked.

"You're cheating!" she accused.

"Oh, am I?" he replied innocently.

"You and Jeremy and Charles bought out the bakery in town—don't try to deny it!"

He folded his arms over his chest with a nonchalance that infuriated her. "I won't. Actually, we bought out two bakeries."

"You—you what?" She was flabbergasted.

He grinned at her wickedly. "We wanted to make sure we'd win the wager."

Missy was tempted to stamp her foot at his contemptible tactics. "Why, you miscreant! So— you stacked the odds in your favor by tripling your expected inventory? And now you have the audacity to undercut your prices, too?"

His wink was totally unrepentent. "That about sums it up."

"But that's not fair!"

He straightened his cuffs. "Well, dear, you know what they say about love and war. And frankly, all of us men are ready to put an end to this nonsense. We're tired of the war and would like a bit more harmony—and love—instead."

Fighting the excitement that swept over her at his words, Missy faced him down furiously. "Don't hold your breath!"

"Don't hold yours," he advised.

"You braggarts only want to call the shots!"

"That, too."

"Well, don't count on victory yet."

He laughed. "Missy, there's no way you and the other ladies can win now. Face it, you're outmatched."

"We'll see," she snapped, turning and storming off.

At noon, everyone paused for dinner, sitting

267

down together at oilcloth-draped tables to share a repast of fried chicken, ham, baked beans, cornbread, pies, cakes, and other homemade delights. The Reverend Ferguson, pastor of the church, returned thanks and made a brief speech in which he thanked all present for their support of the building fund.

Missy had little appetite as she sat with her taciturn friends. Around them, the two elderly couples who shared their table were discussing matters of local interest—an upcoming performance of elocutionists, sponsored by the Thespian Society, and the construction that was just beginning on the Memphis and Charleston Railroad.

Missy stared coldly at the men, who sat three tables away from them, eating like hogs and visiting jovially with other attendees. Missy would have loved to go dump a pitcher of iced tea over their egotistical heads.

Toward the end of the meal, Antoinette gulped as she watched the grinning men get up en masse and head back to their booth. She leaned over toward Missy and whispered, "What are we going to do? They're already so far ahead of us!"

"We're bound to lose now," Lucy put in, sniffing. "And Jeremy will never again let me paint!"

"I'll have to give up my millinery shop, as well," Antoinette added morosely.

"Oh, quit whining, you two," Missy ordered in an undertone. "Have you thought about *my* fate if we lose? I'll have to marry that beast!"

The other two glanced toward Fabian, grimaced, and then murmured their sympathy.

Missy forced herself to pick up a chicken leg and take a bite. "Eat up, ladies," she ordered, her eyes gleaming with steely resolve. "We're going to need our strength for the afternoon siege. It's not over yet."

Yet by midafternoon, the reality of Fabian's prophecy was sinking in for all of them. The women had sold out everything in their booth, and still, the men's booth was the sight of continued pandemonium, given their seemingly endless supply of baked goods at cut-rate prices.

"What shall we do now?" Antoinette asked fatalistically. She was leaning on the empty counter, with chin propped in her hands.

"There's no way we shall win," Lucy added.

Missy, meanwhile, was glowering at Fabian. He grinned back and blew her a kiss. Suddenly, she smiled as a deliciously wicked, outrageous idea occurred to her.

"I know how we'll win!" she announced excitedly to the others.

"How?" they both asked in unison.

Missy leaned over and whispered her idea. Lucy and Antoinette gasped in mortification.

"But, my dear, it simply isn't done," Lucy said.

"We'll all be disgraced," Antoinette added.

"So who cares?" Missy retorted. "There's a first for everything, isn't there? And this is for a good cause, right? Furthermore, have the men played fair with us?"

Antoinette and Lucy exchanged lost looks.

"Well, have they? Do you two want to win or not?"

Lucy and Antoinette implored each other with another glance, then both nodded firmly.

"Good. Now, listen carefully, both of you," Missy ordered.

The three huddled together and whispered for a few moments.

"Way to go!" Missy cried afterward, clapping her hands in triumph. "Now—you two go circulate through the crowd and stir up some customers."

"And what are you going to do?" Antoinette asked.

"I'm gonna pucker up," Missy replied with a wink.

Moments later, Fabian was gloating over his victory when he glanced over at the women's booth and noticed an appalling sight. The area was now a mob scene! At least twenty men milled outside the booth, laughing and waving dollar bills. He spotted everyone from dashing local businessman Robertson Topp to the slave trader Bedford Forest to the aging former mayor of Memphis, Marcus Winchester. Indeed, Fabian couldn't even see Missy past the sea of hats!

What on earth was going on over there? A moment ago, he would have sworn the women had already exhausted their inventory and the men had safely won their bet. Now this!

Fabian left his booth and strode over to see what was going on. He arrived just in time to watch Missy kiss the grinning, portly steamboat captain, Jim Lee, even as Lucy calmly plucked Jim's dollar bill from his pudgy, outstretched fingers.

Missy was selling kisses! Not only that, but she seemed to be having the time of her life, the little minx!

Indignant, Fabian rushed over to her. "Missy, you will stop this disgraceful conduct at once!" he thundered.

Missy and Jim moved apart and stared at Fabian with mild interest.

Meanwhile, the crowd of men was growing impatient. "Oh, don't be a wet blanket, Fabian," one of his friends, W. F. Taylor, called out. "It's for a good cause, isn't it?"

"Indeed, Fontenot, desist!" another male voice exclaimed.

Missy joined in, flashing him a sly smile. "That's right, Fabian, honey, don't be a spoilsport. The end of the line is that way. And it'll cost you a dollar."

"Charge him twenty!" another amused male voice called out, and everyone laughed.

With that, Missy calmly turned to her next customer, a blushing teenage lad who extended his bill with trembling fingers.

Seething with frustrated rage, Fabian stormed off, to the jeers and laughter of the other men.

Damn the little baggage! he thought. She had to best him, even if it meant selling her favors like a woman of the streets!

Then a grudging smile pulled at his mouth, and he realized that, through it all, he had to respect and admire the hotheaded little vixen for her ingenuity. Though it was a big blow to his pride, could he really blame her for resorting to means as devious as his own? He'd gambled on forcing her into marriage, and he'd lost. It was now time to return to his original scheme. After all, this was really his fault, for not setting the spitfire in her place long ago.

Ah yes, her place—that delicious, torrid, wicked place he had in mind for her . . . He would see that she avoided her fate no longer. The day of the Montgomery spring ball would soon be upon them—and *he* intended to be upon one very saucy southern belle.

* * *

When the receipts were tallied by church personnel, the minister joyously informed Missy, Lucy, and Antoinette that their booth had garnered the largest revenues for the day. The three were shrieking their victory and hugging one another when the chastened men came up to join them. Antoinette and Lucy left, smiling from ear to ear, in the company of their grim-faced husbands. Missy was left alone with Fabian.

He acknowledged her victory with a mocking tip of his hat. "So it seems you've bested us, Missy," he drawled.

"So it seems," she returned with a smug smile.

"Are you quite sure you've won?" he added ironically.

Sensing his meaning at once, she lifted her chin and retorted proudly, "Quite sure."

"Do you have a way home?" he continued politely.

"Mom and Dad can take me."

He bowed elaborately. "Then I'll bid you good night."

Watching him stride off into the sunset, Missy felt a trifle disappointed that he had not even offered to take her home. She almost welcomed the thought of a rousing fight, so that she could relish her victory and lord it over him.

Oh, to hell with it! At least she wouldn't have to marry the jerk—she should feel delighted!

Instead, she found herself remembering the soft, menacing tone of his voice and the cynical gleam in his eye—as if to warn her that her triumph might not be so sweet, after all. She wondered what was on his diabolical mind now.

Chapter Twenty-six

During the next couple of weeks, Jeff and Melissa continued to spend as much time together as possible. They shared their lives and discussed the differences in their time periods. While they still passed many happy hours at his family's summer house, they also went out to dinner together and attended movies and plays. Gradually, Jeff took Melissa closer to Memphis proper, driving along the freeways to let her grow accustomed to the daunting tall buildings of the skyline. Although at first she was frightened as they zoomed along the austere concrete highways at such amazing speeds, she gradually grew more accustomed to modern travel and the fantastical superstructures of the twentieth century.

Melissa began to feel guilty that she was keeping Jeff from his duties at his family's business. She involved herself in other activities so he would not feel obliged to spend his every moment with her.

Unlike Missy, who had squeaked by doing as little as possible for church and community, Melissa attended church faithfully, and volunteered for several charitable committees there and at the Junior League. Since, as far as her parents knew, Melissa still could not "remember" how to drive, they hired a driver to take her to her various activities. Melissa also enlisted her friends, Jennifer, Lisa, and Michelle, to help in her altruistic pursuits; while at first the three young women balked violently, ultimately none could resist Melissa's firm yet polite insistence that they do their part to benefit humanity. Of course, all of this meant that Melissa had to venture forth more in her daunting new world; yet she invariably found her joy at the thought of helping others banished her fear of the unknown.

Still, her attitude was that of a tourist, rather than a resident, in the twentieth century. For she was still haunted by occasional glimpses of Missy in the newel button, and she knew that her cousin remained unhappy in the past; thus, Melissa remained resigned to her fate of switching places again with Missy, if the opportunity should present itself.

On a crisply cool late March day, Jeff at last took Melissa for a drive into the city proper. She glanced about them in awe as they drove up and down the crowded streets past huge, looming skyscrapers. "What holds those buildings up?" she asked him.

He chuckled as he maneuvered the car around a corner. "Mostly steel girders and concrete," he replied.

"Amazing."

He pointed out the sights as they moved along—

the County Courthouse, City Hall, the Lincoln American Tower. They zig-zagged through downtown, going along Beale Street, passing the old Cotton Exchange Building and circling Court Square with its lush landscaping and impressive fountain.

"I'll bet all this is radically different from the Memphis you left behind," Jeff commented.

"I should say so," she replied. "When I left Memphis there was only a deserted log cabin on Court Square, and the streets were gravel or dirt. I must say, however, that the shops we passed along Beale Street look a bit more like my time period."

He nodded. "That's because Beale Street is a historic district currently being revitalized. The area dates back to the 1920s. As a matter of fact, the blues were born there."

"The blues?"

"It's a type of music made famous by performers such as Louis Armstrong and B.B. King."

"Ah—I see."

"We'll have to go down there one evening soon."

"Yes, that would be nice," she murmured.

They drove along Front Street, and Melissa studied the amazing bridges crossing the Mississippi and looked down at the public entertainment area known as "Mud Island." The island itself—which Jeff explained was a sandbar, created by a grounded ship early in this century—hadn't even been there when she had lived in Memphis previously!

"So many changes," she muttered, shaking her head. "All those years—and the terrible war. It does make me wonder how my family made out."

"If they got out of Memphis before the 1860s, I'm sure they were fine," he reassured her. Hesitantly, he added, "Do you miss your folks?"

She bit her lip. "This will sound terrible, but . . ."

"No, please tell me."

She drew a deep breath. "I love my parents deeply, Jeff, but we were so ill-suited that it's hard to truly miss them. Do you understand that?"

"Totally. And I know it's because you're so much happier here."

Her smile was bittersweet. "Only, my happiness belongs to someone else."

Both fell morosely silent as Jeff drove toward a nearby hotel, where he'd made reservations for lunch. Melissa's comments pricked Jeff's conscience. He felt guilty because he hadn't told her about the investigative activities he had instigated since learning that she had come from a different century. Jeff had put Mildred Reed to work researching information concerning the Montgomery family in the 1850s. So far, the research had not been particularly fruitful, although Mildred had uncovered one astounding, unnerving fact in the Shelby County records: Melissa Montgomery had married Fabian Fontenot on May 15, 1852!

The revelation had been agonizing for Jeff. Endlessly, he had asked himself the central, crucial question: Which Melissa had Fontenot married? Was it Missy Monroe, or the dear, gentle woman he now loved with all his heart?

Jeff glanced at Melissa, looking so beautiful, yet somehow so ephemeral, sitting beside him. Would he soon lose her? While he certainly didn't understand everything about her time-travel experience, he did accept that she and Missy were living each other's lives concurrently, one hundred and forty years apart. Thus, all his instincts told him that, if he were to lose Melissa, it would be on or before May 15. Indeed, that date now loomed in his mind like a doomsday prediction, making him more determined than ever to marry her—and before May 15!

They pulled up to a stylish, modern hotel; a smiling doorman opened Melissa's door, while a valet came around to Jeff's side to take the car. Jeff got out, tipped both men, then escorted Melissa toward the front door.

"Is this where we're going to eat?" she asked, glancing about in awe as they swept through the revolving glass doors.

"Indeed. I thought we'd go up to the restaurant on the roof."

Melissa was staring, amazed, at the area they were now passing through—a soaring atrium complete with lush plants and a lovely fountain. "The roof? But how will we get there?"

"In the elevator, silly." Watching her features blanche, he added, "Come on, darling. You've got to get into an elevator sometime. They're perfectly safe."

They turned a corner and approached the forbidding gray elevator doors; Jeff pushed a button, then Melissa's eyes widened as the double doors parted as miraculously as the Red Sea.

"Who did that?" she demanded of Jeff, glancing about wildly, trying to determine who had opened the doors.

"No one," he replied, tugging her gently into the car. "It's automatic. The doors responded electronically to the button I pushed."

She gulped as she stared ahead at the atrium area. "The back of the car is glass!"

He chuckled. "I thought you'd enjoy that, darling. You get to watch as we go up."

"Oh, my."

Melissa clung to Jeff's arm as the car lurched into motion, rising by some amazing power of its own. Her eyes were enormous as she stared downward, watching the fountain grow smaller as they continued upward.

"You okay, darling?" he asked tenderly.

"I feel as if I left my stomach downstairs," she confided.

"Everyone feels that way the first time."

"It's all so mystifying. I'm not sure I'll ever get used to all the fantastical devices of this century."

He chuckled as the doors of the car opened, and led her outside onto a carpeted catwalk. "You're doing just fine. Next, I'm determined to get you on an airplane."

"You mean one of these huge birds that carry people into the sky?" she gasped.

"The very same. I want to show you the world. Perhaps we can fly someplace truly romantic—like Paris—for our honeymoon."

Melissa was pensively quiet as they entered the dark, elegant restaurant. A maitre d' showed them to a table near a glass wall. While Jeff ordered drinks, Melissa stared in amazement at the city of Memphis sprawled below them and the Mississippi in the distance.

"What's this?" she asked Jeff a moment later, watching the waiter set down an opened bottle of champagne and two glasses.

Jeff winked at her as the waiter poured two

glassfuls. "Dom Perignon, darling."

"But I don't sip spirits," she murmured.

"Not even on a special occasion?" he teased.

She grinned. "Is today special?"

"I sincerely hope so."

She lifted her glass. "Then I suppose I can make an exception."

"To us," Jeff said as he lifted his.

After they toasted each other, Jeff took out a small black velvet box and smilingly handed it to Melissa.

Throwing him a perplexed look, she opened it. "Oh, Jeff!" she exclaimed. Inside the satin-lined box was the most beautiful diamond ring she had ever seen.

"Do you like it, darling?" he asked eagerly.

"It's wonderful," she replied, then added quickly, "but I cannot accept this."

"Of course you can," he said indignantly. "That ring honors a very important occasion."

"What occasion?"

He took her hand and stared into her eyes. "It's called an engagement ring, darling. When a man and woman decide to marry, the man traditionally gives it to the woman as a symbol of their commitment. The wedding ring itself is added on the wedding day."

"I see," she murmured, feeling a poignant mixture of joy and sorrow. "It's a lovely tradition."

"I'm glad you think so." With a touch of bitterness, he added, "Missy found the custom of the engagement ring to be nonsense, and wanted only a simple gold band on our wedding day." He quickly flashed her a smile. "But I do so want you to have this—and for us to set a new date for the wedding at once."

"Oh, Jeff!" Melissa's expression was crestfallen. "I would like nothing more than to do just that! But can't you see that it's impossible for me to promise to marry you now?"

"Are you back to your impossible scheme of trading places with Missy again?" Jeff asked exasperatedly. "Can't you see that, even though you may feel it's the right thing to do, there's no practical way to accomplish the switch?"

Melissa frowned. "I'm not so sure. I've been reading Mr. Wells' book, *The Time Machine*—"

Jeff interrupted her with a laugh. "That's purely fictional. As I told you before, here in the twentieth century, we've discovered no actual way to travel through time."

"But Missy discovered a way," she put in firmly. "For that matter, so did I."

He sighed. "True. But I cannot help feeling that the two of you switching was some monumental quirk that will never again be repeated."

"Perhaps so." Her eyes entreated him. "But I must be willing to give her back her life."

"And sacrifice the only happiness you yourself have ever known?"

"Jeff, we've been over this and over this. I don't own this life—it belongs to Missy, and I can keep it only with her permission."

"Damn it!" Catching her dismayed expression, he quickly squeezed her hand. "I'm sorry, darling. Look, I want you to marry me. I may never lose you, but if I do, at least we can both take comfort in what we'll have."

Her expression was miserably torn. "I can't, Jeff. Indeed, to be technical, I'm still engaged to Fabian—"

"You'll go back to that beast over my dead body,"

he cut in angrily. "Don't you know that the mere thought of that man within a hundred feet of you drives me crazy?"

She stared miserably at her lap. "I'm sorry, Jeff. It's a matter of honor."

"Melissa, wear my ring," he beseeched. "Then we can announce a new date for the wedding, at the dinner party your parents are giving for their friends next week."

She gazed at him sadly. "Jeff, I'll wear your ring for now if it will make you happy. But we cannot set a new date for the wedding. I must wait and see what develops with Missy. If she finds a way for us to switch again, I must be ready to—to leave you, darling." Her last words were thick with tears.

Jeff's jaw tightened into a rigid line; he slipped the ring on her finger and spoke vehemently. "Not while I have breath in my body, you won't."

"Oh, Jeff! In a way, I wish I'd never come here."

"But why?"

"Because I'm causing you such heartache."

He reached out and brushed a tear from her cheek. "Darling, you must never think that! I wouldn't have missed knowing you for the world! You're so wonderful, so kind, so gentle—in every way, the woman of my dreams! The only problem is, you're too good to be true. It almost makes me wish you were a little more selfish, like Missy was, but then I would never love you as I do."

"Indeed, you wouldn't," she answered in an emotion-filled voice, "for you are a person of honor, too. If you think about it, I'm sure you'll agree that mine is the only way."

Jeff lifted her hand, kissing the finger that bore his ring. "If I weren't such a gentleman," he whispered intensely, "I'd get us a room and seduce you right this minute."

She stared back at him raptly. "If I weren't a lady, I'd let you."

"My God, Melissa, what are we going to do?" he cried.

Their gazes locked, both filled with love and anguish, but no answers.

Later, as they left the restaurant, Jeff clutched Melissa's hand tightly. He knew he *was* a man of honor, just as she had said. But right now, his love for Melissa, his desire to keep her at his side, took precedence over all else. He couldn't lose her! He simply couldn't! Most importantly, he couldn't let her sacrifice her own happiness for Missy, who truly needed a strong man like Fabian Fontenot, much as she might not readily admit it.

Thus, Jeff knew he would fight for his Melissa in every way, fair or foul. Somehow, she would be his—and before May 15.

Chapter Twenty-seven

The eve of the Montgomery Spring ball arrived. After eating an early, modest supper in her room, Missy prepared for the festivities with Dulcie's assistance. The servant styled Missy's coiffure, pinning her blond locks in curls on top of her head and letting a lush cascade fall loose at her nape. Afterward, the slave helped her mistress into her ball gown—a sumptuous, full-skirted frock of sapphire blue satin, with a low neck, lace half-sleeves, a tight waist, and a full, lace-trimmed skirt.

As the two women stood side-by-side before the pier mirror—Missy in her fabulous gown and Dulcie in her slave cottonades—the injustice of the situation struck Missy anew. While Missy had not been that aware of politics or race relations back in her own time, she certainly knew when something was dead wrong.

"You know, you should attend the ball, too, Dulcie," she murmured.

Dulcie's eyes widened in shock. "Me, mistress? That ain't proper."

"And what's not proper about you?" Missy countered indignantly. "You're beautiful, you're very kind, and furthermore, you should be free to do as you please."

Dulcie shook a finger at Missy. "Please, mistress, don't start that freedom talk again. You is goin' to get me in trouble!"

Missy sighed. While she'd had great success in liberating her "friends" here in the past, she'd had little luck in convincing Dulcie that her own human rights were being violated by the institution of slavery. Even though she and the slave had become closer over the past weeks, Missy felt as if an invisible barrier still loomed between them. After trying endlessly to convince Dulcie that there was no need for her to wait on her "mistress" hand and foot, Missy had finally given up in the face of the servant's obviously hurt feelings. How could she convince Dulcie she was entitled to live a life of her own, rather than spending her days pampering some spoiled southern belle? She must speak with her father.

"Missy, dear?"

Missy heard Lavinia's voice, accompanied by her soft rap at the door. "Come on in, Mom," she called.

Lavinia, dressed in a tasteful ball gown of pale green silk organza, swept inside. She eyed Missy with an approving smile. "How beautiful you look, darling." She nodded to the slave. "Dulcie, you did a splendid job on my daughter's coiffure."

"Thank you, mistress." Bowing, Dulcie slipped from the room.

Missy smiled at her mother. "You look quite lovely, Mom. Is everything ready downstairs?"

"Oh, yes. We're expecting the evening to be a grand success. Indeed, it would be perfect, if only . . ."

"Yes?"

Lavinia slanted Missy a chiding look. "If only you would allow your father and me to announce a new date for your wedding."

Missy rolled her eyes. "Mom, I'm not going to marry Fabian."

"Then what will you do with your life?"

"Why should my life revolve around some man?"

Lavinia appeared perplexed. "You mean you intend to become a spinster?"

"And why are we assuming that my not marrying is a fate worse than death?" Missy continued exasperatedly. "Think of all the worthwhile things I could do with my life. I could start a business— or spend my life traveling—or become President of the United States!"

Lavinia stepped forward to feel Missy's forehead. "Are you certain you haven't taken a fever?"

Missy sighed. "Look, Mom, perhaps someday I'll find a man I want to marry. But it won't be Fabian Fontenot."

Lavinia waved her folded fan at Missy. "From the way that darling boy looks at you, my dear, I'd say he has other plans."

"Tough," she replied. Catching her mother's crestfallen expression, she winked and added, "Now, no more talk of the beast, all right? I want to enjoy myself tonight."

"You wicked girl," Lavinia scolded, yet Missy's

remark had coaxed a smile out of her. She eyed Missy's gown speculatively. "Now, what jewels will you wear tonight? I should think your sapphire drop and the matching earbobs would be just lovely with that vibrant gown. Don't you agree?"

After the appropriate jewelry had been selected for Missy, the two women left the room arm-in-arm. As they swept down the magnificent, beautifully lit spiral staircase, its banister bedecked with spring foliage, Missy reflected that there were some things she truly enjoyed about this age—the lovely, genteel homes, the beautiful clothing, the absence of noise pollution. She did adore her spirited new parents, and the continuing battle of wills between herself and Fabian was fun, too, she had to admit, even though she was determined never to marry the scoundrel. Still, she lusted after him more shamelessly every time she saw him, and she often wondered if she might as well throw caution to the winds and go to bed with him, if only to get him out of her system.

On a permanent basis, however, Missy felt she still belonged back in her own time. She could never be truly content here, with her only possible future role that of wife and mother, as Lavinia had just pointed out. She wanted her career back; she wanted to be in charge of her own life and destiny once more.

John awaited them in the central hallway. He appeared quite the dapper gentleman, dressed in formal black velvet with a white ruffled shirt; his eyes gleamed with pride as he watched the two women approach. The scent of his bay rum wafted over Missy as he pecked each of their cheeks in turn.

"Ah, my two favorite ladies in the world," he declared gallantly. "How enchanting you both look!"

"Thanks, Dad," Missy said.

John slanted a questioning glance toward Lavinia. "My dear, will we be making an announcement tonight?" he asked hopefully.

"You won't," Missy answered for her mother.

Both parents groaned.

"John," Lavinia directed sternly, "will you kindly make this wayward girl see reason? I must go speak with the musicians concerning their programme, and make certain the furniture has been moved aside to allow for dancing."

As Lavinia sailed off into the parlor, John winked at his daughter. "Will you join me for a cup of punch, my dear?"

"A splendid idea," she replied, placing her hand on his sleeve.

They strolled into the formal dining room. Missy noted that the room was a feast for the senses, the scents of the flowers vying with the enticing aromas of the food, and the glittering chandelier casting a soft glow over the magnificent furnishings and the fine Persian rug. A sumptuous buffet had been laid out on tables near the back windows, everything from oysters on the half shell to Virginia ham and pickled vegetables to canapes and pastries and *petit fours*.

They paused next to the huge crystal punch bowl and Missy smiled at Joseph as he poured them each a cupful of planter's punch. Then father and daughter strolled off toward the front windows together.

"Tell me, my dear," John began quietly. "Why are you so dead set against marrying Fabian?"

"Because I don't like him," Missy replied bluntly.

John chuckled. "As much as I admire your spirit, any fool can see that the two of you make a splendid pair."

"Hah!"

"Furthermore, daughter, you cannot fight your own destiny."

Missy's eyes widened; her father could not possibly know how truly ironic his statement was to her. "And why not?" she challenged with a saucy tilt of her chin. "Where is it written in stone that I can never be more than somebody's wife and a brood mare for his children?"

John sighed, tossing her a sympathetic smile. "That's simply the way of the world, my dear. Women are destined to become wives and mothers, just as men are meant to handle business affairs and politics." Nodding toward Joseph, he finished, "Just as Negroes are intended to handle the bulk of our physical labor."

Now Missy's eyes shot sparks as his comment reminded her of Dulcie's situation. "That's another thing. I don't like your having slaves here on the plantation."

He uttered an amazed laugh. "I beg your pardon?"

She faced him down unflinchingly. "I think you should free the slaves, Dad."

"You must be joking."

"Not at all."

"Free them to do what?"

"To live their lives as they choose—to have jobs and families like the rest of us."

John's gaze beseeched the heavens. "That's the most ludicrous proposal I've ever heard. If I did free the slaves, not only would we lose our source of labor for the plantation, but the Negroes would be lost without us to care for them and guide them."

"Oh, give me a break!" Missy cried. "Do you actually have the audacity to suggest that black people are incapable of caring for themselves?"

"Well, no, but—"

"I don't like seeing human beings kept in bondage!" she put in heatedly.

John was aghast, glancing toward Joseph, then speaking in a low, firm voice. "Missy, mind the fact that you could quite easily be overheard. Our darkies are not kept in bondage. They're quite well-treated—"

"I've seen some of the men working on Sundays," she argued.

"Only the ones who want to earn extra supplies and rations. Otherwise, the darkies are all given one day off each week, to attend church and be with their families."

"Gee, that's mighty white of you," she snapped.

John colored vividly and spoke in a clipped, cold voice. "Melissa, kindly remember your place!"

"Don't you dare try to tell me my place!"

He shook a finger at her. "You will remember it, daughter, or you will spend the evening in your room, away from civil company! Moreover, I refuse to carry on this absurd conversation with you for one more instant! I advise you to quit meddling in affairs that are none of your concern and to start thinking about setting your wedding date, like a dutiful daughter."

Watching John turn and stride off with dignity, Missy was tempted to stamp her foot.

Soon, the guests began to arrive, and Lavinia

called out for Missy to join them in the hallway to greet their friends. Missy dutifully trudged off to take her place with her parents. An endless parade of charming gentlemen in formal black and gracious ladies in dazzling ball gowns floated past them, and Missy did her best to mouth polite platitudes to everyone. Some of the people Missy had already met at the church bazaar, but a number of others were complete strangers to her. Lavinia tactfully explained to several couples that Missy's memory had not been quite the same ever since her fall. While most of the guests were quite solicitous in inquiring of her current health, she also caught more than a few curious glances. She realized that her antics must be the talk of the town by now—not just her fall down the stairs on her wedding day, but also her organizing her female friends into revolt against their husbands and her selling kisses at the recent bazaar.

Soon, Antoinette and Lucy arrived with their husbands. The men seemed in somewhat better humor tonight, and the small group even laughed over the fact that Philippa and Charles still had not returned from Kentucky. The two couples had just moved past Missy when she heard the sound of a throat being cleared. She turned to see Fabian standing behind her next to the door, looking quite dashing in a black velvet tailcoat, dark trousers, and a pleated linen shirt with white silk cravat. Unbidden, a feeling of excitement swept over her at the sight of him.

"Good evening, Missy, darling," he drawled, stepping forward to take her hand and kiss it.

"Good evening, Fabian," she simpered back.

He dropped her hand. "My, you do look lovely," he went on with silky sarcasm. "Shall we hope that tonight, for once, your demeanor will match you ladylike veneer?"

Missy glowered at him. Ever since she had bested him at the bazaar, Fabian had been even more cold and distant. Since then, she'd seen him only a few times—at church, at a play, and a dinner party she'd attended with her parents—and yet he never missed an opportunity to needle her mercilessly. His conduct made her long to torment him as skillfully as he was vexing her.

"Don't hold your breath," she hissed.

Missy was about to sweep off when an elderly couple stepped up to join them. Smiling at the couple, Fabian said to Missy, "My dear, you remember my grandparents, Annette and Pierre La Branche?"

Staring at the frail white-haired little couple, Missy extended her hand and said awkwardly, "How do you—I mean, I'm pleased to see you both again."

"Enchanted, my dear," Pierre said gallantly, kissing her hand.

"We're so pleased to see you recovered, Melissa," Annette added, kissing Missy's cheek.

Missy chatted with the couple for several more minutes, gritting her teeth when several broad hints were dropped about her and Fabian setting a new date for the wedding. At last she was able to steal off, under guise of helping her mother.

As more and more guests arrived, Missy and Fabian circulated separately, visiting with their friends and conspicuously ignoring each other. When Missy spotted him fetching punch for a couple of Memphis's most lovely young belles, her blood boiled. Soon, the string ensemble began its first set of lilting waltzes. As couples began to swirl about the double parlors, Missy made a point of dancing with every gentleman who asked her. She found she had no shortage of partners—Robertson Topp, Eugene Magevney, David Porter—and she attributed her newfound popularity to her behavior on the infamous day when she had sold her kisses.

She particularly enjoyed whirling about with Robert Brinkley, a prominent local banker and promoter of roads and railroads. She had heard her father discussing Brinkley's various enterprises several times. Brinkley was middle-aged, but he appeared quite handsome and elegant to Missy, with his thick graying hair, his heavy mustache, and the intelligent twinkle in his eyes.

"So, Mr. Brinkley, you're the one who built that nice plank road that runs by our plantation?" she murmured as they glided about to a Chopin waltz.

He smiled in pleasant surprise. "You're speaking of the Memphis and Germantown Turnpike?"

"Indeed," she replied.

"How did you know my company built the road?"

"My father mentioned it."

"Ah, yes. A most observant young woman you are. Most young ladies take no interest in such matters. And I'm glad you find the road convenient, although, of course, its main purpose is to bring the cotton harvest in to town."

"Of course." She bit her lip. "Tell me something."

"If I can," he offered magnanimously.

"With the huge cotton market here in Memphis,

why is it that there are no textile or garment factories here?"

He scowled. "My, what an odd question coming from a young woman like you."

"And your response to it?" she pursued.

"We do have one cotton yarn factory in town," he murmured.

She shrugged. "A drop in the bucket. I'm talking about establishing an entire, viable industry."

A quizzical smile tugged at his mouth. "Textile factories in Memphis. You know, it's something I've never really thought about before."

"Well, you should," Missy said vehemently. "Why not capitalize on the huge supply of cotton you have available locally?"

"An excellent point," he agreed. He shook his head slowly. "I cannot believe this. A young lady with a head for business. How very refreshing."

Missy pulled a droll face. "Well, at least you're not running away screaming, like most men in this town do when they discover a female has something besides air between her ears."

He chuckled. "I must confess, I find you to be quite a different woman following your—er—mishap. I've heard of the mutiny you caused amongst your female friends. Of course, I was present the day you and the others brought down three of our city's fair-haired sons."

She was amazed. "You mean you knew about the bet we all made?"

He winked solemnly. "I think the whole town knew."

"Oh, how rich!"

"Not that many of us minded watching Fontenot and company being hoisted on their own petards."

She giggled. "Did you enjoy your kiss that day, Mr. Brinkley?"

"You mean our kiss?" he teased.

She tapped his arm playfully. "Why you sly rascal."

Fighting a grin, he glanced toward a lovely matron who stood near the archway chatting with Lavinia. "Given my devotion to my dear wife, I'm not at liberty to answer your question. Were I a much younger man, it might be another matter altogether. But I will say that I was impressed with your ingenuity that day."

Laughing, she shot him a look of pure challenge. "Then if I come to you with plans for a textile factory, will you finance it?"

He raised an eyebrow. "You realize, young lady, that you're going against every custom and tradition of our society—"

"I am doing just that. And will you be a pioneer with me—or cling to the safety of convention, like the others?"

He whistled. "I'll take it under advisement. When you're ready—come see me."

Once the dance had finished, Missy wondered at the rashness of her suggestions to Brinkley. What was she doing, considering putting down permanent roots here? Getting involved in textile factories, no less! Not to mention campaigning to have the slaves freed. Wasn't she still determined to return to her old life, her real life, back in the twentieth century?

Watching Fabian whirl about, laughing, with a dazzling blond coquette in his arms, Missy renewed her determination to escape this exasperating age. She continued to dance with every man there except Fabian; she also drank copious amounts of Planter's punch, and felt herself growing tipsy as the evening progressed.

It wasn't until almost ten o'clock that Fabian finally came to her side. "Well, have you finished your flirtations for the evening?" he asked casually.

"Have you?" she responded flippantly.

He smiled tolerantly. "I note that you've danced so much tonight, you've ripped your petticoat in the back. I suggest that you go repair it."

She laughed, trying to glance behind her but unable to see much over her billowing skirts. "I don't see a rip. And even if I have torn the petticoat, who cares?"

"You will, if you end up taking another tumble," he drawled.

"Very well." Shrugging, Missy flounced off. Inwardly, though, she smiled. Even tipsy as she was, she could see straight through Fabian's ploy. She was certain her petticoat wasn't ripped at all. On the contrary, Fabian was simply trying to maneuver her upstairs.

Should she rise to his bait? Had he already risen to hers? Giggling at her own ribald pun, she wove her way up the stairs.

To her amazement, she found that the possibility of imminent seduction by Fabian intrigued and excited her beyond all caution. After all, the two of them had been headed toward this explosion for weeks.

So let it come! As frustrated as she was with her current plight, some good, lusty rolling about in the feather bed upstairs might help clear the air. Fabian might be a fiancé to kill, but she already knew in her gut that he was going to be a lover to die for.

In her bedroom, Missy stood at the pier mirror. She toyed with her coiffure, then removed her earbobs and necklace. After a moment, Fabian entered the room.

She hadn't really expected him to knock.

She turned to him with an eager smile. He stood just inside the closed door, regarding her with a riveting intensity that made her stomach lurch. "Well, Mr. Fontenot?" she queried with bravado. "Have you come to play the role of maid and help me with my ostensibly shredded petticoat?"

He chuckled, turning to throw the lock. "That's not quite the game I had in mind."

The sound of the bolt sliding home was somehow brazenly erotic to Missy. "Then, pray enlighten me," she mocked, over her thrumming heart.

"You and I have been headed for a reckoning for some time now," he said with deceptive mildness, taking off his jacket and laying it across a chair.

She licked her lips in anticipation. "Indeed, we have."

"And I think the time is now upon us."

"Is it? Why tonight?"

"I think the sight of you flirting with Robert Brinkley pretty much decided the issue for me," he drawled. He removed his cravat and began unbuttoning his shirt, and his next words came mingled with husky sensuality and hoarse warning. "If you wish to say no, Missy, I'd suggest you say it now."

Studying the crisp dark curls on his magnificent chest, she felt her mouth go dry. She laughed and began to pull the pins from her hair. "You think I'm not woman enough to take you on?" She again ogled him brazenly. "How'd you get to be such a big man, anyway? You're grandparents are so tiny."

He grinned and tossed down his shirt. "I'm definitely my father's son."

"Indeed, you are. So, come and get me, you big bumpkin."

He did. He was across the room in three strides, hauling her into his arms, kissing her with barely suppressed violence, raking his fingers through her hair. For Missy, the gnawing frustrations of weeks exploded in a cataclysm of white-hot yearning. Fabian's tongue ravished her mouth, demanding a surrender that she eagerly gave; her own tongue teased and parried with his, and she gloried at his tortured groan. She couldn't seem to kiss him deeply enough; she couldn't get enough of him.

"God, woman," he breathed, kissing her cheek, her hair. "I've wanted you for so long. I've never wanted any woman like I've burned for you."

"Not even Melissa?" she asked, kissing him back hungrily.

"Never . . . Not until you became my Missy."

"God . . ." Digging her fingernails into his shoulders, she begged, "Say that again."

"My Missy . . . My love."

They stood kissing passionately for several more electrifying moments. Missy had to marvel at Fabian's seductive skill when he undid the buttons on the back of her gown and loosened the ties on her corset while never losing the rhythm or thrust of his kiss. She was in heaven as he picked her up and carried her over to the bed. He gently laid her down, then positioned his aroused body over hers. She moaned in ecstasy at the hard, hot feel of his body.

His hands took her face and stared down at her with mesmerizing intensity. "What were you talking about with Brinkley tonight?" he demanded.

She laughed. "Did I drive you insane with jealousy?"

"Quite mad, darling. Now tell me what the two of you were discussing."

"Business."

"What business?"

"It's none of yours."

A look of possessive anger flashed in his dark eyes. "Damn it, Missy! I want your promise that you won't flirt with other men again." As he spoke, his hot mouth moved down her throat.

She managed a breathy laugh that ended in a tiny shiver of delight. "Just like you won't flirt with other women?" As he stared up at her, she added, "Fabian, you can't demand my respect or loyalty. You have to earn it."

"Do I?" His hands firmly pulled down the bodice of her gown, and he smiled at her sudden, wide-eyed gasp. "Then perhaps we should begin with this."

Fabian latched his mouth on her nipple, sucking hard, and Missy cried out in rapture, tangling her fingers in his hair. Gone was the teasing, the war of words, leaving only feverish flesh and blazing desire. Missy's senses were on fire with the scent of him, the tormenting wetness of his mouth on her aroused, aching breast. Riveting lust streaked down her body to settle in the very core of her with painful urgency.

She shuddered with rapture as Fabian roved his tongue over both breasts, then kissed the valley between. Pushing down her camisole and corset, he drew his teasing tongue lower, across her stomach. Missy bucked in agonized pleasure, and he clamped both arms across her midriff to hold her still.

His tortured voice drifted up to her. "I'm going to make love to you until you never even think of looking at another man again."

"Please do," she coaxed wantonly, and was rewarded by another searing kiss.

Fabian was shocked but also pleased when Missy pushed him off her and began to draw her own mouth down his bare chest. She smiled at his grunt of agonized pleasure as she drew her tongue over his male nipples. A satisfied moan rose in her throat when her kisses and nips brought gooseflesh rising on his skin. But when her hand moved lower to wantonly grip his hardness through his trousers, his fingers restrained hers.

"Do you want me inside you, Missy?" he demanded.

"Oh, yes."

"How much?"

Her delirious gaze met his. "So much I'd die for it."

"You may before this night is over." Though his words were teasing, they ignited a new torrent of desire in Missy.

Fabian's eyes flashed with a feral light as he pushed her onto her back. As he boldly hiked her skirts and pulled down her pantalets, Missy realized that everything was happening way too fast. Her head was spinning and she could barely breathe. They were both still half-clothed, but suddenly, that didn't seem to matter. The need consuming them both could not be contained.

He knelt between her spread thighs, hooked his

Eugenia Riley

arms under her knees and brought her close. She gasped as she felt his arousal probe against her feminine portal. She was no virgin, but it had been years since she'd made love with a man and he was very big, very hard.

"Trust me, darling," he murmured, and then with a swift, deep stroke, he embedded himself to the hilt inside her.

Missy cried out in wonder and some discomfort. He felt so hot, so huge and vibrant inside her. He watched her mindless response closely, her eager acceptance of him crumbling his restraint. He groaned in ecstasy and drove into her, hard and sure and deep, again and again. All the while, he stared intently into her eyes.

Feelings she had never known before began to stream through Missy, shredding her apart, until she was left sobbing beneath him. She tossed her head, her hands clawing upward to touch his face. When he fell upon her, she threw her arms about his neck, brought his lips down to hers, and kissed him ravenously. His rough chest rubbed her breasts exquisitely as he slammed into her again and again. She could not seem to control her own breathing, her own racing heartbeat, or the intense paroxysms gripping her. When Fabian raised her hips high and rammed himself into her with the powerful strokes of his climax, she met each stroke eagerly, feeling certain she would die of pleasure. Her fingernails scored his back, her hips arched higher to meet him, and her wanton moans only increased the fierceness of his utter possession. By the time he plunged to rest inside her, she had climaxed three times.

They lay locked together for a long moment. She sensed the change in him the minute he rolled

300

off her and pulled down her skirts. "Fabian?" she queried softly.

He stood, buttoned his trousers, and left her to stare at his broad bare back with its blooming welts as he went to fetch his shirt and cravat. After donning both, he returned to her and stood staring down at her with dark, accusing eyes.

"What is it?" she cried.

"That was very good, Missy," he drawled cynically. "You were very hot, very tight. I'd say the best roll I've ever had."

She was enraged. "Why, you—"

"There's only one problem."

"What?" she half-screamed at him.

"You weren't a virgin."

It took a moment for the import of his words to fully sink in on her. In the space of that time, he had already crossed the room, grabbed his jacket, and opened the door.

"You bastard!" she screamed.

She hurled a small vase at him, but it only crashed against the slammed door, and then she burst into tears.

Chapter Twenty-eight

"Good evening, Reverend White, Mrs. White," Melissa said.

"Good evening, dear," the Whites replied in unison.

Melissa was greeting the arriving guests at her parents' dinner party. Dressed in a beautifully fitted teal-green silk dress and matching pumps, with her hair lushly curled and makeup expertly applied, she was a beautiful, exotic splash of color among the burnished antiques in the downstairs hallway.

"To coin a pun, you do look divine, my dear," Reverend White said with a grin. He glanced down at Melissa's hand. "And what a lovely engagement ring! I do hope you and Jeff will be announcing a new wedding date tonight."

"You seem completely recovered from your—er—unfortunate accident," Mrs. White added graciously. "We've so enjoyed having you join us at our Bible study group."

"Thank you both for your kind words," Melissa replied. "I am feeling much improved, and I'm sure Jeffrey and I will set a new date in due course. Now, won't you both join my parents in the parlor for some refreshments?"

Melissa escorted the elderly couple into the living room, where they were graciously greeted by Charlotte and Howard. At the sound of a new rap at the front door, Melissa returned to the hallway and opened the door to admit the next guest.

Aunt Agnes, in a tailored navy blue dress, swept inside. "Hello, honey," she said, pecking Melissa's cheek. "My, you look like a doll tonight."

"Thank you, Aunt Agnes," Melissa replied, taking the woman's wrap. "You are looking quite well yourself."

"Jeff not here yet?" Agnes continued.

Melissa shook her head as she turned to hang the jacket on a hall tree. "Not yet—he must shower and change after work, then go fetch his mother. But he should join us soon, I imagine."

Agnes spotted the ring on Melissa's hand, and let out a joyous shriek. "Let me see that rock, honey!"

Smiling, Melissa extended her hand.

Agnes watched the light play over the fabulous marquis-shaped stone and whistled. "Will we be hearing an announcement at dinner?" she asked with a wink. "Like a new wedding date?"

"I'm afraid not as yet, Aunt Agnes."

Agnes frowned. "Charlotte told me you don't want to marry Jeff until you find all those years you lost. That's nonsense, if you ask me." She quickly hugged the girl. "Don't you know that we all adore you just the way you are? At last, you've become a truly fine human being." Agnes shook a finger at her. "Don't mess it up now, kid."

"Thank you, Aunt Agnes." Watching her aunt walk into the parlor, Melissa felt a sudden rush of sympathy for her distant cousin. If only these people knew the truth . . . It saddened her that no one here seemed to miss poor Missy—even though most of them were assuming that "Missy" was actually her own former self!

As another rap sounded at the door, Melissa turned to admit Jeff and his widowed mother, Irene Dalton. Irene was a pretty woman, tall and slim, and, like her son, she was blond and blue-eyed. Melissa felt very pleased that, over the past weeks, she and Irene had become good friends.

"Melissa!" Irene cried, giving the girl a warm hug. "Jeff told me about that gorgeous ring—now let me see it!"

After Irene oohed and aahed over Melissa's diamond, Jeff stepped closer, hugging and kissing his fiancée. "You're a knockout tonight, darling," he whispered, studying her with adoring eyes.

"You look quite fine yourself," she returned, admiring him in his dark blue suit.

The threesome strolled into the parlor together. After all present had greeted Irene and Jeff, Howard passed around the champagne and then led everyone in a toast. "Here's hoping we'll be hearing wedding bells again soon," he pronounced, and everyone cheered. Jeff winked at Melissa, and she forced a smile, wishing with all her heart that she could, indeed, throw caution to the winds and marry him.

A moment later, her father answered the door and brought in a stranger—a large, middle-aged man with dark, thinning hair. "Melissa, dear, you remember George, don't you?" Howard asked.

Melissa stared at the man blankly, and he in turn eyed her in puzzlement.

"You know, George Schmidt, plant manager of our ball bearing factory?" her father continued kindly.

"Missy?" the man named George now asked, still regarding her confusedly.

She extended her hand. "I prefer Melissa now," she said, shaking his hand. "And I'm pleased to meet you, Mr. Schmidt."

When George glanced perplexedly at his host, Melissa's father explained, "As I believe I've mentioned previously, George, our daughter has suffered from some memory lapses ever since her fall."

"Oh, yes." He nodded to her. "I do hope you're feeling better Miss—Melissa."

"Thank you—and I am," she replied.

Shortly thereafter, the party of nine adjourned to the dining room, where the maids served a fabulous meal, including lemon chicken fricassee, rice pilaf, peas in cream sauce, and wonderful homemade yeast rolls.

Melissa and Jeff sat together toward the center of one side of the table, with George Schmidt seated across from Melissa. As she visited with the others and ate delicately, she was perturbed to note several times during the meal that George was staring at her pointedly.

The conversation was general, ranging from the church membership drive to national politics, the current business downturn in Memphis, and crime in the city. Throughout the meal, George said little and continued to regard Melissa quizzically. Later, as everyone was finishing up their desserts of cherries jubilee, he cleared his throat and said, "Melissa, why don't you join me outside for a smoke?"

There was a moment of strained silence, then Jeff protectively took Melissa's hand and replied to George, "Melissa doesn't smoke anymore."

"Oh, she doesn't?" he asked, laughing. "Filthy habit, isn't it, Melissa? I should kick it, too."

"Yes, I presume you should," she said stiffly.

He winked at her. "But you'll join me outside for a moment, won't you—er, Melissa? We've a bit of plant business to discuss."

Jeff was about to reply in Melissa's place again, when she held up a hand and said evenly, "I'd be happy to join Mr. Schmidt on the veranda."

The two excused themselves and slipped out the back door. For a moment, George smoked silently while Melissa stood tensely nearby. The night was cool and full of sounds—crickets, an owl, tree leaves rustling in the breeze. Beyond them, the softly lit pool gleamed, its surface rippling slightly in the breeze.

"Why haven't you come in to work?" he asked at last.

"Hasn't my father explained things to you?" she asked.

"He has. But the Missy Monroe I used to know would have come in to work—memory lapses or not."

She paced off a step or two. "Perhaps my interests are different now."

He laughed. "By the way, we landed the Wakefield Aircraft account, and that N. C. lathe finally came in from Japan, after nine months. We've gotten it anchored, leveled, and wired, and we're starting the programming now." He paused. "All of this is Greek to you, isn't it?"

Lamely, she explained, "As I told you—I've had these lapses—"

"And I'm the Tooth Fairy," he drawled cynically. He dropped his smoke and snuffed it out. "I think it's all meaningless to you because you're not Missy Monroe."

She whirled to face him, her eyes huge. "What do you mean?"

"Oh, you look like her," he went on, "but you're different. Too young, and radically different in temperament."

"People—can change," she stammered.

"Oh, they can," he agreed. "But not the Missy Monroe I knew."

She was silent, struggling to hang on to her composure. Finally, she asked, "If I'm not Missy, then who am I? And where has she gone?"

He laughed. "Now those are the million-dollar questions." Scratching his jaw, he mused, "I'm guessing you're some distant relative of hers—a cousin, maybe. Perhaps the two of you decided to switch places, as a joke or something. I can see Missy pulling a stunt like that."

Melissa's face burned at the accuracy of his conjectures. "What you're suggesting is preposterous, Mr. Schmidt. Missy—that is, I—would have no reason to pull such a prank. Furthermore, if I'm not Missy, why are all the others accepting me as her?"

He was quiet a moment, then said, "Because they all want so desperately to believe you are her."

She attempted a laugh that came out shrill and forced. "Mr. Schmidt, I assure you you are imagining things."

"Not so," he cut in, stepping closer. "But don't worry. I'll not be the one to spill the beans."

"But there are no beans to spill—"

"Baloney."

She glanced at him in consternation, trying to draw a connection between baloney and beans. At last, she said, "If what you are saying is indeed accurate, Mr. Schmidt, why aren't you telling the others the truth?"

He smiled. "Because you're a very decent human being, Miss Melissa-whoever-you-are. Tonight, I saw at least five people at that dinner table staring at you with utter love and devotion."

Melissa bit her lip. "What if—strictly for the sake of argument—what you're saying could be true? What if there were this monumental quirk of fate, an occurrence so miraculous and powerful that it defies description—and two people were—switched."

He was quiet a moment. "You mean like permanently switched?"

"Perhaps irrevocably."

He whistled. "Damn. So you're saying both people are alive and well, only kind of swapped, like they do in the movies?"

Melissa had no idea what movies he spoke of. Nevertheless, she nodded. "What would you suggest a person like me do under those circumstances?"

He shrugged. "You appear to be where you're supposed to be, so I'd say, why not enjoy it? Everyone here seems nuts about you, and you're happy, aren't you?"

"Yes—but can I seek my happiness at the expense of another?"

He shook his head. "If you're worrying about

Missy, I'm sure that, wherever she is, she deserves to be there."

As Melissa watched in perplexed silence, George turned and reentered the house.

When the dinner party broke up, Jeff asked Reverend and Mrs. White to drop his mother off at her house on their way home, since he wanted to spend more time with Melissa. After everyone said their good nights, Jeff and Melissa strolled out by the pool.

"Tonight was great," Jeff murmured, squeezing her hand. "Only one thing would have made it better."

She smiled as she watched the light from the pool area sculpt his handsome features. "An announcement of a new wedding date?"

"You're psychic," Jeff teased.

She rolled her eyes. "I'd have to be mentally deficient not to have caught all those blatant hints."

He grinned, displaying irresistible dimples. "Who knows? Maybe with enough arm-twisting, you'll give in."

"Oh, Jeff." She glanced at him in uncertainty. "There are so many things I love about being here, but I don't think I can keep up this charade forever."

She felt his fingers tense over hers. "What do you mean?"

She sighed. "George Schmidt knows I'm not Missy."

"What?" Jeff paused in his tracks. "Tell me what he said."

"He confronted me tonight—saying that I'm totally different from her, that I look years younger, and that I haven't fooled him."

"Damn!" Jeff said.

"He told me the others have not truly questioned who I am because they want so badly to believe I'm really Missy."

Jeff nodded morosely. "That's probably true. Still, I must speak with George—"

"Don't worry, he said he would not be the one to—um—toss the baloney."

He fought a smile. "You mean, spill the beans?"

"Something like that." She paused, her expression deeply perturbed. "Don't you see how sad all this is?"

"What do you mean?"

"No one wants Missy back."

He frowned. "If that's the case, then Missy brought this on herself."

"But I really think we're not being fair to her," Melissa continued earnestly. "Even with George— he suspects I'm an impostor, and yet he doesn't seem even to care what's happened to her. Nor is he willing to lift a finger to come to her aid— and that includes not telling Mother and Father the truth."

Jeff pulled her into his arms. "Darling, I think you're being too altruistic for your own good. Fate brought you here and brought us together. Why not simply enjoy what's meant to be?"

She drew a ragged breath. "That's pretty much what George said. But still, I'm troubled."

He pressed her hand to his heart. "Then lay your troubles here, my lady," he whispered fervently. "I promise I'll take care of you."

Jeff pulled her into the shadows of the nearby cabana and kissed her passionately. Melissa kissed him back just as ardently, basking in the scent of him, the taste and texture of his warm lips on hers.

After a moment, they paused to catch their breath, holding each other close and gazing out at the pool. "If it weren't so cool, I'd suggest we go for a dip," he murmured.

Her eyes grew enormous. "And then we'd have to don one of those scandalous bathing suits?"

He winked at her solemnly. "We could always go skinny-dipping."

She was aghast. "Does that mean what I think it does?"

"Of course." As she gasped, he touched the tip of her nose with his fingertip and added, "We'll go buy you a bikini soon. They should have them in the stores by now."

She shook her head vehemently. "Jeffrey, I've managed to adjust to many conventions of the late twentieth century, but I'll never put on one of those obscene devices."

"Never? Wanna bet?" he teased. He backed her into a nearby column and began tickling her. She shrieked and did her best to wrestle away from him. But as her squirming inadvertently brought her pelvis arching into the front of his trousers, all at once the teasing stopped. Jeff gripped her shoulders and pressed her against the post; she felt the hard maleness of him pulsing against her as he stared down into her eyes. Never before had she seen this particular look in his eye; indeed, he appeared ready to devour her on the spot.

"Melissa, marry me," he whispered intensely, leaning over to plant fluttering kisses all over her face. "Please say you will. I think I'll die if I can't have you soon."

"I know, Jeff, and I feel the same way," she

replied breathlessly. "But don't you understand? I can't give you a complete commitment until I'm sure Missy is happy, too."

He sighed heavily, glancing at the nearby door to the cabana. "Then make love with me, darling," he whispered intensely, running his fingers through her hair. "If time—or fate—ever pulls us apart again, at least we'll have that much."

"Oh, Jeff!" Melissa's heart felt torn apart with love and regret. "You must understand that technically, at least, I still belong to Fabian—"

"To hell with Fabian Fontenot!" he cried passionately, gripping her face with his hands. "I'll die before I'll ever let that bastard anywhere near you again. You're mine, Melissa—mine—and don't you ever forget it."

Jeff kissed her hungrily again, swirling his tongue deeply inside her mouth until little whimpers of pleasure rose up in her throat. Melissa found herself reeling with a love and a need that was even stronger than the family loyalty and nagging conscience that bound her to the past. She ached all over with her desire for him, her heart pounding, her every breath seeming to devour his essence, the womanly center of her hungering for his driving heat. She roved her fingers over his back and murmured his name.

Yet when he tugged her toward the cabana, she still hesitated. Jeff detoured to a nearby patio chair, sat down, and pulled her into his lap. She felt the strength of him surrounding her, the rigid length of his arousal pressing against her bottom, and she thought she might die of wanting him.

"What is it, darling?" he coaxed tenderly, holding her close and kissing her cheek. "Are you frightened because you're a virgin, because it's your first time?"

Far from being afraid, Melissa was in such rapture, she could barely breathe. "I'm not frightened of you, Jeff," she murmured.

She felt him tensing. "Don't tell me that Fontenot forced you to—"

She shook her head vehemently. "No, he never tried to force himself on me."

"Then what, sweetheart?" he asked, gently nipping her neck.

She drew a heavy breath and laced her fingers through his. "I'm not used to this time period."

"I know that."

"I mean, in my time period, what you want . . . It would have been wrong."

"Is our love wrong?" he asked, his voice raw with hurt.

Her anguished gaze met his. "Of course not, darling. It could never be. But perhaps . . ."

"Yes?"

Miserably, she stammered, "I know that my friends are—aren't—"

"What?"

She pulled back and regarded him solemnly. "I'm not a sexually liberated nineties woman, Jeffrey. Perhaps I'll disappoint you."

At first, she felt confused when he threw back his head and laughed. He ruffled her hair and said, "Darling, you should know by now that sexually liberated nineties women hold no interest for me whatsoever."

She beamed with happiness. "Really, Jeff? Then, you mean—"

He nipped at her nose. "I mean I'm much more

interested in seducing one nineteenth-century virgin."

Her eyes grew huge. "Are you saying that you're a seducer of young women, Jeffrey?"

"One particular young woman." All levity ended as he kissed her again. "Give yourself to me, angel," he whispered into her mouth. "Tell me you're mine in your heart from this moment on. Trust me, sweetheart."

Melissa could not resist his heartfelt pleas. She realized that he was right. If the forces of time did pull them apart again, they could at least have this one night to treasure in their hearts forever. "I trust you, Jeff," she whispered back. "And I'm yours."

Seconds later, they entered the darkened cabana together; Jeff locked the latch behind them. Melissa found that they stood in a small bungalow with a table and chairs and several chaise lounges. The walls were solid on three sides; the front consisted of rows and rows of drawn shutters that emitted only pencil pricks of light.

"Will we be—uninterrupted here?" she asked.

"Yes, darling. The door is latched, and no one ever comes back here." He laughed dryly. "Indeed, Missy used to pull me in here sometimes so we could neck."

She stiffened in his arms. "Did you and she ever . . . ?"

"No."

"I'm glad," she said, then hastily added, "Not that I had any right to control your life before I came—"

He caught her closer and spoke fiercely. "Listen to me, Melissa, and never forget this. I had no life before you came to me."

And he kissed her deeply, thoroughly, until she sobbed in joy.

The room was cool and drafty, but neither noticed. Standing there in the silvery shadows with mouths and bodies tightly locked, they both grew feverishly hot with desire. While Melissa was normally quite modest by nature, she found to her delight and wonder that she felt no embarrassment at the thought of giving herself to the man she loved. When Jeff began to unbutton her dress, her fingers automatically reached for the buttons on his shirt. He removed her silk dress carefully, laying it and his shirt neatly across a chair. When he returned to her, he drew his lips slowly, tormentingly, over her flesh as he removed her slip, bra, pantyhose, and shoes. She trembled with excitement and caressed his bare chest, his strong neck, his rough face.

Once she was nude, he pulled back and studied her in the scant light. "My Lord, you're so incredibly beautiful," he whispered.

When he leaned over to press his mouth to her bare breast, she cried out in rapture. Her entire body seemed one large quivering mass of gooseflesh.

"Are you all right, darling?" he asked, flicking his tongue over her tautened nipple.

"Oh, yes," she panted, tangling her fingers in his silky hair. "It's just that I've never felt anything like this before. . . . It's like madness—the sweetest madness a body could ever know."

"I know, darling."

When he sucked the tip of her breast into his mouth, a soft scream escaped her, and even madness could not begin to describe the riotous rapture, the tormenting need consuming her. She

Eugenia Riley

arched her breast deeper into the wondrous heat of his mouth and was doubly rewarded when his mouth sucked harder at her breast even as his fingers reached down to part her and stroke her most intimate parts, already moist with her desire for him.

A tortured groan rumbled in his throat as he felt her wet readiness. He pulled her to a nearby chaise longue and pressed her down beneath him. His bare, hair-roughened chest felt divine, so hot and crushing, against her aroused breasts. He kissed her deeply while unbuckling his belt and unzipping his trousers.

His voice was agonized. "Darling, I don't think I can wait."

Even though her need was every bit as blinding as his, a last-minute doubt assailed her. "Jeff . . . could we?"

"Could we what, darling?" came his half-dazed response.

"Well, I was wondering . . . Mankind has made such strides. Is there a way to prevent our having a child together?"

Suddenly alert, Jeff stared down at her solemnly. "Haven't you read about such things?"

She blushed. "Actually, a lady would never . . . Well, that is, when I come across subjects such as—" she cleared her throat miserably—"human sexuality, I always try to avert my eyes while reading."

Despite his advanced state of excitement, a chuckle escaped Jeff as he kissed the side of her mouth and thrust against her brazenly. "Don't you want my child, angel?" he asked huskily.

She gasped in delight at the feel of his rock-solid, hot erection pressing into her. "Oh, yes, my darling! Only, with things so tenuous, I thought perhaps it might be better . . . Is there a way, Jeff?"

Jeff stared down at her, feeling very torn, his heart welling with love and desire for this woman who had brought him back to life again, his soul tormented by the possibility that she might leave him one day. Again, he remembered May 15, the date she might well marry Fabian Fontenot, the doomsday date on which he might lose her. Merciful heavens, he simply could not! A child would be a bond between them, he thought quickly. If he got her pregnant, then she would have to stay—

"Jeff?"

He stared down into her wide, trusting eyes again. He would burn in hell for this one, he thought.

"Sorry, darling, guess we'll just have to chance it," he murmured.

He slipped his hands beneath her hips, lifting her to him. Fastening his mouth on hers, he thrust slowly into her warm, tight vessel. The feel of her squeezing about him was hot and heavenly, and with great restraint he resisted an urge to ram his full length inside her snug sheath. Instead, he made her his steadily, lovingly, whispering soothing endearments in her mouth.

Despite his gentleness, Jeff's heat seemed to split Melissa apart; her pain was intense, yet so was her ecstasy at giving herself over to the man she loved. Her fingernails dug into his shoulders, and she cried out softly as her maidenhead gave way; he kissed her tenderly and pressed home unhurriedly.

"I love you," he whispered, at last fully inside her.

"I love you, too," she murmured, clinging to him.

"What you've given me tonight," he added raggedly, "will shine in my soul forever."

"What you've given me," she whispered back, "will fill my heart for the rest of my life."

When he kissed her again, she could feel the wetness of their mingled tears. Melissa gloried at Jeff's utter possession; even the aching of her own sensitized flesh simply added to the exquisite feeling of oneness. As he began to move inside her, she cried out again at the shattering pressure, arching upward to kiss him eagerly; he responded with several hard, deep strokes that ignited a cataclysm of feeling within her.

His voice came hoarse and tortured. "I shouldn't be . . . Might hurt you . . . Can't seem to stop."

"Don't stop, darling," she urged, then heard his own ragged cry, felt his mouth smother hers as his loins pounded into her, driving them both headlong into the paroxysm, until a torrent of ecstasy convulsed them, leaving only peace and wonder in its wake.

Much later, as Melissa crept back inside the darkened house after seeing Jeff off, she paused by the newel post and again saw her cousin's miserable visage reflected in the newel stone. Missy was shaking her fist and mouthing angry words Melissa still could not understand—although their import was again devastatingly clear.

"What am I going to do?" Melissa cried.

"Get me out of here!" Missy cried furiously. She stood by the newel post, trying desperately to communicate with her cousin one hundred and forty years away. "Can't you understand what I'm saying, you ninny? You've got to help me get out of here! Oh, damn it, you don't understand!"

Missy stormed off up the stairs, to spend the night weeping furiously.

Chapter Twenty-nine

The next morning, Missy was pacing the veranda in a rage after having slept not at all the previous night.

Oh, that bastard Fabian Fontenot! Here, she had given herself to the cad, had done the most unspeakably carnal things with him, and then he'd had the unmitigated gall to point out that she wasn't a virgin! Who in the hell did he think he was? Was *he* a virgin? Had *he* spent his life in a monastery? Who was he to cast aspersions on her character? The very questions made her laugh bitterly. Fabian Fontenot was nothing but a blockheaded Neanderthal who, like ninety-nine percent of the male population, was totally rooted in the prehistoric mind set of the double standard. Well, she'd have a thing or two to tell him—assuming she ever saw the beast again!

Missy re-entered her room, stared at the bed, and then abruptly burst into tears as memories of the previous night swept over her. She threw herself down on the mattress, only to be inundated by the scent of him, which still lingered on the bedclothes.

"Damn you!" she cried, drowning in bittersweet images of their fevered lovemaking. Oh, heavens, it had been so glorious! He'd made her scream with passion. He'd turned her inside out emotionally! And now—

Now, she was hopelessly in love with the biggest jerk in all of history!

In love? With him? Oh, God, she was doomed! Heaven help her! Missy pounded her fists on the pillow and sobbed all the more. What on earth was she going to do?

Elegantly dressed and impeccably groomed, Fabian Fontenot sat eating breakfast with his grandparents in the dining room of the family plantation house.

"Did you enjoy yourself last night, dear?" his grandmother asked.

Fabian all but choked on his coffee, then managed to smile stiffly at the dear little white-haired woman. "I found the evening quite memorable, Grand'mere," he said dryly.

"It was good to see Melissa again," Pierre put in.

Fabian nodded. "Indeed, Grand-pere. And she prefers being called 'Missy' now."

"Ah, so we've noted," Pierre replied, scratching his jaw. "The girl seems vastly different in temperament ever since her fall."

"Quite so," Fabian concurred ironically.

"Have the two of you discussed a new date for the wedding?" Annette asked. "I mean, she does seem completely recovered from her accident."

Fabian sighed. "I'm sorry to disappoint you, Grand'mere, but, suffice it to say, the young lady wants nothing to do with me at the moment."

"But why, darling?" Annette pursued. "What woman wouldn't be thrilled to marry you?"

Fabian lifted his napkin to cover a deprecating chuckle and did not comment.

"We've all dreamed for years of joining our estate with the Montgomerys'," Pierre went on. "After all, it is what your dear departed parents wanted most of all. Furthermore, violating the marriage contract made by your parents would be a most grave affront to the honor of both our families."

"Yes, grandson, you must end this alienation at once," Annette added. She touched Fabian's hand. "Darling, we do not mean to push you so. But as you know, Grand-pere and I are in our golden years now. We do so want to see you settled, and happy."

"And most of all, you'd like to see me provide you with a few great-grandchildren to bounce on your knees?" Fabian asked with a wink.

Annette and Pierre exchanged guilty glances, then Pierre grinned and said, "But of course, grandson."

Fabian was thoughtfully silent for a long moment. At last he said, "Do not worry, Grand'mere, Grand-pere. I'll prevail upon the young lady to see reason. Now, if you'll both excuse me . . . ?"

He stood, kissed his grandmother's cheek, nodded to his grandfather, and left.

The conversation with his grandparents was very much on Fabian's mind as he rode through the sweetness of the April morning toward the neighboring Montgomery plantation. Fabian was devoted to his elderly grandparents. His mother's parents had lived at the Fontenot family home for as long as he could remember; indeed, the couple had emigrated to America from France with his parents long before Fabian was even born. After the deaths of their daughter and son-in-law in the yellow fever epidemic two years ago, all the elderly La Branches had ever asked of Fabian was that he honor the marriage contract his parents had made twenty years earlier.

In fact, Fabian's love and devotion toward both generations of his forebears, and his desire not to besmirch his parents' memory, were the factors that had compelled him to honor the covenant in the first place, even though every grain of his masculinity had balked at the idea of marrying mealy-mouthed Melissa Montgomery—

Yet now "Melissa" had become his hotheaded little spitfire, Missy. His loins tightened as he remembered the ecstasy of their fevered love-making last night. Lord, she had been such heaven in his arms! He'd gloried in every moment of their intimacy—until afterward, when the haze of passion had at last lifted and he'd realized she had not come to him a virgin. Even now, the very thought of her having been with another man made him wild with jealousy.

Because he loved her! The realization hit him like a fist in the gut. Of course; why else would he have reacted in such a fit of passion? He loved the little vixen, and he'd be damned if he'd ever again let another man touch her!

After all, she could be pregnant, he thought, remembering his earlier discussion with his grandparents. There might well be a little Fontenot filling her womb even now. The very thought all but made him reel with a fierce possessiveness, a primal desire to make her his irrevocably.

Thus, he would take her back and marry her posthaste, with a stern warning that he'd blister her bottom soundly if he ever caught her even looking at another man again. Surely she'd be grateful for his benevolence in accepting a less than chaste bride, and would shape up into a proper wife for him.

A self-satisfied grin sculpted his mouth. Ah, yes, his problems were clearly solved. He congratulated himself on his great wisdom and commendable generosity and lit a cheroot to celebrate.

Missy was still sobbing on the bed when her mother stepped into the room. "Missy, dear, Fabian is here to see you."

Missy brought her puffy face up from the pillow. "Tell him to go to hell."

Lavinia chuckled and went to sit beside her daughter, reaching out to smooth Missy's disheveled hair. "Come, now, darling, what is the problem? Why all these tears?"

Missy's lower lip trembled as she sat up to face her mother. "Fabian and I had a fight."

"Then don't you think it's time for the two of you to kiss and make up?"

"No!"

"Now, Missy," Lavinia chided. "You must at least go downstairs and speak with the poor boy."

Missy glowered at her mother for another moment. "Very well," she conceded grudgingly. "I'll go speak with the big bully—but only so I'll have the pleasure of telling that jackass just what he can do with himself."

Lavinia rolled her eyes. "Do you need help with your toilette?"

"Thank you, no," Missy responded with uncharacteristic primness.

"Very well, then, darling. Fabian's waiting for you in the parlor."

Shaking her head, Lavinia left the room.

Missy rose and went to the dressing table. Wetting a cloth with cool water and dabbing her face, she grimaced at her red-eyed, puffy-faced reflection and realized she still looked as if she'd been crying all night—which, of course, she had. Lord, how she hated for Fabian to see her this way, for him to know that she cared enough about him to bawl her eyes out.

Steeling her resolve, she left her room and went downstairs, eager to get this over with. She walked into the parlor, then froze as she glimpsed him standing across from her.

He looked absolutely gorgeous, dressed in a brown velvet frock coat and fawn-colored trousers, his clean-shaven face perfect in every detail, his thick hair gleaming in the sunlight, his deep-set eyes focused on her with a strange mixture of tenderness and uncertainty. An unexpected floodtide of feeling washed over her—anger, fear, love, hate, and a stunning sexual excitement at the very sight of him.

Oh, heavens, why was this happening to her—again? She'd come down the stairs perfectly prepared to set him in his place, and now her equilibrium was sent reeling in his electrifying presence.

"Good morning, Missy," he said tightly.

"Good morning," she returned sullenly.

He moved closer, staring at her with an odd compassion. "You look exhausted, darling."

She wanted to tell him to go to hell, but could only manage a trembling glare.

"You're been crying, angel," he whispered.

Damn him, why did he have to say that to her? The last thing she'd expected from him was this devastating tenderness. She wanted with all her being to tell him not to call her angel, she wanted to tell him to take his nauseating endearments and *stuff* them—and yet she couldn't, for suddenly, to her horror and utter humiliation, tears were flooding her eyes—and then she was in his arms.

"You're crying for me," he whispered against her hair, and she shook with violent sobs.

Fabian's lips took hers fiercely, and Missy clung to him desperately, wanting to kiss him until passion obliterated all memory of the hurt within her. As his tongue plunged sure and deep inside her mouth, the raw eroticism was shattering. Bittersweet emotion and desire welled within her so powerfully that she was left dizzy and breathless, her anger and wounded pride momentarily forgotten. Fabian whispered ragged endearments and feverishly kissed her cheek, her chin, her neck, and then her trembling mouth once more. Little sobs escaped her—cries of irrepressible longing—

Fabian's excitement was in every way equal to her own. The taste of her tears and the honeyeyed texture of her mouth sent desire raging through him. He wanted her so badly he was tempted to take her right there on the parlor floor. Thank goodness everything was getting resolved between them. Perhaps with just a few more words of reassurance, all would be perfect.

"Don't worry, darling," he whispered, nibbling at her ear. "I've decided to forgive you."

For a moment Missy was so lulled by the overpowering magic of Fabian's embrace that she didn't really hear his statement. In the next instant, his words became emblazoned across her brain.

I've decided to forgive you . . .

With a violent, infuriated cry, Missy shoved him away. "You've decided to forgive me?" she shrieked. *"You've decided to forgive me?"*

He gazed at her enraged countenance, his own utterly perplexed. "Why, yes, darling."

By now Missy was trembling so violently, her face was the color of a very ripe beet. "You've decided to forgive me? Why of all the arrogant, conceited, asinine and jackassy—"

"Jackassy?" he cut in incredulously.

She advanced on him, stabbing at his chest with her finger. "You, you great big overblown boor, have probably hiked the skirts of half the females in the Mississippi Delta, and yet you have the unmitigated gall to forgive *me?*"

"It is a man's due to have a chaste bride," Fabian put in pompously. "Furthermore, it is quite generous of me to accept as my bride a woman who is soiled goods."

"Soiled goods! Soiled goods!" she screamed. "How dare you call me soiled goods, you misbegotten son of Satan! Furthermore, you can take your damned generosity and stuff it! And you can take your self and—"

"Missy, what is going on here?" demanded her father's voice.

Missy was about to verbally propel Fabian to the nether regions when both her parents burst into the room. John and Lavinia stared, horrified, at the two people who had been bellowing at each other so loudly, the entire household could hear them.

Magnificent in her fury, Missy turned to her parents. "You two may as well hear this, as well. My marriage to this Neanderthal is off—finished, kaput!" She whirled on Fabian. "And as for you, Mr. Fabian Fontenot—you can go kiss the devil's butt, you boneheaded, conceited, male chauvinist pig!"

Missy heard her father's disbelieving expletive, her mother's stunned gasp. But her parents' reactions were soon forgotten as she watched Fabian advance on her like a raging bull, his features livid. He reached for her and she tried to cringe away, but it was too late—

Before Missy knew what was happening, Fabian grabbed her arm, hauled her over to the settee, threw her down across his lap, and began vigorously spanking her bottom, right there in the presence of her appalled parents.

Missy screamed her lungs out and fought like a wildcat, but it was useless. Fabian ignored the flailing of her hands and legs, holding her pinned in his lap with one hand while pounding her behind with the other. Given the many layers of her skirts, the damage was much more to her pride than to her person. Nonetheless, never in her twenty-five years had Missy been so humiliated. Indeed, never before had she been spanked.

When at last he let her up, she stood trembling in her rage before a white-faced Fabian.

Near-blinded by tears, she still managed to slap him hard across the face. "I hate your guts!" she screamed, turning and running out of the room.

Watching her leave, remembering the stricken look on her face, Fabian stood stunned. He could not believe what he'd just done, the fit of passion that had consumed him. Yet he had little time to wrestle with his own hellish conscience as Lavinia and John advanced on him angrily.

John was shaking in his outrage. "I tell you, young man, I'll not have you striking my daughter again! I don't give a damn what she called you. You touch a hair on her head again, and I swear, I'll call you out, my friendship with your grandparents notwithstanding."

Distraught, Fabian raked a hand through his hair. "You are right, sir, and I humbly apologize. I don't know what came over me. I suppose I lost my head when she called me a pig. But I promise you, sir, it will never happen again."

John glared at Fabian skeptically, prompting Lavinia to intervene. "John, darling, Fabian does seem abject. Like you, I don't agree with what he just did, but Missy did provoke him terribly. We were both certainly witnesses to that."

Fabian extended his hand to John. "Sir, will you accept my apology?"

John sighed and accepted the handshake. "Very well, son."

"Now the real question is, will Missy forgive you?" Lavinia added wisely.

"I know," Fabian concurred grimly. He turned to John. "Sir, I beg you, let me go upstairs and speak with her."

John was instantly irate. "Young man, that simply isn't done."

Again, Lavinia mediated. "Oh, John, let the boy go. They're going to be married, after all. It's obvious the two are deeply in love—"

"Obvious?" John queried ironically.

"Why, they're fighting like cats and dogs. What else could it be?" Lavinia replied stoutly. She turned to Fabian. "Go upstairs and speak to her."

Fabian bolted out of the room and hurried up the stairs, his heart pounding with terrible anxiety. He entered Missy's room without knocking. She lay sprawled across the bed, sobbing her heart out, and his own heart twisted with a mixture of tenderness and hellish guilt at the sight of her.

"Missy?" he queried gently.

She turned to him, her eyes burning with anger. "Drop dead!"

"Darling, we must talk," he pleaded.

"Hah! I have nothing to say to a man who does his talking with physical violence!"

"Physical violence?" he repeated in a stunned voice.

She jumped up from the bed. "Yes. You're nothing but a big, mean bully, Fabian Fontenot, getting your jollies by picking on someone smaller than you are!"

He gulped. "Missy . . . Darling, I'm so sorry—"

Yet she was heedless, advancing on him like an enraged lioness. "Do you know that if we were back in the twentieth century, you'd be locked up for what you just did?"

He appeared mystified. "Twentieth century? Locked up? Woman, what idiocy are you ranting?"

Yet Missy's fury was such that she threw caution to the winds. She began to pace, waving her arms and screaming out her frustrations to him. "You know, I wouldn't even be here at all, except that I got switched with your real fiancée, dear little Melissa Milquetoast, who probably suited you just fine, I presume!"

Fabian stared at her in utter amazement.

"Well, if you want her back, you can go the hell to the year 1992 and try to find her!" Missy continued spitefully. "I'm sure she's still perfectly chaste and virginal—unless Jeff has seduced her."

"Jeff? Who is this Jeff?" Fabian's voice was an appalled whisper.

"He's the man I was supposed to marry—in this very house—until that blasted, devious newel button screwed everything up. Oh, heaven help me, I've got to get out of here!"

"My God!" Fabian gasped as realization dawned. "I've driven you mad!"

"No kidding!" she snapped.

Fabian fell to his knees before her. "Darling, forgive me. I've acted like an utter ass. I apologize from the bottom of my soul. I . . . I love you, Missy."

Missy uttered an anguished cry and shook a fist at him. She hated him, and yet his words were tearing her apart! "Damn you, why did you have to go and say that!"

Now there were tears in his eyes, too. "Because it's true. I do love you, Missy. With all my heart."

"Don't you understand anything?" she ranted. "I don't want your apologies! I don't want your love! I want to go back to the twentieth century!" She fell to her knees beside him, sobbing abjectly. "Only I don't know how to get there!"

"Oh, angel. I'm so sorry."

Fabian pulled her into his arms and kissed her passionately. She sobbed into his mouth and kissed him back.

"Darling, it's all right," he murmured hoarsely, stroking her hair as she quivered and wept against him. "I promise you, we'll get everything straightened out. We'll recover your sanity—somehow—and I swear to you, I'll never touch you in anger again!"

"Oh, Fabian!"

Something snapped in Missy then. She illogically hated him, loved him, and burned with desire for him all in the same moment. She poured all her anguish, hurt, and need into the kiss they shared, desperately needing to bridge the chasm between them. He kissed her back ravenously, as if he would eat her up alive.

Within seconds, she was pulling the buttons to his trousers and tumbling him down on the floor on top of her. "I want you inside me," she panted. "Oh, God, please, now!"

With a tortured groan, he complied, reaching beneath her skirts to pull down her pantalets even as she freed his solid erection. "Missy, I love you," he whispered poignantly as he penetrated sure and deep.

Crying out in ecstasy, Missy coiled her legs tightly about his waist and whispered graphic encouragements in his ear.

Yet he paused and stared down into her mindless eyes. "First, tell me you forgive me—please, Missy."

His words brought fresh sobs welling. Never before had he said "please" to her. "I do," she whispered. "I forgive you."

"Tell me you love me," he added.

"I do."

"Say it."

"I love you, Fabian."

Her words were rewarded with an agonized moan and a hard, driving thrust. Missy arched into his splendid heat and clawed at his shoulders with her fingernails. The intimacy was glorious, shattering, riveting, making her cry out in rapture as her lips feverishly sought his.

Fabian's mouth took Missy's rapaciously, and he felt himself drowning in her, her hot tightness squeezing about him so exquisitely. Her little sobs of pleasure broke his control. Rising to his knees, he pulled her astride him and devoured her with powerful, deep strokes, glorying in her ragged pleas as he brought them both to a quick, explosive climax. His ecstasy was complete as he heard her cry out, then felt her melt in his arms.

He lowered her gently to the rug, pulled down the bodice of her gown, and kissed each of her tautened nipples in turn. Afterward, he stared into her languorous eyes and rubbed a finger across her passion-bruised lips. "I'd best go, darling, before your parents come to investigate again." He withdrew from her gently, righted their clothing, and afterward carried her to the bed. For a moment, he stared down at her with adoring eyes and stroked her cheek. The passion and love in his gaze were frightening in their intensity.

"I promise you, Missy, that from this day onward, I'll do everything in my power to atone for my sins and prove myself worthy of your love," he said fervently. Leaning over, he claimed her lips in one last, soul-rending kiss. "Oh, angel. I can't wait to hold you again. . . ."

After he left, Missy still sobbed. She drew a hand across her wondrously aching lower belly and felt as if her very heart had been ripped in two. She wanted to hold on to her convictions; she didn't want to love Fabian. But being in his arms just now had been so heavenly, his show of abject humility so sweet.

It was becoming harder and harder to resist his spell, and that scared her to death.

Chapter Thirty

The next morning Jeff left work for an early lunch and drove to Melissa's house. He felt horribly guilty for not being completely honest with her last night. Making love with her had been the most glorious experience of his entire life, but he'd been wrong to equivocate regarding her questions about birth control. His desperation to hold on to her—his gnawing fear that he would lose her, on or before May 15—was no excuse for his deceptive behavior.

At the Monroe house, one of the maids informed him that Melissa had just left with her friend, Lisa, and that the two women were supposed to meet Michelle and Jennifer at a local old folks' home. Jeff drove to the nearby home, parked, and went into the lobby. Joy filled his heart as he spotted the woman he loved standing in the corridor with her three friends, issuing orders with the efficiency of a majordomo.

"Jennifer," she was saying, handing the girl a leather-bound volume, "you may go read to Mrs. Dickson from *War and Peace*." As the girl dutifully trudged off with the book, Melissa turned to Michelle. "And Shelley, Mr. Taylor needs to dictate a letter to his daughter. As for you, Lisa—"

"Good morning, ladies," Jeff called, stepping up to join the two remaining woman.

Both Melissa and Lisa turned to him with smiles of pleasant surprise. "Why, good morning, Jeffrey," Melissa said. "What brings you here today? Do you have a friend or relative in the home?"

He leaned over to kiss her cheek, drinking in the feminine scent of her as he wrapped an arm about her waist. "No. You bring me here, of course, darling."

As Melissa flushed with pleasure, Lisa winked at Jeff and teased, "No lie, Dalton. You just can't keep your hot hands off my best friend, can you?"

"Lisa!" Mortified, Melissa scolded, "Didn't you promise Mrs. Ross a manicure?"

Lisa rolled her eyes. "Right, I can take a hint." She pointed a finger at Jeff. "Behave yourself, Romeo."

Laughing, Lisa strolled off.

"What was *that* about?" Jeff asked Melissa with a frown.

She sighed. "Could we talk outside for a moment?"

"Certainly, darling." As they headed out the door, Jeff laughed and added, "I can't believe you've got those three self-centered little debutantes volunteering here at the old folks' home."

Melissa was scandalized. "But, Jeffrey, my friends are not self-centered in the least. They

336

were delighted to help out—"

His hearty laugh cut her short. "They appeared about as delighted as orphans lining up for castor oil. They just can't face the prospect of disappointing you. For that matter, who can?"

Melissa was thoughtfully silent as they seated themselves on a bench in the courtyard. The morning air was fragrant with the perfume of roses; bees droned and a mourning dove cooed in the background.

"Well, Melissa?" Jeff asked. "Why the snide comments from Lisa?"

Her guilty gaze met his. "I'm afraid that when Lisa came over this morning she expressed a lot of curiosity about our—um—relationship. She wanted to know if we'd been . . ." Red-faced and wringing her hands, she rushed on, "Of course, I would never admit such a thing! But I'm afraid her questions made me blush, and then she guessed it all!"

Jeff groaned. "I'll strangle her."

"No, please don't," Melissa implored him. "She brought up some very good points about our—er—situation. She wanted to know if we'd—"

"Yes?" His voice was rising.

In a low, mortified voice, she confided, "If we'd practiced safe sex."

"I'll kill her!" Jeff lunged to his feet. Then, catching Melissa's bewildered expression, he took her hands and stared down at her earnestly. "Darling, I'm just mad at Lisa for being such a busybody. You must know I'd never expose you to anything—"

"But of course I do! I was simply relating what she said—"

"I know." He sighed. "The fact of the matter is,

I've only made love with one other woman in my entire life, and since both of us were virgins at the time, I don't think we need worry much on that account." He laughed ruefully. "Actually, the only thing you're not safe from is the nine-month virus."

"Oh, dear! Nine entire months of a virus?"

Chuckling, he sat down beside her and pressed the flat of his hand against her stomach. His eyes grew strangely glazed as he whispered, "Pregnancy, darling."

She blushed again, then smiled radiantly. "Oh. I see. Then that is one particular virus I do hope you'll give me one day."

"God, you're such an angel!" Unable to resist her for another second, Jeff pulled her into his arms and kissed her hungrily.

Afterward, he gently brushed a wisp of hair from her eyes. "Melissa, are you sure you're all right? I mean, after last night?"

She nodded as they moved apart. "I'm fine."

He coughed. "I have a confession to make."

She smiled quizzically. "A confession?"

"Yes." He drew a ragged breath. "You see, Lisa did raise some valid points. Last night, when I implied that there was no way to prevent—well, your becoming pregnant—I equivocated."

"Equivocated?" she repeated confusedly.

He gritted his teeth. "To hell with it! I lied."

Her eyes widened. "You lied? But why?"

He stared at her in anguish. "Because I love you so much I would have resorted to any trick to make you my wife and keep you here—including getting you pregnant."

Though her gaze was filled with sadness, her smile was sympathetic. "Oh, Jeffrey."

"I told myself it would be all to the good," he continued self-deprecatingly, "that I would save you from your self-destructive impulse of leaving me and returning to the past."

"Poor darling," she murmured.

He clutched her hand. "Are you terribly angry at me? Terribly disappointed?"

She shook her head. "No. Indeed, I understand your wanting to establish such a bond between us."

"I couldn't face losing you," he went on intensely. "But it was wrong of me to try to manipulate you that way. I'm just so crazy about you that I couldn't help myself."

"I know," she said, hugging him quickly. "It's done now, darling. You mustn't torture yourself about it."

"Will you marry me?"

She shook her head regretfully and stood. "I can't."

Jeff shot to his feet after her. "Why?"

A fatalistic look darkened her eyes. "When I returned to the house late last night I saw Missy's face again in the newel stone. She looked so terribly unhappy, and I know she was trying to communicate something to me."

"What?" Jeff asked tensely.

"I think we both know." She touched his sleeve. "She wants her life back."

"Melissa, no!" he cried. "Don't tell me you're still suffering from the delusion that you can switch places with her again?"

She sighed. "I think it's the only way, Jeff, and something tells me Missy will find a way for us to do this."

"Damn her!" Jeff cursed, hauling Melissa close.

"Why can't she leave well enough alone!"

"It's her life," Melissa said wretchedly.

"But what she wants could ruin *our* lives," he said passionately. "Don't you understand, people here need you? I need you, your friends need you, Charlotte and Howard need you! You've had a tremendous impact on all our lives, and none of us will ever be the same again without you!"

Her expression was anguished. "Then you'll all just have to hold my memory in your hearts, as I will treasure yours—always."

"And what is to become of all the good deeds you've done?" he pursued aggressively. "Who will persuade Shelley, Lisa, and Jennifer to volunteer at the old folks' home when you're no longer here to convince them? Who will see to it that Mrs. Dickson gets read to and Mrs. Ross gets her manicure?"

"My friends will still come—I know they will," she insisted through tears. "My legacy will live on."

"Legacy?" He caught her face in his hands and spoke fiercely. "And what if there is a child? What if you're pregnant right now?"

She bit her lip as tears threatened to spill over. "We'll have to cross that bridge when—and if— we come to it. In the meantime—"

"Yes?" He tenderly brushed away a tear with his thumb.

She gazed at him with love and anguish. "I don't think we should risk making love again."

He drew back. "I thought you said you wanted my child."

"I do. But I won't feel free to give myself to you again—not in that way—unless I'm allowed to stay here permanently."

He groaned. "Don't worry, I'll see to it you won't risk pregnancy again. Indeed, I've been thinking—"

"Yes?"

He regarded her solemnly. "I think it's time for you to see a doctor."

She paled. "A doctor? But I'm not ill!"

"Of course you're not, darling," he said with a smile.

"Will I have to get into one of those screaming, monster ambulances and be rushed off to the hospital for X rays?" she cried.

"No, nothing that drastic," he soothed. "All you'll have to do is to go to a doctor's office for an examination, a few routine tests and some shots—"

"Shots?"

He nodded firmly, though a terrible resignation shone in his eyes. "I've been thinking that I may have been rather negligent. What if you are somehow whisked back to your own time? A dozen diseases that are rare here could mean death for you there. We need to see to it that you're protected against measles, mumps, smallpox, and tetanus—that sort of thing."

"Ah—I see. You're speaking of the miracles of modern medical science?"

"Yes. I'd never forgive myself if you somehow went back to the 1850s and we hadn't given you every advantage possible. For all we know, there may not even be time for a complete schedule of immunizations, but we should at least make a beginning."

"I see." All at once, she felt unnerved by his words. "Jeff, the way you're talking, it's almost as if you're resigned to losing me, as if you know something I don't."

341

"Don't be silly," he said gruffly. "I simply want us to be careful regarding your health. Will you go to the doctor, Melissa? Do you think you're ready?"

"If you think it's best, then certainly I shall. Will you send me to Dr. Carnes?"

He mulled that over. "No, it's probably best that you see a doctor who never treated Missy. My mother knows a good man." He pulled her close. "And you can also ask him about birth control."

She smiled shyly. "Very well, Jeff."

He began kissing the contour of her jaw. "For you see, my sweet darling, for every day that we are together, we will make love. I think I'd die if we don't. And furthermore, I won't let you leave me! Do you hear me? I won't!"

Melissa nodded, her eyes welling with tears as Jeff's mouth came down possessively on hers. She now knew in her soul that she must leave him, even though it was tearing her apart. But when the time came, she must be sure not to tell him, for he would surely try to stop her.

Jeff's thoughts were equally tortured as he kissed Melissa with all his being. He would give his very life to keep her here with him, and yet, for her own good, here he was, having to prepare for the possibility of losing her.

Chapter Thirty-one

Missy was styling her hair the following morning when Dulcie swept in bearing a huge bouquet of roses. The servant beamed as she set the arrangement in front of Missy on the dressing table.

"Look what Mr. Fontenot just sent over," Dulcie said.

Trying to swallow the lump of emotion in her throat, Missy glanced miserably at the luscious blooms. There were deep reds, delicate pinks, and pale yellows, their mingled fragrances tantalizing. The flowers were an all too painful reminder to Missy of her devastating surrender to Fabian yesterday, mere minutes after their disgraceful scene downstairs. She'd made herself totally vulnerable to the very man she considered her worst enemy, and since then, every atom of her independent nature had rebelled against his domination—and against the frightening love she felt for him.

Steeling herself against her own traitorous feelings, she lurched to her feet. "I don't want these," she said tersely to Dulcie. "Why don't you just go dump them on the compost heap or something?"

Dulcie's expression was crestfallen. "But, miss, throwing away such beautiful flowers is downright sinful."

"Then you take them!" Catching Dulcie's bewildered expression and feeling a hard twinge of guilt, she quickly desisted. "Oh, never mind."

"Yes 'um."

Missy watched Dulcie walk over to make the bed. Eager to distract herself from her unsettling thoughts, she remarked, "By the way, I spoke with my father the other night about freeing you and the other slaves—but I'm afraid I didn't get very far."

Dulcie laughed. "Miss, please. Not that freedom talk again."

"I tell you, I won't rest as long as you're kept in bondage."

"Bondage?" Dulcie repeated, her expression bewildered.

Missy scowled. "How are you at painting placards?"

Dulcie was too mystified to reply.

"You just hide and watch," Missy went on with determination. "I'll get together everything that we'll need, then you'll see. We've put up with this nonsense long enough. It's high time to blast Dad out of his smug complacency."

"Yes 'um," Dulcie mumbled.

Missy wandered over to the dressing table, where she found herself treasonously inhaling the scent of Fabian's roses, even touching a velvety bloom.

"Damn it," she cursed under her breath. "Don't you dare be nice to me, Fabian Fontenot!"

An hour later, Lavinia swept inside Missy's room, wearing a huge smile and carrying an ornate tin. "Look what Fabian just sent over for you!"

"Not another present!" Missy snapped moodily.

"Why, Missy, I'm shocked at you," Lavinia scolded. "Whyever would you protest such lovely gifts?" She deposited the tin in her daughter's hands. "You've got Fabian behaving like a prince. I swear, that boy must be utterly smitten with you."

"Who cares?" Missy managed sourly, then couldn't resist opening the tin.

"Bon-bons!" Lavinia cried, clapping her hands.

"Chocolates," Missy added dismally. Unfortunately, she adored chocolates! Struggling not to succumb to temptation, she extended the tin to her mother. "Here, Mom, have one. They make my face break out."

Lavinia picked up a morsel, popped it into her mouth and made an ecstatic sound. "Manna from heaven!"

Missy groaned and popped one in her own mouth. "So, okay, they're good."

Lavinia touched her arm. "I do hope you've forgiven Fabian for his impetuosity yesterday. John and I so want to see the two of you married—and producing grandchildren with as much dispatch as possible. For years, your father and I had hoped to be blessed again. Now it appears that we must count on you and Fabian to bring a baby into our lives once more."

"Don't hold your breath," Missy muttered, although the pit of her stomach twisted with nervousness and an appalling sexual heat as she realized that she could be pregnant even now. Leaving Fabian would be one thing, but could she take his child away from him?

Oh, Lord, what was she going to do? One thing was for damn sure—she'd best not let Fabian Fontenot seduce her again! She resolved this vehemently as she devoured her fourth chocolate.

Lavinia smiled wisely as she slipped from the room.

An hour later, a box full of luscious silk scarves arrived.

An hour after that, a bottle of expensive French perfume and a pearl necklace were delivered.

At luncheon time, the amorous suitor himself appeared.

Missy stormed down to the parlor to confront Fabian. Steeling herself against the devastating feelings inundating her at the sight of the gorgeous man standing across from her, she snapped, "Fabian, I want you to stop sending me presents!"

He only grinned. "Quit plying you with gifts? But how can I do that, my sweet darling, when I'm determined to win your favor?"

"Well, you're wasting your time—and your money," she blustered. "It's not going to work!"

He chuckled, crossing the room and kissing her cheek. Cupping her chin, he tilted her face until her tempestuous gaze met his. "My, aren't we touchy today? Obviously, you've been cooped up in the house for too long. Let's go for a picnic."

"A picnic?" This was the very last thing she'd ever expected Fabian Fontenot to suggest!

"Why, of course. What better atmosphere for courting fair maidens?"

She shook a finger at the exasperating devil. "Fabian, don't you dare—"

Flashing her a dazzling smile, he cut in smoothly. "The cook packed me a truly tempting luncheon—ham, potato salad, biscuits, a cherry cobbler—"

While Missy's mouth was watering, she managed a weak, "Fabian, no, I can't—"

Yet her protests were useless as Fabian gently but firmly tugged her from the room and out the front door.

"Damn it, Fabian, are you a certified idiot?" she demanded as he led her down the front steps.

"A lovely day, isn't it, my darling?" he asked gallantly, deliberately ignoring her burst of temper and her struggles as he pulled her toward his barouche. "Ah, the brisk coolness of spring, the scent of nectar in the air . . . how very romantic."

Missy gritted her teeth. "I think you're losing it, buster."

He chuckled. "What quaint, enchanting things you say."

"Fabian, will you please just go home and leave me alone?"

"But how can I woo you and win you, my darling, if I leave you?" he countered patiently.

At his barouche, he easily lifted the protesting female onto the seat. He reached up to touch her bare neck. "You aren't wearing the pearls," he scolded with a wounded expression.

Missy made a strangled sound and tried unsuccessfully to fight the shiver of longing that swept her at his exciting touch. "That's another thing—all those gifts!"

"You did not like them, my love? I'll send others."

"Don't you dare!" she protested. "It's bad enough to be inundated with flowers—and silk scarves—"

"Ah, yes." He winked devilishly. "I could always use the silk scarves to tie you to my bed, couldn't I?"

Missy made another tortured sound as he circled around the conveyance and got in beside her. Damn him, she thought, why did he have to act so masterfully charming? She'd always been a sucker for charm.

Nonetheless, as he reached for the reins, she lit into him with all the bravado she could muster. "I know what you're trying to do, Fabian Fontenot, and it's not going to work, do you hear me? Flowers give me a headache, silk scarves aren't my particular kink, thank you, and as for chocolates, they not only make my face break out, they make me fat."

Yet Missy was stopped in mid-sentence as Fabian pulled her against him. "Enough, Missy."

"Don't you dare tell me enough, you big—"

"You're not going to make me stop loving you," he said firmly.

"What?" she cried.

His determined gaze seemed to impale her. "You can rant like a harridan, you can eat until you become fat and your face breaks out, but you're never—*ever*—going to make me stop loving you or trying to convince you to become my wife."

"Damn it, Fabian!" By now, her senses and her resolve were practically in tatters.

"Why don't you just give in?" he went on with an easy grin as he turned to snap the reins. "You're going to lose, you know."

Ever defiant, she retorted, "I'm not! And you're not going to seduce me again!"

"Oh, I'm not? Isn't it odd, my love, that you are the one to bring up the subject of seduction? Can't you at least wait until we're safely away from the house?"

Fabian's insufferable comments reduced Missy to red-faced silence.

As he drove them down a shady dirt road, Missy's earlier fears returned to nag her. What if she were indeed stuck here with Fabian Fontenot permanently? What if she were already carrying his child?

"Fabian, what are your goals in life?" she abruptly asked.

He turned to stare at her in amazement. "Goals?"

"What do you like to do?" Watching him grin lecherously, she hastily added, "Besides that."

He pondered her question a moment. "I enjoy hunting, fishing, a good bottle of sour mash . . ." He wiggled his eyebrows. "Courting fair maidens . . ."

She uttered an exasperated groan. "That's not what I mean at all! You're talking about leisure activities. What I want to know is, what are your career objectives?"

"Career objectives? I've never heard of such a silly expression."

"Why?" she demanded.

"Why? Because why should one have long-term goals, when the next yellow fever epidemic could come along and sweep us all away into the afterlife?"

"Not if you get rid of the mosquitoes, it won't," she argued.

"Mosquitoes?" He laughed. "What possible bearing could those little pests have on the epidemics?"

Missy spoke through gritted teeth. "As I've already told you and your laughable Board of Health, mosquitoes carry yellow fever!"

"Absurd," he scoffed.

"Oh, you're hopeless!"

"Hopelessly in love?" he teased. "Ah, yes, there I must agree. Now, if you'll just agree to marry me—"

She set her arms akimbo and stared ahead moodily. "I refuse to marry a man without goals."

"Have you forgotten that I raise cotton?" he queried.

She rolled her eyes. "Your slaves raise cotton, and I'm sure you have a reliable overseer to run the plantation. So raising cotton doesn't count."

He shrugged and snapped the reins.

He drove them to a forested area with a grassy clearing that looked perfect for picnicking. As Fabian helped her out of the barouche, Missy couldn't help but feel enchanted by the dappled scene and the many vibrant, blooming wildflowers. A nearby stream rushed with clear, clean water, the sound soothing to her ears. While she went to fill their tin cups, Fabian spread out a blanket on the ground and set out their food.

Sitting on the ground next to Fabian, Missy devoured the luscious meal. Fabian chuckled at her voracious appetite and occasionally fed her a grape or a few strawberries. When his fingertips lingered on her mouth several times, she practically came unglued.

Missy was quickly becoming a nervous wreck. It was impossible being alone with Fabian this way, knowing there was nothing to save her from her own shameless lusts, to stop her from ripping his clothes off. If anything, their earlier fights had only added to the sexual tension.

Covetously, she eyed him sitting next to her. He'd removed his hat, coat, and cravat, and he looked so sinfully gorgeous, with his trousers pulling at his muscular legs and his white shirt partially unbuttoned, revealing the crisp, sexy hair on his chest. The way the wind ruffled his thick, dark-brown hair, the way the light outlined the sensual shadow of whiskers along his jaw, was enough to drive her mad with desire, especially as she remembered him thrusting into her so exquisitely only yesterday. When she spotted him licking his lips, she wanted to lick them for him. When his perfect white teeth nibbled at a strawberry, all she could think of was having those wonderful teeth nibbling at her breast again.

Good grief! What was wrong with her? What had happened to her resolve, her self-control?

As they were eating their cherry cobbler, Fabian said casually, "Tell me about this Jeff you were ranting about yesterday."

"What about him?" Missy asked, instantly suspicious.

Fabian's boot reached out to toy with her slipper. "Was he the one you were intimate with?"

Missy uttered an infuriated cry and set aside her plate. "You're such a jerk, Fontenot."

He smiled. "Am I?"

She tossed her curls and stared at him in defiance. "It's just killing you that you weren't my first, isn't it?"

He shocked her then by pushing her down onto the ground and covering her with his strong body.

A near-frightening intensity glittered in his dark eyes. "I'll tell you something, my sweet darling— I'm going to be your last."

The words were electrifyingly sensual for Missy, especially as she lay pinned beneath him, crushed by his hard heat, inundated by his wonderful scent. Indeed, staring up into his dark, determined eyes, she felt far too inclined to believe him. She could hardly even hear his words over the mad beating of her heart.

"You still haven't told me about Jeff," he continued patiently.

She was silent a moment, attempting a glower. Should she tell him the truth about everything— about Jeff, the family, and the century she'd left behind? But if she did, Fabian would surely think her mad—just as he had yesterday. Still, there might be some benefit to his thinking she was crazy. She must give this subject additional thought.

"Well, Missy?" he nudged. "Did you love him?"

"No!" she hurled at him.

"Were you intimate?"

"Jeff and I were never intimate," she retorted. "There, are you satisfied, Mr. Busybody?"

"Then who . . . ?"

"Took my virginity?" she supplied waspishly. "Damn it, Fabian, it was a long time ago, it was meaningless, and it *is* none of your business! Now will you get off me, you big bully?"

He merely smiled and said, "No."

"And why not?"

He leaned over to nibble on the tip of her nose. "Because I need you so desperately, my darling."

A strangled sound died in her throat as he kissed her. Oh, God, she thought sinkingly, why'd he have to say such endearing things? He was being far too patient, too sexy, and too damned clever. She hadn't even been able to provoke his usual, hair-trigger temper!

"So sweet," he murmured into her mouth. "Sweet as cherries . . . I must have more."

Missy was drowning in his kiss, fighting to hold on to her convictions. "Please—I don't want—I don't need you," she managed weakly, trying to shove him away.

He pressed a hand to his heart and feigned a wounded air. "Princess, you slay me."

Feeling far too vulnerable to him, she used anger to shore up her weakening defenses. "About time. Why do you insist we keep on dating, anyway? You don't even like me—"

He smiled. "Oh, there are things about you that I like."

"Yeah, and they're all to be found from my neck down."

He chuckled. "But that's not true, darling." Leaning closer, he whispered, "You have the most incredible . . . mouth."

"See what I mean?" she cried. "You'd never say I have an incredible mind!"

"But it's not your mind that I want to kiss," he murmured, proceeded to demonstrate at his leisure.

"There, you did it again!" she cried afterward in a quivering voice that betrayed her growing excitement. "You're such a typical man!"

He touched her right breast, smiling when he felt the tautness of her nipple even through the layers of her clothing. Their gazes locked—both fervid and searching.

"And you're not a typical woman?" he murmured.

"Tell me why you need me!" she demanded.

He smiled and began to smooth down her mussed hair. "I need your strong spirit and brave heart. I need your pride and your passion. I need you in my bed—"

"Another sentiment spoken straight from the bottom of your gonads!"

Still, she was unable to provoke him! "But darling," he coaxed, roving his tongue over her chin, making her break out in shivers, "you're such a gorgeous, gloriously wanton creature, so sensuous and so very desirable . . ."

Missy groaned. "What are you doing now?"

"Seducing you," he replied wickedly, lifting her skirts and touching her boldly.

She gasped.

"Why don't you say no, Missy?" he teased remorselessly. "Is it because you can't? Is it because you need me, too?"

"Yes!" she cried.

"Is it because you want me as much as I want you?"

"Yes!" she half-sobbed.

He kissed her ravenously, grinding his aroused loins into her pelvis. She kissed him back so passionately that tears sprang to her eyes.

"Fabian, please don't," she begged desperately. "You're going to get me pregnant."

"I want you pregnant," he whispered intensely, kissing her damp cheek. "I want to get you with my child right this minute, so you can never escape me."

His words were arousing her to a fever pitch, yet still she protested. "Please, don't you have anything you can use in this benighted century? A condom or something?"

He pulled back and glared down at her, at last magnificent in his fury. "Where did you learn of such indelicate matters, woman? In a brothel?"

"Yes!" she declared, half-frantic to dissuade him. "I'm a closet whore."

But he only laughed. "You're no whore, my love. You may have succumbed to a momentary indiscretion in the past, for which I've already forgiven you—"

"Damn you, Fabian!"

"But you're no whore. Indeed, you never knew true pleasure until you found it in my arms for the first time the other night."

She turned away with a cry of anguish.

He grabbed her face. "Well, Missy? Do you deny it?"

"You know I can't!" she cried.

"And do you want to feel that way again?"

"You know I do!"

His hands were beneath her skirts again. Her fingers were ripping at the buttons of his shirt, her lips kissing the hair-roughened texture of his chest.

He spoke vehemently. "I'm going to love you— and make love to you—until you're pregnant, until you promise you'll marry me—until you love me in return—"

"I do love you!"

"I know, darling. And I'm going to keep on doing this until you say you're mine!"

Chapter Thirty-two

A few nights later, Melissa and Jeff stopped off at his apartment after attending a benefit dinner sponsored by the Junior League. She wore a pale blue, glittery cocktail gown with a slit up one leg; he wore a tuxedo. They were dancing about his living room to the strains of Phil Collins on the stereo.

"I can't believe I'm here with you in your apartment," she murmured dreamily. "In my day and age, this would have been considered highly improper."

"I'm liberating you, darling," he teased.

"Liberating?" she repeated.

"Within certain boundaries, of course. As long as you're one hundred percent, positively mine, you can be just as liberated as you please."

"Why, that does sound delightful," she said.

"Tonight was fun, wasn't it?" he added as they glided about.

"Oh, yes. It is always enjoyable to know that one is benefiting mankind."

He drew back slightly, admiring her in the low-necked dress. "You have no idea how you've benefited *this* member of mankind by wearing that sexy little number."

She glanced downward confusedly. "Is there a number somewhere on this frock?"

He chuckled and kissed the tip of her nose. "I'm talking about your dress, silly—and especially about every delightful curve you've poured into it."

She blushed becomingly. "I'm glad I've pleased you, Mr. Dalton."

He winked. "Next, I'm getting you into a bikini."

"The bikini again. Is this more of the liberation process?"

"Within the prescribed limits."

"My, but you're a determined man."

His expression suddenly grew serious. "Where you're concerned, darling, my determination knows no bounds. First we'll get you in the pool and teach you how to swim, and then I'll teach you how to drive."

She feigned indignation. "But if I learn to drive, then my chauffeur, Mr. Duke, will be without a job."

"If I know you, you'll learn to drive just so you can chauffeur him around."

"I suppose it would be only fair for me to drive once in a while," Melissa mused with a thoughtful frown.

"You're becoming more accustomed to the technology of this age, aren't you?" he asked.

She nodded. "I'm not nearly as frightened as

I used to be. And I must admit this age has its conveniences."

"I intend to spoil you so thoroughly with those conveniences that you'll never leave me." Pulling her closer, he added, "Speaking of modern miracles, how did it go at the doctor's office the other day?"

Melissa cleared her throat in acute discomfort. "Well, it was most embarrassing, to say the very least, but then, I suppose a woman must become accustomed to such matters."

"Did you begin your shots?"

"Ah, yes. I told the doctor just what you'd suggested, that all my life, I'd had this—er—path—"

"Pathological."

"Yes. That all my life, I'd had this pathological fear of needles."

"Did he buy it?"

"Did he buy what?" she asked, perplexed.

Jeff chuckled. "Did he believe your story?"

"Oh. Well, to say that he was horrified would be a gross understatement. He delivered the most impassioned lecture, demanding to know how on earth my parents could have been so irresponsible, and how I'd been allowed to get through school without being immunized—for which I had no suitable explanation, of course. At any rate, my argument seemed to be borne out when I swooned during my first inoculation—"

"Oh, no!"

"Oh, it is all right," she said earnestly. "The nurse informed me that many people faint at the sight of needles. Miss Foster was also telling me that Dr. Murchison volunteers one afternoon a week at the free clinic. Indeed, they need some help there answering phones and doing filing, so of course I offered my services."

He buried his face in her hair and spoke intensely. "Of course you did. You're such a darling. You've made your mark here—you've changed lives. Where would we all be without you?"

She was silent, mulling over his words and feeling an aching sadness at the impermanence of her life here, at the forces that could at any time pull her and Jeff apart. As much as she felt bound by honor and duty to the past, she couldn't bear the thought of breaking his heart.

As if summoned by her own turbulent thoughts, the song *Against All Odds* began to spill out over the speakers. She listened to the poignant lyrics for a moment, then murmured, "I like this Mr. Collins on the hi-fi."

"Stereo," he corrected with a grin.

"Ah, stereo. There is something very romantic, and also rather sad, about his music. And I so enjoyed the other night, when we listened to the blues over on Beale Street."

"We'll go there again soon."

"I would very much enjoy that."

"Good. I want you thoroughly addicted to this century."

They continued to dance for a few more moments as the song played out. Jeff held her close and whispered passionately, "That song hits home far too much. It describes just how I'd feel if I lost you."

"I know, Jeffrey, and I'd feel the same way." A shadow crossed her eyes. "Nevertheless, we simply don't know how much time we have left together. Even if Missy should decide to stay in the past, how can I know for certain that my existence here will be permanent? We may be dealing with forces more powerful than either of us!"

"We're dealing with love!" he cried fiercely. "How can you think that our love won't be stronger than anything else? How can you think that there won't be a way for us? You belong with me, and I won't let Fontenot have you! By God, I won't!"

He swept her through his bedroom door, caught her hard against him, and kissed her urgently. She kissed him back, glorying in the scent and taste of him, even as bittersweet tears clogged her throat at the thought of losing him.

"Did you ask the doctor about birth control?" he asked hoarsely.

While embarrassed, she answered forthrightly. "Yes. As a matter of fact, the devise is in my purse even now. I mentioned to him our—er—indiscretion, and he said that, while we can't be certain for a few more days, the timing most likely was not right for pregnancy."

"I'm glad," he murmured, nibbling at her neck. "Not that I don't want a child with you quite badly, but it was wrong of me to try to force the issue."

"I understand, darling."

"I want to make love with you, Melissa," he went on intensely. "Spend the night with me so I can love you every minute."

Even as excitement stormed her senses at his words, her eyes grew huge. "But I can't! Mother and Father would be scandalized!"

"No, they won't. Just call them and tell them you'll be very late, and not to wait up for you." He caught her face in his hands. "Darling, don't you trust me?"

"Oh, yes," she whispered fervently.

"Don't you want to make love with me?"

"With all my heart."

He smiled and handed her the phone. "Do you need help dialing?"

She smiled back. "No. Father's been giving me lessons."

"Good for him."

"And besides, I must become adjusted to these devices if I'm going to help out at the free clinic, mustn't I?"

"Right."

While Melissa made her call, Jeff went to the living room, returning momentarily with her purse. He handed her her small beaded bag as she set down the receiver. "Well?"

She smiled crookedly. "Mother said to take our time."

He grinned. "Turn around." As she complied, he unzipped her dress and kissed her bare shoulder. Smiling at her soft gasp, at the sight of the gooseflesh breaking out on her lovely nape and shoulders, he said in a sexy rumble, "Now, I think you'd best duck into the bathroom, darling, before I throw caution to the winds."

"Ah, yes." She started off with her bag, then hesitated.

"Melissa?" he asked.

She turned to him, biting her lip. "Is this a long-term, monogamous relationship, Jeffrey?"

He laughed. "What on earth brought on *that* question?"

She blushed vividly. "Well, the doctor said that this particular device can only be used in a long-term, monogamous er . . . Is it?"

He winked at her. "You bet your sweet bottom it is."

Smiling radiantly, she dashed off. As Jeff began

undressing, he felt so filled with love for her that his throat ached.

When Melissa returned, wearing just her half slip and strapless bra, she spotted Jeff waiting for her beneath the covers, bare-chested and looking very sexy. His gaze seemed riveted on her as she climbed in beside him. Then her bottom contacted something hard; she pulled out the remote control and stared at it confusedly.

"Sorry, darling," he said sheepishly. "Too many late nights alone, with just me and the TV, I guess."

She grinned wickedly and handed him the device. "I think we'd best put this away in a safe place, Jeffrey. I don't want to cancel, stop, or eject you."

"Just try it, lady!" Jeff howled with laughter, took the remote control, and placed it on the nightstand. He kissed her thoroughly and began unsnapping her bra.

"I was wondering Jeffrey," she murmured breathlessly as he kissed her breasts.

"Yes?" His voice was very husky.

She stroked his muscular arms. "Well . . . while I was in the bathroom I noticed that you have a whirlpool. Every time I try to use the one at home, it shoots geysers at me."

He chuckled. "How can I help, darling?"

"Well . . . can you show me how it works?"

She was rewarded by a fierce kiss that ground their teeth together. "Can I ever!"

Chapter Thirty-three

"Now, everyone, come to attention."

Late Saturday afternoon, Missy stood at one end of the carriage house with a sober-faced Dulcie beside her. Her podium was a small, scarred desk; across it were laid several placards she had stayed up late last night to finish lettering.

In front of Missy, down the long center aisle between the many conveyances, sat most of the plantation's Negroes. Arrayed in a variety of coarse cottonades, the fifty or so men, women, and children huddled together on the floor and listened to Missy in wary silence. Even Missy's call to attention had been absurdly unnecessary, since the mood in the large shed was so morose and somber that a scurrying mouse would have sounded like a cattle stampede.

Missy was aware that the slaves had come here very reluctantly, after she had sent Dulcie over to the "Street" to announce the meeting. However, ever since her recent frustrating argument with her father, Missy had resolved to do something about the unjust institution of slavery here on the plantation. She had been patient with John Montgomery long enough; it was time for action.

Staring at the sea of somber faces stretching before her, she cleared her throat and began her prepared speech. "I've come here today to tell you that it is time that you all take charge of your own lives."

Silence.

She braved on. "I've come to tell you that the institution of slavery is wrong, and since my father will not see reason on the subject, I'm here to encourage you to take matters into your own hands."

Silence again.

"You have no rights as human beings," Missy went on passionately. "You are ordered about, with no choices whatsoever regarding your own destinies. Your children are not taught to read or write, you are not allowed to leave the plantation or even marry without my father's consent. I say that you have tolerated this unacceptable situation long enough, and it is high time that you put an end to this evil."

As many of the slaves exchanged glances of fear or confusion, an older man with silvery hair got to his feet. "Just what are you suggesting, mistress?" he asked.

She coughed nervously. "I'm suggesting that you protest this inhumane system, that you go on strike and demonstrate."

"Demonstrate?" he asked, even as shocked murmurings drifted through the crowd.

"Yes. You must all refuse to work, and carry signs such as the ones I've prepared." She nodded to Dulcie, who hesitantly lifted one of the placards. "There," Missy finished triumphantly, "you must all make more of these."

"But how can we make more signs, mistress," the man asked patiently, "when most of these people can't read or write and don't even know what the signs say?"

"Oh, I'm sorry," Missy muttered, feeling like a complete idiot. She pointed toward Dulcie's placard. "This one says 'Freedom Now' . . ." She grabbed another sign and raised it. "And this one says 'Human Bondage Is Evil.'"

As horrified gasps filtered through the crowd, the elderly spokesman said sternly, "Mistress, do you realize that we could all be whipped or thrown in jail for plotting an insurrection?"

Missy paled to the roots of her hair and hastily dropped her placard. "Oh, I hadn't thought—"

"Missy, what on earth is going on here?" came an outraged male voice.

As the captive audience turned in horror, John Montgomery stormed in through the back door, his features livid as he carefully wended his way through the seated slaves to his daughter's side. "What do you think you are you doing, daughter?" he asked in a furious undertone, glancing flabbergasted from the placards to the slaves, and then back at Missy.

Missy drew herself up and faced her father defiantly. "I'm informing these human beings of their rights."

"What rights?"

"That's just my point!" she declared. "These people have no rights, thanks to you, and I'd say it's high time they demanded their due."

Clenching his jaw, John turned to the assemblage. "Isaac," he said, addressing the spokesman with surprising gentleness, "I apologize to you and the others for my daughter's rash actions. You may all leave."

Murmuring to one another and shaking their heads, the slaves got to their feet and dutifully trooped out.

John turned to Dulcie. "You may go, too, thank you."

"Yessir." Hastily placing her placard on the desk, Dulcie scurried off.

As soon as Dulcie was out of earshot, John shook his finger at Missy. "Young lady, I have just witnessed the most appalling, treasonous . . . ! By damn, when will you remember your place?"

"Don't start in on my place, Dad," Missy snapped back. She heaved a frustrated sigh. "Besides, I fully realize I just made a complete ass of myself."

"You do?" For once, John appeared at a loss. But he recovered quickly, demanding, "And do you realize that you were toying recklessly with the lives of these people by inciting them to insurrection?"

"Yes! And can you honestly say you don't toy recklessly with their lives every day?"

Taken aback, he blustered, "Well, I—"

"As a matter of fact, I'm delighted to get straight to the heart of this problem." She balled her hands on her hips and continued furiously. "Yes, I was a presumptuous idiot to think that the slaves could change things themselves. The truth is, they have no say over their own lives because you've seen to it that they're powerless! The real villain here is you!"

"Now I'm the villain?" he cried, flinging a hand

to his breast. "I've told you, I treat the slaves well—"

"Do you? Tell me—who was that older man who spoke for them?"

An expression of regret crossed John's eyes. "Why, that was Isaac."

"He spoke so eloquently," Missy said. "How did he come to be so well-educated?"

John sighed, flashing his daughter a sheepish glance. "Actually, Isaac and I grew up together. We were childhood playmates, and the tutor taught us both how to read and write. Eventually, of course, we came to a parting of the ways—"

"And now you're the master and he's the slave?" Missy cried. "Don't you see how wrong that is?"

John drew a heavy breath. "Is it right of you to make these people yearn for something that can never be?"

"If that's true, then it's entirely your fault, Dad. You don't have to keep them in bondage."

"Why is this so important to you?" he cried exasperatedly. "You never cared before—"

"I'm a different person now," she asserted. "And you'll have to accept all of me—even the parts of me that you may not like or agree with."

John removed his hat and drew a hand through his thinning gray hair. "My dear, slavery is our system of labor here in the South—"

"That doesn't make it right. Furthermore . . ." Missy's voice broke as she finished, "I can't be your daughter anymore if you continue to have slaves here on the plantation."

"What?" he cried, his expression crestfallen. "How can you quit being my daughter?"

"I mean it, Dad. Either you remedy this situation or you're fired." She thrust a placard into his hands and stormed out of the carriage house.

John's expression was utterly mystified as he watched his daughter leave, then stared down at the placard. He read the message, "End Slavery Today," and gulped.

Outside the carriage house, Missy paused next to an oak tree, leaning against the rough bark for support. She realized she was trembling and perilously close to tears. What was happening to her? Until just a few weeks ago, she had never in her life cared about anything or anyone except herself. Now, she was starting to care about *everything*—about Dulcie and her other new friends, about her family and Fabian, about what was right and what was wrong here in this new world where she'd found herself.

Fabian . . . Oh, God, what had he done to her? He had melted something in her, made her vulnerable, made her open up her heart to the needs of the others around her. Even as she'd lit into her father just now, even with right on her side, she'd felt guilty for the pain and confusion she'd caused him. Of course, it hadn't been his fault, since he knew no better; still, she considered it her bounden duty to educate him and see that he did the right thing.

Why? Who had appointed her the ultimate moral authority here? How had she become so caught up in the fabric of the world surrounding her? Love had taken root in her heart, and now those very roots bound her to this new life.

She was losing herself.

Or was she finding herself?

That was the most terrifying question of all.

* * *

"Oh, my, look at all these books," Melissa cried.

Melissa was with her friend Shelley's mother, Lucy French. Lucy was the head librarian at one of the Memphis branch libraries, and the two women were walking through the stacks together.

"It was so good of you to volunteer to help us today, Melissa," Lucy said.

"To shelve a few books?" Melissa replied. "Oh, it's nothing. Besides, when I overheard you telling Shelley that you are currently short on volunteers, how could I not offer to help?"

Lucy smiled. "You are a fine and generous young woman." She laughed. "Shelley wouldn't be caught dead helping us out."

"Oh, she'll be here on Tuesday afternoon, along with Lisa and Jennifer," Melissa put in firmly.

At first, Lucy was too stunned to reply. Then, as they moved into a new area of shelves, she nodded and said, "This is our fiction section here."

"Ah, yes. This is where you said the books are arranged alphabetically, by the last name of the author?"

Lucy beamed. "Why yes. You catch on so quickly! Do you have much library experience, dear?"

Glancing around, Melissa muttered, "Oh, not for a hundred and forty years or so. . . ."

Looking perplexed, Lucy asked, "I beg your pardon?"

Melissa quickly smiled. "I'm sorry, I was talking to myself. Actually, I've pretty much exhausted my parents' library at home, so I'm quite thrilled to be here."

"Wonderful. Tell you what—we'll have you shelving fiction today, and then next week I'll acquaint you more with the rest of our stacks and our classification system."

"Splendid."

At the edge of the fiction stacks, the two women paused next to a cart full of books parked on one side of an open doorway. "Well, dear, you can begin with these volumes right here," Lucy said.

Melissa, meanwhile, was gazing through the doorway at a small, cluttered room with many ancient-looking volumes. "What is in there, if I may ask?"

"Oh, that's our local history room."

Melissa was instantly all attention. "Local history?"

"Yes. Actually, much of what we have here is genealogical studies of some of the families who lived in Memphis during the nineteenth century."

Melissa paled. "Oh, my goodness!" she cried, gazing raptly into the room. "I had no idea such extensive records were kept! Could I find information about *any* Memphis family in those records?"

Lucy frowned. "I'm afraid records were not kept on every family. But I'd venture to say we have at least some information on most of the prominent families."

"Do you have anything on the family who built the house where I live—the John Montgomerys?"

Lucy mulled over that, then shook her head. "I'm pretty familiar with the material, and that name doesn't ring a bell. However, while we may not have a specific history on the John Montgomerys, you still might be able to gather some incidental information through reading other sources." She smiled. "If you're interested, dear, you're welcome to come back and spend all the time you want."

"Thank you, Mrs. French." Melissa nodded decisively and picked up an armload of titles. Starting off for the stacks, she called over her shoulder, "I'll be back first thing on Monday."

Chapter Thirty-four

As Missy sat with Fabian at the Presbyterian church on Sunday, she wore his pearls. Despite her stylish, sedate veneer—her feathered hat and new spring frock—inside she was feeling far from serene.

Fabian, seated next to her, had the countenance of an angel; from simply looking at him, one would never guess the passionate things he did to her each night. She realized with a sinking feeling that she wasn't just madly in love with him, she was *in lust* with him, up to her eyeballs. Indeed, she did the equivalent of lust's death spiral every time she remembered him kissing her and driving into her with such sweet violence. To make matters worse, he treated her with a devastating charm that melted her heart—and her clothes. Just last night, he'd seduced her again in the little guest house at the plantation, the one she now laughingly referred to as the "gargoyle."

Every day, it became harder and harder for her to resist his magnetic spell. The way things were going, she would soon end up married and pregnant—and not necessarily in that order! Every time she tried to lecture the maddening devil on birth control, he merely laughed and began tossing up her skirts. Her resolutions quickly went the way of her underclothes—discarded somewhere in the netherworld. All her instincts told her that if she were to escape him—and to escape being trapped permanently in the year 1852—she had to act quickly!

But what could she do? She had no real idea how to travel back to the future again. She still occasionally saw glimpses of Cousin Melissa's face in the newel button, and she always tried to communicate that she wanted her life back. Lately, she'd seen a sadness in her cousin's eyes.

Was her message getting through?

Even if Melissa knew she wanted her life back, there was still no practical way to accomplish the switch. No doubt, Melissa, being the more passive of the two of them, was waiting for *her* to point the way.

But *how*?

And, in the meantime, how would she keep Fabian from making her the very new—and the very pregnant—Mrs. Fontenot?

In the past few days she'd reflected a lot on Fabian's bewilderment the day he'd spanked her and she'd dropped her guard and started ranting about the twentieth century. Prior to this, she'd been afraid to tell anyone where she'd truly come from, out of a fear that she'd be locked up as a lunatic.

And Fabian had, indeed, assumed she was temporarily insane. She smiled. Maybe telling him the truth wouldn't be so bad after all. How well would Fabian Fontenot like the idea of being married to a madwoman?

After church, Missy and Fabian had dinner with her parents and his grandparents at the Gayoso Hotel. After the pleasant meal, John invited everyone to be his guests at a hot-air balloon launching that would be held along the bluff near Pinch, to benefit the Masonic Lodge. Fabian's grandparents at once enthusiastically accepted.

Missy, however, demurred. Nodding toward Fabian, she said to her father, "Thanks for the invitation, Dad, but Fabian has promised to take me for a drive along the Public Promenade."

"I have?" Fabian asked in astonishment.

"Yes, we have things to discuss," she added smoothly.

"We do?" he asked.

"I hope it's setting a new date for the wedding," Lavinia put in smilingly.

"Who knows?" Missy replied glibly to her mother. "At any rate, all of you go on and have a good time. I'm sure Fabian and I will be able to see the balloon rising from our vantage point on the bluff."

They said their good-byes, and Fabian was grinning as she towed him out of the hotel. "I hadn't realized you were so eager to be alone with me," he remarked devilishly.

"Oh, you have no idea how eager," she purred back.

Outside, he assisted her into his barouche. As they drove off together, she was silent, gathering her thoughts. They left Exchange Square and turned onto the Public Promenade, following the contour of the bluff northward. They passed numerous other conveyances bearing elegantly dressed couples or families who were on their way to the balloon launching, or merely taking their Sunday afternoon drives.

"Pull over," Missy urged Fabian after a few minutes. "Let's get out and walk."

He obliged, helped her out of the conveyance, and they strolled arm-in-arm through the grass at the edge of the bluff. Wild violets were blooming, and the day was sweet and mild. Beneath them, a river packet moved slowly through the silvery waters of the Mississippi, battling the strong currents as it traveled upstream.

"I see you wore my pearls today," he murmured.

She touched the double strand at her throat. "So I did. What of it?"

He winked at her. "Next, it will be my ring."

"Don't press your luck," she snapped, though she couldn't resist a smile.

"What's on your mind, Missy?" he asked.

She bit her lip. "Do you remember last week, when I spoke of being from another century?"

A look of compassion crossed his eyes, and he reached out to stroke her cheek. "How can I forget, darling? I drove you quite past all reason. I do hope you can find it in your heart to forgive me."

"But the point is, there's no forgiveness needed—at least, not on that score."

He scowled. "Now you're speaking in riddles. You must tell me what you mean."

She nodded. "You see, the truth is . . ." She took a deep breath, then blurted, "I am from another century."

Fabian threw back his head and laughed. "What a delightful sense of humor you have."

She gripped his sleeve, pulling him to a halt, and spoke vehemently. "But I'm not imagining things! It's true! I'm from the year 1992!" Watching him roll his eyes, she rushed on, "Your real fiancée and I were both getting married on the same day, a hundred and forty years apart. Then, through some quirk of fate—we got switched."

Fabian was shaking his head. "Darling, that's totally absurd."

"But it's not! I tell you, it's true!"

"So you got switched with my real fiancée," he drawled cynically, "and you just *happen* to be her exact physical twin?"

"Yes! I mean, more or less," she replied, wringing her hands. "You see, my real name is Missy Monroe. I'm a distant relative of the woman you knew as Melissa Montgomery, which is the reason for the uncanny resemblance."

He chuckled. "So, if this switch you speak of really occurred, then where, pray tell, is the real Melissa?"

Missy was growing exasperated. "Don't you understand anything? She took my place in the year 1992!"

Now Fabian was all but doubled over with mirth. "Come now, Missy. You can't possibly think I'm that gullible! Everyone knows that phenomena such as travel through time are impossible."

"But I tell you, it's all true! I am from the future! And I'll prove it to you!"

"How?"

She pointed toward the river. "Ten years from now, the entire country will be caught up in a Civil War, and Memphis will fall to the Yankees."

"Ridiculous," he scoffed.

"The South will lose the war and slavery will be abolished," she went on. "In the decades following, the economy of Memphis will decline, there will be three disastrous yellow fever epidemics, the city will eventually lose its charter, and then it will rise again as a major cotton market and distribution center."

"Unbelievable," he uttered.

"In the twentieth century, there will be two great wars, and mankind will fly to the moon—"

Abruptly she was hauled against Fabian, to face the anger sparkling in his dark eyes. "Missy, that's quite enough. Stop it!"

"But I'm telling you the truth!"

"No, you're not," he said in a deadly firm voice.

"What possible motive would I have to lie?"

He laughed ruefully. "The same motive you've had all along, my sweet darling—to escape me. And it's not going to work."

She broke away from him. "Damn it, why won't you listen to me?"

His expression turned more conciliatory. "Missy, you've been through a lot—hitting your head, losing your memory. Perhaps all of these inventions you speak of were part of a dream you had while you were unconscious."

She was silent a moment, jarred by his words. What if what he said were true—and all her memories of 1992 were just a hallucination? It was a most unsettling thought.

"Besides, you've spoken the most patent idiocy," he went on. "Even if there is eventually a war over this slavery business, the South will never lose. As for flying to the moon—that's utter nonsense. Everyone knows the sky is strictly for the birds."

Growing extremely frustrated, Missy glanced off to the north, only to smile triumphantly as she spotted the colorful hot-air balloon making its assent into the air. Pointing toward it, she demanded, "If the sky is for the birds, then how do you explain *that*, Mr. Know-It-All?"

He shrugged. "There's a world of difference between a hot-air balloon and a rocket to the moon."

She stamped her foot. "Damn it, can't you at least acknowledge the possibilities I've raised?"

"No."

Missy threw up her hands in defeat. There was obviously no getting through to this man. As always, he was one hundred percent provincial bumpkin—even if he was also her provincial bumpkin, and the man she loved. Oh, what a mess!

Missy strolled off toward the edge of the bluff and crossed her arms over her chest, her expression moody. Fabian came up behind her, curling his arms around her and pressing his cheek next to hers. A little sigh escaped her.

"Marry me, angel," he whispered tenderly.

She gritted her teeth against the floodtide of feeling sweeping over her at his nearness. "Doesn't it bother you that I'm crazy?"

"You're not the least bit crazy. You're simply afraid to surrender to what you're feeling for me." Nibbling at her throat, he finished, "But you'll get over it."

"Oh, will I?" she blustered.

"I'll build you the most beautiful mansion in Memphis," he went on seductively. "We'll take a riverboat to New Orleans on our honeymoon, and make love every minute of the way."

She turned in his arms, her expression eloquent with conflicted emotion. "Damn it, Fabian, I've told you I can never be happy as just your wife!"

He took her hands in his and spoke earnestly. "Why? Are you still in love with this Jeff person?"

"How many times do I have to say it? I never loved him. But that doesn't mean things can work with you."

"Why not?"

"Because you can't give me what I want."

He caught her about the waist, locking their lower bodies together. "Really?"

She groaned. "Okay, it's great between us in bed. But that's not what I'm referring to."

"Then, pray, enlighten me."

"For one thing, you have no goals."

"That again?" he muttered irritably. "Then I'll get some."

She made a sound of extreme frustration. "Even if you could, that still wouldn't be enough."

"What else would you want?"

"To be my own person!"

"I'll let you."

"To travel!"

"We'll do so."

"To run my own business."

He frowned.

"See what I mean?" she cried exasperatedly. "Despite all your high-minded arguments, you're still totally rooted in the thinking of the nineteenth century! You'll never take me seriously, or respect my rights as an individual."

"Missy, I didn't say no," he pointed out.

She harrumphed.

He caught her close again. "Indeed, there's only one issue on which I'll say no to you."

She stared up at him belligerently. "And what's that?"

"I'll always say no on the subject of your ever loving anyone else."

The earnest, vulnerable look in his eye melted her. "Oh, damn it, Fabian, just when I'm working up a good head of steam, why do you always have to go and say such romantic things?"

His answer was a grin, followed by a searing kiss that seemed to last for a thousand heartbeats.

Melissa and Jeff were strolling through Confederate Park at the edge of the bluff. They had just attended church and shared lunch with his mother.

Around them, the huge old trees were leafing out and the scent of spring was thick in the air. Below them, tourists swarmed over the River Walk area of Mud Island, and sailboats were gliding out of the marina.

As they paused before the statue of Jefferson Davis, Melissa found that the image of the President of the Confederacy brought home for her the reality of her situation.

"I met him once, you know," she murmured to Jeff.

He glanced at her in astonishment. "You met Jefferson Davis?"

She nodded. "It was several years ago—in the past, that is. Mr. Davis and his wife, Varina, stopped in Memphis on their way to visit his family in Kentucky. My parents and I attended a dinner party given in their honor." She glanced beyond them at the stone wall and cannon that had been put in place to commemorate the Confederate ramparts during the Civil War. "Jeff, it's still so difficult for me to believe what happened to the South after I left. The more I learn about the war, the more distressed I become. For instance, yesterday, while I was helping out at the library, I spotted a shadow box exhibit on the terrible naval battle fought in the Memphis harbor, when the city fell to the Federals in 1862."

Jeff hugged her quickly. "But darling, your family had left Memphis by then," he reminded her.

"I realize this. But there were others—my friends, the Sargeants, the Mercers, and the McGees. The entire town suffered, for that matter." When he didn't respond, she added, "You don't ask me much about my time. You did at first—but not so much anymore."

He squeezed her hand. "I'm sorry, darling. I guess I felt that if I encouraged you to talk about the past, you'd want to return there all the more."

"Oh, Jeff." As they strolled past the statue, she asked, "Do you remember when you suggested that we try to look up records on my family?" she asked.

"Yes," he replied cautiously.

"I was against the suggestion, because I didn't see how such research could help. Of course, I have read the old family letters I mentioned to you previously, but other than that, Mother has always assured me that there were few records kept on our family."

"Then what's the point?" he asked.

Her poignant gaze met his. "While I was at the library, I happened past the local history room. I was stunned by the detailed genealogies on various Memphis families that are kept there. I just hadn't realized that such extensive records were available."

"Go on," he said.

"Anyway, my point is that you were right. We do need to see if we can find out anything more about my family—after I left them, that is. I should have recognized this before, but perhaps, in a way, I was afraid of what we might discover."

"Amen," he muttered.

Unhappily, she continued, "Yesterday during my break, I spent a few minutes in the room and read a little more about what happened to Memphis following the war—the yellow fever epidemics, the city losing its charter . . ." She finished with a shudder.

"Those years were quite disastrous for the city," he concurred. "It's a good thing your family left."

"But we're still back to the same question."

"Which is?"

Her anguished eyes met his. "Who warned them about the war? Was it me—or was it Missy?"

"That's the critical question, all right."

"Then you were right that we should investigate more, see if we can't find a hint somewhere in the family histories of which one of us—me or Missy—actually remained in the past. Indeed, I've decided to go back to the library tomorrow, and to spend the entire day in the local history room."

All at once, Jeff stopped her in her tracks by pressing his hands to her shoulders. "That won't be necessary."

"But why?"

He nodded toward a nearby bench. "Darling, please sit down."

She complied, while he paced with his hands shoved in his pockets and his expression deeply abstracted. After a moment, he turned to her and said resignedly, "You don't need to do any research, Melissa. I've already seen to that."

She paled. "You've what? What do you mean?"

He drew a heavy breath. "As soon as you convinced me you were from another time, I hired a local genealogist, Mildred Reed, to research anything she could find out regarding your family history. She's been doing extensive work for me on the project for several weeks now."

Melissa's expression was stunned. "And what has she discovered?"

All at once, he avoided her eye. "Very little, actually. It seems your mother was right when she told you few records were kept on your family. As a matter of fact, finding out any information at all has been quite frustrating for Mildred. But when I last spoke with her, she felt certain she was getting closer. She mentioned having contacted some county and state agencies, as well as the Family History Library of the Mormon Church. The upshot is, she has promised to give me a full report within a week."

Melissa rose, her expression a mixture of confusion and hurt. "Jeff, why did you not tell me you were doing all this?"

His regretful gaze met hers. "I'm sorry to have kept it from you, darling. However, as you've already pointed out, I was afraid of what I might find out. Also, I didn't want to give you just a partial report, which might only alarm you unnecessarily."

Her eyes widened in sudden realization. "Then you do already know something!"

He grasped her hands and spoke earnestly. "Melissa, please, don't press me on this. Telling you what little I know at this point would only create more problems than it would solve. Let's not get into this subject in depth until Mildred's report is complete. Can you trust me that much?"

"Very well, Jeffrey," she said reluctantly.

He leaned over, kissing her gently. "Darling, whatever we find out, we'll get through it together," he said fervently.

She forced a smile and kissed him back. "I'm sure we will."

Yet both their expressions were troubled as they strolled through the trees for a few more moments. Privately, each wondered whether Mildred Reed's report would spell triumph or disaster for their relationship. Jeff in particular felt guilty that he had not as yet told Melissa what he knew about her own—or Missy's—wedding date in the past. But he was still holding on to the hope that Mildred would ferret out some detail that would prove that Missy, and not Melissa, had stayed behind and had married Fabian Fontenot on May 15, 1852.

After a moment, Melissa cleared her throat. "Jeff, there's something else I need to tell you. . . ."

He paused, turning to her. "Yes?"

She stared at him with sadness and some embarrassment. "There's . . . there's no child. I found out this morning."

He managed a reassuring smile, even though his own heart was aching. "I'm glad, darling. Not that I don't feel a sense of loss. It's just that right now, getting you pregnant would have been unfair to you."

She nodded. "It's not that I wouldn't adore having your children—"

He pressed his fingers to her mouth. "I know, darling. You don't have to explain your feelings."

Her expression grew wistful as she stared off at the river. "I was thinking of what the minister said in church today—about living each day to the fullest, since we never know what may happen tomorrow."

He caught her close with a groan. "Oh, Lord, darling. Every time I look at you, every time I hold you . . ." His voice broke as he finished, "I wonder if it will be the last time."

She looked up at him with eyes brimming with love. "Then we must make the most of this moment, mustn't we?"

Her words were rewarded with a tender smile and a kiss that seemed to last for a thousand heartbeats.

Chapter Thirty-five

The following week, Fabian took Missy on a carriage ride through town. They had lunch at the Commercial Hotel, and afterward, he drove them over to Front Street, to the area known as "Cotton Row," with its many two-storied cotton warehouses. A spring shower began to pelt their bodies as Fabian parked the barouche in front of one of the looming buildings.

Missy glanced askance at him as he hopped out of the conveyance and hurried around it to offer her his hand. "What are we doing here?"

He winked at her as he helped her climb out. "Oh, I think we'll just duck in here and wait out the storm."

Missy groaned and held on to her hat as she and Fabian rushed toward the building, with its two-story brick facade and rows of tall windows on the upper level. He unlocked the wide front door and they entered the dusty warehouse. Pulling off her feathered hat and shaking raindrops from her hair and clothing, Missy looked around at high ceilings and sturdy brick walls. The entire downstairs was vacant, except for a scarred old desk at the center of the building and a forlorn bale of cotton sagging against one wall. Upstairs, across the front of the building, stretched a loft with tables arranged near the windows for cotton classing.

Removing his hat and tossing it onto the desk, Fabian looked about with a proud grin. "Well, darling, what do you think?"

She glanced at him, astonished. "What do *I* think?"

"That's what I asked."

She rolled her eyes. "What exactly is on your mind, Fabian?"

"Do you really want to know?" he asked wickedly.

"Other than that!" she gritted.

He strolled about and gestured expansively. "Well, didn't you tell me you wanted me to have goals?"

She glanced about the empty building, then snorted derisively. "*This* is a goal?"

His eyes danced with merriment. "Truth to tell, my love, I'm thinking of becoming a cotton factor, and this establishment is available."

"Oh—I see," she murmured with a frown. "That does put a different spin on things."

"And I wanted your advice," he went on innocently.

She laughed. "Fabian, you don't have to indulge me like some precocious child."

He came over and took her hand, staring at her solemnly. "Missy, I'm not indulging you. I really would like to know what you think."

She harrumphed.

"You see, I have been giving much thought to your recent remarks about my lack of—er—productive endeavors. You're right that my duties at the plantation hardly monopolize my time, and after we're married, I would like us to live in town for much of each year. Since I am about to become—well, a family man—I've decided I need to establish an enterprise in my own right."

Missy's expression remained skeptical. "Do you have enough capital to start your own cotton commission house?"

"Indeed, I do."

She shrugged. "Then I suppose it makes sense. Cotton prices should go through the roof after the war."

"Missy, when will you cease this ludicrous talk of the war?" he scolded exasperatedly.

She ground her jaw in frustrated silence. Ever since she had tried to tell him the truth about where she'd come from, it had been an ongoing battle of wills between them. He steadfastly refused to believe she had come from the year 1992, and she adamantly insisted that she had.

He cleared his throat. "So, Missy—do you think my plan will work?"

"Yes, but—"

"But?"

She glanced about with a calculating gleam in her eye. "This is quite a solidly built warehouse. If I were you, I'd turn it into a textile factory."

He appeared amazed. "Textiles?"

"Yes." Stepping toward him, she continued eagerly, "Look at all the cotton produced in this region—and yet I've seen only one cotton manufacturing plant since I've been here."

He appeared taken aback. "Since you've been here? You mean, during your lifetime?"

She waved him off. "Whatever. The fact of the matter is, there is virtually no textile industry in Memphis. Think of all the money that could be saved if the cotton doesn't have to be shipped off to the east or England and could be made into fabric right here—and then sold on local and national markets."

He whistled. "You know, that's a splendid idea."

"If you also broker your own product, you could make a killing," she went on. "You can even set up your own spinning mill to feed your plant." She paused, laying her index finger alongside her jaw. "But I do wonder where we could get the best machinery—power looms, dyeing vats, and so forth—in this day and age. . . . Probably New York or Birmingham. Yes, we'd definitely have to travel to buy our capital equipment."

"*We'd* have to travel to buy our capital equipment?" he repeated, raising an eyebrow meaningfully.

She regarded him steadily. "That's what I said."

He stared at her with a mixture of admiration and caution. "It seems you have quite a head for business, my love."

She drew herself up proudly. "I've told you repeatedly that I'd never be happy here as just someone's wife."

"So you have," he murmured.

She hesitated a moment, then added nonchalantly, "As a matter of fact, I was recently discussing just such an enterprise with Robert Brinkley, and he all but agreed to finance it for me."

Eugenia Riley

He appeared stunned. "And you did not come to me? Or to your father?"

She laughed scornfully. "Fabian, you—and my father—would not have been the least bit interested in helping me establish my own business. Indeed, ever since I've been here, the only thing that has interested either of you is showing me my *place*."

Now his gaze shone with a glint of devilishness. "So far, it does not appear to have worked."

"Hah!" she cried. "If you started a factory here, can you honestly tell me you would want to make me a part of the enterprise?"

He sighed. "Missy, that's asking a lot."

"But I'll never settle for less."

He stepped closer and flashed her his most persuasive smile. "Tell you what, darling. We'll go to New York and Birmingham to look into the machinery—on our honeymoon."

"And then what, Fabian?" she challenged.

He offered her a supplicating gesture. "Give me some time, woman. You're flouting every convention of our society. I cannot adjust to all of this immediately."

Far from mollified, she stalked off, then turned to confront him with jaw clenched. "I'm afraid it takes a little more than just, 'Marry me, angel, and I'll let you see my equipment.'"

He advanced on her, fighting a grin at her double entendre. "Missy, you know I'm determined that you wed me."

"And I've told you, I won't—"

He grabbed her and hauled her close. "Which brings me to my second—and most important—goal in bringing you here today—showing you my—er—equipment." His head ducked down and

390

he claimed her lips passionately.

A protesting cry was strangled in Missy's throat as the heat of Fabian's lips swamped her. She mused ruefully that it was as if he hadn't kissed her in weeks, she was suddenly so hot for him.

With a supreme effort, she managed to push him away. "Not so fast, Romeo! I want an answer—now!"

"Kiss me and I promise to think about it," he said, swooping down again, prying her lips apart with his own, and ramming his tongue into her mouth. His fingers yanked the pins from her hair, then plunged deeply into her golden locks, holding her head firmly to his.

Missy lost it then, surrendering to his kiss and clutching him tightly. All at once, it didn't seem to matter that she hadn't gotten her answer. She couldn't even remember what her question was! Oh, why did Fabian have to taste so wonderful and smell so good? She ran her fingers through his silky hair as their tongues vied and the kiss deepened. Outside, thunder boomed and rain pelted the roof, the turbulence only adding to the tempestuous, romantic mood.

"You're damp," he whispered, kissing her moist cheek, her hair, even as she panted for her breath. His hand reached lower, his fingers stroking her boldly through her dress, his gaze piercing her own and demanding honesty. "Where else are you wet, darling?"

"Oh, God," she moaned, sagging against him.

They stood there kissing each other with voracious hunger. Fabian stroked her aroused breasts through her dress; Missy caressed the delicious hard bulge at the front of his trousers. The near-agonized sounds of his response only heightened the sweet aching between her thighs.

A moment later, he stared down at her intensely. "Take off your clothes," he said urgently.

"Here?" she gasped.

He stalked off to the front door, threw the bolt, then turned back to her with eyes burning with desire. "Yes, here, in the full light of day. This time I want to see you, angel."

Her entire being seemed to twist with lust at his provocative words. Nonetheless, she managed to protest weakly, "But, in a public warehouse—"

"I assure you, no one will see us. That lock is stout, and the windows on the second floor are much too high."

"But—where—"

He grinned wickedly. "There's a bale of cotton against the far wall."

"But then I'll go home with tufts of cotton in my hair—and elsewhere," she pointed out in a mortified squeak.

He drew closer. "Not if you sit on my lap."

Her knees buckled beneath her, and she would have fallen had he not hauled her against him. He laughed and kissed her soundly.

He was still chuckling as he released her and began undoing his cravat. He removed his coat and walked over to the desk, spreading it out. "This surface is splintery—only the best for my lady."

She gulped. "But I thought you said—the bale of cotton—"

"That will be later," he murmured, advancing on her.

Missy would have collapsed again, but Fabian caught her. For a few moments, they stood kissing and tearing at each other's clothes. Soon, her dress and corset, as well as his shirt, lay discarded on the gravel floor. He wore only his trousers and boots, she only her underclothes, when he carried her to the desk and lifted her onto it. Pressing her back, he pulled off her stockings, garters, and pantalets, untied her chemise, and bared her breasts. Missy panted in rapture as his eyes devoured her and his skilled fingers kneaded her breasts. He looked like a god standing above her, with his magnificent chest bare, his hair sensually mussed, and his dark eyes focused on her.

Then, with a sensual grin, he pulled her hips to the edge of the table, spread her legs and buried his face in the cleft between her thighs.

"Fabian!" Electrified, she tried to arch away.

He pinned her back firmly. "Do you know how long I've wanted to do this?" he whispered huskily. He drew back and teased the folds of her femininity with his fingers as his eyes devoured her most intimate recesses. He kissed the birthmark on her inner thigh and murmured, "To look at you, so beautiful, with all those laces and ribbons undone and you so open to me . . . To love you until you beg for mercy . . ."

Indeed, she cried out, but not for mercy, as he buried his tormenting lips in her moistness again. He teased her with his tongue until she went quite mad, clawing his shoulders and tossing her head violently.

She was sobbing with frustration by the time he carried her across the building to the bale of cotton. He sat down with her on his lap, locking his fervid gaze with hers. Before he could join their bodies, she surged downward, taking his erection greedily, uttering a hoarse cry of delight. He felt hot, hard, unyielding inside her, and the pressure was acute and sense-shattering. At her sob of ecstasy, he made a sound of feral satisfaction and latched his mouth on her breast. Missy couldn't bear the pleasure. She moaned and moved with him eagerly, crying out as she soared from one climax to another. He held her tightly and sought his own release with deep, riveting strokes that sent her hurtling over the pinnacle again. With a ragged cry, she sagged against him, totally limp, her face resting against his strong neck.

"Oh, God, Fabian, you're going to make me pregnant," she moaned.

His hands tightened at her bottom. "I've already told you, woman, that I want you pregnant." He pressed her away from him slightly and stared at her solemnly. "I want us to marry."

"Damn it, Fabian, don't do this to me!" she cried wretchedly. "Not now."

She felt him throbbing to life inside her again as he whispered, "What better time is there, my love?"

A whimper of desire escaped her. Her fingernails dug into his strong arms as she laid her face against his shoulder and fought tears at the sweetness of being with him.

She felt his arms stiffening about her. "You're still enamored of this Jeff person, aren't you?" he asked.

She straightened to face him. "No. Fabian, how many times do I have to tell you that I never loved him!"

He nipped at her shoulder as his fingers caressed her tender nipple. "But you can't let go of him, can you?"

The hurt in his voice, combined with the intimacy of their position, shattered her resolve. "That's not true." Leaning over to kiss him achingly, she finished in a breaking voice, "You know that no man has ever made me feel what you do."

He groaned. "You shouldn't say things like that to a man, Missy."

"I shouldn't?"

Abruptly, he pivoted, withdrawing from her body and laying her down on her back on the bale of cotton. "No, you shouldn't. It makes a man want to take you home with tufts of cotton in your hair—and elsewhere."

"Fabian!" As she watched, electrified, he knelt between her spread thighs. Her eyes grew huge and longing flooded her anew as she studied his manhood, fully aroused again, rigid with desire for her.

A gasp of shocked pleasure escaped her as he wrapped her legs high about his waist. The ardor and determination in his eyes quite took her breath away.

"And furthermore, we're not leaving this building, woman, until you promise me your hand in marriage," he said fervidly.

Missy's next protest was drowned out in a cry of agonized eroticism.

As Fabian drove her home, Missy plucked tufts of cotton from her hair and glanced at her fiancé with grudging admiration. True to his threat, Fabian had kept her with him at the warehouse until she had given herself to him in every way possible. Now, she had promised to marry the bumpkin, and even her own normally intrepid soul cringed at his imagined response if she went back on her word.

Eugenia Riley

Damn it all, she felt so torn! Physically and emotionally, she was totally in love with this man, even if intellectually, she still felt they were wrong for each other and that she belonged back in her own time.

But what if that wasn't possible? What if she were indeed stuck here forever?

Studying the devastating devil seated beside her, all at once, she felt that it no longer seemed a fate worse than death.

Still, if she were destined to remain here, perhaps she should get some things straight with Fabian before they married. Thinking of the coming years that they might pass together, she felt a shudder gripping her spine. Whether or not she'd have a career no longer seemed the most critical issue. How would they escape the coming disasters—the years of war and epidemic?

"We'll marry on May 15," Fabian now said. "That will give you several weeks to prepare."

She glanced at him, then said through gritted teeth, "Yes, Fabian." She bit her lip. "But there's a condition—"

"What?"

"I won't allow you to fight in the Civil War."

He laughed heartily. "Are you back to that nonsense again?"

"Just indulge me and promise me you won't fight with the Confederacy."

He scowled a moment. "If there is eventually a war over the slavery issue, I would have to side with the South."

She set her arms akimbo and stared moodily ahead. "Then I won't marry you."

"Missy!"

She turned to him, gesturing vehemently. "I tell

you I won't! Hundreds of thousands of men will be slaughtered, families will be torn apart, and I won't sacrifice you to a war that never should be and will all but destroy this country."

He frowned fiercely. "Missy, we don't even know if there will be a war."

"Trust me, there will be."

"In such circumstances, a gentleman with honor has no choice but to—"

"Oh, you and your honor!" she scoffed. When he glowered back murderously, she quickly held up a hand. "Very well, you can be a blockade runner like Rhett Butler—"

"Rhett who?"

"Never mind! I won't allow you to be a soldier. Furthermore, your family and mine—all of us—will have to find a safe place to ride out the war. We'll need to free all the slaves—Dad's being a real chump on the issue, but he'll come around eventually. And before the end of this decade, we'll all need to move—oh, I don't know, to Nevada or some other place out west—"

"Missy, there's no such place as Nevada."

"Believe me, there will be." She snapped her fingers. "I know, we can all become gold miners! That's it! You know, I once had to do a term paper on the Comstock Lode! We can beat everyone else to Virginia City!"

He rolled his eyes.

"Well, Fabian, what's your answer?"

"What am I going to do with my textile plant if we move away to this imaginary Nevada?"

"You mean *our* textile plant?"

He grinned. "For the sake of argument, call it ours."

She shrugged. "We'll simply make it successful

first and sell out." She gazed at him narrowly. "Do we have a deal?"

"Do I have a wife?"

"Do I have a blockade runner?"

"You are unbelievable, woman!"

"Well?"

"All right!"

Missy turned away, unable to believe the conversation she had just had with Fabian. Not only had she agreed to become his wife, she was now intent on saving him from the Civil War and making him filthy rich—

Damn it all, she was coming to care for him far too much!

What the hell, she was doomed. She was probably right that she might never escape back to her own time. Surely Melissa was about to marry Jeff, too—

Suddenly, Missy sat bolt upright in the seat as a momentus realization dawned. Of course! Why hadn't she thought of it before! She and Melissa had switched places during the marriage ceremonies before—why couldn't it happen again?

But wouldn't that mean they'd both have to fall down the stairs again? And were there any guarantees that this wild scheme would even work?

It had to work! she thought fiercely. Furthermore, she had to take the risk. If she stayed here, she would lose her own identity, lose herself to feelings for Fabian that she couldn't control, and she'd end up giving her entire self over to him. As nice as he had been lately, cleverly claiming that he valued her opinions, she still strongly suspected he would never be content until he had her completely subjugated to him.

That was it, then. She would stage the wedding

ceremony again, and then, with any luck, she and Melissa would switch places—

She paused, totally stumped. How could she ensure that Melissa would also marry Jeff on May 15? This would surely never work unless the ceremonies were staged simultaneously, just like the last time. How could she get a message through to her cousin?

"We'll make our announcement in the newspaper," Fabian was saying. "I'll arrange for a new marriage license—"

"Of course!" Missy cried. "The newspaper! The library! The court house!" She turned to Fabian and gripped his sleeve. "There will be records of our wedding, won't there?"

He glanced at her as if she'd lost her mind. "But of course. Otherwise, it would not be legal."

"Oh, this is wonderful!" Missy cried, clapping her hands.

Fabian nodded, although his expression remained bemused. "I'm glad to see you're coming around."

But Missy barely heard him, so lost was she in her own thoughts. Surely, sooner or later, Melissa and Jeff would think to study records to see if she had remained in the past, or if she and Melissa had switched places again. If Melissa found the date of her wedding, she might even assume that she and Jeff should marry on the same day.

She shook her head grimly. That was much too chancy. Somehow, through the newel button or something, she would get her message through to Cousin Melissa. In the meantime, she would proceed with her own wedding plans.

Now, the critical question was, who would really marry Fabian Fontenot—Missy Monroe or

Melissa Montgomery? And an even more daunting question plagued her—could she really bear to leave Fabian, her parents, and her new life here?

Chapter Thirty-six

Jeff and Melissa stood on the main deck of a jaunty excursion steamboat. Both wore deeply abstracted expressions as they held hands and stared out at the churning gray waters of the Mississippi. The afternoon had turned cool and drizzly, the covering of the promenade deck above them protecting them from the light rain.

Melissa felt a bit awkward today, wearing "jeans," a polo shirt, athletic shoes, and a windbreaker, an outfit quite similar to the one Jeff wore. This was the first time since she'd arrived in the present that she'd dared to don the denim trousers so many women here considered a staple of their wardrobes. While she couldn't help but feel rather scandalous, she had to admit that she liked the feeling of freedom the casual attire provided.

She stared at Jeff, so solemn beside her, and felt the tension of his fingers clutching hers. She knew he had received his report from Mildred Reed, and ever since he'd picked her up for their date, she'd been struggling to get up the nerve to ask him what he'd found out. Finally, she decided she could not stand the suspense for a single moment more.

"Jeffrey, you've been so quiet all afternoon," she began tentatively. "I know you wish to protect me, but you mustn't be afraid to tell me what Mrs. Reed said."

"I know." He turned to her resignedly. "I'm not sure that what she found out will be of that much comfort to either of us."

She regarded him bravely. "Jeffrey, we must face up to this thing. We've both been avoiding the truth for far too long."

"You're right," he admitted. "Well, to begin with . . ." He glanced away, then said hoarsely, "By looking through the county records, Mrs. Reed was able to determine that Fabian Fontenot and Melissa Montgomery were married on May 15, 1852."

"Oh, my!" Melissa cried, even as her heart thudded in despair at the pronouncement. With forlorn hope, she added, "Only, we still don't know for certain whether it was I who married Fabian, or Missy, masquerading as me."

Jeff gripped her shoulders and spoke with forlorn hope. "That's true. It's quite possible Missy is the one who married Fabian."

"And it's also quite possible Missy and I will switch places again before the marriage is performed," she added fatalistically.

"Don't say that, darling," he begged, hugging her quickly.

She sighed. "Please—go on."

He nodded, staring out at a passing barge. "Well, it seems that, just as you thought, both your family, the Montgomerys, and the Fontenots remained in Memphis until the late 1850s. Then both families moved west, to the area we now know as Nevada."

"Everyone left Memphis?" Melissa asked with keen interest. "Then what Mother told me was true!"

"Indeed. Out in Nevada, both families became quite wealthy through various gold strikes. The details are somewhat sketchy, although Mildred was able to determine that you—or Missy—and this Fabian Fontenot had seven children—"

"Seven children!" she gasped.

"Yes," he confirmed grimly. "Mildred also discovered that your parents, John and Lavinia, had another child fairly late in life—a boy, John Jr., who arrived during the years before they moved west."

"My gracious! I have—had—a brother."

"Indeed, darling. Out in Nevada, John Jr. grew up, married, and continued the Montgomery family name. Eventually, his family re-settled in Alabama, and it was during the third generation thereafter that there was only one child, a girl, who married a Mr. Monroe."

"Ahah! So that's how the family name was changed!"

"Yes. Then, as you know, in the late 1960s, Missy's parents, Howard and Charlotte Monroe, moved back to Memphis, established their business, and bought back the old family home."

"I see," Melissa murmured, her eyes filled with awe. "So Howard and Charlotte are indeed distant relatives of mine."

"Yes—very distant relatives, I'd say."

"This is all so fascinating," she murmured with

a thoughtful frown. "Do you know when my parents—when any of us—died?" At his look of sudden hesitation, she held up a hand. "On second thought, I don't think I want to know."

He smiled kindly. "That's probably best, dear. But I can tell you that you all lived long, happy lives."

"I'm so glad," she said feelingly. "What else did Mrs. Reed find out?"

He sighed. "Those are the basics. Mildred did prepare a complete history and genealogical table, which you can look at if you want. However, as we just decided, it may be best that you not learn too much."

"I agree. So where do we go from here?"

He gestured in frustration. "That's why I told you I wasn't sure the information would be of much benefit. It would help tremendously if we knew which one of you married Fabian Fontenot. However, I have a theory—"

"Yes?"

He stared at her, his eyes alive with hope. "I think it was Missy who stayed behind."

"Why?"

He continued with growing fervor. "It's as we concluded before—Missy would have warned both families about the coming war. And this business about moving everyone to Nevada and capitalizing on what she would have known about the gold strikes there. That sounds just like her."

But Melissa only shook her head, her eyes filled with terrible sadness and resignation. "You don't understand, Jeff."

"What don't I understand?"

Her troubled gaze met his. "Just as I told you before, if I went back, I doubtless would have done exactly the same thing as Missy would have—warning my family about the war and the coming epidemics."

"Would you have sent both families gold hunting out west?" he demanded, his expression quite skeptical. "That doesn't sound like you at all—but it would have been totally in character for Missy."

"I disagree again," she said sadly.

"Why?" he cried exasperatedly.

She bit her lip. "Well . . . now that I know how the family history is to be written, wouldn't I be duty-bound to follow this same course if I went back?"

He threw up his hands in despair. "Damn it! You're right! I shouldn't have told you any of this!"

"But how can we possibly search for the truth if you don't tell me what you know?" she pointed out patiently.

Jeff slammed a fist against the railing. "You're right again—but it's so frustrating! The past is like a maze, with every possible clue leading to a dead end—and I'm afraid we'll never find our way out of it!" He turned to her and gripped her hands. "But one thing I do know—"

"Yes?"

"Melissa, I absolutely, categorically refuse to allow you to go back and have seven children by that abominable man!"

Melissa laughed ruefully and rolled her eyes. "Perhaps I wouldn't hate Fabian quite so much—not after having seven children by him." Observing Jeff's stunned expression, she touched his arm and quickly added, "Jeffrey, I was only trying to make a joke."

He hauled her into his arms and spoke fiercely. "It isn't funny, Melissa. Not at all."

"I know, darling."

He stroked her hair. "Lord, what will we do?"

She pulled back and stared at him soberly. "I think we should also plan to marry on May 15, and see what happens."

All at once, his eyes grew bright with suspicion and he shook a finger at her. "You're thinking of switching places with Missy again, aren't you?"

With terrible resignation, she said, "I think if Missy and I are meant to switch again, there may be nothing we can do to stop it."

"No!" he cried. "And yes, there's something we can do about it! We won't marry on May 15, I tell you!" He caught her face in his hands and continued in a voice edged with desperation, "Melissa, marry me *now*, today. We'll hop a plane to Vegas and—"

"No, Jeffrey."

"No? But don't you understand? If you marry me now, you can't possibly marry Fabian Fontenot on May 15!"

She shook her head in resignation. "I think it would be both wrong and naive of us to assume we can change time or destiny. Nor can we run away from our honor. If Missy truly wants her life back again, I must relinquish it. Anything else would be unconscionable."

His eyes were crazed with pain and fear. "Tell me you're not saying this!"

"But I am—I must. We must schedule our wedding for May 15, and then let destiny take its course. It could be that we're meant to remain together. Or it could be—"

He caught her to him tightly. "Don't say it,

woman. I tell you, I won't lose you. I'm going to keep you here if it takes every ounce of strength in my body."

Jeff kissed her hungrily, pinning her softness against his hard, aroused body. She kissed him back with all her being and clung to him as poignant tears filled her eyes.

That night, as Missy Monroe lay in bed, she concentrated fiercely, willing a message to her cousin one hundred and forty years away. Over and over, she repeated the words in her mind, praying that Melissa would somehow hear her plea and follow her critical instructions. Otherwise, she would never be free—she would never escape Fabian.

Melissa slept fitfully. In her dreams, she kept seeing Missy's determined face, and hearing the words, "May 15 . . . schedule the wedding again . . . fall down the stairs again . . . Promise me . . . don't forget."

The message replayed itself endlessly through her dreams, until she awakened with a ragged cry, knowing in her heart what she must now do—and that the heartbreaking conclusion she had reached with Jeff today had been absolutely right. The forces of destiny were at play, and, whatever the outcome might be, there was nothing she could really do to change things.

"I promise you," she whispered convulsively.

She turned into her pillow and sobbed.

In the past, Missy awakened with a cry of realization. Her message had gotten through! Somehow, she knew it had gotten through! She had even seen Melissa's face in her dreams and heard her respond, "I promise you."

Missy knew a moment of deepest triumph, then she turned into her pillow and, illogically, wept her heart out.

Chapter Thirty-seven

Morning found Melissa sitting at her dressing table, staring into the mirror, red-eyed and puffy-faced. She knew now what she must do, after having received her "message"—her instructions—from Missy last night. She must plan to marry Jeff on May 15, and on that date, she must fake a new tumble down the stairs; at that point, she and Missy would switch back again—and she would lose everything that mattered to her!

At the very thought, wrenching sobs burst from her anew. She hated the thought of leaving Jeff and her lovely new parents, or of returning to her old parents and that beastly Fabian. She knew she'd always been a disappointment to those she'd left behind in the past, and that, while she'd bloomed briefly here, when she returned to the year 1852, she would regress to her former self again, becoming a shrinking violet, downtrodden and overshadowed once more by her parents and Fabian.

Still, what was right was right, so she would remain true to her promise. This wonderful life she had lived had only been "borrowed," and had never truly been hers. She must give Missy back the life that ultimately belonged only to her.

And there was no way she could admit to Jeff what he already suspected, for he was certain to stand in her way. . . .

Missy sat at her dressing table, wondering why she didn't feel ecstatic and relieved. She knew now that her message had finally gotten through to Cousin Melissa, in her dream last night. Now, both of them would reschedule their marriages for May 15, both would fake a new tumble down the stairs, and they would switch places again. She was certain Melissa would faithfully follow through on the instructions; indeed, she had seen Melissa's face in her dream, had watched her nod back in assent with a terrible resignation.

It was the memory of that tortured face that haunted Missy now. Dear Cousin Melissa had agreed so readily to follow her orders and relinquish the life—Missy's life—that she was now living in the present—and quite happily so, from all indications. Moreover, from everything Missy had learned, Melissa couldn't have been anything but miserable when she had lived in the past. Both Fabian and her new "parents" had spoken frequently of how insipid and spiritless they'd found the "old" Melissa; once Melissa returned here, the three of them would chew her up and spit her out, their good intentions notwithstanding.

As for Fabian . . . ! Oh, Lord, how miserable he must have been with Melissa before! And how disappointed he would be when he discovered that his former, meek little fiancée had somehow been resurrected! He'd still feel duty-bound to honor the marriage contract, of course, but ultimately, both he and Melissa would be wretchedly unhappy in their marriage.

Could she do this to Fabian? To Melissa?

To herself?

With a groan, Missy got up and began to pace. She remembered the day when she had looked into the newel button and had seen Jeff and Melissa kissing. Lord, they had looked so happy, so right together. If she went back to the present again, she would make Jeff miserable—and ditto, her parents. Indeed, she had a gut feeling that her folks back in the present were much more content with Melissa as their daughter than they'd ever been with her.

Furthermore, once she returned to the present, she would miss Fabian and her new parents terribly. . . .

"But damn it, it's my life and I want it back!" she cried, trying desperately to hold on to her convictions. She was still convinced that ultimately, Fabian would never be satisfied until he dominated her totally. If she remained here, surely she would be doomed.

Yet, the irony of it was, she could no longer just think selfishly of herself—she had to consider the feelings of the others she had come to care for—Fabian, her new parents, and the four people back in the present whose future happiness depended on her own decision. Just as she had recently concluded, falling in love with Fabian must have changed something elemental inside her. She had gone soft—another reason to fight to get back her old life—and her old self—before it was too late!

Missy threw herself down on her bed. She felt so tormented and torn. Maybe she had found her own hell, but Melissa had also found her heaven. Now, could she truly sacrifice Melissa's happiness for the sake of her own?

At breakfast with her parents, Melissa said, "I have an announcement to make."

Charlotte looked up from her coffee, while Howard peered up from his newspaper. "Yes, dear?" they queried in smiling unison.

Melissa smiled back tremulously. "Jeff and I have decided to marry on May 15."

"Oh, how wonderful!" Charlotte cried.

"I'm thrilled for you both," Howard added.

Indeed, both parents sprang up and hurried over to embrace their daughter. Melissa eagerly hugged both parents, smiling stiffly. Once all the congratulations and happy tears had been exhausted, the three resumed their seats.

"Oh, we're going to be so busy," Charlotte continued eagerly. "May 15 is only a few weeks away. Perhaps we can get a rush order through on invitations, or maybe just call people this time. And, of course, we'll have to arrange for the caterers—"

"Before you continue, there's something else I wish to tell you both," Melissa cut in solemnly.

"Yes, dear?" Charlotte asked.

Staring from one dear parent to the other, she fought tears. "I must tell you how wonderful it has been to be here with you—how greatly you have both enriched my life—and how proud I've been to be your daughter."

Both parents beamed with pride. "Thank you, dear," Charlotte said, blinking at tears.

"We feel the same way, darling," Howard added with a catch in his voice.

Melissa twisted her linen napkin in her fingers. "And—I want you both to promise me you'll never forget me," she went on in a choked voice.

Now her parents' blissful facades faded into expressions of bewilderment.

"But, dear," Howard put in worriedly, "you sound almost as if you're planning to leave us."

"She is leaving us, Howie," Charlotte pointed out, wiping a tear. "She's taking a husband."

"But won't we still always be a family?" Howard asked, reaching across the table to take his daughter's hand and staring at her with utter devotion.

"Indeed, we will," Charlotte concurred, reaching out to take Melissa's other hand. "Although we'll understand, darling, that Jeff must come first with you from now on. Still, we'll always be together in our hearts, won't we?"

Melissa managed a quivery nod. "Yes! Oh, you're both so wonderful!"

"And you're going to be so happy with Jeff," Charlotte added.

For a moment, Melissa stared back at her mother, her lower lip trembling. Then she stunned both parents by bursting into a torrent of violent weeping and fleeing the room.

"I suppose she's simply overcome with her happiness," Charlotte murmured perplexedly.

"I wonder," Howard added skeptically.

At breakfast with her parents, Missy said, "I have an announcement to make."

Lavinia looked up from her tea, while John

peered up from his newspaper. "Yes, dear?" they queried in unison.

Missy smiled bravely. "Fabian and I have decided to marry on May 15."

"What splendid news!" John exclaimed.

"And about time!" Lavinia added, clapping her hands.

"Oh, this is so exciting," Lavinia continued gaily. "We'll need to send out invitations, of course, and arrange for the minister—"

"Before you get too deeply into this, there's something else we must discuss," Missy cut in firmly.

"Yes, dear?" Lavinia asked.

Lifting her chin, she looked from one parent to the other, then announced, "Before I marry Fabian, I must ask you both to promise me something."

Her parents exchanged confused glances. "Speak your mind, daughter," John said.

Missy nodded to her father. "I want you to promise me that you and Mother will leave Memphis— and before the 1860s."

Missy might as well have asked them both to dance through the downtown streets naked.

"Leave Memphis?" John cried, his expression thunderstruck.

"Desert our home?" Lavinia echoed in astonishment.

"Please," Missy implored, "you truly must leave Memphis. It's for your own good. I want you both to give me your word that you'll move farther west—and by 1860 at the very latest."

"But why?" Lavinia cried.

"Yes, why?" John demanded.

Missy shook her head ruefully. "If I told you,

you'd never believe me. Please, just say you'll do it. You'll make me so happy if you do." Leaning forward and lacing her fingers together, she added to her father, "And there's another promise I must have—"

"Yes?" John asked, his brow deeply furrowed.

She stared him in the eye. "I want you to free the slaves, Dad."

He threw up his hands. "That again!"

"Dad, please," she urged. "Make it your wedding gift to me. That, and give me your promise you'll sell out your property and move west."

"Daughter, these are most bizarre requests," Lavinia remarked sternly.

Missy swung around toward her mother. "You want to see me married to Fabian, don't you?"

"Are you making an ultimatum, my dear?" John asked ominously.

She pivoted back toward him, suddenly blinking at tears. "No," she replied, surprising even herself. "I'm asking you . . ." As her words grew choked, she paused. "I'm begging you, as someone who loves you, to please do as I ask."

Now, both parents were too mystified to comment.

At last, Lavinia reached over, cupping her daughter's chin in her hand and staring at the girl with deep concern. "Missy, dear, why these tears? Why this tragic tone and all these strange demands? You sound almost as if you're planning to leave us."

"She is leaving us," John pointed out. "She's taking a husband."

"But won't we all still be a family?" Lavinia said wisely. "Won't we all always be together in our hearts?"

Both parents stared at Missy questioningly.

"Of course we will," she replied brokenly, feeling about a hair's breadth away from a disgraceful crying jag. Beseechingly, she stared from one dear parent to the other. "Will you both at least promise me you'll think about my requests?"

Lavinia looked to John for guidance. After a moment's hesitation, he nodded to his daughter. "Yes, Missy we'll promise that much."

She expelled a ragged breath. "Thanks, Dad." Biting her lip, she added, "And there's one more thing. I want you both to know how happy I've been to be your daughter."

Both parents appeared deeply touched. John squeezed his daughter's hand. "My dear, your pride and joy cannot possibly be equal to your mother's and mine in having you as our daughter."

"Amen," Lavinia added.

"Thanks, Mom, Dad." Missy smiled wanly from one to the other. "I—I do hope you'll both never forget me."

"Forget you?" Lavinia cried. "How can we possibly forget you, darling, when we're all going to share each other's lives for many years to come?" She patted Missy's hand. "Now, no more tears. Why don't you think instead of how happy you're going to be once you're married to Fabian?"

Chapter Thirty-eight

Melissa's parents invited about a dozen of the family's best friends, as well as Aunt Agnes, over for a buffet dinner party to announce the rescheduled wedding. Lisa, Michelle, and Jennifer attended with their boyfriends; all three women buzzed about Melissa excitedly. Reverend and Mrs. White were present, as were George Schmidt and Jeff's mother.

Once all were present in the living room with champagne cocktails, Howard and Charlotte pulled Jeff and Melissa to the center of the room, and Howard proudly made their announcement. "Friends, I'm delighted to inform you that Melissa is now completely recovered from her fall, and that she and Jeff have decided to reschedule their wedding for May 15. A toast, to Melissa and Jeff! Happiness always!"

As several guests called out their own cheers or fond wishes, Jeff clinked his glass against Melissa's, and the two silently toasted each other. As she smiled at him shyly, he winked at her tenderly and feasted his eyes on the woman he loved. How he adored her! She looked exquisitely lovely tonight in her sapphire blue dress and gold jewelry. Her beautiful face was flushed from all the attention, and yet he could see a certain sadness in her eyes. When her three friends rushed up to congratulate her, her smile seemed strangely hollow.

Fear chilled his heart. There was something she wasn't telling him—and he had a good idea just what that something was. She planned to leave him. As to just how, the possibility he had in mind was so frightening that it pained him to think about it.

Should he confront her, demand to know what her plans were, demand that they change their wedding date at once? He shook his head grimly. No, if he forced her hand, she'd only feel duty-bound to deceive him—it wouldn't be fair to place her in such a moral dilemma. He could try more subtle persuasions, but a power play would never work.

If he were to save her, then, to save their love, he could count only on his own resources. Should he speak with her father?

Anxiety lanced him anew. Would it do any good to try to stop her, or had she already spoken the truth—that the forces of destiny were stronger than either of them?

Missy's parents invited about a dozen of the family's best friends over for a buffet dinner party to celebrate the rescheduled wedding. Fabian's grandparents attended, as did Lucy, Antoinette, and Philippa, with their husbands. The three women buzzed excitedly around Missy, Philippa in particular regaling the others with tales of hers and Charles's sojourn to Kentucky, from which they had returned only a week earlier.

Once all were present in the parlor with cups of punch, John and Lavinia pulled Missy and Fabian to the center of the room, and John proudly made their announcement. As Fabian clinked his cup against Missy's, he could see a certain sadness in her eyes. Fear chilled his heart. Why was it, just as she had finally consented to marry him, he sensed instead that he was losing her?

He thought of the dramatic change in her over the past months, and of all the joy and love she had brought him. He grinned as he recalled her absurd assertions that she was from another time—that she had been switched with the "real" Melissa. This little spitfire had certainly gone to great lengths to ward him off! Now, if they could just get through their wedding day, she would be his forever. . . .

Their wedding day! Suddenly, Fabian felt all color draining from his face as he recalled that the changes in Missy had occurred immediately after she'd taken that bad fall on their previous wedding day. She had been like a different person ever since. What if what she said were true—what if she were truly from the future and had been switched with the real Melissa?

But that was preposterous, impossible! Still, he felt an irrational, almost superstitious fear of the wedding day to come.

Should he speak with her father?

After dinner, Jeff turned on the stereo, and the younger guests danced gaily in the double parlors, while the older generation sipped coffee, visited, and watched. Much later, after all the guests had left, Jeff asked Melissa to go for a walk by the pool.

As soon as they were out of earshot of the house, he pulled her into his arms. "It's time for our own celebration, darling," he murmured intensely, and kissed her.

Melissa poured all her own emotions into the kiss, thinking of how she must relish every second she and Jeff had left together. She inhaled his spicy scent, ran her fingers through his silky hair, and savored the drugging taste of his kiss, as if to imprint him on her own senses forever.

He pulled back, staring at her with the eyes of a drowning man. "You look so beautiful tonight. Lord, I can't wait until you're mine."

"Me, too," she whispered, though she buried her face against his shirtfront to hide the guilt in her own eyes.

"Melissa, you wouldn't try to leave me, would you?" he asked urgently.

Feeling wretched, she replied in a small voice, "Jeff, I would never want to leave you."

His arms tightened around her. "Before you even consider it, there's something I want you to remember."

"What?"

"This."

With a groan, he caught her hand, pulled her into the nearby cabana, and shut and locked the door behind them. His lips claimed hers, his tongue ravishing her mouth deeply and thoroughly. Then he nipped at her ears and throat, his breathing urgent and rough. She shivered with pleasure and kneaded his back with her fingertips.

When he undid the buttons on the back of her silk dress and then unhooked her bra, she realized he had far more on his mind than just a few kisses.

"Jeffrey, please," she implored, shuddering in delight as he pulled down her dress, slip and bra, and then stroked her bare breasts. "Someone will find us!"

"No they won't," he assured her, holding her firm breasts in his hands as he stared into her eyes. "Come with me, darling?"

The stark need in his eyes sent desire surging and spiraling within her. "Anywhere!"

He pulled her to the chaise longue, sat down and pulled her on top of him, then latched his mouth on her breast and sucked hard.

"Jeff!" Melissa felt scandalized and electrified to be straddling him this way, with his hot tongue flicking over her nipple and driving her insane. She pressed her hand to his face and confessed in a mortified hiss, "I'm not wearing the device!"

She heard his throaty chuckle as he took her hand and kissed each of her fingers, lingering on the one that bore his ring. "Don't worry, darling, I've brought along protection tonight," he soothed huskily, and reached into his pocket.

She stiffened, suddenly intensely curious. "Does that mean we're going to practice safe sex?"

Now he laughed ribaldly. "God, I love it when you talk dirty."

"Jeffrey, be serious!"

She heard more amused rumblings, followed by a crinkling sound, and then he murmured, "Yes, my darling, I intend to introduce you to all the vices and devices of the twentieth century."

Now even she smiled as she leaned over to kiss the firm line of his jaw.

Shoving the empty foil wrapper back into his pocket, he caught her closer and whispered, "I'll be so glad when we're married and I don't have to use these. I want a child right away—don't you?"

Emotion choked Melissa at the sweetness of his words—and the guilty secret only she knew. She was about to reply when she felt her pantyhose being ripped. "Jeffrey!"

"Sorry, darling, but you're dealing with a man in pain." He lifted her and settled her onto his hard erection. She heard him groan ecstatically. "Lord, angel, you feel so good," he said, thrusting himself into her. "I don't know what I'd do if I ever lost you."

Even as Melissa gasped at the wonder of his filling her, his poignant words seared her very soul. As she thought of how she would soon lose forever such glorious, loving moments with him, her tears came, tears of exquisite pleasure and bitter regret. . . .

After dinner, everyone waltzed to the piano music of Lucy Sergeant. Once all the guests had departed, Fabian maneuvered Missy out the back door and onto the veranda. He kissed her there, deeply, druggingly, and she was breathless by the time he pulled her deeper into the shadows of the night.

"Where are you taking me?" she panted.

"Time for our own celebration," came his husky, enigmatic reply.

He tugged her farther into the dusky trees, until they arrived at a bench swing suspended from the sturdy limb of a large oak. He pulled her down onto the swing with him and kissed her again, passionately.

"My, you're ardent tonight," she said with a shaky laugh.

He drew back, the moonlight gleaming in his intense eyes. "Do you have any idea how absolutely gorgeous you look?"

She managed a crooked smile. "You're looking pretty spiffy yourself, I must confess."

He took her hand and lovingly kissed each tapered finger. "Lord, I can't wait until you're mine." As she shivered in delight, he looked deeply into her eyes and asked, "You're not going to try to leave me, are you, Missy?"

Her features blanched, and her guilty gaze darted away from his. "Leave you? Don't be silly! Why would I leave you?"

He shook his head slowly. "I just had this strange feeling come over me tonight—like a chill—right as your parents were announcing the new wedding date."

"Well, your chill was no doubt caused by a draft," she said with more bravado than conviction. "Haven't I promised to marry you?"

Grasping her chin, he tilted her face toward his and stared at her solemnly. "Why do I sense there's something you're not telling me? Why do I fear I'm losing you?"

She gulped, gazing back at him with anguish and love. "You're not losing me," she murmured, her words sounding unconvincing, even to her own ears.

He sighed and pulled her onto his lap. As his teeth nibbled at her ear, he began pulling up her skirts.

"Fabian! What on earth are you doing?"

"I have to feel you're mine tonight," he whispered urgently, reaching for the tie on her pantalets.

"Good Lord! Here?" she cried, feeling scandalized, and yet so electrified with desire that she was trembling violently.

"No one will see us—and even if they do, they'll just assume we're swinging."

She laughed squeakily at the twentieth-century meaning of that, only to gasp as she felt herself being lifted onto to him. His feet pushed them off the ground, and the next thing she knew, she slid deeply onto his erect phallus with a cry of exquisite pleasure. The tightness of their position created a wondrous friction and heat within her womanhood, and made her desires escalate to a fever pitch, until she could have devoured him alive.

"Swinging is rather fun, isn't it, darling?" he murmured as they rocked to and fro.

She nodded violently, between frantic gulps for air.

"Would you like a boy or a girl first?" he went on.

"Oh, my God!" she cried.

"Don't worry—we've plenty of time to decide," he murmured as he nipped her neck and tightened his hands at her waist.

Indeed, he kept her there until his boots had worn a groove in the ground.

Chapter Thirty-nine

The next few weeks passed all too quickly for Missy as she prepared for her wedding day and for the return flight through time that only she knew about. She saw Fabian frequently, and she continued to feel bewilderingly torn at the prospect of leaving him and her parents. For a time, she even feared she might be pregnant, and she knew of no way she could follow through on her scheme to leave him if she were indeed carrying his child—she had to credit herself with having at least that much honor and conscience. Then, when her period came a week before the scheduled wedding, she didn't know whether to feel relieved or disappointed. Now, there was nothing to keep her here—except her own free will and her love for Fabian.

She was still agonizing over her dilemma on the eve of the wedding itself. That afternoon, she and Fabian, as well as the Sargeants and the McGees, were invited out to the racetrack just off Hernando Road for an impromptu horse race. It seemed that a couple of Charles Mercers' former business associates had passed through Memphis on their way to race horses in Natchez—and Philippa, now the proud owner of two Kentucky thoroughbreds—had promptly challenged both men to a race. Philippa had even insisted that the course be run among the principals themselves, denouncing the usual custom of having jockeys race the thoroughbreds.

It was a somber group that sat on benches at the side of the track—Missy and Fabian, Lucy and Jeremy, Antoinette and Brent, as well as a glum-faced Charles Mercer, seated between the wives of his two former associates. Down the track a way beneath a tree were seated several slaves who had been brought along to tend the horses.

Missy tried her best not to smirk as she observed her friend Philippa on the starting line, looking quite regal in her riding habit and perched on her magnificent chestnut thoroughbred. On either side of her were the two men she had challenged, one on a smaller black Arabian and the other on a taller gray racer.

At a signal from Philippa, Fabian rose, ambled out toward the riders, and pulled out a pistol. Counting down from five to one, he fired a shot, and the horses sprang forward.

Missy sat on the edge of her seat as she watched the riders race each other around the track. All three horses were grace personified, their muscles rippling as they seemed to fly down the dirt course. The action was neck-in-neck, and soon Missy could not resist egging her friend on.

Lunging to her feet, she waved her handkerchief and yelled, "Come on, Philippa! Beat the everlasting daylights out of them!"

The men glowered, while Lucy and Antoinette, also caught up in the mood, jumped to their feet and yelled out encouragements of their own.

"You can do it, Philippa!" Antoinette cried.

"Make us proud!" Lucy added.

The men continued to glare.

The race was extremely close, but Philippa pulled out all the stops at the end. When her mighty thoroughbred leaped over the finish line a good length before the others, her three friends along the sidelines screamed themselves hoarse and huddled together joyously. Moments later, after Philippa's groom had led off her horse, she triumphantly rejoined the other women.

"Didn't I tell you all that I could do it?" she cried, grinning widely and waving her crop in victory.

"A woman can do anything!" Missy replied.

"Amen," Lucy added.

As the women hugged and congratulated Philippa, the red-faced losers quickly retrieved their wives, their servants, and their horses, and left. Visiting with her friends, Missy thought of how proud she felt for changing all their lives and freeing them from the shackles imposed by their stodgy husbands. Indeed, she was still smiling from ear to ear as the foursome walked, arm-in-arm, to rejoin the men. Then her smile faded as she observed the grim-faced males waiting for them.

"I hope you're satisfied," Charles snapped at Philippa as he extended his arm.

Philippa accepted her husband's arm, tossed her head high, and swept off with him.

"Have you uttered enough blasphemies for one afternoon?" Jeremy added sanctimoniously to Lucy.

She rolled her eyes and headed off for their carriage without a word to him.

"Next, you'll want to race one of your stupid hats," Brent carped to Antoinette.

She batted him soundly with her bonnet as the two stormed off together.

Fabian stepped forward, smiled cynically, and offered his arm. "Shall we go?"

She stared murder at him. "By all means!"

Missy was still fuming as Fabian drove her home in his barouche. "You men certainly are sore losers!" she declared.

He laughed humorlessly. "And you've certainly done your three friends a lot of good."

"What do you mean by that crack?" she demanded.

He clenched his jaw as he worked the reins. "All you've done is to create dissention in three marriages and make all the couples miserable."

"That's not true! How do you think my friends felt being the doormats of those obnoxious men for so many years? I've merely taught them to assert their rights."

"Because men and women are equal?" he sneered.

"Darn tooting!"

"But you don't want us to be equal!" he argued hotly. "You'll never be happy until we all admit that you're better than us."

"Well, maybe we are!"

"See what I mean?"

"Oh, you're impossible! You'll never change! I'm so glad that I'm not—"

Abruptly, he pulled the horse to a halt. "Glad that you're not what, Missy?" he asked in a deadly serious tone.

She gulped. "I'm glad I'm not entering into this marriage under any delusions," she quickly fabricated.

He laughed derisively. "What kind of double-talk is that?" He pulled her close and scowled down into her eyes. "I'll tell you what you're doing, my love."

"What am I doing, Mr. Fontenot?" she asked with consummate sarcasm.

"You're picking a fight with me so you won't have to marry me tomorrow. And it's not going to work!"

Sensing that he was about to kiss her into submission—and that it was going to work—she shoved him away. "Fabian, take me home. I've got a lot to do before tomorrow, and frankly, I'm not in the mood for your caveman tactics."

With a curse, he turned to snap the reins.

Melissa emerged shyly from the cabana at the Monroe home. She was wearing a very skimpy bikini, and her long hair was caught up in a ponytail. She stared at Jeff, standing across from her on the patio in his swim trunks, his body so tanned, magnificent, and sexy.

He whistled, devouring her with his eyes. "I told you I'd get you into a bikini."

She blushed vividly as she glanced down at the two strips of blue and white fabric that were all she wore. "Jeffrey, I feel naked!"

He winked at her solemnly. "We'll get to that next."

She moved closer and shoved him playfully. "You sex fiend!"

He caught her close and howled with laughter. "Who taught you that particular expression?"

"It is how Lisa always describes her boy friend," she responded primly.

He chuckled. "Speaking of which, when are the three giggly debutantes and their boy friends descending on us?"

"I told everyone we would begin the pool party at five."

"Good. That gives me an entire hour alone with you." He tugged her toward a nearby table and picked up a plastic bottle. "First, we'll coat you with sunscreen—"

"Sunscreen?"

He was already carefully dabbing the lotion on her cheeks, forehead, and nose. "It keeps you from burning, darling. I'm taking no chances with that delectable skin of yours, since I'm determined to bite and devour you to pieces tomorrow night."

She giggled, loving the feel of his hands as they applied the lotion to her neck, shoulders, and the rest of her body.

He recapped the bottle and set it aside. "Now, we must water test that bikini—"

"But Jeffrey, I need to put out the food for the party," she protested. "You see, Mother and I agreed that we should give Mrs. Jackson and her daughter the day off today. They're going to be so busy during the wedding tomorrow."

"You're always so thoughtful." Determinedly, he tugged her toward the pool. "Last one in's a rotten egg!"

"But I don't know how to swim!"

"You'll be at my mercy then."

Both were laughing as they went down the steps into the shallow end. The water felt cool and delicious against Melissa's skin. She lovingly perused Jeff's muscled body in the navy trunks that fit him so perfectly; he stared avidly at her lush curves, which the bikini displayed so enticingly.

Once they were in up to their waists, he pulled her close. "Thinking about tomorrow, darling?"

She avoided his gaze. "Er—yes."

"I can't think of anything else," he said intensely. "I can't wait to get you alone on our honeymoon—and to begin the rest of our lives together."

She ran her fingers through the water and nodded, afraid her voice would betray her.

"Do you like it here?" he continued tenderly.

"Here?" She smiled.

His hand massaged the small of her back. "Here in the pool, of course—but especially here in the twentieth century."

While she didn't hesitate, her gaze was sad. "Oh, yes, I love it here. I was frightened at first, but now I feel—well, such a sense of belonging."

"That's because you belong to me!" he said fervently. "There's so much I want to teach you— how to swim, to country western dance—"

"Country western dance?" she cut with a quizzical smile.

"Sure, there are some places in town that I enjoy. And I'll teach you how to ride in a plane, how to drive, how to spend all my money—"

"Now you're teasing me, Jeffrey!"

"Am I?" Caressing the soft skin of her back, he added solemnly, "Do you realize how much you've changed since you've been here?"

She gazed at him quickly. "Changed how?"

"You've bloomed, my love. When you first arrived here, you were a bewildered, terrified young woman. Now, you've grown into a person in your own right, confident and brave, someone who's ready for this century and all its challenges."

She bit her lip, feeling miserably torn. Hadn't she made these same realizations herself recently? "What are you saying, Jeff?"

"I'm saying it would be a sin for you to regress to your former self."

"Why—why would I do that?"

He caught her to him fiercely. "Don't take my love—my life—away from me, Melissa," he whispered poignantly. "I can try to hold you here, but ultimately, the decision is all yours."

Tears welled in her eyes as she gazed back at him soulfully. "I love you, Jeffrey. Please, always remember that."

His eyes were strangely bright, as well. "I know, darling. And I love you, too."

Melissa clutched Jeff close. She wanted with all her heart to reassure him more—yet she had no further words of comfort to offer him, except for the love that would burn in her heart for the rest of her life. Stretching on tiptoe, she kissed him with all that love, desperately hoping the memory of her kiss would be enough to last him a lifetime.

Late that night, as Missy stood in her nightgown, brushing her hair, she heard a rumbling at the door to her balcony. As she turned, wide-eyed, the French door swung open and Fabian stepped in, wearing a flowing white shirt and dark trousers and carrying a bouquet of flowers.

"Fabian!" she gasped, dropping her brush. "How did you get in here?"

Grinning, he bowed. "I climbed a tree to your veranda, my love."

"But—why?"

He strode over to her and handed her the flowers. "A peace offering."

Feeling very touched, Missy took the bouquet, sniffed the fragrance of the lovely mixed blooms, then gently laid the flowers down on her dresser. "Thank you," she murmured. "They're quite lovely."

For a moment they stared at each other awkwardly.

He shifted from one foot to the other. "Missy, I wish to apologize for today—"

"*You* wish to apologize?" she repeated incredulously.

He nodded. "I had a drink with Charles, Brent, and Jeremy late today, and the funny thing is—"

"Yes?"

He grinned sheepishly. "Well, with the exception of Jeremy, who is a hopeless prig, all of us men agreed that we like you women even better now that you've changed."

"You—you do?" she gasped.

He nodded solemnly. "You're all so much more lively and fun. Only sometimes, your spirit, combined with our determination, puts us at odds with one another. We all need to find a common ground, a point of compromise." He stepped closer, touching her shoulder. "Do you suppose there's such a place for us?"

"I—I don't know," she muttered.

"Can we try?" he asked, staring at her with his heart in his eyes.

Her gaze suddenly could not meet his. "Well, I suppose . . ."

"I think I know a good place for us to begin," he added huskily, advancing on her with a lusty gleam in his eye.

"Fabian, no!" she cried, pressing a hand to his chest to hold him at bay. "As much as I love what we have in bed, we can't solve everything with just sex."

Undaunted, he removed her hand from his chest and began to kiss each soft finger. "I didn't say we could. Let me ravish you thoroughly, and then we'll talk."

Panic and lust seized her, a dizzying combination. "I—I can't."

Now he appeared mystified and hurt. "But why?"

Because I can't leave you if I'm carrying your child. The words she could never say to him clogged her throat with tears.

"Are you afraid your parents will find us?" he asked.

She shook her head in anguish. "No, that's not it. I just . . . can't make love with you again."

"Can't make love with me again? Not ever?" he cried.

She twisted her fingers together. "I mean, not until we're married. I—I'm superstitious about it all, you see." In a breaking voice, she finished, "I want to make tomorrow night very special."

"Ah, I see," he murmured. "You know, that's really very sweet, angel."

Yet he continued to stare at her with intense longing.

"Damn it, Fabian, please don't look at me that way!"

They stood there gazing at each other, desire seeming to ignite the very air between them. Missy stared at the man she loved, taking in every chiseled line of his face, every contour of his magnificent body, and the blazing depths of his dark eyes. As the reality hit her that she would never see him again after tomorrow, never again know his sweet loving, she suddenly knew what she must to do, what she yearned to do.

"But I can do something for you," she whispered.

"You can?"

With tears in her eyes, she said, "Fabian, no matter what happens, please, always remember that I love you."

"I love you, too, darling," he said, though his expression was bemused.

She sank to her knees before him and began unbuttoning his trousers.

"Missy, what are you—"

Before she could lose her nerve, she took him in her mouth.

Fabian was as stunned as he was agonizingly aroused. "Woman, where on earth did you learn to—"

"I didn't," she gritted back. "Believe me, Fabian, this is going to be 'learn by doing' for us both." Glancing up at him in suspicion, she finished primly, "At least, I hope so."

"Oh, yes," he assured her in a rough, trembling voice. "That is, I've never—"

The rest of his words became lost in sounds of tortured ecstasy.

Chapter Forty

On the morning of her wedding, Melissa sniffed at tears as she sat at her dressing table, applying her makeup. Her heart was breaking at the thought of leaving Jeff and her parents later today, even if she knew she was doing the only honorable thing as far as Missy was concerned. Nonetheless, she was giving up not only the three people she had come to love dearly, but the new identity and the confident new person she'd become here in the present. As she stared at Jeff's lovely ring on her finger, it was all she could do not to fall apart as she thought achingly of the wedding band he would never place on her finger and the anguish he would know when he found out he'd lost her. She said a silent prayer for strength to help her get through the coming ordeal.

"Melissa, dear, may I come in?"

Hearing her mother's voice at the door, Melissa called out, "Of course, Mother."

Attired in a lovely lavender silk dress, Charlotte swept inside, smiling from ear to ear and carrying a huge arrangement of yellow roses. "Look what Jeff just sent over for you," she announced gaily. "Aren't these lovely, darling?"

Melissa looked at the flowers and burst into tears.

"There, dear," Charlotte said, setting down the arrangement and patting her daughter's heaving shoulders. "I knew you'd be simply ecstatic."

Missy sat at the dressing table, sniffing at tears as she styled her hair. She hated the thought of leaving Fabian and her new parents today, even though she still felt this was the only solution for her as an individual. Of course, Fabian had acted very sweet, very conciliatory, when he came to her room last night. But the memory of his chauvinistic behavior yesterday at the race track still haunted her. He could be a persuasive devil when he wanted to, but she was still far from convinced that he had really changed. Would he ever truly respect her as an individual?

Still, could she desert him and the others forever? Anxiety stabbed her anew as she considered the coming years of war and epidemic. Would her parents move west, as she had pleaded with them to do? Would Fabian stay out of the Civil War conflict, or make his contribution only as a blockade runner, as she had begged him to do? Or would all of them remain here in Memphis and succumb to the coming disasters?

A bittersweet smile curved her lips as she thought of how she'd changed since she'd come here. For the first time in her life, she was feeling responsible for someone besides herself. She'd developed a heart and a conscience; she had come to really care about the feelings of others. In a way, though, she feared this transformation in herself as much as she feared eventually becoming Fabian Fontenot's doormat.

Who, then, would she save today—herself, or those she had come to love?

"Missy, dear, may I come in?"

Hearing Lavinia's voice, Missy called out, "Sure, Mom."

Attired in a lovely mauve silk frock, Lavinia swept inside and quickly crossed over to the dressing table, laying down an envelope in front of her daughter. "Fabian just sent this over for you."

Frowning, Missy opened the envelope. She gasped as she pulled out the deed to the warehouse she and Fabian had recently toured. A note from Fabian was also included: "Missy, darling, we shall establish your factory. I have booked us passage to England on our honeymoon, and there we shall look into the necessary equipment— when I'm not too busy showing you mine. Love, Fabian."

Staring down at the note, Missy burst into tears. At last Fabian had acknowledged her independence. How could she possibly leave him now? Yet how could she halt the events she'd put into motion?

"There, dear," Lavinia soothed, patting her daughter's heaving shoulders. "I knew you'd be overcome with happiness."

Half an hour later, Missy stood at the top of the staircase in her wedding gown, with her hand on her father's arm. Downstairs, the guests, Fabian, and the minister awaited her.

"Ready, dear?" John asked.

"Sure, Dad," she replied tremulously.

"By the way, there's something I've been meaning to tell you," he added.

"Yes?"

He grinned. "I'm going to free all the slaves. It's my wedding present to you, darling."

Feeling deeply touched, she hugged him quickly. "Oh, Dad! I'm so happy—and so proud of you!"

"I must say, my feelings are precisely the same on this joyous day," he added in a voice hoarse with emotion.

Missy had to glance away to hide the tears in her eyes. As the strains of the wedding march drifted up from the parlor, panic set her pulse to raging and twisted her gut. Here, at last, was her one chance to escape, her golden opportunity to regain her independence. Why, then, wasn't she eager to take the leap?

"Missy?" came her father's perplexed voice.

With the tip of her foot poised to take her tumble, she stared at the father who regarded her with love and concern. Then she glanced downward at the parlor. She spotted Fabian, thought about the deed lying on her dressing table upstairs, and considered how he had finally met her halfway. She glimpsed the love and vulnerability reflected on his face and she froze.

Suddenly, nothing in the world seemed to exist for Missy but the love and need reflected on that dear face. Fabian Fontenot was the man she loved with all her heart, she thought. She couldn't do this to him. She didn't want to do this to him. At last she knew what truly mattered to her, and that was not asserting her own independence, but loving Fabian, being with him—and knowing she would make Jeff and Melissa happy in another time.

In her heart, she felt Melissa would know. . . .

Feeling a sublime peacefulness, Missy glided down the stairs to join the man she loved.

"Ready, dear?"

Standing at the top of the stairs in her wedding gown, with her hand on her father's arm, Melissa nodded tremulously. Below them, the guests, Jeff, and the minister were waiting for her. She heard the strains of the wedding march drift up, and feelings of panic accelerated her pulse and twisted her stomach.

"Melissa?" came her father's perplexed voice.

With the tip of her foot poised to fake her fall, Melissa stared at the father who regarded her with love and concern. Then she glanced downward at the parlor and spotted Jeff, stared at his dear face, and lost herself in his adoring eyes.

Good-bye, my darling, her heart cried out to him. *Please forgive me. I'll love you always.*

Choking back tears, Melissa stepped forward, bracing herself to take her terrible plunge.

Then her father pulled her back almost violently, clamping a hand over her arm. "Oh, no, my dear," Howard said firmly. "We can't have you taking another tumble today."

"But you don't understand," Melissa whispered back, beseeching him with frantic eyes. "I must."

But Howard only chuckled and tightened his grip on her arm. "Don't be silly. Come on now, my dear—steady as we go."

Melissa had no choice but to proceed with her father down the stairs. He was holding on to her so firmly that, if she did attempt a tumble, she would likely take him hurtling off with her— and that was, of course, an unthinkable prospect.

I'm sorry, Missy, she thought guiltily. *So sorry . . .*

At the bottom of the steps, Melissa dug in her heels and turned, staring frantically into the newel button for the answers she so desperately needed. Then, as if by a miracle, the circles began to ripple and part, and she saw an image of Fabian and Missy standing before the minister and staring at each other with utter love and devotion in their eyes.

As tears of joy flooded Melissa's vision, suddenly, she was at peace. Smiling radiantly, she glided to join the man she loved.

"Why did you want to stay here tonight?" Fabian asked Missy.

The wedding celebration had been over for many hours. Mr. and Mrs. Fabian Fontenot were lying upstairs in her bed, kissing and caressing, their bodies outlined in the burnished glow of a lamp.

"Oh, I don't know," she murmured, running her fingers over his bare chest. "It seemed appropriate for us to spend our wedding night here."

"Tomorrow we'll board that steamer for New Orleans," he murmured, nipping at her throat. "And from there, it's on to England, my pet."

"Where you'll show me your equipment?" she teased.

He chuckled huskily. "Indeed."

She smiled at him adoringly. "So you're really going to let me run the factory with you?"

"I will," he promised solemnly. "As long as you give me—and our children—sufficient attention."

She caressed his muscled back. "Believe me, I will."

Fabian was pulling at the ties on her diaphanous gown. "God, woman, I'm so glad you're mine! You know, it's funny, but—"

"Yes?"

He gazed at her starkly. "I had this uncanny fear that I was going to lose you today."

She curled her arms around his neck and stared at him with total love. "You're never going to lose me, Fabian." Wistfully, she added, "You know, I've learned so much in the past two and a half months."

"Such as?" he queried.

She gazed at him solemnly. "I've learned not to be afraid of the changes in myself. I've learned to love you and trust you, without fearing that you'll swallow me up as a person."

He grinned. "There's only one way I want to swallow you up."

"By all means, gorge yourself," she purred back.

He nibbled at her breast. "Indeed, I may never even let you out of this bed. I'm going to strip you naked and kiss every delectable inch of you."

"Don't forget to get me pregnant," she added in a sultry purr, touching his delicious hardness through his pajama bottom. "I want a baby right away."

"Count on at least one each year," he promised in a sensual growl.

She chuckled. "So, when do I get to strip you naked and kiss every delectable inch of you, Mr. Fontenot?"

"Actually, Mrs. Fontenot, I thought you already did that last night," he teased back. "However, I've no objection to an encore performance. . . ."

Later, after many glorious encore performances, Missy sat up in bed, donned her negligee, and handed Fabian his robe. As he glanced at her questioningly, she kissed him quickly and said, "Come downstairs with me, my darling. There's something I must show you."

"Why did you want to stay here tonight, darling?" Jeff asked Melissa.

The wedding celebration had been over for many hours. Mr. and Mrs. Jeffrey Dalton lay upstairs in her bed, kissing and caressing, their bodies outlined in the burnished glow of a lamp.

"I really love this house," Melissa replied. "I've had so many wonderful times here—with you, and with my parents."

"I understand," he said. "I'm glad we're here tonight. And tomorrow, we'll leave for our honeymoon in Paris."

"I can't believe we're actually flying there on an airplane," she murmured in awe.

"Does the prospect make you uneasy?" he asked with concern.

She smiled and kissed his hand. "Not if you're with me, my love."

His eyes lit with joy. "Lord, I'm so glad you're mine!" Solemnly, he added, "I was so afraid that I was going to lose you today."

She curled her arms around his neck and stared at him with utter love. "You're never going to lose me, Jeff."

"I've been dying to ask . . ."

"Yes?"

He stared into her eyes. "What changed your mind about staying here with me?"

She sighed. "You knew I planned to switch with Missy today?"

"Yes, I knew. I even warned your father to keep a careful eye on you."

She snapped her fingers. "So that's why he was holding on to me for dear life!"

He nodded. "Still, like you, I was so afraid we might not be able to control the forces of destiny." He smiled quizzically. "What made you stay, love?"

She squeezed his hand and smiled radiantly. "I simply found out that Missy is happy in the past with Fabian."

"You did? Thank God!" He frowned. "How do you know?"

"Oh, it was something I saw today."

"You saw?"

She kissed the strong line of his jaw and ran her fingertips over his bare chest. "Why don't I explain everything later?" she asked in a sexy whisper.

"Fine with me." He grinned. "Indeed, I may never even let you out of this bed! I'm going to strip you naked and kiss every inch of you—"

"And will you give me a baby?" she asked tenderly.

"Will I ever!" He lifted her gown and buried his face against her satiny stomach. "No more devices, my love. I'm going to do my best to get you pregnant this very night. If Fabian and Missy are going to have seven children, then we must outdo them by having at least ten!"

"I'm with you, darling," she purred.

Later, long after they made glorious love, Melissa sat up in bed, donned her negligee, and handed Jeff his robe. As he glanced at her questioningly, she kissed him quickly and murmured, "Come downstairs with me, darling. There's something I must show you."

Jeff and Melissa stood next to the newel post, gazing into the newel stone. As the circles began to waver, they saw another couple reflected there.

"I'll be damned!" Jeff cried. "It's Missy. And is that Fabian with her?"

"It is, indeed."

Jeff shook his head wonderingly.

Smiling with great joy, Melissa added, "We've so much to discuss, darling. But first I think it's time for us to say good-bye to Missy and Fabian. Something tells me we won't be seeing them again."

Holding each other close, the lovers turned to stare into the newel stone.

In the past, Missy and Fabian stood at the newel post, gazing into the same stone. As the circles began to waver, both saw another couple reflected there.

"I'll be deuced!" Fabian cried. "It's Melissa!" He turned to Missy incredulously. "Then you must have been telling me the truth all along—"

"Indeed, I was, my love."

He was still shaking his head. "But—who on earth is she with?"

"Jeff."

"Jeff?" He raised an eyebrow meaningfully.

Laughing her joy, Missy pulled Fabian into her arms. "I've a very long story to tell you, my darling. But first, we must say good-bye to Melissa

445

and Jeff. Something tells me we won't be seeing them again."

Holding each other close, the lovers turned to stare into the newel stone.

As both couples smiled at each other, the images flickered and and then faded away forever. . . .

Dear Reader:

I wish to take this opportunity to thank you, my wonderful readers, for your enthusiasm and support for my time travel stories!

At the back of my first time travel romance, *A Tryst In Time*, I asked you to write and let me know what you thought of my book, and whether you'd like to see additional time travel stories by me. The results have exceeded my wildest dreams! As I write this, I have received almost 500 enthusiastic fan letters on *A Tryst In Time*, and mail continues to arrive! I can't tell you how touched I have felt to have you share not only your feelings on my book, but also your lives with me.

Bless all of you for encouraging me to continue writing time travel stories! *Tempest In Time* is, of course, the result. I do hope that you've had as much fun in reading about the "star-crossed" lives of Missy and Fabian, Melissa and Jeff, as I have had in writing this book.

I do, of course, continue to welcome your feedback. For those wishing a free bookmark and a copy of my latest newsletter, a long-sized SASE is appreciated.

Please write to:

Eugenia Riley
P.O. Box 840526
Houston, TX 77284-0526

P.S.: If you enjoyed *Tempest In Time*, I do hope you'll watch for my story *Two Hearts In Time*, a Victorian time travel novella that Leisure will publish in its *Old-Fashioned Valentine* anthology, coming in February, 1993.